DEADLY
SWEET
LIES

THE DREAM WAR SAGA

Erica Cameron

SPENCER
HILL
PRESS

Spencer Hill Press

Contact: Spencer Hill Press
27 West 20th Street, Suite 1102
New York, NY 10011

Please visit our website at www.spencerhillpress.com

First Edition: December 2015
Erica Cameron
Deadly Sweet Lies/by Erica Cameron–1st ed.
p. cm.

Summary:
Human lie-detector Nadette is on the run from the Balasura, dream demons intent on acquiring her, when she meets master-of-deception Julian, who must gain her trust through lying if he wants to have a chance at saving her.

Cover design by Michael Short
Interior layout by Errick A. Nunnally

978-1-63392-011-8 (paperback)
978-1-63392-012-5 (e-book)

Printed in the United States of America

For Danielle Ellison and Patricia Riley, who asked the right questions, looked under the right rocks, and helped me create two extraordinary characters who could not have existed without their guidance.

"The truth is rarely pure
and never simple."

–Oscar Wilde, *The Importance
of Being Earnest*

"The truth is not always beautiful,
no beautiful words the truth."

–Lao Tzu, *Tao Te Ching*

One

Julian

The clink of the poker chips against the green felt table sounds a lot like the ice hitting the side of my opponent's whiskey tumbler. He takes a sip and smiles at me over the rim of the glass, the indulgent smile an uncle might give his favorite nephew. I'm not his nephew, though. He doesn't have any nephews.

I've been playing against John Owens for years, long enough to know his tells by heart. Right now, with the glint in his eyes, the way his thumb caresses his tumbler when he sets it down on the table, and the careful distance he keeps from the cards sitting face down in front of him, I know he has a solid hand. Full house or better.

Hopefully my four queens will be enough.

"How's your mother, Julian?" John asks as he tosses a few chips into the pile, seeing the $500 already in play and raising the hand $50.

I shrug and call, adding another $550 to the pot. "Lynnie's good." If you call falling fast into the well of debt, drinking, and decay "good." "She's working at Flash still." At least, she was yesterday.

"Same old Jacquelyn then, huh, kiddo?" Brandon folded early this round and now he's lounging in the armchair like it's a couch.

They've known her too long (she stopped introducing herself as Jacquelyn when she turned thirty) to think she's going to grow up now. They don't know the worst of it, though. To them she's a free spirit, but a good mother. I barely keep from rolling my eyes.

"Always a child at heart," I say, forcing a laugh even though my chest tightens. I really wish she'd grow up.

"I forget." Bai Chang rubs his thumb along his wrinkled cheek, his dark eyes narrow. "How old were you the first time you snuck up here? I fold, by the way."

He places his cards facedown and sits back. I smile. Years ago I distracted the Bellagio's concierge long enough to swipe a master keycard and sneak up the elevator on a night I knew John was hosting a private poker game. Friendly, but not exactly playing for chump change. The guys had been regulars at the hotel long enough that Lynnie knew them and I knew I could get them to give me a chance.

"I was ten."

"Couldn't believe it when you begged us to teach you to play," Brandon says, laughing. "Little imp. Jacquelyn was mad as fire when she figured out you'd found your way up here."

Yeah. Mad because I hadn't brought her with me.

"Gentlemen," John smirks and winks at me, "and Julian, I think this round might be mine."

I stare at the cards he reveals. A straight flush. "Oh Sinatra bless it."

The guys laugh. That stupid phrase I picked up from Lynnie always makes them laugh; it's pretty much the only reason I made it a habitual thing. I flick my useless hand onto the table and smile ruefully at them, pretending to laugh with them, but in my head I quickly calculate the remaining chips in front of me and the odds of convincing them to play another hand. Normally it wouldn't be a problem, but John's granddaughter is in Vegas for the week (a combination trip to visit family and celebrate her best friend's eighteenth birthday in style, apparently) and there's no way I'm talking him into being late to dinner with her.

Only $2,500 tonight. The cards just weren't with me. If I hadn't bluffed my way through most of the hands, I wouldn't have even made this much. It isn't enough. This will cover a payment on Lynnie's more pressing debts, but I'm going to have to find another game this weekend to make rent. Forget food or electricity. That might not happen.

Taking a deep breath, I shake that train of thought off the tracks and refocus. My fault. I skipped two games this month because of the marketing internship I'd been working. Thought it'd be okay, but Lynnie's losses outpaced my gains. By a lot.

John stands, buttoning his suit jacket as he does. That's the signal. It's time to go.

"A pleasure, as always, my friends," John says as everyone cashes out their winnings and pays up any losses. "Same time next week?"

Smiles, nods, jokes, and handshakes follow as Brandon, Bai, and I head for the elevator. Halfway there, John taps my shoulder and holds me back, his brown eyes scanning my face.

"Things really okay, kid?"

Looking up at him, I know I could play this a few different ways. If I laugh and show off the bullet-hole dimple in my cheek, tell him about the (nonexistent) regular who tips Lynnie well, and ask him about his granddaughter, he'll go off thinking everything really is fine. If I hint that Lynnie might be on the verge of losing her crappy job at Flash because of her habit of being an hour or more late, he'll probably spend the next week trying to think about if and how he should help. If I smile (without the dimple), shrug, and play the story down the middle, though…

Smiling, I shrug. "It's been a slow month, but we're good. Really."

John's already thin lips almost disappear as he considers my answer. I hold my breath, waiting. It only takes him a couple of seconds to reach into his pocket for his wallet and pull out a wad of bills. "You're a good kid, Julian."

"John, no." I make my eyes wide and push the bills back into his hand even though I desperately want to shove them in my pocket and run. "I appreciate it like you wouldn't believe, but we'll be fine. Honestly."

He laughs. "That right there proves it. How many fifteen-year-olds would turn down a no-strings-attached wad of cash?" John shakes his head and closes my hand around the bills. The deeply etched lines around his eyes get deeper as he grins.

I force a blush to my cheeks, knowing the freckles across my nose stand out more against the pink and make me look even younger than fifteen. I play it up whenever I need to, because it works. Without looking at the bills, I nod and push them deep into my pocket. "Thank you, John."

He nods, looking pleased with himself and probably feeling both virtuous and generous. Which he is. We leave the suite together and

I listen to him talk about his granddaughter's insanely high SAT score and her long-term agony over the choice between a West Coast school or one in the Ivy League. I comment whenever necessary (which isn't often) and swallow the resentment building in the pit of my stomach. When we reach the lobby, I repeat my thanks and wave goodbye, heading out the doors and north toward the Stratosphere.

On the three-mile walk home, my mind churns. Take time off to travel after high school or plunge straight into life at a fancy college? Please. I *wish* I had her problems.

Sighing, I stop at the edge of the small parking lot in front of the (motel-look-alike) apartment building hidden behind the Stratosphere complex. The paint is peeling and the slightly angled roof desperately needs a pressure washing. Music blasts from one of the apartments, sirens wail in the distance, and the baby in 1-C is screaming again.

I walk up the steps to the second floor, the hand in my pocket fingering the folded wad of (technically illegally obtained) bills that will get Lynnie and me through another month in this disaster of an apartment.

Sinatra save me. What wouldn't I do or give or pay to have *college* be the biggest stressor in my life?

Once upon a midnight more dry than dreary, while I pondered weak and really pissed off with the world in general, a door opened in the wall of my bedroom. I thought I'd fallen asleep somewhere between tearing apart the eviction notice I'd found tacked to the door that afternoon and punching a hole in the cracked drywall, so I stepped through that inviting portal of pale-gold light with only a few seconds of hesitation. Inside, I found a world as different from the deserts of Nevada as possible.

The rocky shoreline stretched for over a mile in a soft crescent shape, outcroppings of rock on either end creating a natural barrier and quieting the waves before they entered the bay. Massive trees (sequoias, I guessed from pictures I'd seen) grew above the rocks, their branches swaying in the cool breeze that blew off the water. Standing in the center of it all was a guy who looked like he was maybe in his twenties. He had an angular face framed by long auburn hair, violet eyes, and a surprisingly soft voice. He introduced himself as Orane.

I've been back to his world (which I sometimes jokingly call Narnia) every night at midnight for the past two years, and Orane has earned my respect, becoming something between a much older brother and a mentor. I trust him with all the grime and secrets in my life and he does whatever he can to help me. I trust him. I do. But oh, by Sinatra's last cigar do I wish I hadn't agreed to this particular adventure.

"Are you sure about this?" I ask Orane as he edges closer to the door. Through the small window inset in the white-painted panel, all I see is pale blue.

He was way more serious than I thought about grinding my fear of heights into dust. Each night it's been a different challenge, and each one has knocked my fear down another notch, but hiking the Rockies or standing on the glass floor of the Willis Tower overlooking Chicago is really not (at all) the same thing as what he has planned tonight. There's facing your fear and then there's insanity.

Skydiving is freaking insane.

"The last test," Orane says with a grin. "If you can face this tonight, no height will ever challenge you."

He opens the door of the plane and the wind whips into the cabin, pushing me back against the opposite wall. The last lingering bubble of fear swells in my chest. I cling to the strap hanging from the ceiling and shake my head. What about that scratch on my cheek I brought back from the dream world last week? Injuries here matter. I may be asleep, but hitting the ground at terminal velocity will still kill me.

"This isn't about heights! It's about not dying!" I shout at him.

"Death is an inevitable part of life. If your fear keeps you from living, you might as well let death claim you now."

Orane holds out his hand. He's barely recognizable in his jumpsuit, helmet, and goggles. His grin is the same, though, and I never have been able to turn down a challenge he's thrown at me. However much I may want to.

Grabbing his hand, I let him pull me across the plane until I'm standing in front of the open door. Ahead I see nothing but cloudless sky. Gulping a breath, I look down and know what a satellite feels like. I think I'd rather be in space. Maybe we can do that instead. I start to turn to ask Orane, but then his head is next to mine and he's speaking into my ear.

"Pull the red cord first." Orane yanks my hand off the doorframe and shoves me out of the plane.

I can't help it. I scream. I scream like a five-year-old as the wind pushes against me but does nothing to slow me down. I'm freefalling. My heart is pounding. All I can hear is the wind. Only fear is keeping me warm against the bite of the air. My hands search for the cord. I can't remember where it is. This feels like a cord. Or is that the strap holding my backpack in place? What if I pull the wrong thing and lose the chute?

Holy Frank Sinatra, I'm going to die.

But not for a while, apparently.

We jumped from miles above the land, much higher than would be possible on Earth without an oxygen mask. But that means I have way too much time to process what's happening. Lynnie went skydiving once and spent the whole next day complaining it was over too fast. I can't say the same thing. It seems like I've been falling for five minutes and the ground isn't getting any closer.

Something shoots past me like a torpedo. I flinch away, the motion sending me spinning through the air. When I finally stabilize, I spot Orane careening toward the ground. His arms and legs are locked together and he's rocketing down even faster than I am.

He's insane! I'm not doing that! I don't even know why I'm doing *this.*

Why not go for it? a small voice in the back of my head asks. *Would Orane really let you get hurt?*

The bubble of fear pops, adrenaline and curiosity rushing in. What must it be like to plummet toward the earth like that? Can I handle it? Am I strong enough? Orane seems to think I am, or he never would have taken me up here.

It's like someone has reached into my mind and cleared away the cobwebs. Or maybe like the last bit of a complicated knot has finally come undone. I feel unburdened. Free. Brave. Sucking in a lungful of chilly air, I fight against the wind, lock my legs together and glue my arms to my sides.

Pointing my head toward the ground, I pick up more speed. I have no idea how fast I'm going. It doesn't matter. I scream again, but this time it's fueled by excitement. Exhilaration.

Experimenting with the currents of air, I spin and dive, tumbling through the sky with no restrictions and no limitations. I see Orane's body jerk as his chute opens and slows his descent to a crawl. But I'm not ready to let go of this freefall yet.

I tumble faster and faster, spinning through the air so quickly I start getting nauseous. The ground is coming into focus at an alarming speed, but the freedom is addicting and I don't want it to end. *Wait*, I tell myself. *Wait, wait, wait.* Only when I realize I can see the spots on a deer running through the enormous clearing do I give in and tug the red cord.

My head jerks forward as the parachute pulls me higher. Or maybe it just seems like I'm going higher. It's hard to tell. And then, suddenly, it doesn't matter.

I've gone from falling to floating. The adrenaline begins to fade and I'm left with a softer sort of excitement. Closer to the wonder I felt when I was a kid before I learned to be constantly on guard.

Wait. The ground is coming closer a lot faster than I thought.

"Oh, crap!" I scream just before my feet hit.

Momentum pushes me forward and I roll, ending up on my back tangled in the lines of the parachute. My face is covered, but before I can attempt to unravel the mess I'm in, a shadow falls over my eyes.

"Except for the landing, I would say you did quite well, Julian."

"Help me get out of here so we can go again!"

Orane laughs and the parachute vanishes, lines and all. He's standing over me with his hand outstretched, offering to help me to my feet. I knew Orane wouldn't let me die. A scratch is one thing, but he always watches out for me.

"So? Can we do it again?"

"I was right, then?" Orane takes his helmet off and tosses it into the air. It disappears before it hits the ground. "Your fear of heights has been vanquished?"

"I don't know. Maybe we should test it and see." I can definitely see now why some people become adrenaline junkies. That was insanely awesome. "Can we do it again?"

"Perhaps tomorrow." He taps the helmet on my head. It fades away and he nods toward the edge of the field, where a picnic table and a huge buffet of food appeared. "Come. I must speak to you about something."

"Oh, no." I groan even as I follow him toward the food. "What'd I do now?"

"Nothing." Orane grins at me over his shoulder. "You are not usually such a pessimist. We must discuss your next goal."

"Oh. Cool." As I slide onto the bench, I pick up a piece of bread and toss it from hand to hand, trying to get it to cool. It's as hot as if it had just come out of the oven. "I thought we'd covered most of the annoying ones already."

In the two years I've known Orane, he's taught me to handle crowds, to quit smoking, and how to gamble well enough to make sure Lynnie and I always have enough to eat. *I* asked him to help me get rid of my fear of heights. The memory of getting stuck (paralyzed, really) on a stupid class field trip to the Stratosphere Tower makes it worth the trouble. One of the kids noticed and it took every trick I know to play it off as a joke. A prank. Like, "Oooooh, haha I got you! You thought I was actually scared of that? Please." It worked, but it was a close call. I've worked really hard to keep my weaknesses hidden. The Stratosphere came too close to blowing that out of the water.

To make it worse, I can see the dang thing from our apartment. Every day there's that reminder of my weakness staring at me from 1,149 feet in the air. I smile thinking about it now. I won't ever freeze again. Not after tonight.

Orane takes a grape and pops it into his mouth. "The work we have done for the past two years has only been leading up to the most arduous task. You will not like it, and it will be extremely difficult for you, but I want you to try."

"That sounds ominous. It can't be that bad, can it?" I bite into a piece of bread and raise my eyebrows.

"I suppose you will have to tell me."

Orane arranges two plates of food and passes me one. Grilled sirloin, seasoned French fries, a salad made of greens I can't even identify—it all smells so amazing I can't resist stuffing a huge bite with a little bit of everything into my mouth. Mmm, it's perfect. But I already knew it would be. Everything here is.

We eat in silence for a few minutes, both of us steadily working our way through first (and then second) helpings. When I fill my plate up for a third time, I finally slow down long enough to ask, "What exactly is this horrible thing I won't want to do?"

"You have a habit of lying, Julian."

"I do no—" His lips press together and I cut myself off. "Okay, fine. Maybe I do. But I've never lied to *you*."

The severity of Orane's expression lessens. He even smiles, but only a little. "True. I am grateful for the trust that represents, but I am the *only* person in your life to whom you have never lied. The only one, Julian. It is not healthy. If you do not learn to speak with honesty, one day your lies will lead you down a path there is no escaping."

I stare at him, waiting for the punch line.

There isn't one.

"*That's* my next goal? Honesty?" I shake my head and push my food around on my plate. "Can't we work on something easier? Like walking on coals or theoretical physics?"

Orane chuckles, but I'm serious.

I don't lie just to lie. I lie to keep myself safe. To protect my life from scrutiny and to keep Lynnie (who's more immature than me) from being shuttled off to rehab or something. It's not even usually *lying*. It's the truth presented in disguise. A twist in wording that makes people see the information I present the way I want them to. Even though Lynnie is a 24/7 disaster area, anyone "just trying to be helpful" and "do the right thing" would completely mess up my life. I've heard the horror stories from kids stuck in group homes or foster care. No one adopts a teenage boy. Honesty could destroy everything.

Lynnie has family, but she's managed to piss every one of them off. There's no guarantee any of them would take me in if the worst happened. Maybe Uncle Frank and Aunt Dana, but they live in New York and they've had more than enough to deal with since their daughter Mariella went mute four years ago. Even if they wanted to, they might not be able to handle me. I think Uncle Frank would try, though. Maybe. If I ever let him know how awful it really is with Lynnie.

Still … "I don't know if I can do that. It's not that simple."

"It could be. You have let lying become a *habit*. You do not just lie to keep people from seeing the truth about your life; you lie simply because it is easier and because people will believe you."

"Not *everyone* believes me," I mutter. But is that even true? I bite the inside of my cheek remembering how I played John and ended up with an extra $500. Thinking back further, I can't remember the last time someone called my bluff when I was manipulating them into something. Some people take more convincing than others, but I usually make them do what I want or believe whatever I say. Or I'm smart enough to know when I can't get away with it.

Orane must see the realization on my face because he nods. "You see, do you not?"

"Yeah, yeah. I see." Sighing, I push the plate away and all of the food vanishes, leaving the table clear. "So, that's it? Just suddenly be all honest all the time?"

"It would be an impressive feat if you could do that," Orane says with a smile. "But no. I would not ask that of you. Not yet. For now I ask only this—if the lie does not directly pertain to keeping this realm or the deficiencies of your mother a secret, tell the truth."

"And if I don't?" I ask. "If I *can't*?"

"I know you can, but if you choose not to …" He pauses and holds my eyes as though he wants to make sure I'm paying attention. His violet eyes seem brighter than usual right now, almost glowing. "If you *choose* not to, this place will be close to you."

My hands drop to the table with a *thud*. "What? Are you serious?"

"Of course I am." Orane frowns and tucks his shoulder-length auburn hair behind his ear as he leans closer to me, his eyes somber and a little sad. "This place is a gift, one that is meant to be used as a tool on your path to self-fulfillment. If you decline to work toward your potential, the doors to this realm will shut. There is nothing I can do to change this, Julian. It is simply the way my world works."

Pushing off the bench, I pace, my steps flattening the grass beneath my feet. "So you're saying if I screw up I can't ever come back here? How is *that* fair?"

The door to the dream world may only open at midnight, but knowing it's there is the one thing that gets me through most days. Just the idea of losing this refuge makes my hands shake and my breath quicken.

Orane steps in front of me and grips my shoulders, leaning down to look into my eyes. "It is not so grim as that. A mistake shall not bar the door. Willfully choosing to ignore the tasks you have been set shall."

"Oh." I take a deep breath and exhale slowly. "Really?"

"Yes, really. There will come a time when I shall ask you to vow that you will live your life in honesty—for this is the last and greatest of your tests, Julian—but, until that time, a mistake shall not lock you away from my world."

My head is spinning. It's hard to focus. How did everything change so fast? I knew the freedom of Orane's realm couldn't last forever, but I never expected the price I might have to pay would be so high.

Closing my eyes, I try to concentrate. Honesty and I are barely on speaking terms. To do as he asks, I'm going to have to pay attention to every single word that leaves my mouth. Geez. What about poker? Does bluffing count as a lie? Or what I said to John this afternoon? Technically, it was true. Mostly. Kind of.

Okay, fine. Barely. It was barely true.

Crap. How black and white is this?

The truth is as variable as the people who speak it. There are so many shades of gray in human interactions and motivations and perceptions that not even a mantis shrimp would be able to distinguish between them all. Just thinking about it gives me a headache.

"Will you do this, Julian? Will you begin to live honestly with yourself and those around you?"

I open my eyes and sigh. "Do I have a choice?"

Orane nods, dropping his hands to his sides. "There are always choices, and there are always consequences. You must decide what you are willing to live with and what you are capable of living through."

The spot under my ribs pinches and then pulls, like someone hooked a fishing line through my diaphragm and started tugging. I rub the spot, but that doesn't ease the twinge that always emerges when the doorway back home opens.

"Time is almost gone." Orane glances over my shoulder, where I know the doorway is waiting, and then back at me. "What is your answer?"

What can I live with and what can I live through? Could I survive two years at a group home if they took Lynnie away? Yeah, more than likely. It would suck in ways I probably can't imagine, but I could survive it as long as I had Orane's help. But if I lost this place? I shudder and try not to think about it. If I lost the dream world, I would lose everything.

The tug turns into a sharp pull and I gasp. "Geez. All right, all right. I'm coming."

"Your answer, Julian," Orane says.

"I can do it. Honesty or whatever. I can do it." I say the words with more confidence than I feel. Orane accepts it and smiles as he ruffles my light brown hair and nudges me toward the doorway.

"Then go. I will see you tomorrow night."

Nodding, I turn and walk through the glowing portal that will take me back to the waking world. Everything is black and empty for a split second—neither cold nor hot and I'm somehow weightless and grounded—but then the hazy flow of my dreams overtakes me and I sleep. But not for long.

I wake earlier than usual tonight. It's only two-fifteen when I check the clock, but I don't feel tired or worn out. As soon as my eyes open, I'm alert. Ready to get up and do whatever I have to do today. And do it all with honesty, apparently.

Groaning, I sit up and swing my legs over the side of the bed. I'm about to stand and grab my economics textbook when I notice something shining out of the corner of my eye. I focus on it, but there's nothing there. Maybe it was just an afterimage from Orane's world. No, wait. There *is* something on my nightstand. That bracelet wasn't there before. Leaning closer, I examine the braided leather bracelet and the clear glass bead dangling from one end.

It's weird enough that the bracelet appeared in my room, but it's even weirder that *this* is the source of the light I saw. The whole thing is covered in a thin layer of mist that dances and sparkles like glitter in a snow globe. Wary but curious, I reach out and pick it up.

And almost drop it in shock when Orane's voice fills my head.

The character within the glass is from an ancient language lost to humanity eons ago. It was a symbol of honesty and truth and trust. For you, let it be a reminder of your promise and what is at stake. Remember what I have taught you and you will succeed in this as you have succeeded in every test I have set until now.

I shudder and tighten my grip on the bracelet. Orane is obviously powerful (I mean, the guy created an exact replica of the freaking Grand Canyon for me last week), but I had no idea he could reach through the barrier between our worlds and leave things behind. Or attach telepathic messages to them like he's leaving a note. It's awesome. (Also, really weird. But mostly awesome.)

Taking a deep breath to calm my racing pulse, I turn on my lamp and hold the glass bead up to the light. There in the center is a looping design that vaguely reminds me of an Arabic letter.

Grinning, I hook the bracelet in place and take a deep breath. Honesty. I can do this. I have to do this. Losing Orane would be a far worse fate than leaving Lynnie.

Since the entire apartment building is usually asleep and quiet at this time of the night, these early-morning hours are when I usually do my homework. It's easier to focus when I don't have to filter out traffic and conversations and TV noise and whatever else is happening. I get through some of the reading and one set of questions for Algebra II when a car door slams in the parking lot.

I can't catch the words, but the tone and the screech is one I know well. Lynnie has finally made it home at—I check the clock—3:27 AM.

Please let them come in and go to sleep, I beg the universe. The universe is apparently not in a mood to listen.

The front door slams open so hard it rattles my doorknob, reminding me once again why I never bothered hanging up anything in a frame. They're screaming at each other, words so slurred and incoherent that I know they're both riding some sort of chemical wave. Getting up quietly, I lock my door. I'm not worried they'll hurt me, but I am not in the mood for them to forget which bedroom is Lynnie's and come stumbling half-naked into mine. Eww.

I shouldn't have worried. This isn't a fight that sounds like it'll end in sex. This one rages on for three hours, dying for short bursts as it fades into something close to a normal conversational tone until one of them says something that fires the whole mess up again. The chaos finally dies just before seven. I'm dressed and ready for school by the time they fall completely silent.

I give it ten minutes before I unlock my door and slide into the hallway. I'm about to step into the kitchen to grab something to eat on my way to the bus when I notice something that shouldn't be there. There's a foot on the floor. A foot connected to the body of Lynnie's current jerk boyfriend Ed. Beside him is a half-empty bottle of vodka and, not too far away, a bottle of prescription pills spilled across the linoleum. It's hard to tell if he's breathing or not.

Should I leave him? I consider it for a second, but only a second. If he dies, Lynnie will be a mess and we'll have cops (and maybe social workers) crawling all over our backs. Not worth it.

"Ed?" Nudging him with my foot, I wait for some response. Nothing. I kick him a little harder and talk a little louder. "Ed?"

His leg twitches, but otherwise he doesn't move. Twitching is an okay sign, though. At least he's not dead yet. He's also barely dressed and I really don't want to touch this guy. Looking around, I grab a plastic bag off the counter and wrap my hand in it before crouching down by his side and shaking him.

"Ed, wake up." He snorts and groans, shifting slightly. Snorting means he's breathing, right? And lying on his side is safer than on his back if he starts puking.

Whatever. Good enough for me.

I step over his body and straight into a puddle of vodka. Pulling the leg of my jeans off the floor to keep it dry, I grab my water bottle from the cabinet and refill it in the sink, snagging a granola bar from the mostly empty pantry. On my way out of the room I turn and survey the mess one last time. At least there's no broken glass. I'll clean everything up later. Once there's not a body blocking half the floor.

The sunlight coming through the tiny kitchen window glints off the set of knives in the corner. Two years ago I was so pissed at the world that I would've been inches away from killing this idiot. Orane saved a lot more than my sanity—he saved my life.

In the living room, Lynnie is sprawled on the couch. Her makeup is smeared and runny, making her look like a clown that got caught in the rain. Her short, dyed-blonde hair sticks out in various directions and she's still wearing her glittery, way-too-short club dress. On the floor, half-underneath the coffee table, Lynnie's monstrosity of a pink leather purse is on its side, contents everywhere. It was probably used as a projectile at some point during their fight. Papers and pills are spread across the linoleum.

Suppressing the urge to wake her up and kick her *and* Ed out of the apartment, I pick up the papers from her purse, peer into the huge bag and pull out anything that looks like it might be important. Doing this at least once a week is the only way I find out about when she's lost a job or who she owes money to.

My heart sinks when I pull out the envelope I used to send the check to the electric company. It's been torn open, and only the stub from the bottom of the bill, the piece with our account number and address on it, is inside. They never got last month's check.

I can't even find the energy to be angry. This happens too often to waste the emotion on. The anger only comes when I find a slip of paper torn from a complimentary Caesars notepad.

J.E.T. 3.9k → H.D. 2wk

That's Harry's handwriting and his abbreviations. Jacquelyn Elizabeth Teagan owes $3,900 to Harry Dougal within two weeks.

How old is this? There's no date so I can't be sure, but it's just dirty and creased enough to hint that it's not a debt she picked up tonight. Something (like a crapload of experience with Lynnie) tells me that this is probably where the money that should have gone to our electric check disappeared to. At least she had a decent reason for swiping it this time. I know what would've happened to both of us if she hadn't made at least a good faith payment on the account. Harry Dougal does not subscribe to the "injured and dead people don't pay debts" school of criminal thought. He'd rather lose *some* money and knock the fear of Harry into the rest of his "clients."

Fantastic. Another few thousand dollars I have to scrounge up out of thin air. Guess I know what I'll be doing with my weekend. I probably should've kept a record of how much this woman owes me, but the number would be so high it'd be more depressing than helpful. Not like I'll ever get any of it back.

Swallowing a burst of somewhat hysterical laughter (seriously—*how* have I found myself in this situation *again?*) I drop everything to the floor and leave, locking the door behind me. At least I'll have eight hours of relative peace at school.

Walking across the parking lot and toward my bus stop, I look up at the Stratosphere.

Vegas is the city of dreams, lies, and possibilities. There are a thousand different ways for you to pretend your life is completely different, but none of them last.

Still, it's hard not to imagine what my life could be like. If I had different parents, if we lived in a place that didn't bleed temptations for someone as weak-minded as Lynnie, if the Fates had been kinder when deciding what I would suffer in my life. Logically I know there are people who have it a lot worse than me, but somehow that doesn't really make me feel any better today.

Two

Nadette

Friday, September 12 – 3:56 PM EDT

Some people think the world runs on money or power or, for the particularly optimistic, faith. It doesn't. The world runs on lies.

Big ones, little ones, black ones, white ones, lies that fool an entire nation, and lies that don't fool anyone but make people feel a little better about themselves for a while. As though all they really need to be able to sleep soundly at night is tell themselves, "Well, at least I tried."

Some idiots talk big about being able to call anyone's bluff, about being able to read any lie no matter how seemingly insignificant. They can't. Even if they catch most of them, they still let themselves believe the ones they like. The ones that fit the way they want to see the world. Or the ones that comfort. Or the ones that are easy.

They don't understand what it's like to actually hear every. Single. Lie. *Every* one. To flinch when people tell you something they know isn't true or, worse, to hear the lies even the people telling them believe.

That was bad enough, but now I wish I could go back to that. It's better than losing my mind completely. It's better than getting struck with insomnia so hard that my creepy-ass dreams start stalking my waking hours.

Six months of seeing a psychiatrist. I thought I'd be used to these appointments by now. Especially since I asked for the first one. But, nope. Doesn't seem to matter. Doesn't even matter that I actually like Dr. Peter Branson. He's kind and relatively non-judgmental and his waiting room is nice, with wood floors and cream walls and beautifully soothing watercolors, but every time I walk into this office, my nerves start buzzing like live wires and I can't stop fidgeting. I can't stop wishing I could somehow give myself amnesia, wipe my brain clean, and start over. As long as it would take this stupid polygraph trick of mine with it.

Mom's latest interior design project must be overwhelming because she's staring at the red silk fabric with white dragons embroidered on it like it's a code she has to decipher. Eyebrows drawn close together, she looks at me and asks, "Are dragons too typical in an Asian-inspired décor?"

"Do the clients *like* dragons?"

"I assume so. They own a company called Dragon Fire Industries." She bites her lip and holds up the fabric, staring at it intently. "Maybe if I found something a little more modern. More abstract. Something with the hint of dragons instead of the shape. If anything like that even exists."

"So make it. Your designs are usually better anyway."

Mom gives me a quick but bright smile, her cheeks a little flushed at the compliment. It only takes her about thirty seconds to throw her lapful of fabric samples onto the coffee table in front of us and pull her sketchbook out of her huge purse. She's about to get lost in the project when the door opens and Peter smiles at me. He's tall with one of those "I used to be athletic when I was a kid" builds, and every time I see him standing in that doorway it strikes me again how similar his skin tone is to the walnut wood of his office door. Mom looks up from her sketchbook, giving the doctor a tired smile.

"How are you, Grace?" Peter asks my mom.

Her bright green eyes flick toward me before she answers. "Tired, but I'm all right."

As he nods his acknowledgement, he gestures for me to come into his office. "You let me know if you need to talk, okay, Grace? Don't wait until you're too overtaxed."

"Thanks, Peter. I'll keep that in mind."

He smiles again, his brown eyes crinkling at the corners, then closes the door behind us, locking us in for the next hour.

"Have you been sleeping, Nadette?" It's always the first question he asks.

"No. Not more than an hour a night."

He hums and makes a note on his legal pad as he settles into the dark brown leather armchair. I plop onto the matching overstuffed leather couch across from him and lift my fingers to play with my necklace. The gesture draws Peter's eye. He leans forward, squinting as though he's trying to get a better look.

"New?" he asks.

"Yeah. Mom gave it to me this morning." I look down. All I can see is the oblong black pendant wrapped in silver wire. I trace the etching on the front of the stone, Chinese characters that mean "protected." "She's working on a house for these clients from China, and I don't know. I guess she told one of them I've been having nightmares."

Peter's head tilts. "So she bought you a necklace to apologize for breaking your confidence?"

My lip quirks up, almost a smile. "No. The woman's mother was an herbalist and medicine woman. According to her, black jade is good for keeping away angry spirits and cleansing negative energy. The lady sells jewelry imported from China. She gave this to Mom to give to me."

"And? Do you feel cleansed?"

I stroke the beads, my fingers bumping from one sphere to the next. "Not really. But it can't hurt, right?"

"No. I definitely haven't heard of black jade having any adverse side effects." He smiles at the joke. I can't join in. I remember too well the side effects of the sleeping pills and antipsychotics he's tried on me. None of them worked. Some only made things worse.

Peter runs a hand over his dark hair. His fingers linger over his ears where the strands are starting to go gray. "So, Nadette, we've been dealing with the recent past since you came here—the insomnia and the waking dreams."

"Which still don't make sense. Not even after the CAT scans and sleep studies," I say.

Peter cocks his head to the side slightly. Almost a sideways nod like he's conceding the point. "Traditional methods obviously aren't going to work for a non-traditional problem. Concentrating on the dreams doesn't seem to be helping, so I want to go back further. Tell me about the progression of your other talent."

"Talent?" As if it's something I honed or wanted. Or have any control over. "You mean the invisible polygraph I seem to carry around in my head?"

"That's a good metaphor for it." Peter grins and nods. "I like that. And yes, the progression—or evolution, rather—of your invisible polygraph."

I bite my lip and tug at the black jade pendant. "I'm not sure what you mean exactly. I've always been able to tell when people are lying. My brain has been weird my whole life."

I was six years old when I finally understood that hearing bells ringing in your head when someone told a lie wasn't normal.

"I know you've always had the bells," Peter says. It took him a month to really believe me when I told him I heard lies. Once he adjusted to the fact that I wasn't bullshitting him or completely off my rocker, he's been quietly fascinated by the concept. "But you've said more than once that your sensitivity has increased dramatically."

Pulling my fire-orange hair over my shoulder, I nod slowly.

"I want you to examine the timeline of that evolution for me. Think back to the first time you remember it changing. Try to remember what you noticed was different and when that happened, okay?" He leans forward, scanning my face and gripping his pen in his left fist.

When *did* everything start to change? "It was just after my sister Sophia's birthday. About nineteen months ago." I bite my lip and try to remember the conversation we were having at the time. My breath hitches a bit. I remember it word for word. *Weird.* Shaking myself out of my thoughts, I refocus on Peter. "She was telling me about this guy she'd met and how excited she was for their date. She said, 'It's amazing a guy like that is still single. I can't believe someone else hasn't realized how perfect he is.'"

Peter nods. "And she was lying?"

"Well, no. She really thought she was telling the truth. She *believed* this guy was single. But I heard the bells anyway." I cringe. "Sophia was *pissed* when I told her she was being played. She went out with him anyway. A month later I found a CD of Schubert's compositions, a shirt of hers I'd been coveting for months, and a gift card to Amazon on my bed."

"So, that was what?" Peter tapped on the legal pad with his pen. "Six months after the dreams started? Seven?"

"Seven, yeah."

Peter's grip on his pen loosens and he makes a note. "That's a pretty significant difference—being able to spot a falsehood even when the person speaking believes it."

"It *sucks*." I slide down the couch a little until my butt is almost hanging off and cross my arms over my chest.

"Bet it helps on tests." A small smile curves his lips.

I snort. "Please. How many teachers are willing to admit they're wrong? Or accept 'Because the bells told me so' as proof?"

Peter's smile slides away. "Hmm. Okay, good point." He takes a slow breath and makes another note before he looks up and asks, "What did you notice next?"

"That's not enough?"

"Is that everything?"

I bite my lip and look away, pushing myself up on the couch again. "No."

"Then it's not enough."

Groaning, I rub my hands over my face. "Six months after that, I started *seeing* lies."

"How do you mean?"

"You know how sometimes you look at someone and you can just tell that they're faking a smile?"

I drop my hands as Peter's nose wrinkles, his grimace not stifled quite fast enough. "My ex-mother-in-law seemed to do that every time she saw me."

A little of the tension in my shoulders eases. I almost smile. That's one of the reasons I like Peter—he's willing to poke fun at himself sometimes too, to point out that not even the psychiatrist has everything figured out.

"Well, six months after I started being able to spot," I pause, searching for the word Peter used, "falsehoods, I was watching a friend of mine smile at her boyfriend. She ... look, this is weird even for me, okay?"

"Okay." Peter puts his pen down and settles against the back of the armchair. "Go on."

Taking a deep breath, I force the words out, even though it feels like I'm wearing an iron corset and someone keeps pulling the strings tighter. "There was this red haze over her face. Kind of like how a rainbow looks on a cloudy day? Color that's kind of there but not there? But the haze was only red. And only over her face. And only until she dropped that fake smile."

"That's ..." Peter's eyes are wide. He swallows hard and shakes his head. "That would be *incredibly* useful in my line of work."

I laugh, a startled, harsh laugh that dissolves into breathless chuckles. I look up at Peter, expecting to see him laughing with me.

He isn't moving. Though his lips are slightly parted like he's about to speak, no sound emerges. His shoulders aren't moving with the breaths he should be taking and his foot is stuck on the upstroke of the rhythm his toes have been tapping on the carpet.

Oh, no. Please, no. Not again. Not now.

I pull my legs tight against my chest. One arm locks around my knees and the other hand wraps tight around the black jade pendant. It's warm in my hand. Warmer than it should be from just my body heat. *Please,* I silently beg the necklace. *Please, please work.* Nothing else has stopped these moments where time seems to still.

The air in front of Peter's large, wood desk shimmers and sparkles. All I can do is hold on to the ridiculous hope that a string of black jade beads will work where medication and therapy have failed.

Where there was empty air a second ago, there's now an arch of white light shot through with orange. Through the door I see a strip of snow-white, powder-fine sand leading down to water the color of turquoise. The warm breeze that blows into the room, ruffling strands of my hair against my cheek, smells like saltwater and tropical flowers.

So often, the worlds that appear through that glowing arch are impossible. Fairylands out of fantasy movies, cities built on clouds, crowded Carnival-like festivals lit by floating lanterns. None of them call to me the way this simple, vibrant beach does. I wiggle my toes inside my sneakers, wishing I could run out onto the sand and let my feet sink into the soft-looking grains. Instead, I force my attention onto the man framed inside the arch.

Syver.

His artfully shaggy hair is an iridescent green-black that reminds me of a beetle's wings. His tawny skin gleams in the bright sunlight of his world and his full lips are almost always smiling. Syver smiles now and steps closer to the edge of the arch, leaning against the strip of light as though it's a solid thing. I relax a little, some of the tension easing out of my shoulders, but I don't let go of my knees. Looking at him is like playing a really complicated find-the-difference puzzle. There's something off, something that makes me itchy, but I've never been able to point to any one word or detail and say, "That."

"Hello, Nadette," he says, smiling like we're friends who just happened to run into each other. "How are you?"

Swallowing, I nod a greeting. "Tired."

Concern lines his forehead as his head tilts slightly. "I think you are wearing yourself too thin."

I shrug. Not being able to sleep and living in constant fear of another time-stopping visit from Syver's world is enough to wear anyone thin.

"Two years and you still don't trust me enough to let me show you an easier way." His sigh sounds so disappointed, but I can't tell if he's more upset with himself or me. I can't tell why it matters so much to him either. "Why do you spend so much of your energy fighting?"

That one is easy. "It's worth it if I can find a way to get rid of this ... whatever it is that's in my head." I want it gone. Whatever it is that created the invisible polygraph and makes me see doors to other worlds and impossibly beautiful people who, more often than not, lie.

Twenty-six different people have invaded my mind since these strange dreams started two years ago, but Syver shows up twice as often as anyone else. And he's the only one of them who has never lied to me.

"Why is it easier for most humans to believe themselves crazy than to see themselves as special? Unique." His voice reminds me of a cello, smooth and melodious. "I thought you would have accepted the truth by now, Nadette."

"What *is* the truth?" I ask, the words escaping my lips before I realize I'm going to speak.

"That what you can do is not an affliction, it is a gift."

My hand tightens around the jade pendant. A rush of nearly scalding heat floods my skin. I can't control the shudder that runs through me. These doorways always send shivers across my skin, but they're never this bad.

"A gift?" Gritting my teeth and tightening my arm around my knees, I shake my head and force myself to keep talking. "I have no friends because I freak people out. Even my family isn't comfortable around me. It's hard to see this as a *gift*."

Syver's head tilts and he studies me carefully. His eyes scan down from my bright orange hair to my black Converses tucked in close to my body. His gaze lingers longest on my throat, his expression tightening and his dark eyes narrowing when he spots my necklace.

"Has it come to this, Nadette? Hiding behind a wall of stone and light?"

What is he talking about? The only stones in the room are the ones around my neck. The only light is coming from Peter's lamps and Syver's white and orange archway.

My ears pop and my vision blurs. The feeling is somewhere between the pleasureful pain of a joint cracking and the rush of an epiphany. What I see when my vision settles sends my pulse beating harder and faster than a drumline.

The solid white border of the archway disintegrates into a tangle of tendrils, orange ropes that stretch out, trying to bind my wrists, my chest, my head. I scream and pull back. The coils of light brush like ice-cold drips of water on my overheated skin. Each one makes me shiver even though they never quite make contact.

There's a layer of white, shimmering light coating my body, pulsing out from the black jade pendant.

The tendrils double, sliding over my skin but never sticking. Never taking hold. My body is trembling, shaking like high-voltage electricity is running through it. My eyes stay locked on Syver. His smile never falters—a polite, vaguely concerned smile. That concern is no longer reflected in those changeable eyes.

"W-what is th-this?" I force the words past my chattering teeth. I can't take a full breath. My chest burns. So do my eyes. I think I feel tears trail down my cheeks. "What is ha-ha-happening?"

"Can you see it now?" His dark eyes widen just a little. "Fascinating."

"Stop!" I beg. "Please, p-please, *stop*."

Syver's head tilts as he considers, a lock of his dark hair falling over his forehead. Then he smiles and shakes his head. "No."

I curl tighter around myself, pressing my eyes against my knees. Sobs intensify the tremors running through me. I can barely remember how to breathe.

Stop! Oh God, please. Stop, I repeat in my head. I'm gripping my pendant so tight the wire wrapping might leave permanent indentations in my palm.

"I am afraid this is a turning point for you. As engrossing as it has been to watch you struggle against us and fight the development of your own strengths, now you have a choice, pet."

That voice is so rich, so compelling. *Forcibly* compelling. I look up, feeling as though there's a hand on the back of my head guiding the motion. When I meet Syver's eyes, that smile is still there, but now his dark eyes glimmer with that same strange green-black iridescence as his beetle's wing hair.

"You have a rather unique—and surprisingly powerful—skill. It deserves to be used and cherished, not feared and hidden. Or erased, as you seem intent on doing."

The green glimmer in his eyes intensifies and it feels like all the oxygen has been sucked out of the room. The jade around my neck grows even hotter. But, it's not enough to counteract the chill surrounding me.

"I will give you some time to decide, but not long. Two choices, pet. Take my hand and willingly relinquish the thing you so despise yourself for having." He extends one slender hand as though beckoning me forward. "Or I will take it from you."

His hand flips and his body tenses. The tendrils shift from slithering, grasping vines to spears of light with glittering, razor-sharp points. Instead of groping for a grip, they attack. They slam against my thin shield of white light and send piercing electric shocks through my body.

I dive out of the way. They follow. The attack intensifies until the black jade pendant in my hand heats past the point of burning. I can't release the stone. A scream rips through my throat and my voice breaks. My vision blurs, fading into a field of white. Something shatters, the sound somewhere between the crack of stone and the tinkle of glass.

Then there's only silence and blissful, peaceful darkness.

Almost every day for the past two years, I've woken up in a sudden burst. I jump from unconsciousness to consciousness in one abrupt leap.

Not this time.

Awareness filters through the fog of sleep in pieces. Over-starched cloth against my skin. The smell of disinfectant and cough syrup and plastic. A handful of voices murmuring in hushed whispers. Something beeping that won't shut the hell up.

Where am I?

I force a deep breath, hissing at the throbbing pain behind my right eye.

"Nadette?"

The voice is familiar. *Who is that?*

Never mind. It doesn't matter right now. Not when my head feels like it's being beaten in with a crowbar and I can't seem to shake that last vestige of sleep.

Wake up, wake up, wake up.

My heart beats a little faster. The beeping keeps time, almost like it's … like it's a heart monitor? I suck another breath. The jolt of pain through my head is enough to pop my eyes open and clear away the last of the fog.

Mom is leaning over me. Her red curls are pulled back in a rough bun, and her green eyes are bloodshot and red-rimmed. Normally her outfits are as carefully arranged as her interior designs. Now, her cream silk shirt is rumpled and there's a small stain on the collar.

"Oh, thank God," she breathes, pressing a kiss on my forehead as she smooths my hair back. "You scared us, sweetheart."

Squinting, I look over her shoulder. There's enough evidence in the room to make an educated guess. My throat is raw and my voice is hoarse, but I manage to ask, "Hospital? Why?"

Mom opens her mouth to answer, but then Peter comes in with a tall, strawberry-blond man in a white coat. His sharp nose and the angle of his chin are instantly familiar, but it takes me a second to place the new guy. He just moved back to town a few weeks ago and I haven't seen him decked out for work yet.

My second-oldest brother meets my eyes and grins, relief turning his crooked smile almost goofy. "Always have to be the center of attention, don't you, Nadie?"

"Hey, Jake," I rasp at the same time Mom lightly slaps his arm and scolds, "Don't you start."

Footsteps thud in the hall, quick like someone is running, and shoes squeak just before a hand catches the frame of the open door. My slightly-out-of-breath father pulls himself into the room, his blue eyes wide. My father was in Washington, D.C. last time I checked.

"Dad?"

"Jesus, honey. You scared the hell out of us." He huffs and tries to smile, running his fingers through his already disarranged blond hair as he steps closer to the bed and leans in to kiss my forehead.

I lift my arm to pull him into a hug. Something white is wrapped around my hand. Bandages? For what? Raising my eyes, I flick my gaze between the bandages and everyone else, silently questioning. It doesn't hurt. What happened? Why am I here?

My parents frown. Jake starts to fidget under my stare. Peter clears his throat and steps forward. "Nadette, what's the last thing you remember?"

His words trigger memories. My pulse ratchets up. I gasp and try to sit. Before I get more than a few inches off the bed, three different hands are on my shoulders, easing me back down. I try to breathe. It's like cotton is filling my lungs. There's no room for air. The short gasps I manage only make me dizzier. Memories of everything that happened in Peter's office rush to fill my head.

Frozen time. The door of light. That tempting beach. Syver. The moment when his claws came out, when everything changed. Orange spears and pain. And then nothing. Darkness and silence. Waking up in a hospital with a bandage around my hand for no apparent reason.

Mom, Dad, Jake, and Peter are all there, watching me and waiting for me to say something. To answer Peter's question.

"I was in your office." I swallow again and this time, my voice comes a little closer to normal. "We were talking about you being able to use my polygraph thing in your practice and then …"

I trail off, my eyes darting between the four concerned faces. For a second, I consider skipping the episode with Syver and asking Peter what he *thinks* happened. I don't. Peter and my parents know all about my crazy. Jake knows more than almost anyone else. Sighing, I close my eyes and let my head drop to the pillow. I slowly pour out the rest of the story.

Fear ripples through me when I picture the orange light wrapping around me. I push it down. I try to tell the story the way I'd explain a movie. Like the memories don't send shivers of ice down my spine. Like I don't hear the stupid heart monitor giving away how fast my pulse is racing.

When I get to the part where darkness takes over and I wake up here, I open my eyes. I need to see light. I need the reminder that I'm not still lost in that blackness.

Mom is biting her lip, but she tries to smile when I look at her. "Never thought I'd say this, but right now I really wish you could lie to me and tell me everything is just fine."

I laugh. It sounds more like a sob. "Yeah. Me too." But I can't. And we both know it. I turn to Peter and finally ask, "What happened after I blacked out?"

"I was about to ask you something when—I don't know. It was like watching a DVD that skipped. You were sitting on the couch, and then you were a foot to the left, curled tight in a ball with your eyes shut." Peter swallows and runs his hand over his short hair. His body is tense, drawn so tight that I know he's more terrified than he's letting on and trying not to show it. "Your necklace was in pieces like it had exploded. You slumped over and I saw the scratches on your neck and the cuts on your palm and I …"

His voice is shaking by the end and he turns away. Jake finishes the sentence for him. "He freaked the fuck out and called 911."

"Jake, language," Dad scolds absently, obviously on autopilot.

Everyone settles into a slightly uncomfortable silence. I shift, trying to resist the urge to shove away these horribly scratchy sheets. When I clear my throat, all eyes lock on me. "When can we go home?"

Another beat of silence. The tension in the room ramps higher.

Jake's jaw clenches and he looks away. "They want to keep you overnight for observation."

"What? No! Just sign me out!"

"I'm not your doctor, Nadette. I *can't*."

"You're *a* doctor."

"I'm also your brother. And you were unconscious for over two hours for no apparent reason." He shakes his head, his blue eyes begging me to understand. "The other doctors aren't the only ones who want to keep you here overnight just to be safe, okay?"

I grind my teeth. Dammit. I can't really fault them for wanting to keep me safe, to make sure I'm okay. If any one of them were in this bed instead of me, I'd be doing the same thing. But that doesn't mean I'm any safer here than I was at Peter's office. Or would be at home. I run my finger along one of the shallow cuts the necklace left behind and shudder even as I force myself to ask, "Can you get me a new one?"

Mom's eyes narrow. "A new what?" But then her gaze tracks the movement of my finger and she pales. "Another necklace? But Nadie, it—honey, it *exploded*!"

"It kept me safe. I don't know how, but it did."

For a second, Mom just stares at me. "*Exploded*!" she insists again before looking at Dad and Jake. "*Ex-plo-ded*!"

"Bombs explode too, but that doesn't mean they aren't used to keep people safe," Jake says.

"Thank you, Jacob. That analogy makes me feel *so* much better."

The bells ring in my head, but softer than when someone lies outright. Sarcasm never sets them off too loudly. My brother winces slightly, still not immune to Mom's displeasure.

Dad sighs. "This is Nadette we're talking about, remember? The girl who quite literally chokes on lies?" He waits until Mom and Jake look at him before he continues. "Grace, if she says she needs another one, don't you think it would be safer to believe her? Hell, I vote we go buy her fifteen of them. Fill her whole bedroom with black jade statues and weigh her down with the stuff if she really thinks it'll make this shit stop."

Mom glances at me. Her expression is silently asking if that's true, if I really think the jade will make the visits go away. I clear my throat. "I don't know if they'll stop or not. He didn't like me wearing it, though. At all."

It only takes her another second to make up her mind. "All right, fine. I'll call Zan and see what else she has in stock."

My parents lean over the bed and kiss my forehead, promising to be back soon. Jake squeezes my hand and follows them out. As they leave, I hear Jake say, "Isn't there that New Age store near the house? Maybe they have some."

Peter smiles gently. "I should get back to the office. I have some appointments I need to reschedule."

"Sorry." I try not to cringe as I say it. I don't think it works.

"Not your fault. I'm just glad you're all right. Scared the hell out of me, Nadette. Thought you weren't going to wake up like—" He cuts himself off and shakes his head. "Try to get some rest. We'll get you out of here in the morning if everything checks out."

He pats my unbandaged hand and then he's gone. I'm alone with uncomfortable sheets, an annoyingly loud heart monitor, and the fear that if Syver shows up before my mom comes back with an armful of black jade, I might finally see what it's like on the other side of that glowing arch.

Three

Julian

Friday, September 12 – 1:15 PM PDT

The cell phone Uncle Frank got me last year beeps with a reminder as I'm walking home from the bus after convincing the secretary to let me sign out early from school—Mariella Teagan's 18th Birthday. I haven't seen my cousin in years, but the reminder still makes me grin. Quickly dismissing the note, I pull up Frank's number and call.

"Heya, kiddo!" He sounds happy. Happier than I've heard him in a long time. "How's it going? Everything okay?"

I open my mouth to sugar-coat everything like I always have (the three hours of screaming this morning, the fight I got into with a friend at school today because I didn't lie when he asked me what I thought about the girl he has a massive crush on, the fact that I still haven't figured out how I'm going to pay two months of electric bills) but then I glance down at the shimmering bracelet on my wrist. Honesty. Orane wanted honesty. But I don't have to lay *all* of that on Uncle Frank, do I?

"Uhm, it's not why I called, but we could use some help with the electric bill."

Uncle Frank sighs. "Is she still dating … um, Fred?"

"Ed," I correct. "Fred was last year." He was the one with the habit of "accidentally" walking off with Lynnie's wallet.

There's a noise over the line that sounds like it was almost a word. Whatever Frank had wanted to say gets cut off, though. There's only a slight hesitation before he says, "Email me the bill and I'll take care of it, okay?"

I swallow and close my eyes, embarrassment making my chest burn. He doesn't want to send his sister the money because he doesn't trust her to use it for the bill. And he's right, especially while she still owes money to Harry. I hate that he's right. This feeling is why I started hiding the truth from Frank in the first place. God, how could two people raised by the same parents turn out to be such opposites?

"Yeah, that'll work. Thanks, Uncle Frank."

"Anytime, Julian. You know that. All you have to do is ask." He's quiet for a beat, like he's waiting for me to say something—or maybe ask something—but a second before the silence gets awkward, he breaks it. "So, if the electric bill isn't why you called, to what do I owe the honor?"

My smile comes back a little. "It's Mari's birthday. I was just calling so you could pass along our birthday wishes."

"Sure thing," he says. "I'll tell her when I see her tonight."

"You guys have something special planned?" I doubt they do. From what Frank has told me over the past few years, Mariella has practically shut herself off from the whole world. Family included.

"Actually, yes." It's hard to tell without seeing his face, but Frank sounds as though he isn't quite sure what he's saying is true. Like it's too good to be real. "Her friend K.T.—do you remember K.T.? I think you met her years ago. Well, she and Mari's, um, I guess you can call Hudson her boyfriend? They planned a day for her."

Whoa. That alone makes me blink. She doesn't talk, but she's got a boyfriend? How does *that* one work? Although I *do* talk and I've never had a girlfriend, so I guess talking shouldn't preclude dating if talking doesn't *guarantee* dating either.

"Hudson is taking her to the art museum up in Ottawa and we're meeting them later for dinner and a concert and, I don't know, Julian." He pauses and takes a breath that almost rattles over the phone line. "Mari still isn't talking, but I think she might actually have fun this year."

"That's good, Uncle Frank. Seriously. I'm glad she's happy. Definitely tell her we said happy birthday, okay?"

"Well, I'll tell her that *you* said happy birthday. I'd be shocked if Lynnie remembers. It wouldn't surprise me if she forgets your birthday sometimes."

I snort before I can stop myself. "She does." Oh, crud. I shouldn't have said that. Why did I say that?

Frank sucks in a breath. "Jesus, Julian. I wasn't seri— I mean, does she really?"

Orane's bracelet catches my eye again. Honesty. Right. I sigh. Orane *did* say I could lie if it was to hide the truth about Lynnie, but there's no helping it now. I opened the door to this particular conversation. "She did last year."

"I'm sorry. Why didn't you say anything to me?"

"I didn't want you to worry. You know how she is."

"Yeah, but—"

I bite back a groan. This is why I never tell him how bad it is with her. It just makes him feel guilty when, really, what is he going to do from a couple thousand miles away unless he plans on stepping in and claiming custody? "Uncle Frank, it doesn't matter. You always remember my birthday, and it's not like I can't take care of myself."

He sighs as I round the Stratosphere and come into view of the apartment building. I scan the small parking lot, but Ed's beat-up black Ford pickup isn't there. Thank Frank Sinatra's ghost.

"Julian, promise me you'll call if you need anything."

I hesitate for a second, trying to figure out how to word my response without lying. "If there's anything I think you can do, I promise I'll let you know."

Frank snorts. "Kiddo, I think you're a born politician. That was one of the best side-step answers I've heard in a while."

"I worked on it," I tell him, smiling a little.

"Well, I guess I'll have to take what I can get."

"Everything will be fine, Uncle Frank. Go get ready for the birthday shindig you're throwing for Mari."

He only wavers for a second. "All right. I'm glad you called, Julian. Don't forget to email me that bill."

"Trust me, I won't. Vegas in the summer without air conditioning? Not something I enjoy."

We say goodbye and I hang up as I unlock the front door and step inside the empty, quiet apartment. Collapsing on my bed, I flick the bead on my bracelet, enjoying the *thwap* when it smacks against the braided leather. I got through an honest conversation with Uncle

Frank and nothing exploded. He agreed to pay the electric bill, and social services isn't about to break down the door to take me away. Maybe Orane was right, and lying has become a habit. It probably won't go this smoothly every time (just the argument today at school was enough proof of that), but maybe I can follow through with the promise I made.

I hope I can, anyway.

The alternative isn't worth considering.

The front door slams so hard that my doorknob rattles and the screaming breaks into the music pumping through my headphones.

"If you say 'It wasn't what it looked like' one more goddamn time, Ed, I swear to everything Sinatra holds holy that I will gut you like the spineless thing you are!" Lynnie screeches. She's trying to sound tough, but I can hear the tears in her voice (she always gets high-pitched and nasally when she's been crying). I cringe hearing her swear to Sinatra. I don't like the reminder that it's a habit I picked up from her.

"Baby girl, you know you won't do that." Ed's wheedling turns to cursing when there's a thump, like he tripped and slammed into the wall. I jump as my nightstand rattles against the vibrating wall. My heart races as I crawl across my bed and lock my door.

"God, you are trashed. Do you even remember my *name*, you fucktard?"

"Jesus, Jacquelyn, now you're just being a bi—"

"Don't you dare call me a bitch!" Lynnie screeches and something shatters. A bottle, I think. A full bottle of something Ed wanted to drink, if the string of curses he releases means anything.

Practicing the meditation techniques Orane taught me is the only thing that keeps me calm. He kept saying that mastering this technique will take care of everything. I didn't believe it at first; it seemed too simple. Deep breaths in cycles of four, emptying my mind of everything except the moment I'm in, creating a happy place inside my head where I can retreat when things get too crazy. I believe it now. Meditation keeps me in my room and out of the line of fire (though common sense would've done that too).

I want to turn my music up and drown out the screaming, but I shouldn't. This one seems like it's going to turn into an actual knock-down-drag-out, and if I block it out I might miss the moment I need to escape. Or call 911. Some nights I can intervene and get them to calm down, but the higher or drunker they are, the harder it is to get them to focus on anything for longer than thirty seconds. From the sounds of it, tonight's not a night I want to try my luck.

After an hour, the screaming changes pitch as they go from fighting with their clothes on to fighting with them off. Ugh. How could *anyone* want to be that intimate with someone they were just cursing into hell and oblivion? Knowing it's my mother making those noises only makes it worse. I shudder and swallow the bile rising in my throat. Oh, Sinatra save me. I need to get out of here.

Pressing my ear against the door, I try to pinpoint where the noise is coming from. Did they make it to Lynnie's bedroom, or decide the kitchen was good enough? The bedroom it is, I think. But where should I go? The Bellagio, probably. Even before I started sitting in on John's poker nights, the hotel was my playground. During the years Lynnie worked there, the dealers taught me blackjack and roulette on their breaks, and the chefs would bring me into the kitchens and let me test their newest creations. It didn't matter that Lynnie was useless at home, because the hotel took care of me. Even after she quit for "better opportunities," that hotel was still my refuge most nights. The Bellagio was home set inside a fantasyland. Despite Orane and the sanctuary he offers, I still need that. Especially on nights like this one.

Unlocking my door, hands shaking and heartbeat stuttering, I quietly pull it open and check to make sure the hall is clear. Lynnie's door is half-open. I can't see anything happening inside (*thank you, Sinatra*) but the noise is definitely coming from that direction. Sliding through my door, I sling my backpack over one shoulder and ease down the hall. I could probably make as much noise as a stampede of elephants and it wouldn't matter, but I don't want to take that chance.

Five feet from the door, it's as though I've hit an invisible Velcro wall. And then my body starts convulsing. I'm choking on nothing. On air that is suddenly too thick or too thin for me to breathe. It feels like someone is standing on my chest. The invisible Velcro releases its hold and I collapse to the floor.

Colors and lights flash before my eyes, hundreds of images and pictures I don't understand, but each one shudders through me like a shockwave. I see Orane standing on a desolate landscape of dead, twisted trees in front of a crumbling stone building. There's someone standing in front of him, frozen in place, but they're blurry. I can't make out their face or even their form. I can barely be sure it's a person.

My throat burns. Am I screaming? It feels like I'm screaming. I can't hear it.

The vision trembles and the world I'm seeing begins to collapse. Orane throws his head back and howls. I still can't hear it, or anything at all, but I feel it like the pressure of riding an express elevator exponentially magnified.

My ears pop and my head pounds. Darkness and light play at the corners of my vision. My eyes are bugging out of my head. Someone is bashing my skull in with a sledgehammer. Needles are poking every inch of skin.

It hurts so much I can't remember what it feels like to be free of this. Agony claws its way inside my head. It burrows so deep I can't shake it loose. Darkness is overtaking my vision, blocking out the light until there's only a small circle of the world left. Is it disappearing, or am I?

The last thing I see is a familiar face.

Lynnie? What is she doing here?

Four

Nadette

Saturday, September 13 – 12:00 AM EDT

I'm dreaming—I know I am—but it's not like any dream I've ever had. Not the normal ones but not the creepy ones either. It's like I'm watching a slideshow where the pictures have been bleached and corroded. I see a huge willow tree and an ornate white stone building in the distance. There's a man with long auburn hair and glowing violet eyes. There's a lake black as tar transforming from a whirlpool into a cyclone. There's an entire world falling apart in still shots, and I'm watching in silence.

At first, it's as though I'm standing inside an empty room watching everything on a screen or through a large window. I feel nothing. I hear nothing. I barely understand what I do see.

The last image is different. In more ways than one.

Three people are in silhouette against the bright darkness of the purple and green sky. A broad-shouldered form tears across the disintegrating landscape, carrying someone much smaller, someone with long golden-blonde hair, in his arms. Behind them, the third person stands with their head thrown back and their arms stretched out. Even without seeing the details or hearing a sound, I can feel their agony and their defeat. It presses against me like a weight until I can't breathe— until I'm on the verge of tears for no reason I can name and fighting back the urge to scream. The whole world pulses and a burst of light shoots across the landscape. Straight at me.

I can't move. My heart pounds as I brace myself for impact.

It hits like lightning, sending crackling energy through my body and blinding me. I'm paralyzed and lost in a world both bright and dark at the same time. Ice flows over me. The cold buzzes against my skin until I go numb. Pain and shock and ice blend together until none of it can be separated. My mind is overloading. When sensation returns, it comes in one burst. I feel like I'm about to explode.

The beeping of my heart monitor is like being trapped inside a church bell. The light of the monitors' readouts is spotlight-bright, and the cotton sheets and thin blankets feel crushingly heavy. The combined scent of disinfectant and medicine and perfume in the air turns my stomach.

And then, as fast as the sensations overwhelm me, they drop away. I gasp for breath. I sit up and drop my head into my hands, hissing when I press against my bandaged palm. I've never had a headache this bad. It feels like my brain is trying to stretch my skull in every direction. Despite being back to its normal dull red glow, even the light from the monitors is too much for my eyes. I have to squint to make out the time from the clock on the wall. 12:01 AM. It's only midnight.

Shuddering, I look down and gasp.

There's a dark stain on my blankets, one that's spreading. My hands move on impulse, searching for an open wound, but the bandages make it impossible to feel anything. I lower them to find my hands covered in blood.

Scrambling to my feet, I ignore the pounding ache in my head and run for the bathroom. Thank God they removed the IV after I woke up. I don't turn on the light. The soft glow from the nightlight is enough to reveal the smears of blood across my face, the torrent still pouring from my nose.

Not a dream. And not a visit. Whatever happened was something new. Something I wish would go away.

Blood is still running out of my nose as I splash water on my face and grab some toilet paper to stem the flow. I shove toilet paper balls up my nose and pinch the bridge, but the position does nothing to ease the pounding in my head.

Stumbling half-blind back to my bed, I press the button that calls the nurse and wait, clutching extra toilet paper in my hands. I try to shake my head to clear it. The motion hurts too much. My neck feels like it's caught in a vise and my body is swamped with heat and nausea.

Oh, God. What is *happening* to me?

Five

Julian

Saturday, September 13 – 9:46 PM PDT

I wake up in a world where everything is white. The only color comes from the dark specks on the ceiling tiles above my head and the TV in the corner playing some reality show. This isn't my room. Or a room at the Bellagio. I was on my way to the Bellagio, wasn't I? Where am I? What happened?

Trying to remember sends shards of pain shooting through my head and I gasp, wincing as a loud beeping near my head picks up its pace. The door opens and a woman in blue enters carrying a clipboard. She's reading it when she walks in, but when she looks at me, she blinks and rushes toward the bed.

She presses a button on the side of my bed and smiles. "Hello. How are you feeling?"

Her voice echoes in my head, each word too loud. It sounds like she's screaming at me, but I know she's not. It's like I'm hearing double—her normal volume, and then the magnified version inside my skull.

"My head hurts," I whisper, hoping my voice is loud enough for her to hear. My throat feels raw and parched, and my voice is so gravelly and rough that it's barely recognizable. I cough, but it burns and makes the dryness worse. "What happened? Where am I?"

"Can you tell me your name?"

I swallow, but there isn't enough saliva in my mouth to help. "Julian Teagan."

Another woman comes in, this one in a white coat. She starts asking questions, silly things like the current year and where I live and when my birthday is. The more they ask, the more confused I get. Are they asking these questions because they don't know, or because they think I won't? Someone brings me water, but the cold liquid against my burning throat hurts more than it helps.

Little by little, they fill me in.

I started screaming and Lynnie called an ambulance. They brought me to Valley Hospital. I've been unconscious for almost twenty-four hours. I had a nosebleed they couldn't even stop with cauterization, and my brain activity was off the charts and completely unclassifiable. The only explanation that made any sort of sense was an aneurysm in the veins between my nose and my brain. The only problem? There's no evidence of it. It's like my head exploded and somehow put itself back together wrong. Which is pretty much what it feels like.

Through an IV, they're pumping me full of something that's supposed to get rid of my migraine, but it's not working. At all. The lights in this room are too bright and everything is too loud. I can't keep my eyes open for more than a few seconds, but sleep eludes me. I can feel every bone and muscle in my body and they all hurt. My joints are tight and achy; my muscles feel like someone is poking me with pins and then running electricity through them. I can't stop twitching, but each twitch hurts. My nose keeps bleeding randomly (in disgusting, sticky streams, not drips). I lose so much blood the doctor decides I need a transfusion.

It takes a while for the memory to return. When it does, I only get fragments. I remember Lynnie and Ed bursting in, the screaming and the sex, and I remember leaving my room because I was going to hide out in the Bellagio. Then I ended up here. But there's something in between I need to remember. I saw something … something … some*one*?

"Argh." I groan and shift, my train of thought disappearing as the pain grows a new set of teeth to bite me with. It hurts. I didn't think I could be in this much pain without dying. If I can survive this, I hope I'm brain-dead before I actually die. Dying must hurt like a mother.

Forcing my eyes open, I try to figure out how much time has passed. When I finally find a clock, it's later than I realized. After midnight.

Wait … *After* midnight?

Orane. Why hasn't Orane visited? I can't remember if he came last night either.

Images of Orane standing under a viciously stormy sky appear, but they don't make any sense. In the memory, he's surrounded by desolation. It's not a world I recognize. Not one he's ever built for me before. So where did that image come from, and why isn't he *here*?

He's never arrived after midnight before, but tonight I hold onto hope. I cling to that fraying thread until after five in the morning.

I need to know he'll be back, so I reach for the only physical proof I have. Forcing myself to move is painful and arduous, especially attached to the IV and sensors. I bring my left hand over to my right wrist to find—nothing. No, not nothing. A bandage. I tear off the tape and rip the gauze off my wrist, fear gnawing at my lungs and making it harder to breathe.

Under the bandage is a line of burned skin, bumpy red and charred black. How did I not feel this? How did it even happen? Where's my bracelet?

The door opens and a guy in scrubs come in. With the lights out, it takes him a moment to see I'm awake.

"Where's my bracelet?" I ask, my voice even raspier than it was this morning.

"Bracelet?" He comes closer and picks up the torn bandages, throwing them into a trashcan on the other side of the room. "What does it look like?"

"Leather with a glass bead. I didn't take it off. I *know* I didn't take it off. "

He checks the papers on the clipboard he's holding, frowning and shaking his head. "I can check the full records, but I don't think you were wearing any jewelry when you came in. I was here when you were admitted last night and I don't remember them storing any personal effects. Your clothes were all pretty bloody and your mom had the ER throw them away."

What? She tossed my clothes? That is such a waste! It could've been washed.

Wait ... what if she tossed the bracelet too?

I hiss as a fresh wave of needle-sharp pain hits, this one accompanied by nausea so strong I heave over the side of the bed. I haven't eaten anything solid since lunch on Friday, so nothing comes up.

Once I stop hurling, the nurse helps me settle back in bed.

Something is wrong. Orane wouldn't abandon me without a word. Not unless something kept him away from me. Not unless something happened. I think about calling Uncle Frank, but I don't have my cell phone and I don't want to worry him. And he *would* be worried.

Lynnie, on the other hand ...

Lynnie (surprise, surprise) doesn't come back until she has to pick me up Monday afternoon.

Six

Nadette

They call my bleeding nose a posterior epistaxis and cauterize it with silver nitrate. It hurts like hell and only adds to the pressure in my head. But it stops me from dying of blood loss by nosebleed, so that's good.

After the weird-ass weekend, the doctors refuse to let me go until Sunday morning. They're concerned about the connection between spontaneous unconsciousness, the sudden onset of a migraine—something I've never had before—and the simultaneous nosebleed. Which is also something I've never had before.

They run me through a bunch of different brain scans. I stop paying attention after a while. They're all three-letter acronyms that mean nothing to me. Finally, the doctors admit I seem fine except for the lingering headache and have to send me home.

Around noon on Sunday, the door to my bedroom opens. My younger brother Linus, the baby of the family who turned fifteen last week, pokes his head in. "Hungry?"

I don't have time to answer before my older sister Sophia flicks him on the back of the head. "Of course she is, dimwit. She's been living on hospital food the past two days. Get in there."

I expect Linus to turn around and dump the contents of the tray over Sophia's blonde curls, but he just shrugs and steps inside. He sets the tray over my lap and sits down on the bed.

"Mom said to tell you that she had to go to a meeting that was pushed off from Friday, and then she's picking up the rest of the ingredients for Dad's sauerbraten."

I almost choke on the sip of water I just swallowed. "Dad's cooking? Really?"

"*Linus*," Sophia groans.

"Oh, shit. Yeah, um, dinner was supposed to be a surprise." My brother's pale cheeks flush pink. "Sorry."

Sophia shakes her head, her short hair bouncing around her face. "Whatever. And don't look so shocked, Nadette. Of course Dad is cooking. You're sick and he knows it's your favorite. Besides, if you hadn't been released today, Jessica and H.G. and Honor and Dorothy and Scott were all planning to come down, too. Jake and Mom have been keeping them updated."

"No Phillip?" I ask, wondering about the only sibling she didn't name.

"Busy, busy, busy," Linus grumbles, a fair imitation of our brother's surprisingly deep voice. "Must rule the world one day!"

Sophia smiles and starts telling me stories about the people we know from school. Linus jumps in whenever her stories cross over into his. Even though there are so many of us—ten siblings total—we're all pretty close in age. Sophia is a little more than a year older than me. Linus a little more than a year younger. Doesn't mean everyone gets along. It's *really* strange seeing Linus and Sophia working together. The three of us are the only ones still living at home, but they usually spend more time fighting than talking. Suddenly they're on the same side, and it's weird.

Whatever truce they've formed lasts through the night. When I mention the weirdness to Jake on Monday, he laughs.

"Oh, trust me. They still hate each other. The truce starts right outside your door and ends as soon as they leave."

He sits with me as I eat lunch, trying to be casual as he watches me for anything out of the ordinary. It makes me extra careful to chew every bite well and clean my plate the best I can. When I finally can't eat any more, Jake gathers everything up for me.

"Try to get some rest, Nadie," Jake whispers as he closes the door behind him, balancing my lunch tray on one hand. For someone who always swore he would never move home after college, my brother's old bedroom has been getting an awful lot of use the past few nights.

I smile and settle back into my pile of pillows. It makes me feel a little better knowing he's here.

In the near-silence that follows, I sigh and close my eyes, trying to force myself to sleep.

Shifting my wrist, I hear the two black jade bangles Mom brought me clink against each other. The weight of my replacement necklace is comforting against my throat, even after the whole exploding thing. Knowing that the nightstand and my dresser now hold carved statues and raw chunks of black jade—plus amethyst, jet, and malachite at the suggestion of the guy at the New Age store—makes me feel even better.

Even with my eyes closed, I sense the change in the room. I feel that moment when the rest of the world goes still around me. I freeze with it.

With my gaze lowered, the first thing I see isn't the doorway to another world, but the shimmering white light coating my body. Just like in Peter's office, the light glitters. This time, though, there are threads of purple and green shot through the white.

I want to keep studying it, watching the pretty lights shift and dance like an aurora borealis, but my skin is itching. Like someone's watching me. Because I *know* there's someone watching me.

There's no smile or teasing light in Syver's eyes now; they glow with an iridescent green light. Behind him, the beach is gone. The once-comforting landscape is now only blackness, an empty void that chills my bones as much as the icy wind gusting through that gate bites at my skin.

"Time is up, Nadette."

His words send a wave of knife-like prickles over my skin. I clamp down on my muscles. *Keep still*, I order my body. No damn way will I give him the satisfaction of my fear. I grip the pendant of my necklace and hold onto the warmth it offers.

"Leave me alone," I try to order. My voice comes out breathless and weak. So much for showing no fear.

"Not an option. You possess something that intrigues me and I will have it with or without your cooperation." He steps closer to the edge of the orange arch. The light of that doorway flares, brightening and reaching outward, reaching for me. "I warned you that you would have to make a choice. The time is now. You can come with me, or you can suffer if that is your wish."

My hand is locked around the pendant so tight I can feel the stone grinding against my bones. The jade heats as the orange tendrils reach out, getting closer and closer. The longest one brushes my cheek. I gasp as a spark erupts from my skin.

Syver's gaze is locked on my throat, and his bronze skin is flushed. "So, you have chosen to fight. Very well. It is a choice you shall regret." Syver's smile is grim. His glowing eyes bore into me. "Your armor is inadequate. You will falter soon enough. I shall stalk your steps and haunt your mind, both waking and sleeping. You shall know fear like you have never felt until you beg me to end your life simply to ease your pain."

The energy touches me again. My jewelry flashes so hot it burns. I grit my teeth and keep my hand locked around the pendant. When the orange tendrils brush my cheek one more time, sparks fly out. Blue and white sparks.

"Come with me and it ends, Nadette." His words wind through my mind like a thread of ice. They twist into all the dark places I avoid and send convulsions through my body.

"Never!" I bite out through the pain. Each touch of the orange light is like being stabbed by an electrified knife. My refusal makes Syver smile. The orange light of the doorway glows brighter.

"Should I reveal to your world exactly how different you are from the rest of these pathetic beings? Do you want to know what would happen to you then?"

Yes, I know. Or I can guess. H.G., my oldest brother, joked once about turning me in to the CIA. He said my talents would be a lot less annoying used against enemy spies instead of older siblings. Mom nearly hit him for it. The fear in her eyes was enough to tell me that the threat existed. That if the wrong people ever discovered what I'm capable of, my life would no longer be my own. Like some variation of the sci-fi movies my brothers obsess over, I'd become an experiment locked in a secret laboratory and only brought out when my talents were deemed useful. But I can handle that. I'd be *willing* to handle that if it kept everyone else safe. Maybe everyone would be better off without my special brand of insanity.

As though my thoughts are written on my face, Syver's eyes flare—glowing almost emerald green for a moment. "Or maybe not. Maybe, instead, I should tempt your brother Linus to join me. Do you think he would heed your warnings against me? Do you think I would be unable to convince him to step into my world just once?"

I surge out of my bed, my chest heaving. "You leave him alone. Don't you *dare* touch him."

"Just him? What of your little niece Sandra?"

"No!" My legs tremble. I have to lock my knees to keep myself standing. Shit, shit, *shit*. I want to believe he wouldn't use a three-year-old girl to threaten me, but ... Oh, God, there's nothing about him that tells me he's lying.

"I would advise you to consider the price of your refusal," Syver smiles, that same pleasant smile I've seen on his face for two years. "I have other things I must attend to, but do not worry, pet. I shall keep a close eye on you. You will see me again soon."

The doorway closes. Syver disappears.

Any sense of peace I might have once possessed is gone. Shattered.

The stones around my throat finally begin to cool as the shimmering white light fades away. I look down. My hand and my neck are bright red—sunburned almost—but the skin isn't blistered or scarred. I guess the heat the stones give off isn't the kind that burns. But they also don't seem to be enough to keep Syver the hell away from me.

I need more.

Mom bought me a book from the New Age store—*The Book of Stones*. My hands shake as I flip through it. The more I read, the more frustrated I get. It's a useful encyclopedia of gemstones and crystals. If I want to know the mineral hardness of hematite, I'm all set. There's also a lot of shit about connecting to the higher planes and your inner self. Not one goddamn word I find tells me how to *stop* that from happening.

Syver is backing me into a corner. I don't know what he is or where he came from, but that doesn't matter as much as figuring out how to keep him away from my family.

I shudder at the thoughts spinning through my head. The possibilities I see are all grim as hell. I have to do something, though. To protect Linus. And my nieces. And everyone else. I refuse to let the people I love suffer if I can stop it.

I *will* find a way, even if it means somehow taking myself out of the picture.

Seven

Julian

Tuesday, September 16 – 11:16 PM PDT

If I'd ever doubted Orane enough to fear his disappearance, the past few days would've been straight out of my nightmares.

It's only been a day since they released me from the hospital, but I haven't seen Orane since Thursday night. I thought maybe the hospital kept him away (interference from the machines and the people and the drugs), but I skipped my medications last night, suffered through the pain, and he still didn't visit. I woke up with a headache nearly as bad as the one I had in the hospital this weekend. And another nosebleed.

Lynnie is freaked out by my illness. She makes herself feel better by checking on me to be sure I'm still alive in the morning, but then she says, "I'll just go so you have some nice quiet time to sleep."

I'm glad she goes. Seeing her makes me want to throw something at her head and scream "Where were you this weekend?" and "How could you leave your only child alone in the hospital like that?" But I let her go, and I don't ask because I know the answers will only make me feel worse. The truth is we're not family. Never have been. We're barely cordial roommates. I'm so tired of pretending otherwise.

I can barely move, but I have to drag myself out of bed to force food down my throat. Migraine or not, I've lost too much blood in the past few days to skip meals.

For most of the day, I lie in bed with a wet washcloth over my face. Light hurts, sound hurts, moving hurts, swallowing hurts, *breathing* hurts. Not breathing hurts too.

It sucks because I can't point to one part of my body and blame an injury. I have no injuries. No wounds, scars, scrapes, or cuts except the ring of burned skin on my wrist, but that doesn't even hurt. The burns killed most of the nerves, I guess, because all I feel is a dull itch. Almost pleasant compared to the crushing weight of the rest of my aches. Maybe they're psychosomatic, a physical manifestation of Orane's abandonment. I hope that's not true because it's not an explanation.

This day has crawled. Inched. If today was an animal, it would have lost a race with a slug, a sloth, and a snail. I have nothing to do, no one to distract me, and the pain (it feels like a pike stuck straight through my temples) makes each second last an hour. Limited mobility leaves me stuck and haunted by questions I can't answer until the ache in my chest is almost as bad as the one in my head. Where is Orane? I still only have snippets of memories from whatever happened Friday night, but I can't shake the feeling it had something to do with Orane. But what? And why can't I make myself remember?

Lynnie still hasn't come home by 11:57 (and she probably won't at all since it's ladies night at her favorite hell-hole bar).

Sinatra bless it, I think. *Maybe I should let John and Frank know how horrible she is. I don't want to do this anymore. Even a group home has to be easier than trying to corral Lynnie.*

Through my closed eyelids and the thin washcloth, I see reds and golds dance like flames. I can't tell if I'm awake or asleep. Everything starts to warp and brighten, the colors getting stronger until curiosity urges me to carefully open my eyes. I expect the brightness to hurt, even through the washcloth. It doesn't. My room is drenched in light, but I don't have to look away or squint to bear it. Hearing something behind me, I pull the cloth off my forehead and tilt my head back as the wall above my bed splits open. A glowing white arch appears, revealing an impossible world beyond.

Bright, glittering birds sparkle as they fly over jewel-green hills that lead down to a sapphire-blue lake. Like Orane's world always is, everything here is too bright to be real, but it's beautiful. It calls me like a familiar song. Relief rushes through me. Maybe I was wrong about Friday night. This is a door into Orane's world! He has to be fine.

For the first time in days, I can breathe without a fight. My head doesn't hurt quite as bad, and when I brush my hand under my nose it comes away blood-free. It takes me a second to force my aching body to stand, but I don't hesitate before stepping inside this gorgeous place.

Except for the birdsong and the wind rustling through the trees, it's quiet. Peaceful. I scan the area, looking for Orane, but he's not here. I don't see him anywhere. I don't see anyone, actually. For a moment, I think I'm alone, but then a woman steps out from behind a large tree, her hair—deep pink at the roots and fading slowly to almost white near the tips—flowing in the breeze and her white dress fluttering around her legs. She smiles at me, the expression slightly hesitant, and walks across the open field between us, the train of her white dress following. I step closer, my chest tightening.

She's like Orane. She has to be one of his kind. I knew he wasn't the only one of his people, but I've never met anyone else. For her to appear now…

I've seen movies about military families where someone overseas dies. That moment when they see the uniformed officer approaching and know, just *know*, that something horrible has happened? I hate watching those scenes because they always hurt, but this is the first time I've been able to really empathize with that pain. It feels like a sumo wrestler is sitting on my chest. My vision starts to blur with tears I can't seem to hold back.

She stops walking a few feet away from me, still smiling her serene, peaceful smile.

"Hello, Julian. My name is Pheodora."

I open my mouth, and though there are a million things I could say and a billion questions I should ask, there's only one thing I need to know right now. "Do you know Orane? Do you know what happened? Is everything all right?"

Her sage green eyes darken, and her smile fades. Pheodora holds out her hand and I take it, hoping the comfort of someone else's touch will keep the ice working its way into my chest at bay. I don't know which I'd rather hear—that he's left me willingly or that he didn't have a choice.

"Julian, I am afraid what I have to say may come as quite a shock." Her eyes glisten with tears, and one escapes to roll down her cheek like a drop of liquid diamonds. "Orane was not what he seemed. Not at all. He was part of a group of our kind who do everything they can to spread discord and pain. I tried to warn him that his ways would catch up with him—we were friends once, a long time ago—but he would not listen."

I try to make sense of the words. It's like she's speaking a language I can barely translate. What is she saying? Orane was a *bad guy*? Is she insane? I try to pull out of her grip, but her hands tighten and I can't escape. I try to demand that she let me go, but a block of ice has taken up residence in my throat and I can't speak around it.

"He is gone now, Julian," she says, her voice soft, her eyes full of concern. "He is gone and he cannot ever hurt you again."

The ice in my throat shatters, scraping my insides raw. "What! No. *NO!*" I yank away from her and stumble backwards, almost tripping over my own feet. "I don't know who you're talking about, but it's *not* Orane. He *never* hurt me."

Instead of shock or hurt, Pheodora looks sad. Almost pitying. "He did, Julian. He hurt you so badly; you simply did not realize it. You escaped just in time to save yourself from what he had planned for you."

Heart pounding, I take another step backward, turning to leave. I don't have to listen to this.

The door home is gone. There's an expanse of open field littered with a rainbow of glittering wildflowers. Nothing but open space until the land begins to climb—fields becoming hills becoming mountains the further my eye goes. So much room to run. Nowhere for me to run *to*. No way for me to get home.

Clenching my hands, I take a deep breath, begging my body to stop trembling. For the first time in years, I can't get myself under control. The wall I built to keep my emotions and my reactions hidden has cracked. It feels like my chest is cracking with it.

"Let me go," I demand.

"I will, Julian, I swear it. But, please, listen to me first? Please?"

I want to cross my arms over my chest, but defensive posturing won't help anything. Locking my arms by my sides and forcing myself to breathe evenly, I turn to Pheodora. I scan her face, searching her eyes for any hint of deception and cataloging every muscle that twitches under her skin. I've always been good at reading people. Orane made me better. If I can stay calm and focus, I might be able to figure out the truth.

"Everything you've said so far has been a lie," I bite out. "Why should I listen to *anything* else you say?"

"The burn around your wrist."

My left hand automatically moves to cover my right wrist. I don't say anything, but I don't think she expects me to. She sucks her lips in, her eyes darting away for a moment, but all I read in the gesture is regret and pain.

"You wore a bracelet there, a gift from Orane after he demanded a promise from you. One that would have been incredibly difficult for you."

Breath catching in my throat, I stare at Pheodora. She shifts, her dress fluttering around her legs. The expression in her eyes is completely serious. Right now it's hard to believe that Pheodora isn't being completely honest. Plus, as much as I've had to lie to the world, it's rare that the world has lied to me.

Sinatra help me, I want her to be lying.

"He has done this before—to countless children over the last millennia of your time. I tried to warn so many of them, but I could never break through the cages he locked around his victims." She sniffs and looks away, glittering tears lingering in the corners of her eyes. Wrapping her arms around herself as though trying to stay warm, Pheodora takes a deep breath and continues to chip away pieces of my soul. "Orane would bewitch them, befriend them, and then ultimately betray them, stealing the most treasured pieces of their souls and leaving them broken and bleeding behind him."

Orane was like a father, an older brother, and a best friend rolled into one person. He's the only person who truly cared about me except for Uncle Frank. The only person I ever *let* care about me.

I take a deep breath and force down my growing panic. There is no way I'm going to believe that everything Orane has done for me the past two years—the times he spent working with me to master my fears and all the nights he sat and listened to anything I needed to talk about—were paving stones on the road to some sort of epic betrayal.

"You're *lying!*" The words burn my throat.

Pheodora flinches slightly, but she doesn't back down. "Do you remember what happened that night? Do you remember what you saw?"

It's almost as though someone is reaching into my head and rearranging the pieces of memory from Friday night, clicking them into the right order. All the missing bits are suddenly there, unlocked and falling into place.

Images flash through my head: Orane standing in a dead landscape, a figure draped in shadows, and a scream that burst across the barrier between worlds.

Oh, no. My knees tremble and I fold in half, my arms wrapped around my stomach and my hands locked in fists as I gasp for breath and try to hold on. How could this happen? And how could I *forget* what I saw? And why couldn't I do anything to help him? After all he's done for me, why couldn't I step in and help him the one time he was in trouble?

Small hands wrap around my shoulders and haul me upright. Pheodora is a lot stronger than she looks, practically lifting me off the ground.

"Do *not* cry for him, Julian. He does not deserve it."

You don't understand! I want to protest, but the words are trapped inside my head. Orane was my retreat and he gave me a place to escape reality. His world was my safe haven and he was my closest friend. Now, if Pheodora is telling me the truth, he's gone.

"His actions caught up with him at last," Pheodora says, her voice strong but still sympathetic. "One of Orane's victims turned against him and destroyed him."

Destroyed him.

That's it. The last cut of the knife, the one that digs in and hits every single major artery in my body, leaving me drained and cold.

My legs buckle. Only Pheodora's grip on my arms keeps me from collapsing. The tears I was barely containing escape, cutting warm tracks across cold skin. Pheodora wraps her arms around me, making soothing nonsense noises and stroking my hair. Her touch only reminds me of what I lost, of Orane and everything I'll never have again.

"Leave me alone!" I scream, shoving her away. She could probably stop me if she felt like it, but she releases me. "The only thing I believe is that Orane is g-gone." Speaking the words almost breaks me, but I force them out, taking shallow, gasping breaths and trying to stay on my feet. "Because if h-he were still alive, he'd n-never let you near me."

It's there again in her eyes, the empathy and the pain, but this time it's tinged with pity. "Julian, that is truer than you know, but not for the reasons you imagine."

There's still not a single twitch in her expression to give me hope. Nothing to make me think she's not telling the truth.

"No. *No.*" I back away, giving in to the impulse to wrap my arms around myself. Not for warmth—I'm shaking so badly it feels like my arms are all that will keep me together. "You said you'd let me go. Let me *go!*"

It's the only coherent thought left in my head.

Let me go, let me go, please, please, let me go.

Though Pheodora sighs, tears still hanging from her pale eyelashes, she nods, relenting.

"I will return, Julian. Every night for as long as it takes to prove the truth to you." She waves a hand. I risk a glance over my shoulder, feet itching to run as I watch the glowing arch appear behind me. My crappy bedroom lies beyond it. Without waiting for permission, I flee.

The air changes as soon as I leave the dream world behind, thickening until I can almost feel it pressing against me. But is it welcoming me back or trying to push me away?

I dive for my bed, holding on to it like a life raft on the open ocean, and each gasping breath burns like salt water on an open wound. My head spins and my thoughts crash into each other like waves in opposing currents. Everything Pheodora said echoes, the words ringing in my ears no matter how hard I try to push them away. I hope she's gone. Please let her be gone.

Peering back, all I see is the blank, dingy wall of my bedroom. No glittering birds and no glowing white doorway and definitely no lying, pink-haired witch.

But, it wasn't *all* lies, was it?

The tears start again, still feeling far too warm against my skin. Dragging in shuddering breaths, I dig my hands into my hair and curl over, screaming into the mattress. He's gone. Whether Pheodora told the truth about what Orane wanted or not, he's gone.

My best friend is dead.

Eight

Nadette

Wednesday, September 17 – 12:18 PM EDT

I never really got the phrase "catch-22" before. In a vague sense, I recognized it meant you're screwed whatever way you go, but I never found myself in a situation where that applied. I couldn't understand it.

I sure as shit do now.

Option one: I can give in to Syver, cross into his world, and probably never come out again.

Or option two: I can plant my feet and resist, putting everyone I love at risk.

Neither choice seems sane.

I don't want to step into Syver's world, but I will. I will if it means keeping Linus and Sophia and Sandra and whoever else Syver might end up targeting safe. I'll do it … if I can manage to keep my legs from trembling while I'm sitting down thinking about it.

Technically, there's a third alternative. Technically. But killing myself before Syver does it for me, taking myself permanently out of his reach, would destroy my family. And probably piss Syver off. And there'd be nothing to prevent him from taking that rage out on my family.

Dammit, I need to find a fourth choice. Fast.

My nerves are buzzing from a repeat visit from Syver. His speech was almost identical, but the menace in his eyes was heavier, the emerald light brighter, the prods of that orange light stronger. Thoughts spinning, I search for another way out. A fourth option. A different goddamn door.

Someone knocks at my door. I jump, my pulse rocketing into unsafe speeds when they open it without waiting for me to answer. Mom pokes her head in, already on the verge of saying something, but then her head tilts. Her lips press together. She swallows before trying again.

"You used to sit like that with your teddy bear."

I look down at the large amethyst geode in my lap. "It's not as cuddly, but my teddy bear can't protect me from nightmares."

Shifting my weight, I try not to wince when a sharp edge on the bottom digs into my ankle bone. Or notice when Mom shudders.

"Peter is here to see you, Nadie," Mom says after another beat of tense silence. Only then do I notice him peering around the half-open door. As Peter slides into the room, Mom bites her lip and begins to retreat. "I'll be downstairs if you need anything."

Then she's gone and I'm doing my best to avoid Peter's perceptive brown eyes.

"Your collection has grown." He steps up to my dresser, his fingers tracing the different stones laid out on top. "Are they helping? Do they make you feel safer?"

I laugh, but the sound is half-choked by the lump stuck in my throat. "Not enough." Maybe they would if I could build every single person in my family a house made of crystals and gemstones to keep them safe from Syver, but I can't.

Peter shifts closer. I finally look up, seeing him full on for the first time. The words I was about to say are wiped from my mind the moment I spot the faint orange glow seeping through his shirt.

"W-what is that?" I scramble back until my head hits the headboard. "What are you wearing?"

His face furrowed, Peter looks down at himself. "Wearing? I don't— What do you mean? What do you see?"

"The necklace." My hands are shaking so hard I have to press them against the amethyst geode to keep them still. "Where'd you get that necklace?"

"What?" His hand rises quickly until he's covering whatever is hanging from the thin golden chain around his neck. "It's … it was my daughter's."

"Take it off." My voice starts out hoarse and low, but each word gets stronger. And louder. "Get rid of it or smash it or melt it or whatever. I don't care. Just get it out of my house!"

His hand tightens around the pendant. The glow doesn't disappear. It spreads to encompass his entire fist. "Melt it? But I— Nadette, *why?*"

Calm down and start making sense or he'll think you're losing it. I clamp my mouth shut for a second and then try to speak without shrieking. "What happened to your daughter?"

"She's in a coma." His answer comes slowly. "She has been for a little over a year."

I swallow, trying to get a breath that actually contains oxygen. "What's happening to me happened to her," I finally whisper. "That necklace is glowing the same color as the doorway into Syver's world."

Peter pales and yanks the necklace off, holding it out in front of himself as though it's turned into a dead rat. "It's glowing?"

"Orange."

"Jesus," he mutters. Peter shifts his weight like he's going to walk out the door. But then he stops. His nose wrinkles and his lips tighten. So does his hand around the necklace.

"Shit. You really don't want to get rid of it, do you?"

I don't wait for him to answer. Reaching into the top drawer of my nightstand, I pull out a velvet bag the size of my palm. It's filled with smaller bits of jet and amethyst and malachite and quartz. Mom brought it back from her last stone-buying spree. I didn't know what to do with the smaller bits. No holes drilled for me to put them on a necklace or something, and they're too small to just leave sitting on my nightstand.

"If you're not going to get rid of it, keep it in there." I toss him the bag. I'm not one hundred percent sure this will work, but Peter's reluctance to part with something that belonged to his daughter is pretty clear. He fumbles a little bit but manages to keep from dropping it. His relief is so strong it's like watching a literal weight lift off his shoulders. He still doesn't look happy. At least he doesn't look as pathetically lost and confused as he was a second ago.

His mouth opens, then shuts before any words escape. Swallowing, he slips the strings closing the velvet bag onto his wrist and opens his mouth again.

This time, it's not Peter who keeps himself from speaking.

The air shimmers like waves of heat rolling up from a sidewalk in summer before the glowing arch appears. Oh, shit. Twice in one day? *Twice?* I still haven't shaken the shudders from Syver's last visit. He told me he'd be back, that I could never hide from him, but I'd hoped for a twenty-four hour reprieve.

When the world beyond the orange arch clears, I blink. *What the hell?* I lean closer for a better look.

Which the stupidest thing I've done in a long time.

I back away fast, but curiosity still burns.

It isn't like any scene I've ever seen through those arches. No glittering birds, no fantastical creatures, no picturesque landscapes. No black void, either. Instead, there is a solid wall of white stone lined with what look like mirrors. The large, square pieces of glass *seem* like mirrors, but none of them reflect anything. Not even when a man with dark eyes and sky-blue shoulder-length hair, streaked with white like wisps of clouds, crosses in front of them.

"Listen closely, Nadette, because I don't have time to explain this more than once."

"Explain wh—"

His eyes narrow, but otherwise there's no sign he heard me speak. He barrels over my words. "Syver isn't going to wait much longer. Two days in your time, maybe four if we're lucky. It depends on how long it takes him to deal with—"

Shaking his head, the stranger presses his lips together to stop the words. The *true* words. My heart races. I try to pick through what he's already said, try to guess what he's going to say. Who is this? He doesn't even speak in the same stilted, almost Victorian-style English as Syver and the others who have invaded my life over the past two years.

"That doesn't matter," he says after a second of silence. "Let's just say I'm trying like hell to keep that bastard busy."

My jaw goes slack. My racing pulse stalls, stuttering as though unsure how to react. Speed up or slow down? Is this guy for real, or has the stress of Syver's threats finally broken my invisible polygraph?

"You need to leave, Nadette. Warn your family to protect themselves with the stones—as many as they can carry with them *at all times*—and leave."

"*Leave?*" The word pops out of my mouth. "Where the hell am I supposed to go?"

"Alaster, New York," he says, glancing over his shoulder as though checking on the reflectionless mirrors. "It's one of the only places you'll be safe."

True. Every single word. Hope rises in my chest. The warmth spreads out and beats back the chill Syver's visits always leave me with, but I can't trust it. Not yet.

"Lie to me," I demand, needing to be sure.

His lip twitches. I can't tell if the expression he suppresses is more amusement or annoyance. "I am going to betray you."

Bells. Glorious, loud, clanging bells.

For the first time in days, knots of tension leave my shoulders and my stomach doesn't feel like it's being eaten away by its own acids. "It's safe there? I can keep my family safe there?"

"No. Nadette, you can't tell anyone where you're going."

I tense at his clipped words and stiff expression. All that stress rolls right back into my body. "Are you serious? Syver is going to *hurt* them."

"If you don't appear in Alaster alone, they won't help you at all." His lips are pressed tight together, but I think I can spot sympathy in his dark eyes. "Leave a letter to warn your family, tell them to keep an especially close eye on your nieces, but don't waste time. Don't delay. If you do, nothing I'm capable of will save you. Or them."

"How am I supposed to get to New York alone?" I ask as he glances over his shoulder again. I follow his gaze. Colors dance across one of the once-empty mirrors.

The stranger curses and the doorway begins to close. "They've almost found me. Run, Nadette. Warn your family and *run*. And tell Peter to keep a close watch on Tessa."

I push to my knees, knocking the amethyst geode off my lap as I reach out and call him back. He doesn't wait. The orange arch disappears. The world around me resumes.

"Is there any—*Jesus*!" Peter jumps back, his breath coming in quick gasps. "Holy shit."

"I'm sorry, I just..." Plopping on my bed, I shake my head and rub my hands over my face. Tiny tremors shake my muscles and scatter my thoughts, but not enough to make me forget the stranger's warning. *Tell no one*, he said. But he also gave me a message. For Peter.

"Are you okay?" Peter asks, seeming to shake off a little of his shock. "What did Syver say?"

I swallow to clear my throat, but my voice is rough when I speak. "It wasn't Syver."

"Is that a good thing?" He bites his lip, worrying at the skin with his teeth so much I almost expect it to start bleeding.

Pulling the amethyst geode back into my lap lets me stall for another few seconds. Eventually, I have to force myself to say the words. Harder are the words I have to lock away. *Tell no one*, I remind myself. I wanted a fourth door; I should probably be happy to have found one. Even if the price may be higher than I want to pay.

How can I leave them all behind without telling them where I'm going? Or that I'm safe?

Speak, I order myself. "I don't know if it's a good thing." I think it is, though. I hope it is. All I have to do is find a way to reach Alaster. "I didn't know him—I've never seen him before and he didn't tell me his name—but he had a message. For you."

"Me?"

Nodding, I look down. Avoiding his eyes makes it impossible to ignore the way my hands are shaking. "He said to keep a closer eye on Tessa."

When I look up, his face ashen. Voice hoarse and only a couple decibels above a whisper, he asks, "He mentioned Tessa?"

"Is that your daughter?"

He nods, the motion slow, almost hesitant.

"I'd recommend buying as many of these as you can," I say, holding up the amethyst geode, "and filling her room with them."

"Will they... will she wake up?"

I close my eyes, my heart aching. God, I would give anything to keep the hope in his eyes alive. But I can't. "I don't think so. But they'll keep her safer."

"From Syver, or the one who visited you today?"

"Syver." The blue-haired guy is on my side. I think.

When I open my eyes, Peter is staring at my dresser as though he's cataloguing everything laid out on the flat top. I let him look, wondering if he'll follow through on my advice. He's adjusted to the weird shit that follows me around, but this might be crossing the line. This time, I'm throwing his comatose daughter into the same insanity that's caught me. I had to warn him, though. What he does with that warning isn't my responsibility.

When he picks up my gemstone book and takes pictures of a few pages, I relax. A little bit, anyway. He's going to listen.

The blue-haired man knew Peter's daughter. He wanted to protect her. Blue told the truth and gave me a way to keep my family safe. He's obviously the same kind of being as Syver and the others, but comparing the two seems as fair as comparing Mother Theresa to Ted Bundy. Sure, they're both humans, but it doesn't seem as though the list of similarities would go much farther than that.

Following Blue's advice is going to suck. But I have to do it. It's the fourth door I was looking for.

I blink to refocus my eyes. Peter is staring at me, concern furrowing his brow. There's an expectancy hovering around him like he's waiting for an answer to an important question.

"What'd you say?"

"I asked if you were all right." He swallows. The concern lines don't smooth out. "You looked like…"

"Like what?"

He glances away. When he meets my eyes again, the lines in his face are etched deeper. "The expression on your face. It reminded me of my cousin. He had leukemia. Terminal. I remember the day he finally accepted it all, made peace with the fact that the remainder of his life would be painful and that, in the end, he wouldn't make it another year. You… your face looked just like that."

Did it? That's a little… disturbing. "As far as I know, invisible polygraphs aren't terminal." At least, they didn't seem to be until I started receiving supernatural death threats.

Peter opens his mouth, but a soft knock on the door cuts him off.

"Sorry," Dad says as he steps into the room. "I was going to make lunch. Do you know what you want, Nadie? And you're more than welcome to stay, Peter."

Peter shakes his head. "I need to get back to the office. I have an appointment soon."

I give Dad my lunch request and he edges toward the door. Peter steps closer, puts his hands on my shoulders, and leans down to look into my eyes.

"I don't know what you're not telling me, but I want you to promise me something, Nadette." He pauses as though expecting me to agree. I hold back, waiting to hear his request. "I want you to promise you'll call me if you need help."

There's no way I can promise that. But I don't think he'll leave without an assurance of *some* kind. "If there's anything you can do, I'll call you. Promise."

His eyes narrow. I know he caught the significance of my wording, but he doesn't say a thing. Peter leaves, talking softly with my father as he closes the door—probably whispering about how I'm keeping secrets and urging my parents to keep a close eye on me. I'm left alone again. This time, though, I have a small glimmer of hope. I have a fourth door. Now all I need is a plan.

Everyone is already on high alert around me and Peter's warning will only make it worse. How in the hell am I supposed to get from South Florida to New York without getting caught?

Nine

Julian

Thursday, September 18 – 6:41 PM PDT

Pheodora kept her word, dragging me into the dream world last night to spin her lies again. She knew everything about Orane and the world he created for me, and the longer she talked, the harder it was to convince myself she was lying. I don't want to believe her, but one point her visit definitely drove home is the one I wish I could forget—Orane is gone.

In my waking hours, I still ache. On the plus side, it's downgraded from I-think-I-might-die level pain to wow-this-headache-sucks. Pills still do nothing. It's so bad that if Lynnie actually paid attention, she'd probably force me back to the hospital. She still seems to think whatever I have is catching, though, because she's barely been home since Monday.

After school on Thursday, my first day back, I swing by the Bellagio and cajole the chef at one of the restaurants into feeding me. She's one of the holdouts from the years Lynnie worked here, and when I tell her about my hospital trip she fixes me something she promises will cure my aches and pains. It doesn't, but it's delicious anyway.

The hotel is full of families today, little kids who stare up at Jean Philippe's chocolate fountain with sugar-lust in their eyes and parents who spend half an hour trying to figure out how the Bellagio's botanical gardens are even possible. I've seen thousands of families come through this hotel. Hundreds of thousands of people. All I can think when I see them is that almost any one of them would've taken better care of me than Lynnie has. There are so many decent people in the world and I got stuck with her.

I hang around as long as I can, but the closer it gets to dark, the more my head aches. I need to go home.

All the lights are on in the apartment, but I don't hear any music. Weird. I turned all the lights out when I left and when Lynnie and Ed are here, there's always some noise blasting out of the place—music, TV, or them screaming at each other. Sometimes all three.

When I walk in the door, Lynnie is sitting on the recliner with her knees pulled in to her chest, her phone clutched in her hand and her eyes locked on a blank wall. Her pupils are blown wide, her skin has a gray tinge to it, and her entire body seems to be trembling slightly.

Crap. She's on something heavy. Meth, maybe? Maybe a mix of things. I want to turn around and walk straight back to the Bellagio, but something about the lost look in her eyes worries me. I don't want to take care of her anymore, but I don't want her careening completely off the deep end either. Approaching slowly, I keep my voice soft. "Lynnie?"

She looks up and surges to her feet when she sees me. In a couple of long, shaky steps she's crossed the room and locked her arms around my neck, hugging me tighter than she's held me in years.

"Ju, Ju, Ju, Ju," she whispers over and over again.

She smells like sweat and beer and cigarettes, and the tremble I spotted while she was sitting becomes almost seizure-like now. I recoil from the stench and her touch, but she clutches me tighter. Not knowing what else to do, I pull her toward the couch. My head is throbbing, but I push the pain away long enough to get her to calm down. She's crying and I have no idea why.

"Lynnie? Jacquelyn?" I tug her off my shoulder and hold her far enough away to look into her eyes. They're red-rimmed and she's staring at me like she hasn't seen me in years. Which I don't think she really has. I shift under her scrutiny, not sure what to do with this level of attention from her. Clearing my throat, I try again. "Mom, what happened?"

She starts sobbing. "I got a—got a call from—your grandma."

"What? Did Pops die or something?" I try to bring myself to care, but I've only met the man a few times in my life. I know people I pass on the street every day better than the people who raised Jacquelyn. We visit Frank more often than her parents, and we haven't been to Swallow's Grove in three and a half years.

Lynnie shakes her head, her fingers picking at invisible spots on her skin and her leg bouncing. "Mari is … It came out of nowhere, you know? A coma. Crazy. She fell asleep and never-ever-never woke up."

Before I had Orane's world to escape to, my fantasyland was with Uncle Frank and his family in their small town, a place called Swallow's Grove in upstate New York. Every time we visited Frank, Dana, and Mariella, I marveled at how perfect their life was. They had home-cooked meals every night and music was always playing. Good music at a normal volume. Aunt Dana is a music teacher and she and Mari would spend hours playing piano or cello or guitar and singing. Mari was always singing.

In my daydreams, I wasn't Mariella's cousin, I was her brother. In my daydreams, I didn't have to leave at the end of a couple weeks, I got to wave goodbye to crazy Aunt Lynnie as she got on a plane and disappeared. I got to stay with someone who actually took care of me in a place where I didn't have to hide and gamble and manipulate to survive.

For the last few years, Dana and Mari have stayed home when Frank comes to visit us in Vegas. I haven't seen Mari in forever. Apparently, that doesn't matter, because my chest feels like it's cracking when I think of her trapped in a hospital bed. I was just there. I know how awful it is. Swallowing hard, I force myself to stay calm as I ask Lynnie, "How long?"

"I don't know … I don't—what did he say? A week." She nods, the motion jerky. "Yes, yes. A week. Almost. Almost a week."

A week. A *week*? Why didn't Frank call and tell me?

Chills creep into my chest and a tremor starts to build. It's been almost a week since I ended up in the hospital. Tomorrow, it'll be exactly one week.

Shudders shake through my body. A week ago, Orane disappeared. And I went to the hospital. And my cousin slipped into a coma she may or may not come out of.

Geez. I close my eyes, but that doesn't block out the possibilities running through my head. I blacked out that night and didn't wake up for over a day. What if *I'd* fallen into a coma? Would they have been able to get me out of it?

"Wait. If it happened a *week* ago, why are we just finding out now?" Oh, wow. I have to call Uncle Frank. He's got to be a mess over this.

Lynnie's twitching ramps up again as she swipes angrily at her phone. "The phone company—the fucking bastards screwed me over again. Downloaded some goddamn spy software on my phone. Shut it down completely!"

Translation—she didn't pay the bill for her crappy cell, one of the few bills I never bother covering. I close my eyes and take a breath. Yelling at her will do me no good. It never does.

Before I have a firm grip on my temper, Lynnie surges forward. I freeze when her hands cup my face, her palms still damp. "What if it had been you?"

Then you'd have to figure out how to take care of yourself, I want to say. But I don't.

For a split second, I hesitate before lying to her, but then I glance at the scar on my wrist. No one is holding me to my promise of honesty anymore. Plus, Lynnie can't handle the truth. And most of the time she doesn't understand it anyway. Sinatra help me, I cannot wait until I'm eighteen and can get out of here. For now, I force a smile and tell her what she wants to hear.

"It wasn't me." I make my voice as soothing as possible, holding her face to make her meet my eyes. "I'm fine. And Mari probably will be too, Mom."

With just those words, Lynnie's troubles begin to melt away. She laughs a little and lightly whacks my shoulder. Even that slight tap sends ripples of pain through my head. "Oh, stop it. You know I hate it when you call me that."

And I don't like calling her that either.

She looks around and frowns, her eyes clouding over as the drugs running through her brain erase most of the reassurance I managed to impart. "Where the fuck were you? You weren't home. You shoulda been home. I came home and you weren't here." Her eyes widen. "Ju, did they—did someone come and take you back there? What did they do to you? Are you okay?"

Lingering headaches, random drips of blood still falling from my nose, a woman telling lies (*please, let them be lies*) about my only friend, and now I'm worried that the only family who's ever tried to take care of me is suffering and I can't do anything to help. *Yeah, Lynnie, I'm just peachy. Thanks for asking.*

"No one took me anywhere, Lynnie. I was at school. I'm fine."

"Right…school. School is good. You should go to school." Sitting straighter, she takes a deep breath and shakes herself. Sometimes I really think that's all it takes for her to rid herself of everything she doesn't want to think about. "Do you need lunch for school? We should order something. Chinese? Oh, let's get Chinese!"

I think about our dwindling cash and how hard it will be to focus on the poker game tomorrow with this headache. I'll have to find a way, though, because I still need to make up for the money she's blown this past month. And the medical bills that will be showing up soon from my hospital stay. Right now I don't have the energy to talk her out of it.

"Yeah, sure," I tell her. "Sounds great."

As soon as she's on the phone and distracted, I retreat into my room and grab my phone out of my pocket. I don't like using it around Lynnie because I don't want her swiping it from me.

Why didn't Frank call me last week? Especially when he couldn't reach Lynnie. Then I check my call history. Fifteen missed calls on Saturday, but my phone hadn't shown me notifications for even one of them.

I dial Frank. He answers on the first ring. "Oh, God, Julian, I'm so sorry." I blink in surprise. That was not what I expected him to say. Frank sounds hoarse and absolutely wiped out. I hear him take a deep breath and then he's off again before I can say anything. "I meant to call earlier this week and check in on you, but I just…I forgot, kiddo. Jesus, I'm sorry."

"Check in on—oh! The hospital. You knew about that?"

"Yeah. By chance only, I think," he grumbles. "That asshole Ed answered your phone on Saturday when I called about a hundred times. He told me what happened."

I close my eyes. Ed probably cleared all the alerts too, the jerk. At least that explains why I missed all the notifications. I'm just glad he didn't steal the phone.

"He probably made it sound worse than it was." Frank has enough to deal with. I don't need to add the pressure of a mini-coma due to a dream world and a death, a meth-addled Lynnie, and a massive pile of debts.

"I was worried, kiddo. You know I would've flown over there, but …" He sighs.

"Uncle Frank, I know. That's why I'm calling. I just heard. How is she?"

"We're moving her home on Saturday," he says, his voice even heavier than before. "We've, um, got this specialist—his name is Dr. Carroll. He's going to monitor her at the house because there's really nothing the hospital can do."

My heartbeat slows and the world around me seems to slow with it. I collapse onto my bed, those words reverberating through my head. *Nothing the hospital can do?* "Oh, God, Frank. Is she—is she really not going to wake up?"

"What? No! Shit, I'm sorry. I didn't think about how that sounded." He groans and I hear something thudding on his end of the line, almost like he's banging his head against his desk. "We're nearly positive she's going to wake up. Carroll says we just need to give her some time."

"Oh." Air rushes back into my lungs and the world no longer seems stuck in slow-motion. "What happened? Did she, like, fall or something?"

"She, um …" Another sigh. "We don't really understand what happened. She went to sleep Friday night and didn't wake up again."

Last Friday. Not long after I called to pass on birthday wishes. "Wow. Not the best birthday ever, huh?"

He laughs, but it's not really a happy sound. "Not really, no. Though, actually, until the end there, it was probably the most fun we've had with her in years."

I prompt him for details and he gives me the whole story, how Hudson and Mariella spent the day in a canoe on the river instead of in the museum, how the entire restaurant sang "Happy Birthday" to her, and how Mariella couldn't stop smiling that day.

When he runs out of ways to reminisce about Mari's perfect birthday (the pre-coma part, anyway), Frank digs for more details on my hospital stay. His questions are a lot more specific and knowledgeable than I would've expected, but I guess he's picked up more than a few things about neurology and hospitals and persistent unconsciousness in the past week.

The conversation starts to wind down, but I get the feeling there's something else Frank wants to say. He's hesitating too much to be done.

"What is it, Uncle Frank?"

He sighs. "This is gonna sound like a weird question, but just roll with it, all right?"

"Yeah, okay." Frank sounds nervous, and he almost never sounds nervous. He's one of those people who somehow found a way to become absurdly comfortable in their own skin and he just radiates calm confidence. Or, at least, he always seemed that way to me.

"Have you, um, have you ever had a dream where you were visited by someone who made you promise to give up something important just to stay in the dream?"

My heart clenches and I force a laugh. "Wow, Frank. Could that be any vaguer of a question?" My voice comes out calm and even, but inside my mind is as chaotic as a dust storm. The denial is automatic, drilled into my head every night for the past two years. Orane made me swear, repeatedly and on pain of banishment, to never reveal his world. But the way Frank is asking that question … Can there be any other explanation except that, somehow, he knows about the dream world?

Frank laughs, this time sounding a little relieved. "It seems vague, but, trust me, kiddo. You'd get it if you got it, know what I mean?"

Yeah, I know what he means. But I say, "Kind of?"

"To be honest, I'm glad you don't have a damn clue what I'm talking about. It's about five hundred kinds of messed up. Trust me."

I get chills, coldness that sinks deep into my chest and spreads across my body, and my pulse picks up as though trying desperately to beat back the ice. Years of practice hiding my emotions (from Lynnie, from social services, from kids at school who thought I'd be an easy target, from the guys I play poker with) helps me keep my voice even as we say goodbye, but when I hang up the phone my brain short-circuits completely.

Is Pheodora right? The way Frank talked, there's no chance he was hinting at a dream world version of Disneyland. The thought of the dreams scared him. But if he *was* talking about my dream world, how did he find out about it?

But maybe that's not the most important question. My cousin and I fell into unconsciousness almost at the *same* time on different sides of the freaking country. I haven't taken statistics yet, but it's still pretty dang clear the odds of that happening are astronomical. And I've never heard of persistent unconsciousness being hereditary.

My thoughts spiral, one leading to another until I have one question ringing between my ears—could Pheodora be telling the truth about Orane? About everything?

For a while, my contemplations consume me. It feels like it's only been a few minutes, but I must've lost track of time. When I head out to get dinner, the kitchen and living room are a mess, Lynnie is gone, and all that's left of the Chinese she ordered is half a serving of fried rice.

I hate fried rice.

It's stupid and childish and ridiculous, but it's the fried rice that tips me over the edge. I keep glancing at the half-empty carton as I pick up the clothes and the spilled glass of vodka and try to get the dried soy sauce off the small rug in the kitchen. There's not even any anger burning in me. I'm numb. And tired. And completely done. We've ordered Chinese together about five hundred times in my life. How hard is it for her to remember I don't like fried rice?

Tonight I need to talk to Pheodora (instead of blocking her out). Tomorrow I'm going to swallow down a lifetime of habits and lies and pride and ask John and Uncle Frank for help. Because I can't take care of Lynnie anymore. I don't want to.

Ignoring the dry burn in my eyes, I pick up the container and a plastic fork, trying not to gag as I choke the stuff down. I need to eat something, and I need to calm down until Pheodora shows up. *If* she shows up. After yelling at her for lying the last two nights, I wouldn't be surprised if she's given up on me. I hope she hasn't. There's so much I need to ask her.

I try to stay awake, but I can't. This week has been draining. Add everything from this evening on top of it and I feel like my brain is balancing on a poorly built house of cards.

Despite my worries, I open my eyes and find myself in the dream world, lying on bright green grass under a cerulean blue sky.

A deep breath brings the scent of jasmine and, even more so than the past two nights, my headache clears. Another breath as I sit up and it's practically gone. Physically, I feel almost normal for the first time in days.

Pheodora is sitting in front of me, her white dress spread out around her like a patch of snow on the grass. Though she's absolutely motionless, there's tension in the way she watches me shift and adjust, as though she isn't sure if I'm going to attack her or run screaming.

"Do you know my cousin, Mariella? I talked to her father today and I think … I think she …" The words clog up my throat and I swallow, trying to free them. "Do you know her?"

Pheodora nods slowly. I watch her face carefully for any reaction, so I notice when a glimmer of light, almost like hope, fills her eyes. "I told you that one of Orane's victims turned against him."

"That was Mari?" My hands clench and it takes far too much effort to stay sitting. I want to pace and break something. I want to hurt Mari for destroying my only friend. I want to hug her for risking herself to save us both. I want to curl up into a ball and forget any of this ever happened. Instead, I force myself to meet Pheodora's eyes. "Why didn't you tell me before?"

"You were not ready to listen, Julian." Her voice is soft, reassuring, like I haven't been screaming at her, calling her a liar and a fraud for the past two nights. "You had to hear part of the truth from someone you trusted before I could reveal the rest."

I swallow and a lead weight settles in my stomach. I still ache to deny it, but what could Pheodora possibly gain by lying to me?

Watching Lynnie live life in a near-constant haze of drinks, drugs, and denial has given me a sharp distaste for people who won't see a truth staring them in the face.

My vision whites out for a second, almost like a blood rush when I try to stand up too fast, and warmth rushes through me. It's dizzying. I take a shuddering breath and try to focus. The last of my headache eases, but that pain is replaced by a sick twist in my stomach that makes it hard to keep my fried rice down. Sinatra bless it, she's really telling the truth, isn't she?

"What did he want from me?" I finally ask. "If it's true that he was just trying to steal something from me, what was it? I don't have anything to steal."

"It was nothing tangible." Pheodora speaks slowly, as though she's carefully considering her words. "Those of my kind who hunt humanity target children who have some special gift, a talent that, given the right push, could become something your species would consider almost magical."

"Then what did he want from *me?*"

Her pink lips twitch, suppressing a small frown. "Julian, you have a talent for convincing others to see the world the way you would like them to, for painting a picture with words that makes others doubt what they know to be true. You have a gift for manipulation. For deception, child."

All the air rushes out of my lungs. Deception? Is that the only thing worth recognizing in me? It's a backhanded compliment for sure, kind of like being nominated for Most Likely To End Up In Prison Before Thirty. Should I be grateful for being good at something, or offended that, because of my childhood, my most likely career choice is con artist?

And, come on. How often do I really deceive anyone? My lies are more like verbal self-defense than anything.

But wait … "Why was Orane trying to convince me to be honest?"

"In order to recognize and hone a talent developed unconsciously, you must know what it is like to be without it. To recognize its worth, you must feel its loss. To learn how and when to use it, you must forego it for a long stretch of time. Do you understand?"

It doesn't make me feel much better, but I guess it makes sense. Taking a deep breath, I meet Pheodora's eyes. "What do *you* want from me?"

"Nothing." She smiles and gracefully rises to her feet, her movements as fluid as water. When she offers me a hand up, I hesitate before finally taking it and letting her pull me to my feet. Her grip is strong and her skin is warm and soft. She squeezes my hand and a little jolt of electricity shoots through me, like the static electricity that constantly pops up in winter. It travels up my arm and makes me shudder, but when the feeling fades, I feel almost whole. Healed. Peaceful in a way I haven't felt ... ever, maybe.

I want to believe her, but my only experience with her kind was Orane. Who apparently spent our entire relationship trying to steal my soul. Besides, no one wants nothing.

As though she can hear my doubts, Pheodora takes my other hand, peering down into my eyes. "Julian, if you saw someone lying in the street, alone and in pain, would you help them?"

"Of course." I blink. "I mean, I'd try."

"And would you expect payment or favors in return?" One of her pale pink eyebrows rises, waiting for my response.

"Oh." Heat steals up my body, flushing my skin pink. Is that how she sees me? Alone and in pain? Guess it's not exactly untrue.

"You have been through a great trial because of my kind. A rogue member, true, but it would not be fair to leave you alone to deal with the consequences of his actions." Her smile turns sad as she guides us toward the lake, her arm linked through mine. I don't pull away. The gesture feels normal, almost like we've been taking nightly strolls down this very path for years.

I shake myself a little. *Go slow,* I think. *Even if she is telling the truth, you need to be careful.*

"I want to help you heal and to make sure you have what you need to—"

She jerks to a stop, frozen mid-step with her head cocked to the side. Kind of like a cat listening to something only cats can hear. After a few seconds, her expression clouds. Creases appear around her eyes, stress and worry etching themselves deeper and deeper until, finally, she sighs and glances down at me.

"What is it?" I brace myself. Sinatra bless it, I am so not ready for something else to go wrong.

She shakes her head as she begins to walk again and smiles, but her lips are too tight and her shoulders are too tense. "Nothing to worry you."

"If you say so." Curiosity bites at me. Orane was always so secretive about everything outside of his little corner of the dream world. That should've been a clue right there. I'd thought (hoped, even) Pheodora wouldn't do the same. Pasting on a neutral expression, I shrug. "I'll listen if you want to talk about it, though."

She stops walking and her hold on my arm pulls me to a stop as well. For a second she merely scans my face, but a smile slowly appears, growing until it stretches into the widest grin I've seen her wear yet. The expression doesn't last long before that shadow of frustration reappears.

"Julian, you said you would assist someone in trouble if you could. Did you mean that?"

"Of course. I mean, there's not much I can do to help anyone, but I'd try."

"You underestimate yourself far too often." She strokes my hair like Aunt Dana always did when I visited her. "However, this particular favor may be more than I can fairly ask of you."

"Won't know until you try."

She takes a long, slow breath, and her grip on my arm tightens just a little. "There is a girl, only a few months older than you, who is in danger."

"What kind of danger?" I ask, my chest tight.

"Much the same kind you were in before Mariella saved you." Her green eyes grow distant, as though she's seeing something beyond her world. "Her name is Nadette and she is being pursued by someone like Orane, a vicious man who will destroy her if he can."

There's still a small bite of denial, of agony, at hearing her talk about Orane like that, but I can't push the truth away forever. It's spread too far. Frank knows, Mariella knows, and this girl Nadette knows. They all have seen the dangers of the dream world, dangers I never noticed until someone stepped in to save me. Maybe, just maybe, I can pay that debt back by helping someone in trouble. By saving Nadette.

My skin heats as my smile grows. I'd never pictured myself as the white knight in any kind of scenario before, but I gotta say that the concept is growing on me.

"What do you need me to do?"

"I believe she has been frightened into running from home, but I do not yet know where she will head. One of the others has pointed her toward a safe haven. I cannot reach him to find out where." She looks away, worry lines appearing around her lips. "I fear he may have been caught helping her."

"Where is she now?"

Pheodora's eyes return to mine, but the worry doesn't ease. "Florida."

"Florida? *Florida?* Pheodora, that's a couple thousand miles away from Las Vegas." How in the world does she expect me to get *across the country?*

"You underestimate yourself again." She puts her hands on my shoulders and peers into my eyes. "Your mother does not have a steady job, does she Julian?"

My face heats, but even though I try, I can't look away. "No."

"Then how does she pay rent and feed you and clothe you each month?"

"I gamble." Lynnie lost her last decent job—the one she quit the Bellagio for—three years ago. Playing poker with John is what has kept us from ending up homeless.

"Would it hurt you to leave your mother behind?"

I have to bite my lip to keep from snorting. "No."

"Then will you help me find Nadette and keep her safe?"

Taking a breath and holding it to push the tingling nerves in my stomach down, I nod. "What do I need to do?"

"Tomorrow, gather as much money as you can without raising suspicion. As soon as I am sure where to send you, I will let you know." She squeezes my shoulders and lets go, continuing our walk. "I also do not know how long this task might take."

"So prepare for anything, then?" 'Cause that'll be a cinch.

She smiles and nods.

We walk closer to the water while I try to process everything that's changed tonight. There's so much to consider and so many questions I should ask. One of them seems crucial, though. "Pheodora, why are they after her? What do they want?"

Her hesitation lasts so long I start to think she won't tell me, but then the words spill out. "Nadette is extraordinarily gifted. She has the ability to read lies, even when the person speaking believes they are telling the truth."

Oh, wow. That would be so useful. I'd be able to call any bluff in the world. It'd be awesome, but (considering how often people lie) probably kind of suck, too. "Guess I shouldn't try lying to Nadette, huh?"

"I do not know how your ability will interact with hers, but honesty is always best, Julian. The only thing I must ask is that you do not tell her my name."

"What? Why not?"

"Because there are others like Orane, and they work constantly to hunt down those who help humanity. Tell her everything I have told you—everything about Orane and your cousin and the ones like me who will help if they can—but you must keep my name a secret." Her grip on my hand tightens and her eyes burn with an almost bioluminescent green light. The light is hypnotically beautiful. "Will you promise me this, Julian?"

I swallow, my head spinning a little. "Yes, of course."

Pheodora's hold on me relaxes and she smiles. "Thank you. You have no notion how much your help will mean."

Breathing the jasmine-scented air deep, I smile at Pheodora. When I wake up, I'll pack and play one last game with John and the guys. Maybe I'll let it slip that Lynnie decided to head back to the east coast so they don't go looking for me. Soon enough after that, I'm leaving Lynnie behind. Maybe for good. And without dragging Frank and John into my problems.

There is *no* downside to this plan.

Ten

Nadette

My escape plan involves three things—money, transportation, and the influence of spy movies. Money isn't a problem. Not if I empty my savings account and pull cash off my credit card. As for transportation, after some research, I pick the train. It's the only way I'm getting out of the state without taking too long or passing through *way* too much security. I just have to wait for a window of opportunity to get myself to the station.

The spy movies came into play when I found my older sister Jessica's ID stuffed in my nightstand. She gave me her old one last year when she moved out of state. A test, she said, to see if it was even possible for me to get into real trouble. I doubt she would have guessed I'd use it for this. I figure that if I use my ID to get to Trenton and hers to get to New York, it'll take them a while to sort out the details.

Friday morning, Mom knocks softly on the door and pokes her head in with a tired smile.

"How are you, sweetheart?"

I bite my lip and shrug. As soon as I see her, guilt and fear make my stomach roll, my chest ache, and my hands start to shake. Can I really leave her and Dad? And Linus and Sophia? And Jake? He's always been on my side. No matter what. God, if they ever find me, Jake is going to be so pissed at me for running away.

I can't tell her I'm fine, because I'm not. Lying to someone else is as impossible as someone lying to me; as soon as I even *think* the lie, the bells clang louder than ever. It's obnoxious to the point of pain. To everyone else, it looks like I'm choking on thin air.

"I hate to leave you alone, but your father had to head up to Palm Beach for a meeting. Jake is supposed to be here, but he's running late, and I have to leave now to make it down to Miami in time for my appointment." She strokes my hair with a gentle, sure touch. She's shifting her weight, though, and there are too many lines around her eyes. "I can…I should wait. I'll just call them and tell them I'm running late."

I see my window. All I have to do is jump before it closes. "Is this an important client?"

Mom bites her lip and nods, her green eyes—only a few shades brighter than mine—troubled.

"Will being late cause problems for your firm?"

"Nothing that will be too bad. Plus, Linus—"

The bells in my head start ringing. I raise an eyebrow at her, loving her a little for that particular lie. So many of my friends' parents put their careers over their kids. No matter what. Not my mom.

"All right, fine." She sighs and runs a hand over her red hair. "It would cause problems."

"Then go. Really." I pull her down into a hug. I can't smile. I can't pretend to be happy when my heart feels like it's been replaced by a marble replica. My nerves are all so numb I can barely feel her in my arms. "I love you."

"Oh, sweetheart. I love you too."

Though she stalls for as long as she can, it's only a few minutes before Mom is calling goodbye. Her car hasn't even pulled out of the driveway before I have my packed bags out from under my bed. Then I'm stuffing every single gemstone I own into one of my brothers' old camping backpacks. I leave a letter I wrote last night for Mom under my pillow. She won't find it right away, but she will eventually. I just hope she can forgive me eventually.

Across the hall from my bedroom door is a large family picture surrounded by a wide black frame. It was taken a few years ago—before I'd ever heard of the dream world. It's one of the only pictures that includes all twelve of us—ten kids and two parents. It's a sea of blondes and redheads with dancing blue or green eyes. By walking out the door today I'll be hurting every single one of them. Plus my grandpa Horace, my aunts and uncles, my cousins…

Throat tight, I close my eyes and head for the stairs with my head down. I don't want to see anything else that will drive a knife into my chest like that.

I hear something—almost like a voice saying my name—but the sound is distant and warped. When I look up, I realize why. Directly in front of me, where the rest of the stairs should be, an arch ringed in orange light threatens to lead me into velvet-black darkness and Syver's waiting arms.

"Going somewhere?" His smile is grim. He reaches out, his hand almost leaving the confines of the archway.

Heart pounding, I turn to run up the stairs, throwing my arms out to keep my balance. My backpack thuds against something solid. Someone screams. It's not me. The doorway collapses.

I have a split second of frozen time to see what's about to happen.

Linus is there with wide eyes and his mouth open. He's wearing pajama pants and a T-shirt from our high school's football team, his hands clutching a box of tissues, a plate with a sandwich, and a bottle of water.

My stomach flips and bile rises up my throat. I reach for him, desperate to make contact. Time restarts. He slips through my fingers.

I watch my brother tumble backward down the stairs.

Each thudding, cracking impact resonates through my body like I'm feeling the blows with him. Linus slides the last three steps until he's lying dazed on the floor. His left arm is bent at an angle that makes my stomach turn. Blood oozes from a gash on his head. The bright red spill against the white marble floor shocks me out of my paralysis. I drop my duffle bags on the landing and run, barely catching myself in time to keep from barreling straight through the orange gateway bursting open in front of me.

Tendrils of orange light grab for me, trying to drag me the last few inches into the other world. My collection of stones bursts to life, their light blooming around me like a force field. Syver stands there and laughs. Like I'm putting on a fucking slapstick show for his entertainment.

He leans closer, his face nearly pressed against the invisible line dividing his world from mine. "Keep fighting and you will hurt them all. One by one, you will bring pain to your friends. Your family. You will destroy everything you love with your own hands until you stand in a ruin of your own making. Run and I will do it for you. Surrender, pet, and save them so much pain."

The orange light gets brighter, the tendrils thickening into a pure white so bright it's blinding. It burns my eyes. My vision washes out completely. I falter. I reach out for the railing to keep myself from collapsing into the void. My hand closes around something solid. *Please let this be the railing. Please tell me I haven't already fallen into his world.*

It feels like I stand there for hours. My brain overloads. The sensations pile higher and higher until something in my mind tugs free. Then I'm above it all, floating and watching. Tones echo through the surrounding haze. Although the cadence sounds like a voice, the words are lost. That doesn't stop the sound from sending shudders through me.

The shudders grow and spread, getting stronger instead of dissipating into the mist. In a flash, it changes. Shakes turn to shocks. Electricity jolts through my mind and I'm back in my body, gasping for breath like I've been held underwater.

In front of me, the door to Syver's world is fading. It collapses into itself until there's only empty air. And then my brother groans, a sobbing, pain-filled sound that hits me in the chest like a bucket of acid.

"Linus!" I tear down the rest of the stairs just slow enough to jerk myself to a stop if another of Syver's doorways opens. No more light shows appear between me and the first floor. I leap from the last step over my brother's body. The backpack of stones throws me off-balance. I slide down, catching myself on the floor and kneeling by his side. "I'm so sorry! I didn't mean to!"

"Wh-what?" His blue-green eyes are glazed. Blood runs in a thick river from his head. "Nads?"

"I'm sorry! I'm *so* sorry!" Tears run hot and thick down my face. I flutter around him, my mind so twisted I have no idea what to do.

"Nads, what happened? Why's my head hurt?" His voice is soft and he looks so confused.

Oh God, oh God, oh God.

I dig my hands into my hair and curl forward, biting back the scream that wants to rip free of my throat. What am I supposed to do? If I don't leave now, I'll never get away; they'll watch me so closely it might as well be a maximum-security prison. But how can I leave with Linus hurt? Hurt because of *me*.

Syver's threats still ring in my ears. So do Blue's promises. There's somewhere I can be safe. *If* I can get there. My family will be protected if they follow the instructions I left for them. Linus will heal. And maybe, one day, forgive me for hurting him. For hurting all of them.

Oh God, I have to leave *now*. But I can't. Not yet.

Pushing to my feet, I run into the kitchen. I grab the cordless phone and a roll of paper towels, dialing 911 as I dart back to Linus.

"911. What is your emergency?"

"My brother fell down the stairs!" I swallow and try to keep my voice from cracking. Pressing the towels against the cut on the side of his head with one hand, I can barely hold the phone in the other hand. It's shaking too much. "His arm looks broken and he hit his head hard. He's bleeding."

"Where are you—?"

I rattle off our address before she can finish the question. "Send the ambulance, please!"

"Ma'am, please stay on the—"

I hang up the phone and toss it aside.

"Nads?" Linus's left shoulder twitches like he's trying to lift his arm. Spasms of pain flash across his face. He curls around his arm, protecting it. The motion only seems to makes it worse. Tears flow down his face and his breath comes in gasps. His eyes are unfocused. Each second only digs the guilt-sharpened knife in my chest deeper. I can't stay with him much longer. I'm running out of time. It may just be my imagination, but I think I can hear sirens.

Imagined or not, the sound prods me into motion. Running up the stairs, I grab my two duffle bags and barrel back down, unlocking the front door for the paramedics on my way to the kitchen. Sophia is grounded for sneaking out to a party. Her keys are on the hook in the kitchen and her Jetta Hybrid is waiting in the garage.

As I drive away, my hands are shaking. I pass the ambulance as I'm turning onto Federal Highway. Seeing it, knowing where it's headed and why, breaks open the floodgates. Heavy tears nearly blind me. Luckily, I only need to get to the bank a few blocks from our neighborhood.

Parking in the back of the bank's lot, I rest my head on the steering wheel and try to shut my brain off. The last half-hour keeps repeating in my head. Syver, Linus, leaving. I feel like I'm drowning under the weight of everything I've done wrong. The pain I've caused. My chest is so tight, getting a full breath is nearly impossible.

It takes a few minutes for the tears to slow. I force my lungs to expand. I force my mind to sink into itself, building a buffer between myself and reality. Wiping my cheeks, I wait until my eyes don't look quite as bloodshot and then head inside.

The teller gives me suspicious looks when I remove $2,618 from my savings account in addition to the $2,000 I pull off my credit card. Suspicious or not, they complete the transactions and let me leave. Outside, I call a cab with my cell phone. And then I toss the phone in the front seat of the car. They're both staying here.

When the cab arrives, I dump my bags in the back and climb in.

"Where to?" he asks.

"The train station, please."

In the rearview mirror, I see him blink in surprise. He turns around to get a better look at me, glancing at my bags with bushy eyebrows raised. "Long trip?"

"Jersey." I can't lie to him, so I give him a different truth. "Emergency, but I don't want to fly."

He stares at me for another few seconds, then shrugs and puts the car in drive.

"My wife is terrified of planes," he says as he pulls out of the parking lot. "Makes it really hard when we have to visit her family in California."

I let him talk for the rest of the drive, filling in the moments of silence with the expected responses. Before too long, we're pulling up at the Amtrak station. A minute later, the driver is disappearing the way he came.

"I need a ticket on the next train to Trenton, New Jersey, please?" I try to sound less than completely freaked out. Maybe he'll think I'm excited?

The guy behind the counter barely spares me a glance before plugging something into his computer. "There's a train that leaves in an hour. You'll be in Trenton tomorrow afternoon."

"*Tomorrow?*" I must have read the times wrong. I thought it would get me into New Jersey sometime late tonight.

He glances at me, his eyebrows raised. "You want today? Go to the airport."

Shit. That's more than enough time for them to catch up to me if they figure out how I traveled. But what choice do I have? After this morning, I'll never get another escape window again. I know I won't. Taking a breath, I try to keep my hands from shaking. "Are there seats left?"

"A few." He types something else in. Once he gives me my options, I end up paying for a private room. It's an extravagance I probably can't afford, but if I'm going to be stuck somewhere for the next twenty-five-plus hours, I need to be away from other people. As much as possible. Especially after what happened to Linus.

Ticket in hand, I order pizza. Two of them. And bribe the driver with the promise of an extra tip to get here in twenty minutes. By the time I board the train and lock myself in my room, I have everything I need to hide until I arrive in New Jersey. Or hide as much of the time as possible, anyway.

After I set out my stones in a circle around the room, I settle into the chair and watch the world roll past my window. Tomorrow afternoon, I'll be pulling into my Grandpa Horace's hometown. I haven't talked to him in months. Haven't seen him in almost a year. Time somehow slipped away and I kept forgetting to pick up the phone and call him. Now I'm going to pass through Trenton like a fugitive to add another layer of mystery to my disappearance.

Curling my legs closer to my chest, I let my curly hair fall in front of my eyes. The strands tint the whole world orange. I shudder. Is this what it'll look like if I fall into Syver's grasp?

Blue said there would be people who could help in New York, but they can only help if I make it there alive.

I hope my luck lasts that long.

Eleven

Julian

"Nadette is on her way to Trenton, New Jersey," Pheodora says as soon as I walk into her world. "It is not her final destination, but you should be able to meet her there."

I haven't ever had an urge to visit New Jersey before, but Pheodora could ask me to go to Kansas or Antarctica or an unnamed island in the South Pacific and I'd agree. One of the reasons I never ran from Lynnie before was that I had no idea where to go. Now I have not only a destination, but a mission exactly when I was ready to head for the hills and hope for the best.

"I should have enough to live on for a couple of months even after the plane ticket," I tell her.

Pheodora nods and smiles. "You did well today."

I shrug. After the poker game with John, I used some of the money to clean out the guys who usually spent their nights hustling tourists on The Strip. Conning street hustlers isn't quite a badge of honor, but I don't exactly feel guilty about it either. Plus, keeping them away from the families from Utah and North Dakota and wherever else is practically my good deed for the day.

"How will I find Nadette? I don't know what she looks like."

Pheodora flattens her palm and sweeps her hand across the air as though she's cleaning steam from a bathroom mirror. The air warps and then an image appears. "This is Nadette."

A girl with long, bright red curls sits on a narrow bed, her head resting against the wall but her eyes wide open. Her head is tilted toward the ceiling, her green eyes catching a shaft of light. Two pizza boxes are stacked on a small table and two large duffle bags take up most of the floor space. Nadette hugs a huge backpack to her chest like it's a teddy bear, and her eyes are red-rimmed. It's hard to tell in the low light, but I think there are tears on her cheeks.

The window closes quickly. It doesn't matter. I won't forget her face.

"You must leave as soon as you wake up, but I have something to give you first." Placing her hands on either side of my head, Pheodora closes her eyes and whispers, "I do not know what or who you may face along your journey, so I will help you in the ways I can."

Energy buzzes through my head, not as strong as an electric shock but powerful enough to leave me a little weak-kneed. When she releases me, the colors in her world are brighter and everything is louder for a second. Although it fades quickly, the disconcerting buzz stays with me a while longer. Shaking my head to clear it only makes the buzz worse. It feels like there's something loose and rattling around inside my skull.

"Two things you now have, Julian—privacy and connection. I will be able to find you wherever you may go and speak to you even in your waking hours, but your thoughts will be your own, no matter who you may face."

"What do you mean? Who am I going to face? I thought I was just helping Nadette."

"You *will* be helping Nadette, but I am not yet sure what that will mean or who you might meet. There are those in both my world and yours with the power to delve into your thoughts, whether you wish them to or not," Pheodora says. "Close your eyes and focus inward."

Following her instructions, I breathe in fours, the meditative cycle Orane taught me. My chest burns at the memory, but I push the betrayal aside. It should be harder, impossible even, to pretend he meant nothing to me. Maybe it would be if Orane was the first person to let me down. He isn't; he's just the one I never saw coming.

"Imagine yourself standing in a large room with shelves along the walls," Pheodora says.

Her voice is almost doubled, as though I'm hearing it through my ears and inside my mind. It's surprisingly easy to follow her instructions. Within seconds I'm standing in a wide room with blonde wood shelving in geometric designs along all four walls, the spaces filled with books, framed photos, and pieces of art. The floor is the same pale wood, but the walls behind the shelves are a rich burgundy color. It feels warm and comfortable, the entire room exuding safety. It's what I always imagined "home" would feel like.

"Within this room are representations of your thoughts, your memories, and your mind," Pheodora explains. "Now, I want you to imagine a wall dividing the room in half."

I open my mouth to protest (cutting the room in half seems wrong) but then I realize she never said what I had to build the wall out of. Focusing, I picture a thick wall of unbreakable glass running through the center of the room.

"Now, add two doors, Julian. One on the far wall and one within the dividing wall."

Again, I do as she asks, adding a pale wood door to the wall across from me, on the far side of the room, and a steel-lined door to the glass wall, adding a strong lock without really knowing why. I feel better once it's there, though.

"This wall will be your protection." Something shimmers on the other side of the glass wall, a ripple of light that coalesces into a ghostly image of Pheodora. "Everything you wish to protect from prying eyes, you must keep on that side of the wall." She sweeps her hand toward the side of the room I'm standing in.

I snort. "In that case …" I take a breath and everything around me shifts and moves, the glass divider retracts from the burgundy wall before sliding forward. On either wall, the shelves and display spaces shift and rearrange until they're on my side of the divide. Quickly, Pheodora's side of the room empties and the room changes shape, lengthening until it's simply a burgundy hallway leading to solid glass wall and a metal door.

Pheodora's lips quirk into a smile. "Thorough."

"I'm used to privacy."

Pheodora smiles and presses her hand to the wall. Light flares around her palm and spreads out in thin veins, winding through the walls on either side of the room. When she lifts her hand away, a swirling design of softly glowing golden light is left behind. It's abstract, a symbol of some sort that reminds me of the character from Orane's bracelet.

"This will help me find you wherever you go, but I'm afraid this is all the help I can give." Her smile turns sad. "Open your eyes, Julian."

When I do, we're still standing in the open field by the brilliantly blue lake. Externally, nothing has changed, but my head feels strange. It's as though there's a spot of brightness dancing on the edge of my peripheral vision, something I can't quite catch a real glimpse of, but my mind feels calm and quiet and organized, focused almost. It takes a few seconds for the residual glow to fade. The golden light vanishes completely just before I feel a tug under my ribs. Without looking, I know the doorway home has opened behind me.

Pheodora places her hands on my shoulder and kisses the center of my forehead.

"Rest, Julian, then pack and prepare to leave before first light. You have so very far to travel."

By the time the plane lands in Trenton, I've been gone for about ten hours. I'll bet Lynnie hasn't even noticed.

Breathing deep, I wonder how air can smell like freedom. Does freedom have a scent? Right now, it's a mix of jet fuel and recycled oxygen, Cinnabon and pine-scented cleaning solution. Tomorrow, who knows? Maybe that's what makes it smell like freedom. The fact that it's different every breath you take simply because you've decided to leave the place you were before.

In the middle of a Saturday, I thought the airport would be busier, but I guess that after growing up with the crowds of the Vegas Strip, everything seems empty in comparison. I wind through the terminal with my backpack and my carry-on, trying to focus on the signs hanging from the ceiling, working my way through the maze of tunnels and terminals to find an exit.

The world around me lurches and stalls. I almost crash into the person in front of me.

I jump and have to take a deep breath to calm myself. Everything and everyone around me has frozen. It's like standing in a really detailed (and really creepy) wax museum. The second before the doorway to Pheodora's world opens feels endless, and I have to fight not to shudder. When I step closer to the border, she shakes her head.

"I only came to give you directions," she says. "Nadette will be arriving at the train station in town soon. You must meet her there."

"And then what?" As willing as I am to throw myself into the fray to help someone, even a girl I've never met, I don't actually know what Pheodora expects me to do. The conversation ended last night before I remembered to ask. "How am I supposed to help her?"

"The girl has been forced to leave a family she loves behind for their safety and her own. Nadette needs someone who understands what she's running from and why. She needs information and support and friendship, someone to stand with her when others don't believe her story. She needs *you*."

Well *that's* incredibly non-specific. I open my mouth to ask for more details, like what exactly I can do to help her run, but Pheodora disappears, the doorway closes, and the world around me restarts. Reeling a little, I don't move fast enough. Someone plows into my back. My bags clatter to the floor

"Oh, damn! I'm so sorry! I'm *such* a klutz," the woman mutters as she scrambles to gather our things. "You were walking and then I looked down to check my phone and I didn't see you stop. I'm *so* sorry."

Smiling, I promise her it's all right. She's flustered and overly concerned. Just in the few seconds we spend talking, I know I could easily take advantage of that concern, play injured, and get free lunch out of her, if nothing else. But I don't have time to waste.

I have to wait at the taxi stand for a while. It's a struggle to keep myself from bouncing impatiently. This all seems like it's gone too easily, so it's hard to stay optimistic when I start garnering curious looks from the other people in line.

Over the years I've noticed that when adults spot a kid on their own, it tends to bring out concerned parental instincts. Even in people who have never been parents. They want to help and protect and *save* the poor lost child. The innocent kid schtick is one I've played to the nines most of my life, using the freckles and the dimple and the smile to open a lot of doors (and even more wallets). It's great in theory, but right now I need to be ignored and the taxi stand guy is eyeing me with mild curiosity like he's trying to decide if I'm traveling with the older black couple in front of me or the two twenty-something Asian girls behind me. I can talk my way out of it (with the help of a convincing fake ID and a well-rehearsed, slightly funny story about how being short is the bane of my existence), but thankfully, even when I climb into the back of the cab alone and shut the door, he doesn't ask.

"The train station, please," I tell the cabbie before I sit back and watch the city roll by. Trenton is sprawling like Vegas, but not as cluttered. During certain sections of the trip, all I can see are trees on one side of the road and the Delaware River on the other. A real river. Vegas's most notable water feature is the fountain show at the Bellagio.

Sooner than I expect, we're pulling in to the train station and I'm adjusting my grip on my rolling suitcase and my other bag before heading inside. Maybe my expectations are skewed from watching too many movies, but as I wander through the station I really believe I'll find Nadette sitting right out in the open. I look, peering into alcoves and out onto the tracks, but I don't see anyone with her distinctively bright red hair.

Great. I'm here. She's not. Now what?

After feeding my grumbling stomach at a café across the street from the station, I head back inside to wait. I pick up *The Count of Monte Cristo* (assigned reading for my English class; why did I bring this with me?), but most of my attention is on the other people passing through the station. While some sit in the lobby, most walk out the door, moving quickly to get back to their lives. Several times families pass by; I watch them closely. Each time, it makes me want to pull out my cellphone and call Frank. Each time, I remember I left the thing in Vegas.

I'm watching a little girl, her hair done in thin tight braids ending in bright pink beads, dance around her older brother when everything freezes for a second.

Her train is arriving, Pheodora whispers in my head.

And then, just like that, the world resumes. The little girl's hair clicks as the beads hit each other and her brother looks up at their parents, begging them to make her stop. But my attention isn't on them anymore. Now my eyes are locked on the platform, where a northbound train is pulling in to the station.

Dozens of people pour out of the train, most of them talking on cell phones as they grab their bags. No one looks like Nadette. The flood slows until there's almost a minute where no one disembarks. My heart starts beating faster. What if something happened to her? Did I miss her? I scan the faces surrounding me, but there's no one who even remotely resembles Nadette. Unless she gained fifty pounds and dyed her hair blonde sometime in the past twelve hours.

Taking a breath, I glance at the platform as Nadette appears.

Her hair is piled on top of her head in some kind of messy bun and she's wearing a black hooded sweatshirt with the sleeves pushed up to her elbows, several bracelets lining each wrist. The large backpack she clutched so tightly last night is on her back and she's balancing two large duffle bags, one on each shoulder. Her luggage is more than twice as wide as she is. She pauses for a moment on the platform, blinking like she's trying to get her bearings or adjust to suddenly bright light; when she starts moving, she travels fast. I jump up and grab my bags, ready to follow her out the door, but she doesn't leave the station. Instead, she stops at a display of maps and buys one of New York, unfolding it as she moves toward the board showing departure times for the rest of the afternoon.

The more I watch her, the more I realize that everything about this girl screams "Don't touch me! Don't talk to me! Stay away!" Her shoulders are pulled up tight and her movements are tense and jerky. She glances around every few seconds as though she's expecting an attack. I can talk to almost anyone, but there are some moods you just don't approach people in. This level of paranoid fear is one of them.

After another minute, she shakes her head and crumples the map in one hand before heading to the window to talk to the attendant.

They're too far away for me to make out what they're saying, but she folds the map back and points to something. The man behind the counter peers at it before shrugging and pointing to something else. I can't see the expression on her face, but Nadette's shoulders slump before she finally nods. It only takes another minute for her to walk away, stuffing the map and a ticket into one of the pockets of that monstrous backpack.

She turns toward me, but she's looking down, fiddling with the black bracelets on her wrists. When she reaches an empty stretch of seats, she drops her duffle bags and kicks them under the chairs, linking her hands together and stretching her arms over her head. Should I go over and say hi? Ask her for help with something? Wait for her to come to me? Geez. I have no idea. And the longer I wait to make a decision, the harder it's getting to come up with something that doesn't seem ridiculous or doomed to failure. But if I don't act soon, she may end up getting on her next train without me.

I'm watching her out the corner of my eye when she drops her arms and sighs, her eyes shut tight. Digging into her pocket, Nadette pulls out a little black orb and starts rolling it between her palms. Her movements vary between slow and weary and quick jerks of sudden energy, and the circles under her eyes are dark and deep. It seems like she's running entirely on adrenaline or caffeine.

After a few seconds of slowly pacing back and forth between her chair and an empty spot a few feet away, she opens her eyes. It only takes a second for her gaze to lock on me.

Nadette's eyes open so wide it seems like they might pop out of her head. The black sphere falls from her limp hands. It cracks against the wood floor and rolls. Her mouth drops open and her hands start shaking. The only thing I can think to do is dive after the black orb, pick it up, dust it off, and offer it to her.

Her motions are almost mechanical as she reaches out and takes the sphere, but her eyes never leave mine. Mouth opening and closing like a fish, she stares at me until I start to shift under the scrutiny.

Say something! part of my brain screams at me, but my words are all gone. The quick thinking and the smooth lies that have carried me through the past decade mostly unscathed have completely deserted me now.

There's something about her eyes. The color reminds me of peridot, Lynnie's birthstone, but there's an intensity to her gaze that makes me think she sees everything for what it really is. I remember what Pheodora told me about her and realize that might be true. Maybe those eyes *can* strip away illusions faster than a sandstorm could rip the skin off your bones. It makes me very aware of how many illusions I live surrounded by.

"Who are you?" Nadette finally manages to ask.

Her voice is higher-pitched than I expected, soft and incredibly girly for someone who looks like she might be able to beat me up. She's taller than me (about five-seven to my five-five, I'd guess) and although she's thin, she seems strong. Tough. Even if she also looks so scared she might shake out of her skin at any second.

Smiling, I consider holding out a hand for her to shake. Then again, maybe not. Somehow I think the gesture wouldn't be taken well. "My name is Julian."

Her eyes narrow and her head cocks to the side, but she doesn't say a word.

"Okay, well, right …" Maybe giving her space will help. I step back, retreating toward my chair and my bags.

"You've seen them?" Nadette asks, her eyes darting around the room.

I stop. Is she looking for doorways into the dream world, or checking to make sure no one is close enough to overhear? I can't be sure. I'm also not positive she's asking what I think she's asking. "Seen who?"

"The ones who show up in your dreams." Her voice is soft and shaky and intense. "The ones who won't let you go until you give them what they want. You've seen them, haven't you? You must have."

I open my mouth, an automatic denial on my tongue, but at the last second, I wipe the words away, close my mouth, and nod slowly, more than a little confused. I recognized Nadette because Pheodora told me how to find her, but … "How did you know?"

Her eyebrows furrow, and the expression that crosses her face makes me think she's wondering just how stupid I am. Before I can ask the question again, she leans closer and whispers, "Because you're glowing."

"I'm *what?*" My words echo around us and Nadette cringes, but my nerves are buzzing too hard for me to care right now. I look down at my hands, but all I see is skin. I blink hard, trying to see whatever it is she's seeing. There's nothing there. My hands are only covered in skin. "What are you talking about? I'm not glowing."

"You can't see it?" Nadette's eyes get even wider. "They got to you, didn't they? How long have they been coming to see you?"

"He's—um, they're not anymore, but…" Geez. What is it about this girl that makes my tongue so clumsy? I clear my throat and try again. "About two years. It's been about two years."

Nadette stares at me. Up close, the circles under her eyes are even darker than they looked last night, and her skin seems too pale, even for a redhead.

"Are you running away?" she asks after a second, sitting down carefully.

"Yes. Kind of."

"From Trenton?" Her gaze flicks toward the doors leading out to the city and back.

"Uh, no. I've never been to Trenton before today."

Her head tilts and her forehead is still furrowed. It looks like she's studying me and finding me lacking. I really don't like the feeling. "Where are you from?"

"Vegas."

Her jaw goes slack and her eyes pop open wide. "*Vegas?* Like, Las Vegas, *Nevada?*"

"Is there another one?"

"I don't know." She bites her lip, her entire face scrunched up. "That's really far. What are you doing in Trenton?"

I open my mouth, a story about heading to New York to meet family ready to spill off my tongue. Then my brain clicks out of neutral and I glue my mouth shut, swallowing. She can read lies, I remind myself. Telling her that I'm here to help her might freak her out, but lying to her about why I'm here would be an even stupider move. But then, I've always been good at finding ways to judiciously apply the truth. "I'm supposed to meet someone here."

Her head tilts and I get that she's-studying-me feeling again, but then she shrugs and seems to accept the answer. Which is good and bad. How in the world do I get from here to telling Nadette that I'm here to meet *her*?

I look down at my hands, flipping them palm-down and then palm-up, but there's really nothing there. Glancing at her, I bite my lip, forcing myself to ask the question. "So, you said something about a *glow*?"

Nadette leans back, pulling her knees in to her chest. "Did they ever give you anything?"

I look down at my wrist and the scar on my skin. It's less red now, but it still looks awful. Like someone kept me tied up with ropes for weeks until the skin rubbed completely raw. Holding my arm up, I show her the mark. "I had a bracelet once. It burned my skin off the night I blacked out."

Reaching out, she takes my arm to get a better look. Nadette's trembling gets worse as she stares, and her face is really, *really* pale. So much so that I start thinking she's liable to pass out at any second and I'll have to give her CPR in the middle of a train station. She swallows hard, seeming to get a hold of herself, and lets go of my arm. "What did it look like to you? Did it have, like, an orangey … Wait. Did you say *blacked out*?"

"Yeah." I swallow and tear my eyes away from hers, running my thumb along the scar. "A week ago yesterday I—"

"Had a fucked-up dream and woke up with a migraine and a nosebleed?"

I stiffen and have to grip onto the arm to keep from jumping off the chair, my heart pounding. Mari in New York, Nadette in Florida, and me in Vegas all had the same dream on the same night? But she said she *woke up* that night with the nosebleed. That's not what happened to me.

"I didn't wake up that night. Plus, it was only nine, so I wasn't asleep. It hit me like a hallucination and then I blacked out completely. My mom took me to the hospital. I was there for two days. My cousin … Mariella, my cousin who lives in New York, she dropped into a coma that night."

"A *coma*?" Her eyes bug out again and her hands start shaking. "Just like Tessa."

"Tessa? Who's Tessa?"

Nadette blinks, refocusing on me. I think that, for a second, she completely forgot I was there. "Sorry. It's complicated. She's connected to the same thing, I think, but she's been in a coma for over a year."

Another victim? How many of them are there? I look up and shudder. My chest tightens, my eyes burn, and hysteria fizzes through my body. I almost laugh. This is an insane conversation to be having in the middle of a train station.

"What happened to her?" I ask, not sure I want to know.

"I don't know." Nadette shrugs, still trembling a little even though it seems like she's trying to control it. "I've never met her."

"But you just said—Know what? Never mind." If Tessa has been in a coma for a year, there probably isn't anything I can do to help her. Nadette is here now and I'm supposed to be the one calming her down and helping her get where she's going safely. Which means I should probably figure out where she's going. "If you're running, too, where are—?"

"Why do you talk like that?" The words burst out in a rush like she couldn't hold them in any longer.

"Like what?"

"You sound like ..." Her nose crunches and her eyebrows pull together. "You sound warped. Like a bad auto-tune. Like someone fucked with the cadence of your voice."

"What? No I don't." My voice is a solid countertenor, according to the choir teacher at school. And no one has ever described my voice as warped.

Her eyes narrow and her head tilts. She's looking at me like I'm a puzzle piece or a science project again. It's only a few seconds before I start squirming under her stare.

"Lie to me."

I freeze, my heart skipping a beat before it starts pulsing faster than a hummingbird's wings. "What do you mean?"

Nadette rolls her eyes. "What do you *think* I mean? Tell me something that is untrue. *Obviously* untrue. Something everyone knows is wrong."

"Why?"

"Because I'm testing a theory."

Pheodora said she wasn't sure how our abilities would interact with each other, but I never really believed I'd be able to fool a girl who can hear lies. Trying to hide my nervousness, I do as she asks. "Gravity doesn't exist and the moon is made of whipped cream."

Her lips twitch into a smile for a second, but that smile barely lasts a breath before she's standing up and grabbing my hands, pulling me off the chair.

"Do it again," she demands, staring into my eyes.

"Okay, umm…" My mind goes blank. Scrambling, I glance around the room until I see the TV mounted to the wall. "Television was invented by cavemen and the first car was built by Caesar."

"Holy shit. You can lie to me. You can *lie* to me!" Her grip tightens on my arms and her face starts flushing red. I'm so thrown by this whole conversation I can't even read her face anymore. Is she upset? Happy? I have no clue.

"Uh, I'm sorry?"

She runs closer to the TV and focuses on the reporter. Before more than a minute passes, she cringes and turns away. Her face is unreadable as she walks toward me slowly. A minute passes and then two, and the silence between us starts to feel oppressive and strained. Maybe it would be a good idea to give her some space. If I leave, I can talk to Pheodora and get some advice. Picking my bags up, I step backward. It feels like I shouldn't turn my back or make any sudden moves around her right now.

Crap. I have never needed someone to trust me this bad and been so completely lost on how to make it happen.

Before I can open my mouth to say goodbye, Nadette spins. "Where are you going?"

"Oh, uh, it just seemed like you wanted me to—"

"No, where are you going? From here. After you meet your friend, where are you headed?"

"I—" Oh, Sinatra bless it. What in the world am I supposed to say now? I haven't blushed accidentally in years, but I feel my cheeks heating up under her stare. "I, um, I've never met the person before today. I got a message. I'm supposed to meet someone here who knows where to go."

"You traveled all the way across the country to find someone you've never met? Do you even know what they look like? Or their name?"

This question is a little easier. I take a deep breath and nod. "They described someone who looked a lot like you, actually. A girl around my age with red hair and green eyes traveling alone. They told me she'd know where to go and I should follow her."

"God, my life just keeps getting weirder," she mutters, running her hand over her hair and fussing with her bun. "Who told you this?"

"Someone who found me after I blacked out. She told me that there are some of their kind who hunt humans and others who are trying to help. Told me to leave and find … someone. You?"

"Maybe. Sounds like it. Wish he'd told me to expect company, but he did kind of leave in a hurry." She seems like she's half-talking to herself. Before I can ask who "he" is, she jumps tracks again and asks, "How much amethyst or jade or whatever do you have in those bags?"

"Uhh …" I have to replay that in my head a couple of times before I can be sure I heard her right. "Amethyst? Like, the gemstone? None. Why?"

"What stones are you using to keep them away?" Her eyes are too wide again and her skin looks a little green.

What is she talking about? It doesn't seem like some rocks would protect anyone from anything. "Um, none?"

Nadette gasps and glances at her backpack. "But if they told you to come here, didn't they warn you how to stay off the radar?"

"N-no." Should Pheodora have told me that? "I think they planned on keeping an eye on me until I found you."

"Ugh. This is insane. We're going to have to get you some of these." She pulls her backpack into her lap and opens it. Inside is exactly what she said—a lot of stones.

There are some black rocks, a chunk of something green, and a few purple crystals that are probably amethyst. Pretty, but they don't look particularly protective. Unless they're ammunition in a slingshot aimed at someone's head. Nadette seems convinced they can hide her, though. Maybe there's more to these rocks than it seems.

Nadette is silent for a while, her lips moving slightly as though she's having a conversation with herself. I shift closer to the edge of my seat, tingles of nervous energy making my stomach churn.

"Do you have cash?" she asks after a few seconds.

"Yeah."

"Then buy a ticket on the next train to Saratoga Springs." She grabs my bags and places them under the bench of seats, resting her feet on top as though she's standing guard.

"What's in Saratoga Springs?"

"Nothing that will mean anything to us. We're headed to a town called Alaster."

I smile. "Sounds like a deal. I just have one more question."

She arches one eyebrow and waits.

"What's your name?"

It takes a few seconds, but then she gives me a slight smile and holds out her hand. "Nadette Lawson."

"It's nice to meet you, Nadette. I'm Julian Teagan." Her hand is shaking slightly, but her grip is strong.

She nods and nudges me toward the ticket counter. "Go buy your ticket then, Julian. We've got a ways to travel tonight."

Twelve

Nadette

I've never had to rely on my judgment instead of my bells to get a read on someone. I'm not sure I actually *have* judgment. Or instincts. I think disuse made them shrivel up and disappear. No matter how hard I try, I can't get a handle on Julian. Especially because the light show surrounding Julian is trippy—swirls of blue and orange hover in constant motion just over his skin. It's weird. Weirder than all of the other weirdness that is part of my life.

Weird or not, he's here and I can't tell if he's lying. I had to make a snap choice. I hope letting him come with me is the right one. Keep your friends close and your enemies closer, right? I'm still not entirely sure which camp Julian falls into. If he's a friend, he needs help. If he's an enemy, he'd probably follow me anyway. Better to know where he is. And letting him travel with me at least until Saratoga Springs will give me time to get to know him.

Luckily, Julian doesn't seem to have a problem with story time. Including the transfer at Penn Station, the whole trip takes almost six hours. He spends the first two catching me up on everything that's happened to him in the past two years. The more he talks, the more I begin to trust him. Especially when I realize that just because I can't read Julian doesn't mean everything he says is shrouded in mystery. When I ask him questions or repeat what he tells me in my head, it all rings true. When I try to change it, testing the theory, the bells start clanging. So far, it seems like everything he's told me is true.

Eventually, the tables turn and I have to explain how I ended up in a train station in Trenton, New Jersey. Despite the strange, warped inflection of his voice, Julian is fun to listen to. He talks with his hands when he gets into a story, playing up the dramatic bits even when the memories must hurt. I can't do that. Not yet. I rush through the basics of my tale, pushing away thoughts of my family as much as I can.

God, they've got to be *frantic* by now.

"You're lucky, you know," Julian says when I finish.

"I don't feel lucky." I close my eyes and lean my head back. My hands clench into fists as though that'll stop the ache in my chest from getting any worse.

"Are you *kidding*? I mean, sure, the last few months have probably been stressful, and seeing a therapist is not my idea of a good time, but …"

I open my eyes when he doesn't keep talking right away. The setting sun shines through the window, bringing out the hints of blond and auburn in his hair. The freckles across his nose seem darker and his cheeks are slightly pink. His brown eyes are intense and focused and despite how young and small he looks, those eyes can almost convince me he's the one who's older than me.

Julian takes a breath and glances away, but his gaze quickly returns to mine. "Do you know how often I wished I'd been born into a different family? Or that my uncle had convinced Lynnie to let him and his wife raise me?" He shakes his head. "I would bet my nonexistent fortune that Lynnie hasn't even noticed I'm gone yet. I know it sucks and I'm sorry you had to leave your family behind, but honestly? I wish I had someone—anyone, even someone not related by blood— back in Vegas I missed that much."

The ache in my chest gets worse, but this time it's not because of me. Shit. What the hell can I say to that? I can't imagine being so alone in the world. Even if I wanted to be, I don't think my family would ever let me be truly alone.

Not knowing how else to respond, I nod mutely. He's right. Everyone deserves to have someone in their life who'd miss them.

"Sorry for the melodrama." Julian glances up at me, his lips quirked into a smile. "It's just been a while since I've talked to anyone who might actually, you know, *get* it."

"Yeah, well, I'm sorry Lynnie is a basket case. Maybe you should stay on the train and just show up at your uncle's. It seems like he'd take you in."

"Probably, but I think he's dealing with more than he can handle already. They transferred Mari into home care, remember?"

"Which means they could use some help, sounds like. And you said you thought he knew about the dream world."

Julian opens his mouth, but closes it before he says anything. His eyes narrow and his head tilts. "Are you trying to get rid of me already?"

"No."

He frowns. I don't think he believes me.

"Really, I'm not. It's just that I don't know exactly what or who I'm going to find in Alaster. If you have a safe place to go, somewhere people will actually understand what's happened to you, it might be better than following me into the unknown. That's all."

It takes a few seconds before his expression softens. He shakes his head, smiling again. "I can always go there later."

He closes his eyes and rests his head against the seat, humming happily to himself. I relax a little and watch the scenery roll by. Gotta say that it certainly feels more than a bit better heading to Alaster knowing I have someone with me.

The train pulls in to Saratoga Springs just before eight and it doesn't take us long to grab our things and jump off.

"So." Julian looks around and grins. "Where to?"

"Hotel, I guess." There's a display of information about the town just inside the building, so I grab a few different brochures. "Hate to waste money, but I don't know how to get from here to Alaster yet."

Julian shrugs. "We'll figure it out. Though, honestly, a cab is probably our best bet."

I nod toward an open patio on the side of the building. It's near the parking lot and almost empty. Probably because it's cold and dark and all the normal people are staying warm inside. Julian follows, still grinning, but I'm a little worried. What I saw of the building was pretty new and well-maintained, with high ceilings, huge windows and just enough unnecessary touches—like the baby grand piano—to make me wonder. Out the front windows I only saw trees, and the view on this side of the building isn't any different. If the rest of the town is like this...

"Do you think they have a motel that won't demand a credit card in this city?" I ask as we settle onto a couple of the benches. "This place looks a little ... quainter than I expected."

He glances at me with a raised eyebrow and a smirk. "And these days, 'quaint' demands credit?"

"Doesn't it?"

"Wouldn't know. I've never experienced quaint or credit. Just cash."

The patio is well-lit, but it's still noticeable when a pair of headlights sweep into the lot. I look up and watch an old Bronco pull in from the drop-off circle. I glance at it, noticing the tiny rust spots in the silver paint and the too-loud rumble of the engine. Then the parking lot's overhead lights catch the passenger's face.

Her hair is a soft brown, like dark honey or caramel. She has large eyes under thick eyebrows and eyelashes. Her nose is upturned just the slightest bit and her top lip is thinner than her bottom one. It's hard to tell from a distance, but I think there might be a small cleft in her chin. Overall, her face seems a tad lopsided for conventional beauty, but there's something about the expression in her eyes that grabs me. I can't look away. She's gorgeous.

And she's glowing. It's faint, but her entire body is surrounded by a cerulean blue light. The same shade of blue as half the lights surrounding Julian.

"Nadette?" Julian walks back to me and waves his hand in front of my face. "You okay?"

I suck in a breath and blink, finally breaking eye contact with the girl in the SUV. Before I can tell Julian what I saw, the car pulls into the space and the girl gets out. So does the guy with her, a blue-glowing, fallow-skinned, dark-haired giant who's so broad he'd be obese if he wasn't so friggin' tall. The girl smirks and glances at her friend. If I didn't know better, I'd bet she heard what I was thinking.

"You'd win that bet, Nadette," she calls.

Shit. *Shit.* Only Syver has ever been able to dig into my head. Knew she was too goddamn good to be true. I grab Julian's arm and drag him back into the station, darting toward the women's restroom. I shove him in and slam the door shut behind us a split second before the girl and her giant friend reach us. My hands shake when I flip the lock.

Julian glances around the thankfully empty bathroom. "I don't think I'm supposed to be in here."

Someone knocks. I back away from the door.

"I'm sorry! I shouldn't have said that." Her voice is muffled, but the walls aren't thick enough to keep her words out. "It was stupid, but I didn't think you'd freak out like this, Nadette," the glowing girl calls.

"What's going on?" Julian whispers. "Who are they? Do you know them?"

"I don't know, I don't know, and *obviously* not," I hiss.

"We're here to help you, Nadette."

Not a lie. I think. Unless she's like Julian and she can lie to me, too.

"The sky is green and I'm here to kidnap you."

My bells clang like crazy and I cringe.

"Shit! Oww!" the girl hisses. "What the hell?"

"What happened?" a deep voice asks. Probably the brute.

"I'm fine, I'm fine. Just wasn't expecting that." I hear the tones of conversation then, but not the words. Then the girl asks, "You hear that *every* time someone lies?"

"More or less. Sometimes more, sometimes less." Is she really reading my mind? It seems impossible unless she's like Syver. Then again, maybe not. How can Julian lie to me? How can I do what I do?

There's a moment of quiet and I think I hear her sigh. "Nadette, I swear, it's okay. We're here to bring you the rest of the way home."

My heart picks up. "Home is Florida," I tell her, wary. "And I can't go back there right now."

"Not Florida, *our* home. We came to bring you to Alaster."

"Worth the risk?" Julian whispers. "That can't be a town many people know."

He's probably right. And she wasn't lying when she said it was home. Or that she was here to help. Pressing my forehead against the cool wood door, I take a breath. I can't stay in here much longer, not without gathering way too much unwanted attention. Grabbing my duffels, I open the door slowly. I step out of the relative safety of the bathroom, and yep. They're both still glowing blue. As soon as the door closes behind us, the girl smiles; both her smile and her teeth are adorably crooked.

"Thank you," she says, her cheeks suddenly tinged with pink. I feel my own face heating. Dammit. She heard that, didn't she? Clearing her throat, the girl looks away. "I don't know how you avoid having a migraine every second of every day. Those bells carry some serious echo."

Julian steps closer and the mind-reader glances at him, her dark eyebrows furrowed and her lips pursed. Why do I have the feeling she can't read him?

"Because I can't." She shrugs, her wavy hair spilling over one shoulder. "It happens every so often. I've met three before him that I couldn't read."

"She's really reading your mind?" I nod and Julian shudders. "Creepy."

"I don't know. It almost seems like some sort of cosmic balance. I always know people's secrets. Maybe it's only fair there's someone out there who can ferret out mine."

The girl smiles again and I notice she has a dimple. Jesus. Are you kidding me? A dimple too? She laughs and I want to disappear. This could get annoying fast.

Her laughter dies. So does her smile.

"Sorry." She swallows. "I turned it off." She meets my eyes. Her eyes are a shade of mossy green that almost matches the long skirt she's wearing. "Um, my name is Lexi, and this is Clarke."

She's blushing a little—and damn, that's cute—but she meets me stare for stare. No, I decide. Her eyes are a little more green than her skirt. And they're sprinkled with specks of gold.

"Are you hungry?"

I blink. Not what I expected her to ask.

"There's a few restaurants nearby. We'd have to drive there, but it's close." She shifts the backpack she's wearing; it looks heavy. Clarke has one that's almost identical. "We can eat and fill you in and then you can decide if you want to come with us, okay?"

"Food sounds *so* good," Julian mutters to me. I nod my agreement and we follow her out to the lot. She's right about the restaurants, and within fifteen minutes we're seated at an Irish pub in the middle of town.

Neither Lexi nor Clarke says anything at all, even after we're crowded around a small table. She wasn't hesitant like this before, but she had her mental eavesdropping to rely on then. Clearing my throat, I decide to start this on even footing. "You can turn your mental X-ray back on."

Lexi blinks and looks at Clarke before her eyes meet mine again. "Are you sure?"

"Yeah." I look down at the table, fiddling with the roll of silverware. "It's not really fair if you don't. I can't turn mine off."

"It's not about fair, Nadette. It's about you being comfortable long enough to listen to what I have to tell you."

I look up then, wondering how old she is. She talks like she's much older, but she looks like she might only be a year or two older than me. When I finally realize I'm staring—again—I look away and shrug. "I don't mind. I'll listen whether it's on or off."

"All right."

Then we all fall silent again and that silence quickly morphs into a sleeping dog that no one wants to disturb.

Lexi laughs, a low, throaty chuckle that—*No*, I scold myself, my hands clenching under the table. *Stop it, stop it, stop it.*

When Lexi leans forward, I expect her to begin with how she knew where I was. Instead she turns to Julian and asks, "Who are you? When did you get here?"

Julian sits back against his chair, as far from the table as he can get. After a few seconds, he glances at me and back at Lexi. "I'm Julian Teagan. I'll be sixteen in a few weeks. I got to Trenton this morning from Vegas, and then I met Nadette. Came to Saratoga Springs with her. My mother is incompetent, I never knew my father, and a week ago I collapsed with a nosebleed and the worst migraine known to man—the same night my cousin here in New York fell into a coma." He raises his eyebrow and stares her down. "Want my Social Security number too?"

Clarke snorts a laugh and Lexi smirks. "Chill, kid," she says. "You'll see why I asked in a second."

There's a pause as the waiter comes to take our order, but as soon as he's out of earshot, Lexi looks at me. "Clarke and I are envoys of a sort. We were sent out to find you by a girl who can see the future. She lives with us near Alaster, part of a group of people who've survived run-ins with creatures we call by a dozen different names."

"Evil fucking bastards," Clarke mutters, his hands clenching. Lexi pats his hand. I can't tell if it's more comfort or reprimand. Her lips twitch, but she doesn't laugh this time.

"*We* call them many things," she says. "But they call themselves the Balasura."

Balasura. I take a breath and let that word sink into my thoughts. Should naming them make them less scary? Isn't that what's supposed to happen? Peter once told me that identifying your fears leaches away some of their power.

Lexi shakes her head. "It's not that easy."

"Yeah." I shrug, not bothering to hide my exhaustion. She's inside my damn head. She can see exactly how tired I am. It's been an extraordinarily sucky week. "Wishful thinking."

"The Balasura use their power to slip inside your head and steal whatever power, special ability, or talent makes you special," Lexi explains. "Different from everyone else."

"Better than," Clarke adds.

Lexi's lips tighten. "Matter of opinion, Clarkey. And sometimes it's better to keep your opinions to yourself."

Our food arrives before either of them can say another word, and we all fall silent again. Clarke nearly drowns everything on his plate in salt, then spears a fry with his fork and eats it with shocking delicacy. Blinking, I glance at Lexi. She only peppers her mashed potatoes before beginning to eat.

"Anyway," Lexi says after a minute. "Our little seer Kelsey had a vision that Nadette would be here. She said you would need help. Guidance. A safe place to rest. She didn't know *Julian* would be here, though. It's the biggest lapse she's had in months."

My shoulders sag. They're offering safety. And *rest.* "Damn, rest is so foreign I've almost forgotten what it feels like. I haven't slept more than a couple of hours a night in months. Will it be different in Alaster?"

Clarke snorts. "No. That's one thing we don't ever get back."

I expect the clearer explanation to come from Lexi. Julian speaks first.

"It's a side effect of spending time in the dream world." He's speaking to his plate, pushing around a piece of steak with his fork. "Orane never explained why it happens, but he told me that much."

"Essentially, yes. The same way being there heightens our gifts." Lexi smiles and keeps talking. "So we can't offer sleep, but Johanna—she's the one who kind of watches over everyone—she sent us here to see if you wanted to stay with us. We offer food and shelter and a place where the Balasura can't find you."

Just like Blue said. I close my eyes and bite back the relieved sigh working its way up my throat. Maybe it'll be worth leaving everyone behind. Maybe it'll be worth everything except Linus and—No. Dammit! I don't want to think about that. But now the door is open. The memory replays. The orange arch, Syver, Linus falling, Syver's threats, and the blood. So much blood.

Lexi gasps. My eyes fly to hers. *Shit.* She just saw all of that. I expect to see recrimination or horror or judgment in her eyes, but she's near tears. All I see is empathy.

She holds out her hand, her gaze steady. I can't stop myself from taking it. Warm and soft, her touch quiets me as soon as her fingers curl around mine.

"I'm so sorry." Her voice is so quiet I can barely hear her. "It's not your fault. When you're in their hands, you're no longer yourself. You don't have control anymore."

I'm holding her hand so tight it has to be on the verge of painful. I can feel Julian and Clarke watching us, but I really don't give a shit. God, I didn't realize how much I've missed touching someone. My family is full of huggers. Suddenly going without that quiet reassurance, even for just a couple of days, has me going through a withdrawal I didn't notice until now.

"Come with us to Alaster," she says, running her thumb along the back of my hand.

"What would I have to do for you guys?" Nothing is free. Especially not something as wonderful as this.

Lexi shrugs. "Become a part of the family. Help us fix things that break and keep our home clean. Help us keep everyone safe."

"*Everyone?* How many people are there?" Julian asks.

Clarke laughs. Lexi doesn't let go of my hand. I don't want her to.

"A few," Clarke says as he finishes off his steak. "It's been a while since we've gotten anyone new though. 'Specially not as a two-for-one like this."

Lexi closes her eyes for a second and shakes her head. "Ignore him. We'd love to have you come with us. Both of you."

Ducking my head, I take a breath and squeeze Lexi's hand just a little tighter. "Won't traveling with this many of us attract..." My eyes flick up to the ceiling. "... the wrong kind of attention? I only have one backpack of stones. I feel like all four of us together is like painting a target over our heads."

"It won't be that dangerous," Lexi says. Pulling her hand from mine, she lifts her backpack out from under the table and unzips the main portion. Like mine, it's stuffed with different gemstones and clusters of crystal. "On top of these, the car is kinda overloaded with stones. There's a chunk of malachite in the trunk the size of my head." Winking, she crosses her arms over her chest and puffs up like she's trying to look tough. "We don't travel unprepared."

Smiling, I glance at Julian. When he notices my attention, he smirks. "It's like car service and bodyguards in one! And it'll save us a bunch on cab fare."

Lexi nods. "Pretty much." Within a couple minutes, she's polished off the rest of her meal. She drops some cash on the table before I can offer and nods toward the door. When we reach the parking lot, Lexi glances at Clarke. "Guess we're off to see the wizard."

Clarke shakes his head, muttering, "If you start singing, I'm throwing you out of the car on the highway. At full speed."

"Don't mind him." Lexi's fake whisper is more than loud enough for Julian and Clarke to hear. "He grows on you. Kind of like a fungus!"

Clarke flips her off without turning around. Lexi laughs. And then starts humming songs from *The Wizard of Oz*. Loudly and off-key.

As painful as it is to think about everything I left in Florida, I can't help hoping. Hoping that Alaster won't just be a safe haven. Hoping that I might find a place I can *not* be seen as a freak of nature for the first time. Ever.

Thirteen

Julian

Clarke drives like a maniac, and what should be an hour's drive takes us only half, pulling into Alaster around eleven that night. The town is off the highway and nestled in the foothills of the Adirondacks. Honestly, I think calling it a town is generous. This is a village. A really tiny, postcard-worthy village. At least Clarke's insane need for speed dies down once we enter the city (*village?*) limits.

Most of the businesses are lined along a literal Main Street and, if I'm remembering Uncle Frank's lessons on architecture right, the houses all look like they could have been built as early as the 1890s. Some of them maybe as late as the 1940s. Maybe. Everything is old and charming and well-restored. It's so well-kept that the modern lines of the Hondas and the Toyotas and the Fords parked along the side of the road all look out of place. A classic Model T would fit right in, though.

Clarke passes through the decidedly quaint town, turning down a dirt road that looks like it leads to nowhere. Towering pines and other trees I remember from visiting Frank and Mariella line the narrow one-lane road. Can't identify them, especially in the dark, but their presence is oddly comforting; they've always been in the background of my fantasy childhood with Mari and Uncle Frank.

It's a mile or so through a tight, winding road before we reach a clearing where a few other SUVs are parked, most of them ancient but, I'm guessing, all-wheel-drive capable. I look around, peering into the trees, but there's nothing else here. Nothing that I can make out in the darkness, anyway.

"Leave your heavier luggage for tonight. We'll pick it up when there's some daylight," Lexi says as we all get out of the car. Nadette grabs her backpack of stones, so I grab mine. There aren't any magical crystals in there, but I do have a couple changes of clothes and some food. My money is in my pockets and there's nothing in my bigger bags it'd kill me to lose.

Closing the doors behind us, Lexi asks, "You guys are both wearing sneakers, right?"

I lift a foot encased in beat-up Skechers I got at Goodwill, and Nadette nods even though she looks a little confused at the question. The motion of her head makes her long red curls fall over her face and she huffs as she pushes them back behind her ear.

"It's still a little bit of a hike from here," Lexi explains. Nadette must have thought something, because Lexi glances at her and smiles. "I warned you we worked hard to hide this place."

"We have to hike? At night?" I look at the thick forest surrounding us. Through the initial line of trees there are … more trees. And some rocks. I don't see anything that looks habitable, though. Especially not for as many people as Clarke and Lexi hinted live here. But they have to be here somewhere. Unless I've walked into a horror movie and these two are bringing us into the forest to murder us and get rid of the bodies. Okay, sure. Not *literally* or anything, but still.

"Yeah, normally we'd do this in the daylight," Lexi says with a sigh as she clicks on a heavy-duty flashlight. Beside her, Clarke does the same. "But, you know. Needs must and all."

They start walking, but I hesitate. I'm usually willing to believe (theoretically) that people are, if not straight-up decent, at least somewhere on the morality scale between chaotic neutral and chaotic good. Still, giving these strangers this level of trust this fast has got to be tempting fate.

Nadette swore they were telling the truth, I remind myself. And it's true that Pheodora told me Nadette would know where to go, but really? Backwoods New York? *Really?*

Ugh. Whatever. If I die, I'm coming back to haunt all of them.

I take a step and nearly jump when light blooms in front of me. In the middle of this dark forest, barely lit by a waning moon, the pure white light of the doorway to Pheodora's world is bright as a lighthouse beacon, but not nearly as blinding. Even looking straight at it, my eyes don't need time to adjust.

For the first time, Pheodora doesn't smile. Her eyes are wide, her long hair windblown, and her body tense. "We do not have much time, Julian. The others are close to finding me. Quickly, child, tell me what you have learned."

I barely pause for a breath as I recap everything that's happened in the last twelve hours. Only when I'm done does a question occur to me. "You usually see everything that happens to me. Why couldn't you—?"

"The stones they carry," she says, the words spoken so fast they almost run together. "They keep the children safe from the Balasura, but they also keep those trying to offer aid from finding them."

That seems more than somewhat pointless. "How are you going to help someone you can't reach?"

"In your world, are there not electric fences?" Pheodora makes a sharp gesture with one hand, the expression on her face somewhere between exasperation and earnest intensity. "They keep out those who might rob or vandalize a building, but they would also deter someone from helping if, for example, a fire endangered those inside. The stones do much the same for us."

Huh. That kind of makes sense. It sucks, but it makes sense.

She glances over her shoulder and I notice a mirror hanging in midair, hovering over the lakeshore. There's nothing but a smooth silver reflection. Pheodora relaxes a little, but she still seems tense when her attention returns to me. "Stay close to Nadette, Julian. I fear trouble may be brewing and I do not yet know from which direction it will come."

"How can I find you if I need help?"

"Away from the stones' protections, step across the wall in your mind and touch the mark I left there. If I can, I will come to you." I open my mouth to ask what she wants me to do now that I'm here, but the doorway is already closing. Pheodora's smile turns sad. "Be careful, Julian."

And then the light is gone, the world around me jolts back into motion, and I realize the others are quickly leaving me behind. Alone. In the barely moonlit forest. Crud.

Despite the worries now spinning through my mind, I catch up fast, which is a good thing because the hike starts climbing up the hillside (mountainside? Are we on a mountain?). It grates on my nerves knowing that I'm holding my own on the hike only because Orane took me climbing most nights. Nadette isn't doing quite as well. She slows and even stops a couple of times. I wait for her to catch her breath and take her arm, helping her up the next part of the path.

"Thanks," she huffs. "To think I used to *complain* about Florida being flat."

I laugh and catch her as she tilts slightly off-balance. "It just takes some getting used to."

She grumbles something under her breath, but I can't make out the words. I help her stay balanced until we reach a plateau and Clarke starts heading toward a solid rock wall.

"Holding up okay?" Lexi asks, grinning at us both. She and Clarke aren't winded at all, but I have the feeling they've walked this trail often enough they probably don't even need the flashlights.

"No," Nadette mutters, her voice as dry as the leaves and twigs crunching under our feet. "Are we almost there yet?"

Lexi nods toward the wall of rock. "Almost. Just around the corner."

Clarke looks much more at home in the woods, a lot less tense and grouchy than he seemed at the station. There's practically a smile on his face. It definitely turns into a smile when his flashlight shines on a dilapidated wood shack that's bumped right up against the rock wall.

Oh they can't be serious. *This* is their super-secret hideout?

"What's wrong with that place?" Nadette's voice comes from behind me. Only after I hear it do I realize she's stopped walking. She's too busy staring at the shack, her eyes squinted, irritation obvious on her face. She's also rubbing at her arms like she's been doused with itching powder.

"You can *see* lies too?" Lexi looks back at Nadette and laughs. "Good lord, girl. Johanna is going to get a *kick* out of you! No one has been able to see through her illusions ... ever."

Nadette blinks and looks away from the shack. "Illusions?"

I'm looking at the same building, but I don't see what the fuss is about. It's a wood hut about seven feet tall, and I'd bet a sizable amount of money (against really long odds) that only its proximity to the rocks is keeping it from tumbling down. One good gust of wind in the wrong direction could probably fix that. The boards are rotting away and the sign on the door reading "DANGER: DO NOT ENTER" is barely legible. The red and black paint has been worn down by time until it's hardly a stain on the wood plank across the entrance.

"Hey, kid. Catch."

A glint in the darkness is the only warning I get. I barely duck in time to avoid the rock hurtling toward my head.

"Clarke!" Lexi snaps. "Would you *please* act your age for once?"

Clarke snorts and shines his light on the rock. "Pick it up and check out your new home."

This has *got* to be some kind of joke. Clarke seems like the practical joke type, but I hadn't thought Lexi would play along like this. She's rolling her eyes, but he's smiling, waiting for me to do what he said with this light of expectation in his eye. And not the pleasure I see when people are watching their pranks play out, but the kind of look parents in movies get on their faces when they're about to surprise their kids.

I glance at Nadette. She's still staring at the shack, her head tilting from side to side. Her red curls swing as she moves, falling into her face, but she's so entranced by whatever she's seeing that she doesn't seem to care.

Whatever. Might as well see what kind of game he's playing. Walking a few steps, I pick up the rock and turn around.

Holy Sinatra and all the blessed Rat Pack.

The stone falls from my limp fingers and the image I thought I saw disappears. The dilapidated shack is back. Of course it is. There can't be anything else. Not here. Not in the middle of nowhere.

Slowly, keeping my eyes locked on the shack, I bend to pick up the rock. As soon as my hand closes around the stone, the run-down house vanishes, replaced by a stone and metal entrance about seven feet high and four feet wide. The arch is set with chunks of glittering purple stones and a girl with soft brown, freckle-scattered skin and jet-black ringlets cut close to her head is watching me with her arms crossed over her chest.

"Was there a two-for-one sale?" she asks, one eyebrow high.

Nadette jumps and I pass her the rock. Whatever she can see, it's obviously not what I see when that stone is in my hand. She gasps as soon as her hand closes around the thing.

Without the rock, both the arch and the girl are gone.

"Guess you need another key, huh?" Her voice seems to come from everywhere and nowhere, and I try not to jump. She's standing in the arch I can't see. It's there. I'm not hearing things. Maybe. Wow this is weird.

The door of the shack wavers and there she is. As she comes closer, the flashlight beams show me honey tones in her skin and streaks of lighter brown in her hair. She looks tiny standing next to Clarke, but Clarke is freaking Paul Bunyan tall, so she's probably average height. When she's within reach, Clarke leans down and whispers something. Her eyes flick to me and she nods. Filling her in on the change of plans? This must be Johanna, then. By their descriptions, I kind of expected her to be bigger. The protector and all.

Johanna passes Clarke, her light brown eyes locked on me. She's not smiling, but she doesn't look peeved either. Her expression is carefully neutral. So neutral I don't ever want to play poker with her. This girl has control.

She stops in front of me and holds out her hand. Sitting in her palm is a clear crystal-like stone. Quartz maybe? I didn't get a good look at the stone Clarke chucked at my head, but when I take this in my hand it feels the same. Over her shoulder I can see the gray stone arch come back. This is their key?

"How long has it been?" she asks me.

"What?"

"Since you escaped. How long has it been?"

I open my mouth and close it again. I didn't exactly give her envoys a lot of details and I don't think I have time to go into the full story now. How do I explain everything in ten seconds or less?

"I didn't," I tell her after a beat of silence. "Someone else freed me."

Johanna's eyes widen just a touch. "Guess that explains the light show. Half-in and half-out of their world."

I look down at my hands. Is she seeing the same glow that Nadette mentioned? Whatever it is, I still don't see it. I've never seen anything glow except the doorways to the dream world and the bracelet Orane gave me. The way everyone else is talking about it, though, I think whatever is going on around my skin is a lot stranger than that.

"You were attached to the one who died last week, then?"

My stomach rolls. I fight off the rush of pain and the shame that follows in its wake. How long will it take for me to stop feeling like a complete idiot for not seeing the truth behind Orane's mask? How long will it take for that shame to erase the lingering pain of losing someone I thought was my best friend?

Taking a breath, I give her the highlights of the past two years, a slightly extended version of the twenty-second bullet-point overview of my life I gave Lexi and Clarke, just enough for her to understand. It's really freaking weird to talk about my life to strangers, to admit out loud that Lynnie was a basket case and that we only made rent most months because I was a master of the bluff. It's as though I told the lies for so long they became the truth, and now telling the truth feels more like lying.

I mention Mariella's coma, but I hold back the fact that Mari is the one who stepped into the dream world and broke me free of chains I didn't know I was wearing. The way Johanna's face tightens when I bring up my hospital visit makes me think she isn't too thrilled about what happened that night. Or overly fond of the person who caused the trouble.

When I stop talking, I feel like I've been the center of attention for hours, but it can't have been more than ten minutes.

Johanna grimaces and shakes her head. "We were lucky. Everyone here was safe, but even we felt that backlash last week. I wouldn't be surprised to find a lot more stories like yours. And your cousin's."

Maybe that wasn't anger or disgust I saw in her face. Maybe that was regret. She talks about it like she's seen it before, like she knows a lot about what's happening. Hope rises in my chest. "Can you help her? Can you bring Mari back?"

Clarke freezes behind Johanna. The expression on her face is completely unreadable. With nothing else to do, I count the seconds as they pass. I get to fifteen before Johanna takes a breath, shakes her head, and looks away.

"You two want a tour? You'll need to learn your way around if you decide to stay."

Lexi hisses. "Johanna, don't."

The hint of a smile slowly spreads across Johanna's face. Her eyes are on Nadette, not Lexi. "That good, huh?"

"Kels was right." Lexi's statement draws Johanna's attention. She looks at Lexi with her arched eyebrows raised and then pointedly looks at me. Lexi shrugs. "Okay, *mostly* right."

Johanna meets Nadette's eyes and they stare at each other for a moment, each one weighing the other on who knows what kind of scale.

"We don't get to decide if we stay," Nadette finally says. "You do."

Johanna nods, her hands on her hips. "It's not a very nice thing to say at a first meeting."

Nadette snorts, her tiny nose wrinkling. "You don't care about nice."

"You're right. I care about *safe*." She steps forward, her movements tense but her voice level. Her eyes, though—her eyes almost burn, even in the low, indirect light of the flashlights. "I care about the people who call this place home because they can't go anywhere else. I care about making sure this sanctuary is here for everyone who needs it." She pauses and glances at me. "Anyone can live here as long as they're willing to play by my rules."

Nadette exhales slowly. She even smiles a little. "Fair enough."

"So, how 'bout that tour?" Johanna asks, turning toward the arch.

Everyone follows Johanna, so I hurry after, but it seems too easy. "Aren't you worried about showing us too much before you decide we can stay?"

Johanna glances over her shoulder, Clarke's flashlight picking up a smirk on her lips I don't think I like. All she says is, "No."

I step into the shadow of the arch and take one last look at the little bit of moonlight filtering through the trees. It's dark as the desert at midnight out here, but at least it's open space.

Sighing, I turn into the tunnel and wonder if I have a clue what I've agreed to do.

Fourteen

Nadette

Saturday, September 20 – 11:46 PM EDT

In the back of my mind, I had an image of a safe haven. An abandoned house, maybe. Something vaguely creepy. Possibly with a haunting legend attached to keep people away. Like the shrieking shack in Harry Potter or one of those enormous houses in Scooby-Doo. Almost anything would've made more sense than a bunch of people living in a cave.

Johanna—who, like Lexi and Clarke, is surrounded by cerulean light—leads us through a tunnel that gets tighter before suddenly spreading out. It's weird, but even though all three of them are glowing, that light doesn't cast shadows. The only way I can see anything in front of us is the beams of their flashlights.

The farther we get from the entrance, the more absolute the blackness surrounding us becomes. In the darkness, the gleam of the flashlights is more jarring than comforting. It takes more effort than I want to admit to keep walking, because the last time I was faced with a wall of solid black broken only by brief flashes of light was the last time I saw Syver.

I shudder and press forward. *He's not here*, I remind myself. *You're safe here.*

To help keep my balance, I trail my fingers along the surprisingly smooth walls. They're not perfect, but all of the roughest edges have been worn away. The roof is as high as the top of the arch—a good seven or eight feet—and in random places the stone seems to … sparkle? I look down at the quartz in my hand and back at the walls. Crystal deposits? Otherwise, there's nothing special about this place.

Nothing that makes me feel safe. Nothing that even seems weird except that illusion guarding the entrance.

My skin itches. It's an all-over thing that makes it a fight to keep from fidgeting. At least it's not as bad as it was outside the caves. Even before I noticed the slight waver to the wood and the reddish tint to the air surrounding the ramshackle hut, it felt like there was itching powder in the air or spread inside my clothes. My nose twitched, my eyes felt dried out, and my skin prickled. Now that I've stepped inside the layers and layers of illusion poured over this mountain — and have the quartz key thing—the intensity has died down. Thank God.

After a few more feet, I see a larger cavern ahead. And I feel a faint breeze. There's light, too. Where's it coming from? Looking up, I see a pale shaft of moonlight spilling through the sizable skylight in the roof. There's still no signs this place is inhabited, though.

Lexi's hand catches my arm.

I look down and stumble backward. Shit! I almost walked right off a ledge!

"Thanks," I whisper, staring at the ten-foot drop that would've hurt like hell.

Lexi smiles at me, squeezing my arm gently before letting go. "Anytime."

Taking a breath to calm my jumpy pulse, I search for any sign someone could and does live here. The stone is a little rougher in this area. Everywhere except for the six-foot-wide ledge circling the cavern's walls. That ledge slopes higher on one side to reach a tunnel almost directly across from us. It dips lower on our right to meet another tunnel. Otherwise, this cavern is empty.

Until a girl appears in the mouth of the tunnel to our right.

She's small and looks young. Her skin is deep brown and her eyes are dark, but her smile is bright and white. And *she's* glowing blue, too.

I glance at Julian, at the swirls of orange running through the cerulean light surrounding him. If the one-color thing is normal, then what happened to Julian?

Johanna said something about being half-in and half-out of their world. It makes sense in a way. Everyone here—everyone who's *escaped*—seems to be blue, but the gateway and Tessa's pendant are orange. If Julian never *decided* to leave their world, if he was booted out of it instead…

"Everyone is waiting when you finish," the stranger says. Her voice echoes across the cavern. The tone reminds me of a clarinet. "Don't worry, Nadette. I don't snore."

With those strange words, she turns and disappears down the tunnel.

"Why the hell should I care if she snores?" I wonder. Lexi laughs, but Julian and I look at each other, confused.

"*That* was Kelsey," Lexi says as Johanna leads us up the curving walkway to the left. "She's been the neophyte of the group for almost a year now, so she's excited to pass the torch."

"How did she—" I cut myself off. Kelsey…the seer they mentioned? "She's the one who told you how to find me?"

"Yep, and I think she plans on claiming you as her new roommate," Lexi says.

"Oh. Um, okay." I guess. It's been a while since I shared a bedroom with anyone. It's been even longer since anyone *wanted* to share a bedroom with me. Mom thinks I don't know that she had to bribe Sophia to bunk with me. She thinks I didn't hear Sophia say she was tired of not having any secrets. As though I stole them from her. As though I wanted them.

Lexi places her hand on my shoulder. I blush, refusing to look at her. As misunderstood as I felt by my family sometimes, they're still my family. I love all of them. Not sure how much I like someone else knowing all our dirty little secrets.

Lexi hears the thoughts running through my head. I know she does. But instead of pulling her hand away, she links her arm through mine and ducks her head to whisper, "Most of us haven't seen our families in a long time. Even the best intentioned people don't know how to deal with things they can't understand."

I stop walking and look up into her eyes. In the faint glow from her downturned flashlight the gold flecks in her eyes seem to glitter. She smiles and squeezes my arm.

"No one is going to make you spill secrets you don't want to share, but you may be surprised by how many people can tell you the same secrets using different names."

Lexi breaks eye contact before I can process what she said. Keeping her hand around my arm, she pulls me forward until we catch up with the others.

Ugh. She's right. And thinking otherwise is stupidly self-centered. Hell, I *already* know life could've been worse. Julian's childhood may not have been an absolute horror story, but thinking about everything he told me makes my chest ache.

Thoughts of Julian fly out of my head when I see the first sign of civilization.

Let there be light.

If it was earlier in the day, I'd think it was the sun beaming through a skylight. This is different than sunlight, though. Whiter. Brighter. It's coming from a bare light bulb hanging from the roof by a chain, a coppery wire winding from the bulb and up through the links.

"You guys have electricity?" Julian asks, staring up. "In a *cave?*"

"Only for light," Lexi says. "Thanks to two of our residents."

My eyes are locked on the light as we pass underneath it. How anyone could rig electricity for an entire cave in the middle of nowhere I don't know, but I'm so glad to see it I don't really care how it got here. I didn't like walking through the darkness. It reminds me too much of the absolute blackness of Syver's world that last time. Those flashlights were barely enough to guide us.

Once we pass the first light, they appear every ten feet or so until the tunnel widens into a cavern that's freaking huge. An intricate chandelier of light bulbs and pieces of lamps illuminate a combination living room, library, and playroom. Books line the walls in shelves carved out of the stone. Couches, armchairs, and beanbag chairs are scattered around the center of the room. They've even got a Ping-Pong table off in a corner. All of it is so mismatched it's obvious the furniture was salvaged from yard sales and thrift stores. The chaos in this room would drive Mom's designer instincts crazy, but I kind of love it.

"This is the Whatever Room," Johanna says.

"The Whatever Room?" Julian asks.

"Because we use it for whatever," Clarke says. He shrugs as he picks up a book from one of the end tables and puts it back on the shelf.

The way Johanna rests her hand on the back of a couch is almost possessive. "Everyone needs a place without expectations. This is one of those places."

One sharp nod punctuates the end of the sentence before she leads us through another tunnel into what she calls the Dorm. Caves with curtained entrances are centered around an open space and a huge, crackling fire pit. Until the heat of the flames reach me, I didn't realize how cold it had gotten in the caves. I shiver and step closer to the fire, holding my hands out. Why is it so freezing?

"We're pretty far underground now."

Jumping a little, I turn around. I didn't hear Lexi come up beside me, but she's standing there offering a coat. It's sapphire-blue and thick. I have no idea where she pulled it from, but I slip into it gladly. With my next breath, I get a whiff of coconut and cinnamon. Is that the jacket? It smells good. She tosses a black sweatshirt to Julian and he smiles gratefully.

Johanna leads us up and down and around, left, right, and every which way. The tunnel is curvy as hell, but there aren't many offshoots. Which is good. Otherwise I'd be completely lost by the time we reach what Johanna calls the Training Room.

"It needs to be pretty far away from the main living areas in case of, um, accidents," Lexi explains.

"What kind of accidents?" Julian's eyes are locked on a huge gouge in the stone on the other side of the room.

"Depends on who's training," Clarke says. "With Kels you just have to worry about finding out your most likely death is by heart attack at fifty-three. With Brian you might end up buried in a rockslide."

Julian pales and glances at me, then Clarke. "A *rockslide?*"

"Yeah. But that hasn't happened in ..." Clarke glances at Johanna. "Five years?"

"Six in December," Lexi says.

"This is where we come to learn how to control whatever abilities or skills we've got," Johanna glances at Julian, but her eyes rest on me when she says, "We don't know much about the mechanics of it—the neurology—but we know that life gets easier when we master whatever is inside us."

And then, without a gesture, word, or glance, Johanna vanishes.

Julian stumbles backward. My eyes start burning again. The prickles running across my skin aren't as bad as they felt in the forest. I can track the waver in the air around her form and the very faint red light. I never lose her. When Johanna releases the illusion, she's standing in front of me with a broad smile. The first real one I've seen on her face.

"You really *are* good," she says. "C'mon. It's time to introduce you to the family."

We leave the Training Room and take another long, curving tunnel. I try to remember all the twists and turns. "Are we walking in a huge-ass circle?" I ask Lexi.

"Yep," Lexi whispers back. "It's almost impossible to get lost here because all the caverns connect to each other. Brian helped us make sure of it."

"The guy with the rockslides?" I kind of hope the answer is no.

She laughs. "Don't worry. We're as safe here as we can make it."

The tunnel takes a sharp turn. For the first time, I hear voices that aren't ours echoing off the rocks. Still distant, but definitely a sign of life.

Johanna leads us into yet *another* cavern. This one is smaller, but it's jam-packed with stuff and people. Long tables line the center of the room with mismatched chairs surrounding them. Stone shelves carved into the walls hold cereal boxes and bread and vegetables and everything else you'd need to feed a large group of people. A huge stone oven in the corner heats one end of the room, and a fireplace is at the opposite end. Just as we enter, a kettle starts whistling. A tall guy with brown hair and broad shoulders grabs an oven mitt. He swings the kettle away from the open flame before grabbing the handle and carrying it over to the table.

He looks us over and smiles, but his gaze lingers on Johanna. "Tea, anybody? Or coffee? I think we have some left."

I do a quick count; there are twenty-two people gathered in the kitchen. Some of them are sitting on chairs, and others swing their legs as they perch on the tables. It's hard to guess ages, but it's obviously a wide spread. Prophet Kelsey seems to be at one end of the spectrum.

The brown-haired tea drinker looks like he might be close to the other. No way is he a teenager. He's got to be closer to thirty than twenty. I follow his gaze to Johanna and wonder where she falls on that spectrum. Judging by her face alone, she could be anywhere between seventeen and twenty-seven. But everyone else seems to defer to her, even the tea drinker.

She's twenty-one, -two, -three ... I think, rolling through the numbers until I hit one that doesn't set off the bells. Twenty-six.

Johanna ignores the offered drinks and looks over the group until everyone quiets down. It doesn't take long. They're all staring, but their focus seems to be on Julian.

"This is Nadette and Julian." Johanna points us out like they couldn't guess which name belonged to who.

"What happened to you?" a blonde girl asks. "That light show is ridiculous."

I glance at Julian. He scratches his hand as though he'll be able to see the lights if he just peels away a layer of skin. Everyone except for Julian and me is glowing blue. Like Violet Beauregarde before she gets all round. Or radioactive Smurfs.

Julian glances at me before shifting away from the crowd slightly. I want to help, but I don't know how much I can. These people have a right to be cautious and curious about the strangers they're considering inviting into their home. Still, I step closer until his shoulder almost brushes mine.

Julian takes a deep breath and shrugs. "If any of you can give me an explanation, great. I have no idea why I'm glowing."

"You didn't escape, did you?" The question comes from a guy with light brown hair and dark eyes.

"That's Brian," Lexi whispers to me. Right. The rockslide guy.

Brian shakes his head. "There's no way you fought your way out if you're still all orange like that."

Julian blinks and looks down at his hands. He glances up at me. "Orange? You never told me I was orange. You just said I was glowing."

Didn't I? I totally meant to. "You're glowing orange. And blue."

"*And* blue?" He brings his hands closer to his face then drops them. "I still don't see it."

Jaws drop and eyes bug out of heads. Some look worried, others confused. Only a black-haired kid in the back says, "You don't *see* it?" his voice mocking and skeptical.

Tense, expectant silence descends. No one verbalizes the questions, but I hear them anyway. And so must Julian because he slowly begins to tell them about his life. He talks about Orane. About waking up in the hospital the night after Orane died. They listen and throw questions at him, but there's judgment on more than a few faces. He was released. He didn't fight his way free. It's like that distinction turns him into some kind of goddamn second-class citizen around here. The way they're weighing and measuring us both, it's starting to feel like facing a jury for a crime I don't remember committing.

"Are we sure they should even be here?" the guy with black hair asks, his dark eyes boring into mine. "Neither of them seems like one of us."

The damn bells ring. I close my eyes until they fade. I hear Lexi groan and I whisper, *Sorry* to her in my head. She waves off my apology, too busy glaring at the dissenter. Before I can say anything, a girl gets up.

She's tall and one of the few people I've ever seen who seems perfectly described as willowy. Everything about her except for her sandy blonde hair is long—even her fingers—and she sways as she moves like some breeze is pushing her forward. Her hazel eyes— steady as they look me over—are intense. She walks closer slowly, stopping two feet away.

"This is Beth," Lexi supplies in a soft whisper.

"She definitely belongs here," Beth says, her voice soft and soothing. "Look closer. She's glittering like starlight."

What? I look down at my own hand, pulling up the sleeve of my borrowed coat to expose more skin. It takes a second to pick out, but she's right. It's faint. Subtle. It reminds me of a lotion Sophia had when we were younger. It had iridescent glitter dust swirled into the cream so that when she spread it on her skin, it would sparkle slightly in the light.

"Ho-ly shit I'm sparkling."

Lexi chuckles. "I would've pointed it out earlier, but I thought you knew."

"I don't spend much time in front of a mirror," I mumble, staring at my hands.

Clarke comes closer and stares at my cheek. "Wow. *I* didn't even see that before."

That's all it takes. Everyone jumps off their seats and crowds around. They're gawking at me like some exhibit at a zoo. My breath comes quicker and my skin heats up.

"Step back!" Lexi shouts. She jumps in front of me, shoving everyone away. "She's a person, not a painting. She doesn't want to be gaped at!"

They scramble back, most of them staring at Lexi like she just threatened to eat them. My guess is she doesn't yell much. But she's doing it for me. I reach out and touch her arm, silently thanking her and letting her know it's all right. As they shift back a bit, the flush of heat and the rising panic subsides. I can breathe easier.

Lexi steps aside, but doesn't retreat with the others. Soon, it's just Lexi, Julian, and me at the center of attention again.

"How long did they have you for?" the blonde girl who first commented on Julian's light show asks.

"Sarah," Lexi whispers. "Her name is Sarah."

"What do you mean 'have me?'" I ask Sarah.

Her head quirks to the side a little. She seems as confused by my question as I am by hers. "Like, after they first showed up. How long was it until you realized they were full of shit?"

I remember the first guy who showed up around my fourteenth birthday. It had been a bad day, one where I'd managed to annoy or flat-out piss off almost everyone in the house. Everyone I came in contact with, actually. Then a guy with shamrock-green hair and bright green eyes shows up in the middle of the night...

"Hello, Nadette. I am Isasius," he says.

Whoa. Green hair, green eyes, and a green field behind him. He's like a really tall leprechaun. I back away from the glowing white portal.

"Do not fear me." He holds out his hand like he's going to try to stop me. I skitter back another foot. "Your family doesn't appreciate your gifts, Nadette. I am only here to help. I would like to be your friend."

It's a lie. All of it but his name has been a lie.

"Come with me," Isasius says.

Dream or not, I know the answer to this question. Don't talk to strangers. Especially creepy, lying, green-haired ones. Shaking my head, I scoot back on my bed until my back presses against the wall. "No. I'm not going anywhere with you."

His eyes burn neon for a moment before he vanishes. In a puff of green smoke.

Sitting there in the dark, listening to my sister's quiet breaths, I try to figure out what just happened. It isn't until the next month— after six more visits from different people—that fear begins to sink under my skin. Maybe these *aren't* just dreams.

"I realized it on day one," I tell Sarah.

The dark-haired kid who called me out on my bluelessness— "Vasha," Lexi whispers—laughs. "Yeah, right. No one sees through their illusions on day one."

I open my mouth to protest. Johanna beats me to it. "She saw through mine."

Everyone freezes. Some people stare at me. The rest stare at Johanna. None of them look like they're ready to believe me.

"Try her," Lexi says, smirking. "Everyone tell her something. Truth or lie. I bet you all a week of chores that she calls out every single liar in the bunch."

"Done." Vasha stands up and stares at me. "I could make your heart stop if I wanted to."

No bells. I shift closer to Lexi even though I doubt she could help if he decided to put that power to work. "Um, I'd rather you didn't."

"My mother abandoned me in a Walmart," a girl in the back says. Bells, but only on Walmart.

God. That's awful. "It wasn't in a Walmart, but I'm still sorry."

"I can read your mind," Sarah says.

"Lie."

"I'm allergic to dogs," says the brown-haired tea-drinker.

"That's Tanner," Lexi adds.

"True."

"Kids under the age of five freak me out."

"King Tut's tomb was discovered in 1910."

"*Justice League* is the best cartoon ever created."

"James Buchanan was the twentieth president."

"Malcolm Reynolds is my brother."

They throw statements at me rapid-fire and I try to keep track of them all. I close my eyes and tick off the truth and the lies on my fingers.

When there's finally a break in the stream, I open my eyes and count off the statements. "Truth, lie, opinion, lie, and really? He's a TV character, so lie."

Some people laugh and Lexi throws her arms up and dances in a circle, her long skirt flowing out around her. "Free! I'm free! What am I going to do with all my free time next week?"

The laughter quiets quickly. Before more than a few seconds has passed, everyone is staring at me. Even Vasha, who can apparently stop my heart.

"Wow. So you really saw right through them?" Beth asks. "They never pulled you in?"

I shrug. "I didn't know what they were or what they wanted, I only knew they were lying. All of them except Syver." I shudder saying his name. Truth didn't matter in the end. Not with him. Syver always told the truth and had always been ten times worse than any of the others.

"So you—wait..." Vasha's mouth is hanging open a little. "What do you mean, *all* of them?"

How many meanings can those words *possibly* have?

Bit by bit I tell them everything that happened over the past two years. The dreams, the lack of sleep, the daylight stalking. I tell them about Peter and his daughter Tessa. I describe Syver and his threats. I tell them about Blue's message and how Syver tricked me into hurting Linus. I tell them about meeting Julian, too. I only stop when Lexi and Clarke come into the story.

"And so I'm hoping you guys can fill in all the pieces I'm missing because, honestly, I still don't have a goddamn clue what's happening to me."

When I stop talking this time, There are no outbursts. No questions. Everyone stares at me in silence. A terrified, heavy silence.

Fifteen

Julian

"It wasn't a message from Aisling? The *Balasura* told you to come here?" Johanna has been perfectly controlled and nearly unreadable since we met her outside the caves, but now there's a flush on her cheeks and her hands are clenched so tight the skin over her knuckles is white.

"Who's Aisling?" I ask at the same time Nadette quickly says, "Not the ones like Syver." Her voice is even, but physically she's pulling back, curling her shoulders a little like she's trying to hide. "The other ones, the—"

"There are no other ones!" Johanna cries. Lexi hisses and Nadette flinches, but Johanna doesn't seem to notice. Her voice gets louder with every word until it's nearly echoing off the walls. "Their kind is like a disease and they've been plaguing humanity for who knows how long. Their entire world deserves to be *nuked!*"

I'm standing close enough to Nadette to feel her flinch at almost every other word out of Johanna's mouth. I should check on her to make sure she's doing all right, but taking my eyes off Johanna seems like a bad decision.

"This place has been safe for fifteen years! And now you're telling me they *know?*"

"Someone does." Nadette's voice trembles, but she forces her shoulders back and stands tall. "But it's someone who wants to help. He was trying to keep me off Syver's radar and he—"

"What's his name?" Johanna demands. "This helpful 'friend.' What's his name?"

Nadette bites her lip and shakes her head. "I don't know. He had to leave. Said they'd almost found him."

"And you expect us to believe that one of the Balasura is actually trying to *help* us?"

This time, Nadette doesn't hesitate or waver. "Yes. I wouldn't have made it here without him."

Johanna's entire face purses, but she doesn't immediately bite back. In fact, except for creaking of chairs and shuffling of feet as people shift uneasily, the whole room has gone quiet.

"Tanner," Johanna says, her face still looking like she bit into a lemon coated in wasabi.

The tall guy who offered everyone tea before this mockery of a town hall meeting started gets up, his expression tense. When he's standing just off Johanna's right shoulder, he reaches out as though he's going to put his hand on the small of her back. He never completes the motion, tucking his thumb through his belt loop instead.

Johanna doesn't even glance at him. "Go into town and ask Aisling to come up. Take Clarke with you."

"Sure thing," he says softly. Clarke is already halfway to the tunnel that, I think, leads to the exit.

Their footsteps haven't even faded completely before Johanna is back to issuing orders.

"Lexi, Vasha, Brian, Sarah, and Beth, stay. Everyone else, out. Now."

No one grumbles as the ones commanded to leave get up, but almost all of them cast glances at Nadette and me over their shoulders. Confusion, worry, fear, distrust—geez. I look down at my shoes to avoid their eyes. I thought finding others like me would be ... well, better than *this* at least.

Once the room clears out, Johanna nods toward a table in the center of the room, silently directing us to sit. I hesitate (leaving my back against a wall seems like a *much* better option), but Nadette sighs and walks forward. Okay, then. I guess we're moving.

I stay close to Nadette, waiting until she picks a chair so I can slide into the one next to her. Someone passes close behind me and my skin prickles, the hair on the back of my neck standing on end. I don't turn my head to look, but out the corner of my eye, I see the black-haired kid who can stop hearts walking around the far end of the table, his dark eyes on us. His steps are slow and deliberate and he's rubbing his hands together, the motion too steady to be a nervous fidget. When he reaches the chair opposite us, he uses his foot to pull it away from the table, then sits, scooting closer and resting his elbows and hands on the surface. The sleeves of his hoodie are pushed up to his elbows and I eye the marks on his forearms. Tattoos? Scars? Early-onset varicose veins? Whatever they are, the pinkish-white pattern looks like lightning bolts.

He catches me looking right before he slowly pulls his hands apart and smiles.

I almost jump out of my skin when a bolt of blue-white lightning leaps between his palms.

"*Vasha!*" Lexi scolds. "Enough."

Vasha rolls his eyes and settles back into his chair, but his smile (his more than slightly eerie smile) is still in place and his hands stay in plain sight.

Fantastic. Electro-shock treatments. I guess that's how he'd stop our hearts.

Only years of practice hiding my reactions (from Lynnie and kids at school and pretty much everyone else) allow me to stare him down without giving away how fast my heart is pounding, like it's trying to remind me it still works.

"You wouldn't hurt us on purpose," Nadette says.

The words break our staring contest. Vasha blinks and switches his attention to her. "You think so, huh?"

Nadette releases a long, shaky breath and (surprisingly) smiles. "I do now. It's as impossible for me to lie as it is for other people to lie to me. If you were willing to hurt us on purpose, the bells would've gone off," she says, tapping a finger on her temple. "I wouldn't have been able to say that."

Vasha rolls his eyes and grumbles something I can't make out. It doesn't sound like English. After that, no one says a word. Not to us, anyway. Lexi and Johanna are whispering together on the far side of the room, their eyes cutting in our direction every so often.

Nadette groans and rubs her face. "I was kind of hoping for a shower when we got here."

"Uh, yeah. I'll pass. With how popular we are right now, I picture that ending as well as it did for the girl from *Psycho*."

Nadette snorts, trying to stifle her laugh, but it breaks free. She keeps laughing and drops her forehead to the table, her shoulders shaking. I cover my mouth with my hand and hold my breath, trying not to join her, but all it takes is a glance at the scowls forming on Vasha and Johanna's faces for me to crack up too.

Once our laughter dies, the room is silent except for the faint cracks and snaps coming from the fires. After almost an hour of silence that seems physical (like a weight that's carrying their distrust and dropping it on my shoulders), I can't take it anymore.

"I like being ignored better than being hated," I mutter to Nadette. "Can we just go? You can come with me to Swallow's Grove. I swear they'd help us and—"

I cut myself off. There are footsteps approaching, echoing off the walls of the tunnel Tanner and Clarke disappeared down earlier. Everyone else's attention focuses in the same direction. When their two messengers appear, they all seem strangely disappointed.

"She didn't come." Johanna says it and I have to bite back a sarcastic, "Well, obviously."

Tanner can't seem to meet Johanna's eyes for more than a second. "Um, no."

Johanna's lips tighten. "Did you tell her what they said? I can't believe she wouldn't even come for *this*."

"Her words were, and I'm quoting directly here, 'I already told Jojo when she sent Kelsey down a few days ago that there wasn't enough time for me to go collect the redhead. Tell her to keep them or send them to me. Make a choice and then get over it. Not on your life am I climbing that stupid-ass mountain after dark, especially for something this ridiculous.'" Tanner clears his throat, his cheeks slightly flushed. "End quote."

Johanna's eyes pop open wide. "Ridiculous? *Ridiculous*? Shit. Why do we even talk to her anymore?"

"Because she's *Aisling*, Jo," Tanner says. I raise an eyebrow at Nadette. The way he says the name is like the way some people talk about Jesus.

"Right." Johanna's shoulders rise and then drop as she rolls her neck, like she's forcing the tension out of her body. "So, keep them or send them to live with Aisling at Martha's? Those are the choices?"

Clarke nods. "Pretty much."

"Those are shit choices," she mutters.

"Johanna," Lexi says with a sigh. "She's *not* lying. She *can't* lie."

"Everyone lies."

"Sure," Lexi agrees. "Everyone *except her*."

They stare each other for a minute, only the shifts in Lexi's expression and the small shakes or nods of her head giving away that they're still communicating. When Johanna finally turns toward us, her expression remains wary, but she seems to have lost the edge of fear that was there before.

"I guess I should be the first to say 'Welcome to Abra,'" Johanna says.

I blink. "As in 'cadabra?'"

A muscle in Johanna's jaw twitches, but Lexi stifles a laugh.

"As in the Spanish word for open," Johanna says. "Abra is open for everyone who needs it, a place safe from the Balasura and the rest of the world."

"The rest of the world?" Nadette asks.

"Not everyone comes from a family as decent as yours," Lexi says when Johanna doesn't answer right away.

"Or we had to leave *because* we came from a decent family," the slightly shorter blonde girl, Sarah, says. She snaps her fingers and flicks her wrist. Nadette and I both jump when her entire hand is engulfed in flames. It burns bright and strong, but it doesn't spread farther than her wrist. She doesn't look at it at all, doesn't ever look away from us. "Some of us use Abra to keep the rest of the world safe from us, not the other way around."

"What happened?" I ask. There's pain in her voice that reminds me of what I hear in Nadette's voice when she talks about what happened to Linus.

"Had a fight with my mom one night. Went up to my room and fumed. Lost control. Almost burned the whole house down." Sarah's hazel-green eyes are bleak. "With my entire family stuck inside."

"And this place really keeps you safe?" I look around the room. Except for the chandelier above our heads (which looks like an amateur attempt at junk art), the place is simple and almost all stone. Stone counters run along some walls, stone shelves have been dug into others, and the place smells like tomato sauce.

"There are amethyst deposits in this area." Lexi moves closer to us, taking the chair next to Vasha. "Small ones—not worth mining—but enough to create a shield that hides us from the Balasura."

And from the ones like Pheodora and Blue who are trying to help, I want to remind them. But I think bringing that up again would only stir up unnecessary trouble. Looking around the very obviously lived-in cavern, I decide to try a different tack. "How long do you guys plan on hiding up here?"

"Forever." Johanna leans against the wall, her eyes glinting and her jaw tense. She's still pissed off enough to be readable. "Once you're marked out by the Balasura, they don't leave you alone. If you let them catch you out there, unguarded …"

The heavy silence after she trails off is practically an explanation in and of itself. If they catch you, you end up like Mari. Or Nadette's friend Tessa. Or whoever it is Johanna has lost.

"But … what do you *do?*" I've spent the last six years consciously trying to be as busy as possible. They're essentially trapped here, though. I think I'd rather face the danger of the Balasura than face a life only a few steps up from a prison sentence.

"We work and cook and hang out, same as everyone else in the world," Lexi says with a crooked smile. "And we try to figure out how to find other survivors who need help."

"Have you found any?" Nadette asks.

Johanna's grunt is on the verge of annoyed, but her face is back to placid and unreadable. Lexi glances at her, lips pursed, then shrugs. "It's a work in progress."

A noise from another tunnel draws my attention. Kelsey is standing there, peeking into the room. "Can we come in yet?"

Johanna relaxes just a little as she nods. "Yeah, come on."

Everyone she kicked out of the kitchen an hour ago files in, curiosity shining in more than one pair of eyes.

"Cookies and story time?" Kelsey says. She words it like a question, but she's already moving toward a shelf and pulling down ingredients.

"Story time is depressing," Vasha mutters.

"Which is why it always comes with cookies." There's a faint smile on Lexi's face as she says it.

"Who's going first?" Kelsey asks once the cookies are baking over the fire.

"I already went," Sarah says from her seat on the counter. "Before you guys came back."

"Wasn't the full story," Beth says. I look between the two of them, realizing how much they look alike. Blonde hair, hazel eyes (though Sarah's are greener), and sharp features. Beth is taller, though. And thinner. And when she meets my eyes she doesn't seem as angry. In fact, she stares at me like I remind her of someone. Someone she misses a lot, if I'm reading the sadness in her expression right.

Sarah's eyes harden. "It was close enough."

"It should probably be my turn anyway," Johanna says, her voice slowly losing intonation until she's as inflectionless as Nadette seems to think I sound. "My mother died when I was little and my father and step-mother were abusive. I learned how to hide in plain sight really well growing up, but eventually I got the hell out of there."

Johanna holds her elbows and her eyes seem to slide a little out of focus. "Hiding came in handy since I was on my own at fourteen, but it wasn't always enough. The Balasura found me, and it took me two and a half years to figure out they weren't any better than what I'd left."

I glance around, but everyone seems lost in their own thoughts. The only resident watching Johanna is Tanner. When the pause in her story goes on long enough to become a true silence, he frowns and shifts his weight like he's going to walk closer. But then Johanna takes a breath, her story moves on, and Tanner stays where he is.

"Aisling found me three months after I broke free and brought me here. It wasn't like this back then. It was more cave and less house. Just a place to sleep and hide, basically. When I took over eight years ago, we started making it a home. And here we are." Johanna glances at Nadette and me, almost like she's checking in, before her gaze slides across the rest of the room. "Volunteers?"

There's only a brief pause before someone says, "I'll go."

Brian leans against the counter next to Sarah. He's tall enough to be able to comfortably rub her back without jumping up on the counter next to her, and his brown hair looks like it's growing out from a buzz cut. Sarah smiles at him and rests her head on his shoulder as he faces the group. "So ... from the beginning or just the interesting bits?"

"Highlighted version," Lexi decides.

"They had me for almost four and a half years," Brian says. His hand is still moving up and down Sarah's back, but the motion has become tense and jerky, more like he's taking reassurance than offering it. "She showed up when I was thirteen, but I didn't figure it out until ... until a few months before it was too late."

Sarah whispers something to him and Brian takes a long breath, relaxing a little.

"I got out alive, and lo and behold. My one-time obsession with rocks and dirt has turned into this." He puts his hand on the counter next to him, curling his fingers like he's trying to scoop out a piece of the stone. And then he actually scoops out a piece of the stone. Even from ten feet away, I can see the dark gray rock soften under his fingertips until his fingers sink into the counter completely and Brian is holding a fist-sized chunk of rock. "Awesome, right? Until the weekend my older brother took me camping and we ended up running from a bear. I completely lost my shit and almost killed us both in a rockslide trying to scare the damn bear off."

Brian looks at the rock in his hand and then presses it into the hole he created. When he lifts his hand away, the stone looks whole, as though nothing happened.

"That was ..." The words are out before I realize I'm going to talk. Everyone looks at me and I try to think of something to say. Anything. "Um, if I have to do tricks like that to join the club, you guys might want to kick me out now. I got nothing."

Well, I have *something*, according to Pheodora, but being a masterful liar isn't exactly a trick I want to start bragging about—it's not a skill that inspires much trust. I lied out of necessity at home, but here? I don't want to lie. Not unless I have to.

"Oh, not everyone is as flashy as all that," another girl says. Her long hair is black with streaks of red, blue, pink, and white running through it. "I'm an artist. That's it. Just art."

My eyes narrow. "Did you hurt someone with a painting?"

The girl smiles, but it's a sad smile. "No. Kind of wished I could sometimes, though. I was sixteen and on the street by the time I freed myself from the Balasura, and I still couldn't stop painting."

Her eyes follow Kelsey as the girl checks on the cookies, but she never stops talking. I can tell it's a story she's told many times before; there's a quality to it that's almost rehearsed. "I was down in New York City then, and there was this old woman who always had a booth at those local craft fairs. She would let me sell my paintings in her booth and never took a cut of the money. It wasn't enough to get a place, but it kept me from starving, you know? Then, one day, this girl comes up to me and says she knows a place I can go where the dreams won't come again." She shrugs. "What'd I have to lose? I followed Aisling here three years ago and I haven't left since."

She's barely done before a guy picks up with his own story of betrayal and desperation. Then there's another. And another.

My eyes get wider and wider as the stories pile up. Even though it's strangely comforting to know that I'm not the only one with a really sucky childhood, it seems too easy for these people to spill their life stories to strangers. But they do. All of them. Apparently, once you officially move in to Abra, no one bothers keeping secrets. It makes sense, I guess, with a telepath and a fortune teller (and now Nadette, the walking polygraph test) in the group, but it still feels jarring to me.

It makes it easier when their eyes turn toward me. Knowing that everyone in this room will understand lying to hide the truth about your life and scraping together whatever resources you can find, I tell my story in almost as much detail as I did when Nadette and I were on the train a few hours ago. I even tell them that I can lie to Nadette. I would've told them anyway, I think, but it really would be a stupid thing to try hiding when Lexi can see inside Nadette's head.

Nadette takes her turn after me and then the torch passes back to the others. Slowly, the stories lose their horror. Maybe it's desensitization. Maybe it's because everyone here can empathize. Maybe it's because the whole thing eventually feels like a contest—

who has the worst memory? Maybe it's because after a while, we're hearing these stories and chewing almost-too-gooey triple-chocolate-chip cookies. I'm not sure the reason matters. Within the space of a couple of hours, I know this room of people better than I ever knew the kids I grew up with and, for the first time in a long time, I feel like I might have found somewhere that I can call home.

Sixteen

Nadette

Sunday, September 21 – 4:34 AM EDT

The stories bite at me at first. I've seen the statistics. I know there are millions of kids in this country who are abused or neglected or mistreated. That's statistics. Meeting so many of them at once? Hearing them all talk as though the pain they've suffered in their short lives is normal? As if it's *expected*? After the sympathy pain stops poking at me like a white-hot branding iron, the guilt sets in. I've had a good life. I know that. Sometimes I guess it takes being faced with the opposite to really *understand* how good something is.

Lexi gets up after a while, her eyes downcast as she walks toward the shelves on the other side of the room. Picking up an apple, she carefully cuts it into even slices. Her head is tilted vaguely in the direction of the person talking, but it doesn't seem like she's really listening. Then again, she's heard these stories before. Probably more than once. And she has all the additional details she picks up from their minds.

Then it's Lexi's turn. She glances at me before she says a word.

"My full name is Alexandriana George, and my parents died when I was three. Went on a trip to volunteer in Africa for a month, caught some illness they couldn't shake, and died within days of each other. I got passed around to different family members through most of my childhood until I ended up with a distant cousin when I was thirteen. She decided I was worth keeping around as a free babysitter for her twin daughters." She pops the last bit of apple into her mouth and chews slowly. Her eyes are distant. Almost disconnected. Has she shut off her mind-reading? I think I would in her shoes.

"Maybe it was the constant moving around and having to adjust to new families, trying to guess what would piss them off fastest, but I was always good at reading people. It took two years for me to see through the Balasura, but after I finally escaped my ability to read people was a lot more literal." She shrugs and rubs her hands together. "Ran away after a few months of listening to my cousin bitch about me in her head. Ended up in Albany. Met Aisling at a street fair and then …" She spreads her arms, seeming to silently add, "here we all are."

It's true, the whole story. Still, there's the feel of something missing in her words. Like she scrubbed off some of the dirt and rounded out some of the edges and made the whole thing just a bit prettier than it really was.

Lexi meets my eyes across the room. Her smile is sad as she shrugs one shoulder. The gesture seems to be part apology and part acknowledgment. I smile back, trying to let her know it's all right. I can understand wanting to clean up your past.

After Kelsey finishes passing out the cookies and cleaning up, she plops down on to the seat next to me, scooting it closer. Her black hair is held out of her face in two thick French-braid pigtails and every time she catches my eye, she smiles like we're sharing a secret. I don't know why she seems so attached to me. Doesn't mean I can stop myself from smiling back at her. She's nearly pocket-sized and absolutely adorable.

When the stories wind down, people start wandering off in small groups.

"You guys go through this *every* time someone new shows up?" If that's the case, no wonder they added cookies to the tradition.

"Yep." Kelsey turns a full-on grin in my direction. "Trust me. It's better to get all the messy bits out of the way early. Once we get you settled in our room, I'll show you where we get cleaned up and everything and—oh! But Lexi is going to talk to you first."

By the end of that rambling sentence, my mouth is hanging open. "Do I get a choice in any of that?" I ask, starting to smile. "Or has my night been planned for me?"

"Planned to a T! Comes with the territory. Remember? I'm like the younger sister you never had." She grins at me, but the brightness of that smile fades when she notices the confusion on my face. "Oh. Crap. You haven't said that yet, have you?" She sighs, biting the inside of her lip. "Stupid mixed-up time streams. Now you won't say it."

"I won't?" I glance over at Julian, who is biting back a grin.

"Nope. I changed things. Again." She looks down at her hands and mutters, "At least nothing broke this time."

"Broke?" Julian asks.

Kelsey's nose wrinkles. "Okay, *fine*. Exploded."

Julian's eyes widen. "*Exploded?*"

In my head, I can hear my mom freaking about my necklace. I trace the beads with my fingertips and swallow down the regret that's threatening to build again. I had to leave. I *had* to.

"I thought I was helping!" Kelsey's insistent words break through my guilt. "How did I know that keeping my dad from breaking his leg in a factory accident would make the damn place blow up?"

Julian and I just stare. What do you say to that?

Before I can figure it out, Kelsey shrugs. "Anyway, that's why I try very hard to keep from changing things unless I know how the new path is going to unfold. But sometimes ... I don't know. It just happens."

She sighs again. The sound is so sad and world-weary that I have to do something. She's worried about messing up the time stream, right? Worried I won't ever tell her she's like a sister?

"Kelsey, I'm pretty sure you're going to be exactly like the younger sister I never had." Or like any of the older ones I *do* have.

Her mouth drops open. Then she laughs, throwing her arms around my shoulders. "Oh, I knew I was going to like you!"

Kelsey is still wrapped around me when Lexi sits down at our table again. She's trying to look happy, but it's not working. The smile on her face is tinged with red. Like glowing lipstick. "Kels will get you settled in her room, Nadette, but Julian..." She bites her lip and shrugs. "The only empty bed we have right now is in Vasha's room."

Julian's eyes narrow. "Oh, come on! I have to room with the psychopath in training?"

Lexi's lip twitches. "He's not that bad. Honestly," she says when Julian scoffs. "He's just *really* protective of this place."

"Good for him. Doesn't change the fact that he's got a grudge against me for not dealing with Orane on my own and obviously hates that you can't read my mind and Nadette can't pick out my lies. As a bonus, I'm violating his entire worldview and possibly his religion with my belief that there are good Balasura out there somewhere. Oh, and he can *stop my heart.*" Julian raises an eyebrow. "That all seems like a great combination. I'm sure all it'll take is making us roomies for us to be automatic BFFs."

"It's really the only option," Lexi says. "All the other guys have roommates already."

"He had to room by himself for a long time," Kelsey butts in, her head still resting on my shoulder. "Roommates weren't a possibility until he finally stopped sending off sparks while he slept."

"*What?* No. No, no, *no.*" Julian shakes his head and crosses his arms.

Kelsey straightens, her eyes wide and earnest. "No, it's fine! He hasn't done that in months!"

"Know what? Don't need a room." He's still shaking his head, the motion sharp and adamant. "I barely sleep more than an hour or two a night anyway, so I'll just nap on the couch in the other—the Whatever Room. It's fine."

"Coward," Vasha mutters as he walks past.

"Psycho," Julian responds.

"Antagonizing him probably won't help," I whisper.

Julian flushes a little. "He freaks me out."

"Yeah? Well, you freak him out, too. It'll be a learning experience for both of you," Lexi says.

It takes a few more seconds, but Julian finally caves. "Yes. Okay. Whatever. But if you guys find me dead one morning…"

"C'mon," Tanner says as he walks up to the table. "I'll make sure Vash plays nice."

Julian glances at me and sighs, but pushes his chair back and moves to follow Tanner. "If I don't show up for breakfast, send my body to Swallow's Grove."

I get up to give Julian a hug. He stiffens for a second before wrapping his arms around my waist.

"Thanks," he whispers.

"Don't worry. You'll be fine."

He rolls his eyes at me, but he's a little more relaxed as he follows Tanner through the tunnel that I would have sworn led to the Training Room.

"It does," Lexi says. Kelsey doesn't even raise an eyebrow when Lexi answers a question no one asked. I guess Abra's residents have gotten used to it. "But the tunnel splits and you can also head to the Whatever Room and the Dorms. This place is a huge circle with the Training Room at the center. That tunnel," she says, pointing to the arch almost directly opposite the one Julian left through, "will take you either to the entrance or the Dorms and that one," this time pointing to the tunnel at the apex of the three, "runs between the entrance and the Whatever Room."

"It still seems pretty confusing. And the tunnels all look the same! How do you guys keep from getting lost?" I look between the three tunnels.

"Elephant memories." Kelsey says it as though the phrase should mean something special.

Lexi laughs and, thankfully, explains. "You know the saying, right? An elephant never forgets? Haven't you noticed that you don't really forget things anymore? Like, ever? Anything?"

Although I open my mouth to say no, I close it before the word leaves my lips. I can't say no. I *have* noticed that. Especially in the past six months or so, I've been able to repeat conversations nearly verbatim and account for almost every minute of my days. Even if I'm thinking about it a week or a month later.

"Another side effect," Lexi says. "Like the permanent insomnia."

Kelsey nods. "The ones who spent more than two years with them sleep maybe two hours a day. The less time you were exposed to them, though, the more sleep you need. The memories seem to work on the same sliding scale. It's weird. We'd need someone with a pretty intricate understanding of neurology to explain it better than that."

"Huh. That's a lot of extra time each day. What do you guys do?"

"The ones over eighteen—the ones social services can't swoop in and 'reclaim,'" Lexi says with a grimace, " we have jobs in Alaster and a couple of the nearby towns to pay for food and gas and new shoes and whatever else we need up here."

"The rest of us get stuck in school all day," Kelsey groans.

"You've got four more years to suffer, Kels." Lexi reaches across the table and pats Kelsey's head, grinning when Kelsey shakes her off. Lexi looks at me, her eyes still sparkling with humor as she says, "We all switch out on chores, too. Cooking, keeping the fires fed, cleaning, laundry runs, whatever. And Johanna always has a couple of people out on the mountain keeping watch."

"Keeping watch on *what?*" I ask. "This place is the definition of 'middle of nowhere.'"

"Which is exactly where hikers and spelunkers and drunk teenagers like to come play," Lexi says.

"Oh. Good point."

"The illusion keeps most of them from finding the entrance to the caves, but Johanna likes it better if they don't make it that far in." Kelsey's grin looks slightly evil.

"Damn. What do you do to people who make it past the border?"

"We send Beth to meet them." Lexi's gaze shifts. I follow it, watching Beth catalog the contents of the shelves. Her blonde hair is choppy, barely brushing her shoulders, and she keeps absently flicking it out of her face.

"She accidentally wiped a friend's memory, didn't she?" I ask as though I don't remember the story word for word. Beth was trying to console a friend whose boyfriend died in a car accident. While trying to ease her grief, Beth ended up erasing it instead. Three years of the girl's life were gone.

"Beth can control it now," Lexi says. "Erase only specific memories and implant different ones in their place. Whenever someone who shouldn't find us does …" She trails off and shrugs. "It's better than people coming up here asking questions about why a bunch of kids have commandeered an uncharted cave system."

I nod before the full impact of her words hit. "That's what would've happened to us, isn't it? Julian and me. If Johanna had decided we weren't allowed to stay?"

"Since Aisling decided to claim you both, no." Lexi's lip twitches enough that one of her dimples appears. "In a normal situation, though … yeah, pretty much. Or she would've tried, anyway. I don't know if it would have worked on either of you."

"Why not?"

"Julian's mind is like a vault—seriously. It's a little weird. I think Beth would've had a hard time getting through those walls. And you." She smiles wider, the light in her eyes almost ... almost fond? Whatever that look means, it warms my chest and makes me want to lean a lot closer. "Beth may have been able to erase your memories, but I don't think she would've been able to replace them. You're too good at spotting fakes."

I shudder. "I'm glad I'm not gonna find out if you're right."

"Yeah." Her cheeks are tinged with the slightest shade of pink. Her smile gets a shade warmer. "Me too."

The blush on my own cheeks has to be obvious. I don't care. I keep staring at Lexi, hoping for I don't even know what, until Kelsey jumps up from her chair.

"Let's go see our room!" She grabs my hand and pulls me away. "You'll get plenty of time to talk to Lexi later. Not like she's going anywhere."

True enough. The thought makes me smile wider as we slip back into the tunnels.

Seventeen

Julian

Tuesday, September 30 – 1:14 PM EDT

Between "school" and chores, I haven't had much downtime in the past nine days. Every time my mind has a chance to wander, though, it travels back to Pheodora.

She wanted me to protect Nadette on the journey, but the trip is over and I wasn't all that helpful. With or without me, she would've ended up in Saratoga Springs just fine. If that was it, then mission accomplished. Gotta admit, I kind of wish that my grand act of heroism consisted of more than a flight out of Vegas and a train ride with a quasi-stranger.

Maybe Pheodora has something more planned for me, but that's a question I'll never find an answer to if I don't get out of these caves long enough to talk to her.

"I hate being the new kid," Nadette mutters, yanking my attention back to the present. "They give us all the bitch work."

Rolling my eyes, I adjust my grip on the firewood we're carrying from the entrance tunnel to the kitchen. "Back in Vegas, I was the one who cooked, cleaned, *and* paid the bills every month. Trust me, this is easy."

"Right." She takes a deep breath, a pink flush rising on her pale cheeks. "Sorry."

"It's fine." A breeze gusts through the skylight in the entrance cave and down the tunnel, stirring up the cool air and making me shiver. "Besides, I'm not used to the cold. I'd rather haul the firewood myself and *know* it's there than hope someone else does it and we run out."

"I guess." Nadette glances at me out of the corner of her eye. "But you do know you're not in Vegas anymore, right, Julian? They aren't Lynnie. You can trust them, I promise."

We reach the kitchen and it's empty for once. Just the two of us in this huge space. The clatter of the wood in our arms tumbling into the stone fire pit echoes across the room.

"I trust *you*," I tell her. "But it's hard to trust the others when the feeling isn't mutual. I still think Vasha is trying to figure out how to kill me without getting caught."

Nadette bites back a smile. "He is *not*. I think he may actually like you now."

"This morning, he called me a *predatel'*." She raises an eyebrow at me and I can see the question in her eyes. I shake my head. "It's Russian and it doesn't exactly translate to 'best friend ever.'" It means traitor.

Nadette's gaze shifts toward the ceiling and her lips move without sound for a second. It's something I've noticed she only does around me, and it took me a few days to realize she was repeating some part of what I said, testing it for truth. At first I hated watching her do that because it felt like she didn't believe me. Eventually I realized asking Nadette to give up poking at the world to find the truth would be like asking someone else to willingly give up sight. Her ability is too large a part of her. Even if she could temporarily shut it off the way Lexi does, I'm not sure Nadette could handle life without those bells.

Nadette's nose wrinkles. "*Definitely* doesn't mean 'best friend ever.'"

I laugh, warmth spreading through my stomach. "That's what you were checking?"

"Well, yeah." She looks at me, her eyes a little narrow and her head tilted to the side. "Why? What'd you think I was checking?"

"I don't know." I shrug and bend down to adjust a few misaligned pieces of wood. "I'm not the mind reader, remember? I never know what you're checking."

"Hey." She kneels down next to me, her peridot eyes locked on me. "I trust you now. You know that, right? I may not be able to hear it when you lie, but it would show up when I tried to tell the story to someone else. You told me the truth in the beginning when you didn't know me at all, so … I trust you. Really."

The tension that had been building in my stomach unknots and eases away. My shoulders drop and I exhale. "Thanks. I'm glad you—"

"Good. You guys are together."

We both jump. My mouth snaps shut and we turn. Johanna is standing a couple feet away, her expression as neutral as ever. Nadette glances at me, and I shrug as we stand up. I haven't learned how to predict what our fearless leader might want.

Johanna hands Nadette a piece of notebook paper and a wad of cash. "You're probably both going a little stir-crazy by now, so I figured I'd give you the grocery run. Do you mind?"

I want to jump into the air and cheer at the thought of getting *out* (and maybe, hopefully, finding Pheodora) somewhere beyond Abra, but Nadette stares down at the list in her hand, her face pale.

"Um, I don't—I mean … is it safe?"

Johanna's expression softens. "I wouldn't ask you to do this if it was dangerous."

Nadette looks up from the grocery list, her green eyes wary. She's adjusted so fast here, fit in so well, it's easy to forget that she's still the twitchy, paranoid girl I met in Trenton. I hate knowing that there's something out there that still scares her this much. Syver can't reach her here, but there's knowing that fact and then there's believing it. Getting her to safety doesn't mean much if she doesn't actually *feel* safe. A warm rush of excitement spreads through me. Maybe *that* was what Pheodora actually had in mind for me.

I have to ask her. There has to be a way to erase the last of the fear that haunts Nadette.

"It'll be fine. Like you said, we can trust them." I put my hand on her arm and she looks over at me, her eyes still too wide. "C'mon. We both need a little fresh air."

Her hand tightens around the list, making the paper crinkle, but after a slight hesitation, she nods. "Yeah, okay. I can do it."

It's a bright, clear day and although the breeze is cool, the sun is strong enough to keep me warm. After a week of shivering in the caves, an air-conditioned grocery store holds no appeal. The town itself is practically deserted (or maybe it just seems that way because I keep comparing it to the Strip), but the shops lining the street are all open.

"Hey, you want to go explore?"

Nadette turns, her hands on her hips. "Explore *what?*"

"Everything. Let's go see what's here." I tilt my head back to the sun and feel my body uncoil. "Even moles come up for air every once in a while."

Nadette hoists the strap of her backpack (the one Johanna stuffed full of crystals) higher and looks over her shoulder at the store. "I think they expect us back soon."

"C'mon. This isn't exactly Manhattan. Do you think it'll take more than twenty minutes to walk from one end of Main to the other?"

Her lip twitches. "No."

I step backward toward the town center. "So? You coming?" She's still hesitating, but I really need to be under the open sky for at least a little longer. It's not really manipulating someone if you can tell they kind of want to do it anyway, right? Right or wrong, I know how to get her to agree—play up the adorable. Clasping my hands in front of me, I make my eyes wide and mouth, "Pleeeease?"

It works. Nadette laughs and shakes her head. "All right, all right, fine. Damn. How do you go from sarcastic cynic to anime character like that? Thought Linus was the only one who could pull that off. You two would probably get along like gangbusters."

As fast as the smile appeared, it's gone. I don't have to ask why; I know what happened with Linus.

Sinatra bless it, I hate this. She's so easy to talk to most of the time, always quick to laugh, but when she gets trapped in her memories and the guilt she's carrying around, she gets quiet. She withdraws into her own head and stays there for hours if someone doesn't pull her out of it. I've gotten good at it. Lexi is better, though. Of course, she's got insider information.

Clearing my throat, I raise an eyebrow and ask, "Gangbusters? What are you, like, eighty?"

As a diversionary tactic, apparently this one sucks. More color bleeds out of her face and her head tilts down, her shoulder hunching over as she shakes her head. "It's just something my grandpa says."

Okay. Time to change the subject. "What do you think the people around here do for fun?"

Nadette's head comes up a little, but she's still too pale. "I don't know? Hike? Hunt?"

"Hunt what? We've been up in those mountains a week. Have you heard anything bigger than a bird?"

"No," she admits.

I grin. "Maybe everyone in Alaster is a robot. Or a *clone*. Maybe Johanna set up an entire fake town to hide the caves!"

Success! Nadette laughs. "I think she would if she could."

We keep walking, peering into shop windows. Nobody we pass seems surprised to see two teenagers wandering around in the middle of a school day. I want to ask Nadette what she thinks about it (or if she's even noticed), but I keep the conversation light. Unimportant. Ridiculous, even. She's nervous enough being out of the caves. No need to add extra stress.

When we reach the north end of the street, we head back. I want to walk to the south end too, but Nadette stops.

"We should go back."

"Oh, no." I grab her arm and tug her a couple of steps south. "You promised me a tour. I'm taking a tour."

This time she holds her ground and shakes her head. "Let's go."

I look at her and finally see the way she's biting her lip. Her eyes dart around like she's expecting an attack. She may be more relaxed than the day we met, but that doesn't mean being out in the open isn't grating on her nerves. I could probably convince her to keep going, but it'd be pushing the line too far. It'd be wrong.

Easing up, I nod. "Yeah, okay. Let's go."

She smiles, really smiles, and it's worth giving up a little sunlight.

"Hey, kid! Yo, Glowstick! Hold up!"

We both jerk to a halt and turn around. A girl with long hair the color of blue Curacao runs toward us. She's thin and tall, but when she gets closer the only things I see are her eyes. Her irises are solid black and they stand out against her pale skin. Her nearly *translucent* pale skin. On her hands and forearms I can see the pattern of veins running under her skin clearer than I've ever seen on anyone. Add that oddity to her eyes? I've seen people with really dark brown eyes before, but nothing like this. It's strange. Even compared to the things I've gotten used to seeing in Abra.

She shakes her head and stares at me with wide eyes. "Wow, maybe I *should've* come up to meet you guys when Johanna flipped her shit."

Before I have a chance to say a thing, she glances at Nadette. Her eyes almost pop out of her head.

"Holy hell!" She grabs Nadette's hand and lifts it to her eyes, a grin on her face. "Wow, honey. If you hadn't been walking next to Glowstick here, I would've been running after you instead."

Nadette's mouth drops open and her cheeks turn a little pink before she yanks her hand away and hides it behind her back.

"Who *are* you?" she demands, taking the question right out of my mouth.

"Aisling." She says it as though we should already know, like everyone knows who she is. And she's right. The people in Abra talk about her a lot. "Jojo usually brings all the noobs down to meet me."

"Noobs? Seriously?" I feel like I should be insulted, but I'm not entirely sure.

Aisling grins. "You two are *totally* noobs. In more ways than one. C'mon."

She spins, her hair twirling so far out behind her it smacks me in the face, and jogs a few feet. It must be obvious we're not following because she stops and turns, beckoning us forward.

Why do I feel like the victim of a hit and run? I glance at Nadette and it makes me feel a little better to see her looking as stunned as I feel.

"She's telling the truth," Nadette offers.

I roll my eyes. "Fantastic. At least the crazy blue-haired girl is honest." Nadette smiles and shrugs. I jerk my head toward Aisling who is headed into a store called Martha's Magic Market. "Might as well see what she wants. I mean, since she's *Aisling*."

Nadette's smile turns into a grin as we follow Aisling to the store. "Smartass."

I haven't spent a lot of time in New Age stores, but this one feels like it was constructed off a list of stereotypes.

Red velvet window display of crystal wands, dreamcatchers, and Wicca books? Check.

Wind chimes tied to the door and meditation music playing in the background? Check.

Too much incense burning? Check. Probably more than one type, too. (I'm trying not to sneeze.)

On one shelf behind the register, there's what I hope is a *fake* human skull. The rest of the shop is full of crystals and candles and I don't even know what.

"Are you a survivor?" I ask Aisling. She's a pretty active part of Abra, even if she doesn't live there. She has to be connected to the dream world somehow.

"Oh, honey." She laughs as she settles onto a stool behind the register. "You're cute."

"*Are* you?" Nadette asks.

"In a way, yes. And in a lot of other ways, not in the slightest." She leans forward, her dark eyes intense as she stares at me. "Enough about me. I'm *much* more interested in your story, Glowstick."

My teeth grind together. "Julian. My name is Julian."

"Oh, I know. And you're Nadette," she says, grinning. "Like I said, Jojo usually brings me the noobs. After that visit from Tanner and Clarke, I expected to see you two down here the next day. I don't know why she held onto you so long. She should've known I'd want to dig right into those shiny heads of yours."

Nadette steps back, her hand lifting to her black jade necklace.

Aisling laughs. "Not like that. It's just been a while since she had anyone interesting enough to bring me up to the compound. I usually avoid Abra like the plague, but you two ..." She takes a deep breath and shakes her head, her long hair falling over her shoulders and standing out bright against her black tank top. "*You two* are worth that hellish climb and—well, everything else I have to deal with up there. Come, now. Tell Auntie Aisling absolutely everything."

Nadette and I both stand there staring at her. This girl is one of the strangest people I have ever met. And I grew up in Vegas and have spent the last week with a human lie detector, a telepath, a guy with an affinity for rocks, and a roommate who literally sparks when he gets mad.

"Oh, come on!" Aisling tilts her head back and I can't tell if she's more amused with us or frustrated. "I want to hear how a human lie detector and a professional liar became BFFs!"

I stiffen and step back. Nadette steps forward.

"I'm not a professional liar," I say at the same time Nadette asks, "How did you know I'm a lie detector?"

For a second, Aisling is silent. She glances at me, one blue eyebrow raised, but then looks at Nadette. "Lexi told me."

"No she didn't," Nadette spits back.

She shrugs. "Of course she didn't. I haven't seen her since before you guys showed up. I wanted to see if you'd catch the lie, though." A smile spreads across her face. "And you *did*. Color me impressed. And remind me to be really careful what I say around you."

"Why? You have secrets?" I ask.

Aisling looks at me and I feel like someone is holding my head in place. I can't look away. I can't even blink. Those dark eyes are locked on mine and there's no escape until Aisling finally closes her eyes, a strange expression somewhere between a smile and a glare on her face.

"Of course I have secrets. Everyone does. You of all people should know that. What's that thick-ass wall in your head doing there if not protecting secrets?"

I want to ask what she means by that, but at the same time … I shiver and look away. I'm not sure I want to know how those eyes see what no one else seems to notice.

"The scrawny, silent type, huh?" I glance at Aisling, my stomach turning a little when I see the smirk on her face. "Careful what secrets you hold onto in Abra, Glowstick. They don't take kindly to secrets up there."

"Is that why you don't visit?" Nadette asks.

The smile drops off Aisling's face and she nods. "One of many reasons. To really be a part of that group, you have to give your entire life up to them. It's a lot to ask someone to do."

A breath of time passes and all I hear is the soft, lyric-less music playing in the background. I don't know what to say. Neither does

Nadette, apparently. Aisling must notice, because she's the one who breaks the silence.

"So … Tanner mentioned a demonic message." Her dark eyes sparkle as she leans closer. "Care to share?"

I glance at Nadette and back at Aisling. "Are you going to freak like they did? Because I kinda don't want to go through that again. I felt like I was trying to convince a bunch of POWs that the people holding them captive weren't *that* bad."

Aisling snorts. "Glowstick, you don't know the half of it. Secrets aren't the only reason I've never moved up the mountain."

I don't know what to make of that cryptic comment, but at least it seems like she's going to listen. Nadette launches into her story first, briefly running through the last two years. Aisling's eyebrows furrow when Nadette tells her about Blue, but she doesn't comment. On any of it. It's not until I fill in my side of the story and Nadette and I tell her about Johanna's reaction to the "demonic message" that Aisling releases a frustrated huff.

"It's not like they don't have a reason to hate the Balasura," Nadette says, shrugging. "But they had a hard time trusting me when I told them Blue wasn't evil."

"Little bigots," Aisling mutters, crossing her arms.

Nadette raises an eyebrow. "Bigots?"

"Yes." She nods once, the motion decisive. "They're like alien kids who decide to judge all of humanity on a cross-section of serial killers."

I laugh. "Kids? Some of those alien kids are older than you."

Aisling raises an eyebrow and smirks. "You'd think that, wouldn't you?" She runs her fingers down the opposite arm and coyly lifts one shoulder. "What can I say? I age well. Good genes." Aisling grins, flashing her perfectly even, perfectly white teeth. "Tell Jojo she was smart to let me find you guys. I'll come visit soon. Maybe."

That's more than enough of a dismissal for me. It's rare that I can't read someone, but Aisling kept throwing me off. I spent the entire conversation catching up with her instead of anticipating her and I don't like it. Now we've got more questions than we started with. I grab Nadette's arm and ease toward the door. "We'll tell her you said hi."

What was that comment about her age? And Aisling already knew about the other Balasura, the ones trying to help us. Plus, somehow she knew to pin deception on me. Everyone else assumes my "ability" is some kind of mental shield that keeps me safe from other people's gifts. I never corrected them. (Really, why would I? Who wants to be known as a liar?) Besides, I haven't lied once since I left home. I've barely even kept secrets. Just Pheodora's name. But Aisling still called me out on it, like deception is written into my bones and sunk under my skin.

I shudder, trying to clear my head.

"Can you believe her?" I ask as soon as we're outside. Glancing over my shoulder, I see Aisling come up to the window, her dark eyes trained on us. "Those eyes give me the creeps."

Nadette gives me some vague agreement, but she's still looking back at Martha's Magic Market. Her lips are pursed and her face is scrunched up. Even when she starts paying attention to where she's walking, she's quiet. Too quiet. This time I can't think of a single thing to say that will get her out of her head. Worry gnaws on my stomach like a rat as we walk into the supermarket's chilly air conditioning.

"Do you really have secrets?" Nadette asks as we wind our way through the store.

I shrug. "Like Aisling said, everyone does."

Nadette tenses. "I don't."

"You're not everyone."

She pauses with her hand on a box of crackers, then picks up the box and tosses it in our cart. "How many secrets?"

From her? "Just one."

"Is it a dangerous secret? Will people get hurt because you're keeping it?"

"I'm not the one who can see the future," I point out. "But I don't think this particular secret will hurt anyone. And it's more of a promise than a secret."

She barely blinks and I make myself hold her stare as steadily as possible. It takes a few seconds for Nadette to nod, her expression relaxing. I turn our full cart toward the cashier.

"Not all secrets are bad, you know." I place everything on the conveyor. "Surprise parties, for one, are kind of awesome."

Nadette freezes with a head of lettuce halfway to the conveyor and stares at me for a second before her mouth slowly curves into a smile. "If you say so. I've never had one before."

"Yeah, me neither, actually," I say as we finish unloading the cart for the cashier. "There wasn't ever anyone to organize it. I had big plans for next Monday, though. I was going to talk Lynnie into taking me to the DMV."

Once I had a license, I could start scraping together enough money for a car. Though, honestly, the car part probably wouldn't have worked, since it'd be something she could sell out from under me when she found herself in debt again.

Nadette hands over the cash Johanna gave us and I help the bagger refill our cart, smiling my thanks at the cashier before we head to the car.

"Your birthday is next Monday? Your sixteenth?" Nadette asks once we're outside.

"Sunday the fifth, actually," I correct.

We load the groceries into the trunk of the Bronco and shut the gate. It's not until we're back on the dirt road to Abra that Nadette speaks.

"You know, Lexi or Beth would probably take you driving if you wanted."

"Beth?" Lexi wasn't a surprise, but I didn't expect Nadette to suggest Beth. I've only seen her a couple of times since we arrived.

Nadette shrugs. "I think you remind her of her little brother."

"I'm short, not infantile, you know." I cross my arms, suddenly hating my height and my freckles and my dimple. I played up the cute thing in Vegas, but it doesn't help me much here. Everyone in Abra seeing me as some little kid just makes it too easy for them to write me off.

"Her 'little' brother is nineteen, not nine," Nadette says with a slight smile that fades all too quickly. "Anyway, it's just an educated guess. I know what it's like to miss your family. I recognize the look on her face when she sees you sometimes."

A thought pops into my head and my heart drops a little. Why is it so disappointing to think that I might remind Nadette of her brother? Is this ... is this what a crush feels like? I've never had a crush on anyone before. "I don't ... I don't remind you of Linus, do I?"

Thankfully, she laughs. "Not really. He's a year younger than you, but about three inches taller. You're a lot more reserved than he is. And more responsible. And, yeah you've never really been out of Vegas, but you know more about how the world really operates than he does. All of that shows up in your eyes, did you know that?"

"No." The wash of confused relief that she doesn't see her brother when she looks at me is strong enough that takes a second for the rest of her words to register. "Is that a good thing?"

"It's not good or bad." She pulls into the small clearing-slash-parking lot and shuts off the car. "It's just how it is."

I was going to try to escape for a while when we got back (I have *got* to talk to Pheodora soon), but Lexi, Beth, and Tanner are waiting at the edge of the clearing. As we unload the bags, I notice Lexi watching Nadette, her expression shifting like she's having a conversation I can't hear. What is Nadette telling her? Or maybe the more accurate question is what is Lexi overhearing? Part of me wants to teach Nadette about the wall thing Pheodora showed me (the idea of someone going through my head still makes me feel like I need a shower), but I honestly don't think Nadette minds the intrusion. Maybe being the second youngest of ten has already taught her to tolerate a constant but mostly benign invasion of privacy.

We bring everything into the kitchen and Tanner starts getting things ready for dinner (some stew recipe that he says will have to simmer for hours). He always seems happiest in the kitchen. Or in whatever moment Johanna is paying attention to him.

"We should probably leave him to lord over his domain," Beth says, smiling wryly.

"Yes, you should." Tanner brandishes a wooden ladle like a sword. "Now, scat. All of you! I have spices to measure."

"Tanner?" Lexi puts her hand on Nadette's arm and leaning closer to whisper something. Tanner meets Lexi's eyes and she nods, probably answering whatever question he had floating around in his head. Sighing, he sets aside the ladle and casts a longing look at the ingredients laid out on the counter.

"No one touch anything," he orders as he follows Nadette and Lexi out of the room. None of them look back.

Okay. Guess I'm not invited. I sigh and turn toward the Whatever Room. Maybe I can get ahead on my reading for "school." Which is kind of structured and kind of a "get all the young ones in the same room and see who knows something about a school-related subject" system. It's strange, but a lot more fun than any normal class I've ever had.

I'm turning in that direction when a hand on my shoulder stops me.

"Hey. Want to see something cool?"

I look back at Beth, at the soft look in her eyes, and remember what Nadette said about Beth's little brother. I change my "Not right now" to, "Yeah, sure. What is it?"

She smiles and jerks her head toward the tunnel leading to the entrance cavern. "This way."

The tunnels, smooth though the walls and floor might be, are not by any means in straight lines. They meander through the mountain, sloping up and then declining. Simply walking from room to room in this place is a solid workout.

"I know you haven't spent a lot of time with her, but you remember Anya, right?"

I blink. Why can't I match a face to the name? "Anya?"

"The artist."

"Oh, right. With the multi-colored hair. I don't think she said what her name was that first night." And I haven't seen her much since then.

Beth cocks her head. "She didn't, did she? I think half of us didn't. Of all the things to skip, huh?" She shakes her head and looks up as we enter the entrance cavern, her smile growing wider at the streak of sun pouring through the large skylight. "Anyway, she's been getting really bored with canvases lately, so she kind of took over a wall."

"A whole wall? What'd she paint?"

"That's what I want to show you."

We walk the pathway around the edge of the cavern, skirting the ten-foot drop that Nadette almost fell victim to that first night. Is that why they leave it there? To catch the uninitiated unawares?

Beth leads me to the secondary tunnel, one that will take us deeper underground and end in either the kitchen or the Dorm. I don't know why, but I never really use this section of tunnel. No one seems to. There's this unspoken rule that you should avoid it if possible. Maybe that's why Anya claimed it. The lamps light our way once we're past the first turn. Last week, Lexi explained that the lamps and the electric generators that power them are Vasha and Nicole's pet projects. I think she was trying to make me hate him less. It didn't work.

We keep walking until we reach a long, smooth, softly curved wall that has been completely covered with paint. As soon as I see it, my breath catches in my throat and my eyes burn like I'm about to cry.

"Oh, wow."

"I know, right?" Beth says, taking a breath that sounds more than a little sniffly.

"What … I don't even know what it is." The painting is huge and full of riotous color. Reds, pinks, oranges, purples, blues, greens, yellows, and everything in between swirl and dance across the once-gray wall. There doesn't seem to be any shape or reason to the design (or even a true design), but just looking at it makes me feel happy. Hopeful. Looking at this painting is kind of like looking at clouds and being able to pick out the shapes you like, but only good ones. It's like Anya trapped every good feeling in my life in a painting so I can look at it whenever I want.

"She can do paintings that look so realistic you'd swear you were looking at a photo," Beth says. "But when she does *these*? God, I can't even fathom how she does it. It's like …"

"Emotion trapped in paint," I finish for her. "It's amazing."

"Yeah. And it's nice to have a reminder that sometimes good things come out of what happened to us." She sighs and runs her finger through her short, pin-straight hair. "Elephant memories, and it's still such an easy thing to forget, you know?"

I snort. "Yeah. I know." Before I can think of all the reasons I *shouldn't*, I ask, "What do you think about when you see it?"

The silence stretches for a couple of seconds, long enough for me to open my mouth to take the question back, but Beth starts talking before I can.

"It reminds me of the time before the car accident took my brother and my grandmother." She stops to take a breath, and a nostalgic smile flits across her lips as she looks at me. "Grams was a compulsive baker. Her entire house smelled like fresh bread and brownies even if she wasn't making anything. It had just seeped into the walls. She loved making things that made people happy, but she didn't really have much of a sweet tooth, so she'd make things for us when we came over or take huge trays to the families in her neighborhood."

Another breath, this one a little longer and followed by a smile that is a little sadder. "What about you? What do you remember?"

Only fair, right? I asked her, so of course she was going to ask me. Somehow the question still catches me off guard. "I, uh … I remember Uncle Frank and his family and the people at the Bellagio. Nadette and the people here, too. Or, well … *most* of the people here, anyway." Vasha, for example, isn't going to be making it into my mental happy place any time soon.

She doesn't press for more than I gave her, and so we stand there in comfortable silence examining the wall of color for a while. When Beth turns toward the kitchen, I follow automatically.

"How do you think things are going back in Vegas?" she asks quietly, so quietly that I know she's giving me an out—she'll let me pretend I didn't hear her if I don't feel like answering.

I shrug and shove my hands in the pockets of my jacket. "Lynnie must know I've gone missing. The school has probably called half a dozen times to ask why I'm not in class. And my Uncle Frank probably started freaking out when he couldn't reach me."

I clench my fists inside the pockets, wishing I could erase the guilt that thought brings up. I've had years to perfect the art of not thinking about things that bother me, but the tears Anya's art already pulled to the surface weaken my usual walls. If Frank knows I ran, he's going to freak. Really freak. And he already has so much stress with Mariella's coma.

Which reminds me … Maybe Beth can answer the question Johanna didn't.

Clearing my throat, I glance up at Beth. "Has anyone ever woken up from a coma? One caused by the Balasura?"

Beth frowns and shakes her head. "But your cousin isn't the usual case, Julian. She didn't give up; she fought her way out. She caused a mess and that puts her in the running for Johanna's least favorite person ever, but it kind of proves that what happened to her isn't the same as what happens to the others, right? So, to answer your question, no. But I don't think that's the right question to ask about Mariella."

"What's the right question?"

Beth smiles. "If she's strong enough to bring down Orane, is she strong enough to fight her way back to consciousness? Personally, I'm betting the answer is yes."

I glance back toward Anya's painting (even though the curves and the decline of the tunnel have already blocked it from view), and cling to that sliver of hope.

Eighteen

Nadette

When Lexi leads me away from Julian and Beth, I hope she just wants to hang out. We do that sometimes. Just talk. For hours. She likes hearing stories about my siblings and Grandpa Horace and some of my mom's crazy clients. I ... Well, I can't really say I *like* hearing about Lexi's life before Abra, but I like that she's willing to tell me the stories at all.

That's where I hope she's taking me. To a couch in the Whatever Room where I can listen to her low, soothing voice for hours. But nope.

Instead, Lexi leads me into Johanna's room. She's the only one with her own room. Half the cavern is set up like an office, with a battered wood desk and a squeaky office chair. A dresser, a mattress, and a beat-up nightstand on the other side create a bedroom. When we walk through the curtain, Tanner follows us in. Kelsey, Clarke, and Johanna are already stuffed into the space. None of them are speaking; they're just waiting. For us?

Why do I feel like I'm walking into an intervention?

Lexi's hand rests on the small of my back for a moment, her touch warm and solid and sure. "It won't be that bad," she whispers to me as she guides me to an empty space on the mattress. She eases herself down next to me. Her calm warmth makes it a little easier to believe that it *won't* be that bad.

Johanna isn't smiling, but she doesn't look angry, either. Though, with Johanna, it's hard to be sure. Tanner is watching Johanna, not me—because he's *always* watching Johanna. The others have me in their sights and don't seem inclined to let me out of them. Lexi leans closer, her arm pressing against mine from shoulder to elbow.

"Did you know that you're only the second person who hasn't been brought here by Aisling?" Johanna asks. She must not want an actual answer because she doesn't give me a chance to speak. "Since you got here, we've been trying to figure out what to do now that we know we aren't as hidden from the Balasura as we thought."

I swallow hard. "But Blue wasn't like—"

"Yes." Johanna holds up a hand to stop me. "I know. I get it. He wasn't like the others. But damn, kid. Can't you see why that doesn't really matter? If one of them can figure out where we are, how safe can we really be here? Kelsey is the *only* other person who found their own way here. You two are it. And *you* were led here by the same creatures we're trying like hell to stay away from."

"I …" My throat feels tight. I swallow and try to speak again. "I don't know what you want me to say." Because I'm not exactly sorry for saving my own life and protecting my family.

"Look, you did what you had to do in a tough situation," Tanner says, finally looking my way. "We're not blaming you for that. At all. If we hadn't reacted the same way, none of us would be here."

"I guess." But they weren't the ones who revealed the location of Abra to the enemy. Or revealed that the enemy has known where they've been hiding all along. "So, I don't get it. What is this about?"

Johanna leans forward, the desk chair squeaking like a dying mouse. "We would appreciate it if you could go back through the whole story. Everything, from beginning to end. In excruciating detail. Even the little things you saw or heard that didn't seem to matter at the time." She takes a breath and glances at Tanner. There's a strange look on her face. Almost like she's asking him if she did all right. When he smiles slightly, she faces me again. "Would you be willing to do that?"

I don't have a damn clue what they think they're going to learn from it, but there's really only one answer I can give. "Yeah, sure."

And so I do it again, tell the story I thought I was done reciting. I start two years ago and tell them about Isasius the freaky leprechaun. Then I tell them about all of the ones who came after. All of them. It seemed like a never-ending parade of new faces and new worlds for a while, with only Syver repeating. I tell them about the last six months at home when the midnight dreams started following me around in daylight. And when I finally broke down and told Mom what was happening. I tell them about Peter and Tessa and the hospital and the stones. Then, finally, I tell them about Blue. I repeat our conversation word for word, including when I tested him and asked him to lie to me. I explain about the mirrors that didn't seem to really be mirrors and his abrupt departure when one of those mirrors started reflecting color.

By the time I finish, I feel like someone has hooked me to a machine that pulled all the energy right the hell out of me. My chest feels empty and my body sags. Taking a breath, I try to meet all of their eyes. "So? Does it make any more sense to you guys? Because I'm still pretty fucking clueless here."

Lexi slides her hand around my elbow. It doesn't quite link her arm with mine, but there's enough pressure to let me know I'm not alone. God. The idea of having someone else know *all* of my thoughts has taken some getting used to, but sometimes it's amazing. I lean into her, soaking in her warmth and the comfort she's offering. *Relishing* it.

Johanna looks at Kelsey first. "Anything?"

Kels shakes her head, the bright gold dangly earrings she's wearing today jangling as they swing. "Up close, like the next couple weeks or so, everything seems normal. The farther away I try to look, the fuzzier everything gets. A month out it's all just … static." She shivers, pulling her head down and the collar of her leather jacket up. Like she's a turtle trying to retreat into her shell. "I don't like this, Johanna."

"I know." Johanna's lips press together. "I don't like it either. Shit. How bad are things going to get if the future doesn't even *exist*?"

"'From this day onward call the prophet blind,'" Tanner mutters.

Johanna snaps a glare at him that could melt ice. "Goddammit, Tanner. Really? You want to start quoting tragedies *now*?"

Tanner's face flushes a deep red. His eyes lock on the floor. "Sorry."

"In context, that quote doesn't even work in this situation," Clarke says.

Johanna opens her mouth, her eyes still sharp. Lexi cuts her off. "Johanna, stop. We're all stressed, and snapping is just going to make it worse, okay? Breathe. Relax. Change tracks."

For a second Johanna turns that glare on Lexi. I have to fight the urge to jump between them. Lexi's grip on my elbow tightens, saying thanks without saying a word, but also saying don't. Then Johanna exhales. Some of the edges in her eyes fade, some of the anger dissipates.

"We've all fought them once already." Exhaustion seeps into her voice and her shoulders sag under some invisible weight. "I really don't want to do it again."

"We might not have to," Clarke says. "It's been what? Ten days? So far, nothing. And you know how much time that is in their world."

"Four thousand eight hundred days." Tanner's voice is so quiet I can barely hear it.

Clarke nods. "Exactly. *Years* have passed in their world. More than enough time to plan some sort of … *something*, if they knew where we were." Clarke's voice is resolute, but his expression is strangely hopeful. Like he really wants someone to jump up and cry, "My God! You're *absolutely* right!"

Instead, he gets Johanna.

"That doesn't mean they're not working on something. Or that they won't start. They're practically immortal. They've got no reason to rush." Johanna stands up so fast her chair slams into her desk. The whole thing rattles. "And that possibility, even the *possibility*, means that all our plans to find survivors are shot to shit. No way am I bringing more people here if I can't even protect *us*."

Everyone shrinks back, trying to stay out of her way when Johanna starts pacing in the limited open space. "Those things are fucking immortal. Or close the hell enough to it. They'll still be around long after we all die, and you think we're safe because *ten days* have passed without a sign? Really?" She stops walking and glares at Clarke.

He flushes and looks away, his gaze settling on the wall across the room.

"Does it matter?" It's not until everyone's eyes are focused on me that I realize I spoke. But the words are out there now. I'd better finish the thought or Johanna's next explosion is going to be aimed in my direction.

"I just … It seems as though we're as safe as we can make ourselves here, right? And we don't take unnecessary risks. Traveling alone or, you know, anything like that." I swallow and glance at Lexi. I breathe a little easier when I see resignation, not anger, in her eyes. "Does it matter if they're planning something? If we can't do a thing to make ourselves any safer where we are, does it *matter?*"

Johanna's face flushes and her mouth opens. Then something in her expression shifts. Her head tilts and the flush begins to fade. She sighs. "It *does* matter, but you're right. There's nothing more we can do. Lockdown rules as of today: no one leaves the mountain alone— and no trips out unless *absolutely* essential; everyone carries their weight in crystals; newcomers are screened as best we can. Unless Kelsey's timeline changes, we've got about a month before the future disappears. In the meantime, we just have to stay wary and ... and hope, I guess. Hope that I'm wrong."

"You're not usually wrong," Tanner mutters, his eyes still locked on his shoes.

Johanna glances at him, sadness in her almond eyes. "Yeah." She turns and walks out of the room her words trailing behind her. "This time I want to be."

When Lexi and I walk into the Whatever Room, Beth and Julian are curled up on opposite ends of a couch with books, each of them completely burritoed in blankets. Julian looks up when he hears us come in and smiles when he sees me. That smile vanishes quickly.

"You okay, Nadette? You look pale ... *er* than usual."

I cringe and rub my hands over my face, trying to force some color into my cheeks. "Avoid Johanna for the rest of the afternoon."

His book snaps shut. "What happened?"

Glancing at Lexi, I silently ask, *Can you handle this, please?*

"Johanna wanted to talk to her about Blue." Lexi tells them the important bits of the story, namely Kelsey's static vision and Johanna's bad mood. "There's not much else we can do. But it still seems like a good idea to—"

Lexi's mouth shuts so fast I worry she might have bitten her tongue in the process. Her lips purse and her forehead wrinkles. She's staring at Beth, obviously confused. It seems to have brought her entire thought process to a halt.

"Just a stray thought, I swear." Beth shifts uncomfortably under Lexi's scrutiny.

"Yeah, but … has anyone ever *asked*?"

"Would *you* want to ask?" Beth's eyes go wide. "Because I don't plan to."

Lexi shakes her head slowly. The creases around her eyes and across her forehead etch deeper bit by bit.

Julian crosses his arms as he watches Lexi and Beth. "Do we get to be part of this conversation or should we start playing twenty questions to figure it out?"

"Sorry." Lexi glances at Beth one more time. "She was just wondering if anyone has ever asked Aisling *how* she tracks down the people she brings to Abra."

My eyes narrow. "No one knows? I figured she was like Kelsey."

"I think we all 'figured' something," Beth says. "But no one has ever asked her."

Lexi is biting her lip. "She's always kind of … been there. And everyone who gets here accepts that as the way things are."

"What about her eyes?" Julian asks. "Has anyone ever asked her about *those*? Because they're kind of freaky."

"Her eyes?" Lexi looks puzzled. "They're dark, but I've never thought they were worth asking about. I mean, I wouldn't ask you why your eyes are brown."

"I guess." He says it slowly, like he's still skeptical.

Beth shakes her head, as if brushing off that tangent. "It would just make sense if Aisling had insider information."

"Like how Kelsey has information? Or more like how Lexi does?" Julian asks.

"Um, neither," Beth says. "More like how Nadette got it."

My jaw drops. "You think she's getting tips from *Blue*?"

Beth's nose wrinkles. "I don't know about him *specifically*, but from someone *like* him."

That statement filters through the silence that follows like a fog. It touches everything past and present, coating it with possibilities.

What would it mean if that was true? The reality is impossible to grasp. Julian is the one who finally clears the haze away.

"So, just to recap, the Balasura may or may not know where we are, and they may or may not be planning something dastardly and Aisling may or may not have known about these 'good' Balasura the whole time and we may or may not be about to go on lockdown for the foreseeable future. Which, according to the latest from Kelsey, is somewhere between two weeks and a month." He raises one eyebrow. "Does that sound right?"

Lexi bites her lip and nods. "Uh, yep. That about covers it."

Julian takes a long, slow breath. "Right. Okay then." He slides his hands into his pockets and nods. "I'm going for a walk."

"If you go alone Johanna will be seriously pissed," Lexi says.

"As opposed to her normal sunshine-y disposition?" Julian snorts. "Yeah, I think it's worth the risk."

In the silence that settles over the group, Julian tenses. He inches toward the tunnel, his shoulders rising closer to his ears and his lips pressing into a thin line. It's got to be such a change for him, going from essentially living by himself to being part of this commune-like community. For me, it's practically normal. It felt weird the last couple of years as my older siblings moved out one by one and then there were only four people in that big house. It felt wrong. Empty. *This* feels so much better.

"He'll be fine," I tell Lexi. "He can take care of himself."

Julian's shoulders drop and he smiles at me, a soft, relieved smile. It takes another second for Lexi to relent.

"Promise me you'll be careful," she says as she passes him a backpack of gemstones. "No wandering so far you don't know how to find your way back, okay? And don't be gone too long."

Julian laughs. Taking the bag, he slips it over one shoulder. "You know, I think that's the most maternal thing anyone has ever said to me."

"Call me 'Mom' and I'll tell Vasha to zap some sense into you," she warns. But she's smiling as she says it.

"Please. I don't call anyone 'Mom.' I'm not about to start with you." With that, he waves and scurries away.

Nineteen

Julian

Tuesday, September 30 – 4:39 PM EDT

My heart is beating fast and my hands are shaking. It'd probably be a good idea to swing by my bedroom and pick up another jacket before I go outside. I don't. The room means Vasha, and I don't think I can put up with his muttered Russian insults right now. And they *are* insults. Traitor, coward, liar, crazy. And those are just the tame ones. Some of his more creative insults don't seem legal or anatomically possible. I've been teaching myself Russian from some tapes and books Lexi picked up for me from the library in town. One of these days I'll surprise Vasha and snipe back in his mother tongue, but for now I just feel better knowing what he's calling me under his breath.

Vasha doesn't matter now. He's a minor (nearly negligible) player in a much larger game. I need to talk to one of the people who make the rules. I've spent so much time under the cover of Abra's protections that I haven't been able to talk to Pheodora since I got to the mountain. I was going to try earlier today, but then we met Aisling and all other plans went out the window. Then everyone was waiting for us when we got back and …

Ugh. Sinatra bless it, I'm not used to people constantly checking in with me and wanting to know where I am. It's nice, I guess, but there are times when the warm-fuzziness of the family thing they have going on makes me feel like I can't breathe. I'll probably have to make up for breaking lockdown when I get back, but if I talk to Pheodora she might be able to fill in some of the blanks. Either ease some of Johanna's fears or confirm them. Either one *has* to be better than hanging in limbo.

Dead leaves and dried-out twigs snap under my boots as I walk west in a straight line. It's a little warmer than I expected, but I know that once the sun goes down it'll cool off fast. And it'll be a lot harder to find my way back without tripping over some hidden rock or root. Ducking low-hanging branches and skirting fallen trees, I keep walking. A mile or so away from Abra, I set my backpack in the hollow created by two overgrown root systems, close my eyes, and envision the mental room Pheodora helped me create.

The picture forms around me easily. I walk through the thick glass door into the narrow burgundy hallway and close it behind me. Reaching for the glowing golden symbol, I press my palm against it. The glow brightens as soon as I make contact and it's warm to the touch, as soothing as sitting next to the fire in the kitchen. Pressing harder, I glance at the wood door at the end of the short hall and call, "Pheodora?"

For a moment, nothing happens. I press harder and try again. "Pheodora?"

This time the response is almost immediate. The air around me shimmers like someone dumped a bottle of incandescent glitter from the ceiling and Pheodora's voice fills the space. *Open your eyes, Julian.*

I do as she asks. The doorway to her world is open in front of me. It's the same landscape as always—the large lake, the rolling fields of grass, the mountains in the distance—but no birds fly through the sky this time. And the mirrors that reflect nothing (the same ones Nadette describes when she talks about Blue) are hanging in midair again.

"I have been worried, Julian. It has been so long." She smiles, relief and fatigue obvious in her eyes. Then she glances over her shoulder at the reflectionless mirrors, her shoulders tense. "I do not know how much time we have, so speak now and speak quickly."

"We made it. But … are we safe?" She looks even more nervous than she was the last time we spoke, the furrows on her forehead etched deep. "Do you even know where I am?"

"Everyone in this world is aware of the survivors' camp, but no one can reach it. You are safe for now." She glances over her shoulder again, the movement tense. "But you may not be for long."

I close my eyes, willing my stomach to stop rolling. Willing my head to stop spinning. Oh God. I thought it would be better to know for sure one way or the other, but it's *not*. This *sucks*. Knowing danger is coming only helps if you can do something to *stop* it.

Forcing my body to still, I focus on Pheodora. "We have to help them. *I* have to find a way to help them."

"Such a brave boy. There is so much you do not know, Julian. So much about our world." Another quick glance over her shoulder. The mirrors still reflect nothing. "Recent events must suffice."

"What recent events?"

"Orane's defeat, child. He was a leader of the hunters. His destruction sent shockwaves through our world, upsetting the already precarious balance. Realms that were once safe are chaotic. The rebellion is making tremendous strides, capitalizing on the destabilization as much as possible."

Hope blooms in my chest. I step forward, my toes nearly brushing the edge of her world. "Can you keep the Balasura away? And why haven't you ever approached any of the people here? So many of them could have used your help."

As she opens her mouth to answer, she glances at the mirrors once more. This time, something bright blue and white shimmers at the edge of one of the mirrors. Her entire body tenses as though she's stepped on a live wire. When she turns back to me, her eyes are wide and nearly frantic. "Quickly, Julian! The pack you carried out of Abra. Show me what it looks like."

Biting back my frustration (fantastic, another session cut short before I actually get answers), I close my eyes and bring up a mental image of the backpack I carried out here, making sure it's on the other side of the glass wall in my head, the side Pheodora can see. As soon as my eyes open, well before I can ask why she cares, the air near my feet shimmers and sparkles, the glittering light getting darker and thicker until it coalesces into a near-perfect replica of my backpack.

"Take what is inside and hide them within the caves," Pheodora says, her words rushed and running together, her eyes locked on the mirror farthest to my left as colors slowly spread across the surface. "Do not tell a soul, not even Nadette. You saw how they reacted when you revealed us. They would never accept our help. Nadette might believe you, but she would not be able to keep the secret from the others, especially Alexandriana."

I remember Aisling's words this morning (God, was it only this morning?). "They can be little bigots sometimes," she said. And she's known them a lot longer than I have. If even Aisling thinks that, Pheodora might be right about keeping this a secret.

"Hide them all and hide them well, all along the edges of the occupied caves."

"What will they do?"

She gasps as the colors on the mirror get darker and a streak of red flashes through the blue and white swirls. "Good luck, Julian," she calls as the doorway snaps shut.

The world around me restarts. Above my head, a little bird finishes its song and takes off, fluttering to another tree. And I'm left with a backpack of *something* that I'm supposed to hide around Abra. Somehow. I'm not clear on exactly how Pheodora expects me to keep something like this a secret from Nadette and Kelsey. Especially Kelsey. I mean, come on. The girl can literally *see the future.*

Guess I better find out exactly what I'm hiding.

Crouching next to the bag, I unzip the top. *Weird.* The thing is almost bulging at the zippers in places, but it feels so light that a sharp wind might be able to pick it up. Leaning closer, I peer inside.

Empty? No. Not empty, just dark. The same matte-black as the backpack, but not fabric. Then the branches above me shift and a shaft of light from the setting sun glances off the contents of the bag.

"Oh, wow." This can't be real.

The entire backpack is full of crystal clusters that look like they'll fit perfectly in my palm. In the light, the dark crystals come alive like opals, the brightest, most colorful opals I've ever seen. I carefully remove one to look at it in the light, marveling.

It looks so dull and empty in the dark, but bring it to the sun and it's practically alive. Swirls of iridescent colors dance not only across the surface, but through the inside of the crystal. Reds, oranges, blues, greens, golds—an entire rainbow trapped inside a stone that, in the shadows, seems to have no color at all.

The longer I stare at the crystal, the more I want to grab the whole bag and run into Abra to show them to Nadette and Lexi and Beth and anyone else who would care. Anya would *love* the colors in these. But

I suppress that impulse, place the cluster back in the bag, zip it up, and ease the surprisingly light bundle onto my back.

On the way back to the caves, I pass the hollow where my other backpack is hidden.

Come back and get it tomorrow, I decide. If I can get out of Abra tomorrow with an empty backpack, I can sneak this extra one back in. It'll be easy.

The hard part will be that, for the first time since I met her, I'm going to have to lie to Nadette. Keeping Pheodora's name a secret was one thing, but this?

There's no way I can pretend this is just a lie of omission.

I almost run straight into Nadette in the tunnel between the Dorm and the Whatever Room. She stops short just before we collide, relief in her green eyes.

"Johanna announced the lockdown right after you left. She was pissed you weren't here."

I keep my face blank as I lift my shoulder to hitch the strap of my backpack higher. "I'm back, though."

"Are you okay?" she asks, her eyes scanning my body like she's looking for injuries.

"Yeah, I'm fine. Why?"

"Because you're … more orange than usual."

I look down at myself even though I know I won't be able to see the glow. Is that because I was talking to Pheodora? Does just touching the energy of her world bring that color back? Huh. Johanna did say the colors were like I was half-in and half-out of that world. I guess still having any connection to the place leaves marks. Good to know, I guess. "I still can't see it."

"Right." Nadette eyes the air around my body for another second before shaking her head. She runs her hand over her hair, sweeping the long strands over one shoulder. "You should check in with Johanna. Just in case."

My hand on the strap of my bag tightens. "Uh, sure. I guess. I'll find her."

Nadette opens her mouth, but footsteps in the tunnel make us both turn. Lexi appears there, a wide smile on her face. "Hey, Nadie. You still going to help with dinner?"

The way Nadette smiles back at Lexi makes me pause. It's soft and almost longing and it only lasts for a second. The expression is gone before I can be sure I read it right.

"Yep. Told you I would, didn't I?" Nadette waves as she passes, smiling at me almost the same way she smiled at Lexi.

I never had friends. Friends want to be invited into your life, into your house, and there was no way I was going to risk exposing anyone to Lynnie and whoever she was dating at the time. So no friends. And definitely no girlfriends. No one but Orane (and, to a lesser extent, Uncle Frank) ever knew about my life.

For the first time, that's not true. Nadette knows. And even though I don't think she can fully grasp what growing up with Lynnie was like (not coming from her family), she doesn't judge me for any of it either. Doesn't think I'm low-class and doesn't even seem to hate me for playing illegal poker to pay the bills or constantly lying to school and social services.

I watch her walk away and have to fight back the urge to grab her hand and keep her here with me. But then the bag on my back shifts, a sharp edge of one of the impossibly light crystals digging into my spine, and I let her go. Besides, even if I wasn't carrying a secret on my back, what am I supposed to say to her here and now? I'm not even sure I want to call this a crush. And if *I'm* not sure what I'm feeling, there's no way I'm saying anything to Nadette. Nadette, who *has* to be honest. Contemplating that conversation is about as scary as base-jumping without a parachute, hoping the water far, far below will be enough to help me survive the fall.

Sighing quietly, I turn and keep walking for the Dorm. Along the way, I look for places to hide the small clusters. There aren't many possibilities. I place five of the stones in dark corners and hard-to-find hollows, and then I head to my room, hoping Vasha isn't there. I need to store the rest of these for now.

My hopes are dashed as soon as I push the curtain aside. Vasha is lying on his twin mattress with a book. His dark eyes flick up to meet mine for less than a second before he huffs and mutters, "*Oranzhevyy urod.*" Orange freak.

My control snaps.

"*Mudak,*" I bite back at him. Asshole. His eyes widen and he sits up sharply, his book falling off his lap and snapping shut. Whether he's more shocked by the word (spoken in a language I'm not supposed to even understand) or my tone, I don't know. I keep going, still spewing angry Russian. "I don't know what your deal is, but I'm here and I'm not going away, so you better deal with it somehow, dammit!"

Vasha's jaw drops, but he closes his mouth fast. His eyes narrow and he stands. The guy is just shy of six feet and he's a lot bulkier than me, with these faint, lightning-like marks all over his body. He also comes off as more than willing to pound my head against the stone wall until I never wake up. Or just shock me with however much voltage there is running under his skin. My hands start shaking when he steps closer, but I force them to still, standing my ground under his glare.

"You need to learn how to lighten up," he finally mutters (in English), his eyes dropping. "You don't know how to take a joke."

"It's only a joke if it's funny, *mudak,*" I mutter back.

His eyes flash to meet mine for a beat and his lips press into a thin line. "Whatever."

When he brushes past me, he tries to jam his shoulder into mine and knock me off-balance, but I turn with the pressure, letting him spin me around to face the door instead. Vasha doesn't look back as he blows through the curtained doorway. I watch with a small measure of satisfaction as he mutters to himself and runs his fingers through his dark, shaggy hair. Frustration. It feels good to know I finally got a dig in. A little bit of payback for ten days of slights and insults.

The satisfaction slides away fast. It leaches out of me and leaves me chilled, standing weary and alone in a room I'm supposed to feel safe in. A room I'm supposed to be sharing with someone who gets why we're both here. Instead, I just made him hate me more than ever. And on top of that, I'm keeping a secret now. A big one. One that would probably make him follow through with all those threats he's made since I got here.

I *should* go check in with Johanna like Nadette said, but it's not like she can get any more pissed off at me. No need to rush another reckoning.

The mattress doesn't sit on a frame, just a box spring, so when I collapse to it, it's a long way to fall. The backpack thuds next to me, the remaining stones inside clacking together like marbles. I grab it and pull it onto my chest, trying to calm down. Trying to warm up. Even when I pull the pile of blankets on the bed over me, wrapping myself up in them completely, the chill remains.

If I can't fit into a place where *everyone* is a freak, where in the name of Sinatra's grey ghost am I supposed to go?

Twenty

Nadette

It takes me a few days to figure out what to do for Julian's sixteenth. There's no way I'm letting it pass unnoticed, but beyond that I'm a little lost. I consider getting everyone together for a surprise party, but I change my mind. Some of the others are still a little wary of Julian. Between the light show and the fact that most of their powers don't work on him, they can be a little pissy sometimes.

So, maybe it should be just the two of us.

Once I have a plan, I have to get permission from Johanna to actually do it. She gives me the okay... with a small catch. While we're in town, I have to ask Aisling where she gets her information. Considering how vague and confusing my last conversation with her was, I'm not sure what to expect this time around.

On Sunday, I track Julian down in the kitchen, digging through the shelves in the far corner of the room.

"What are you doing?"

He jumps, slamming the back of his head into one of the stone shelves. I wince with him. The thud echoes through the cave.

"Mother of Sinatra's ghost," he bites out, rubbing the point of impact and collapsing to the floor. "Wow, that hurt."

"Sorry." I crouch next to him. "Didn't mean to scare you."

"More startled than scared." He cringes and rolls his shoulders. "Oww."

Trying not to laugh, I help him up. "What were you looking for?"

"I don't even know," he mumbles, crossing his eyes and letting his head drop to the side. "I think the blow to the head knocked it right out."

I smile. If he's already making jokes about it, he's fine. "Not a great way to start your birthday, huh?"

"I don't know." Still rubbing his head, he shrugs. "Not the worst I've had, but not the best ei—" His head pops up and his eyes widen. "My birthday?"

"You mentioned it last week. Didn't think I'd forget, did you?"

His face flushes a little. "No, I just—uh … I didn't think anyone would bother doing much with the information."

Damn. That has to be one of the saddest things I've heard come out of his mouth in a while. We've been happy here. People have pretty much accepted us both into this dysfunctional, non-traditional family. But he still doesn't see why anyone would bother doing something nice for him just because. I brush over that part as best I can and smile back at him.

"How about lunch to celebrate? We'll let someone else cook and clean and everything."

Julian's brown eyes light up. "Really? You hate going into town."

"Yeah, but *you* don't." And today that's the important bit.

Yesterday made it exactly two weeks since we arrived at Abra. I haven't seen, heard, or felt Syver once. Johanna and the others are still worried about the possibility of something awful, but I'm so happy to be with people who *get* it that those worries feel a long way off. Being wrapped in the security of the amethyst-lined caves has taught me how to breathe again. For Julian's birthday I can risk the real world.

There is exactly one restaurant in Alaster, a place simply called The Diner. So that's where we go. Considering Julian grew up eating at the Bellagio, I don't expect him to be very impressed. I'm wrong. He doesn't stop grinning the whole time we're there. Guess it's been so long since Lynnie made a big deal about his birthday that even a burger in a mom and pop diner seems awesome. I buy him dessert and talk the entire diner—all four other people in the place—into singing "Happy Birthday."

When we walk out, he's still grinning as he loops his arm through mine.

"Nadette, that was so cool. Thank you."

I squeeze his hand where it's resting on my arm and smile. "Glad you liked it. I was considering a surprise party, but I thought you might like this better."

His cheeks gain a little color and he nods. "This is definitely better. I'm surprised Johanna let us escape for this, though."

"Well, there is a price," I admit. "Johanna wants to know if Beth was right about how Aisling found everyone, so we have to stop by Martha's to see Aisling."

"It's been days since Beth realized that. Why hasn't anyone else asked?" Julian's freckled nose crinkles as he tries to puzzle it out.

"Because I asked Johanna for permission days ago. And she said I probably had a better chance of getting a real answer out of her than anyone else."

"You do?" Julian's eyes flick from me to the sky as he sighs. "Why do I have a feeling this conversation is either going to be really entertaining or horror-movie scary?"

I grin and pull him in the direction of Martha's Magic Market. "Nothing like a birthday adventure, right? Let's go find out."

Aisling dragged us into the store so fast last time that I didn't get much of a chance to see Martha's from the outside. From a distance, there isn't anything but the wind chime hanging under the narrow red awning to set it apart from every other store on the street. All of the buildings on Main Street are two stories with sloped roofs and large front windows for light. Close up, it's obvious Martha's is different. It's not like the small furniture and hardware store on the end of the street, or like The Diner where you can get home cooking you don't have to cook. It's not even like the surprisingly upscale art gallery that seems out of place in a town this small, even though their sign claims they've been in business since 1956.

Martha's is the only business on the street to completely block out the front window. Faded and slightly sun-bleached red velvet falls in thick waves from above the window. Set out on small pedestals is an artistic display of crystals, books, wands, and incense. As we pass under the thick metal rods of the chime, I raise my hand and brush against them, setting off a soothing chorus of notes. When I push the door open, another set of tones joins the ones still clanging outside.

"Glowstick and Sparkles!" Aisling calls out. She's wearing a bright yellow hoodie, but it's still no match for her shockingly blue hair. Before I can say hello, let alone tell her why we stopped by, Aisling beckons us closer. "C'mere, Sparkles. I was going to come up to Abra to give this to you today. You saved me a trip."

She ducks behind the counter and comes up with a long, thin black box.

"This came in and I thought of you."

Aisling opens the box and shows me a silver charm bracelet. Instead of symbols or figures, this bracelet has small, wire-wrapped pieces of black stone. About twenty of them. Reaching out, I run a finger along the links of the chain.

"What kind of stone is it?" I ask. "Black jade?"

Aisling nods. "Some. It's also obsidian, jet, and black spinel. Like it?"

I really do. I've gotten used to wearing the stone bangles Mom bought me before I pulled my vanishing act. This one is different, though. It's delicate and jingly and really pretty.

Since moving into the caves, I haven't spent a ton of money, except the chunk I gave to Johanna to contribute to the food fund. I should have enough left to afford a bracelet. It's not like it's a completely self-indulgent purchase, since the stones are all protective. It's adding to my defenses. Plus, it's *really pretty*.

"How much is it?" I swing my backpack around to take out my wallet. Aisling shakes her head.

"A gift." She lifts the bracelet free of the tiny elastic bands holding it to the velvet display box and grabs my wrist before I can protest. "As long as you promise me something."

"I don't mind paying for it." How am I supposed to interrogate her about the rebel Balasura when she's giving me a present? I try to pull my hand away. Or blink. I can't. Her black eyes lock on mine and it's like we're connected. Like my eyes have turned into windows and she's peering into my head. My heart starts beating faster, but everything else seems frozen.

"I don't want your money, I want you to promise me something." Her voice almost echoes around me, like I'm hearing it in this room and then again from somewhere farther away.

"What is it?" I hear myself ask the question. I don't remember telling myself to talk.

"If you promise you'll never take it off—not to shower or exercise or clean or anything—if you promise me that, I'll let you have it as a gift."

"That's a lot to ask." Julian's voice is even more distant than Aisling's. "How will you even know she follows through?"

Aisling's head swivels toward Julian. I almost stumble forward. Pulling air into my lungs, I blink to ease the slight burning in my eyes. Not a pre-tears burning. An oh-my-god-did-I-really-forget-to-blink-for-that-long burning.

"Nadette can't lie. If she promises she'll keep it on, I believe her."

Julian meets her stare for stare before he lifts one shoulder, his shrug almost dismissive. "Just seems excessive is all."

"Hush, Glowstick. Your turn comes next. I'm talking to Sparkles now." Aisling looks at me, but this time I don't get stuck. She dangles the bracelet between her thumb and index finger, swinging it like a pendulum as she leans on the glass counter. "What do you say?"

"I really don't mind paying for it."

Aisling shrugs. "I know, but it's *really* not for sale. It's promise or nothing."

It's such a strange request. If she hadn't said anything, I probably would've worn it all the time without thinking about it. Why is it so important I never take this off?

"It's important," she says after a few seconds of silence.

Not a lie. For some reason, this really matters to her. "Yeah, okay. I promise."

Grinning, Aisling takes my hand and tugs until my arm is extended over the counter. "Don't move, okay? This is gonna pinch."

"Wha—Oww!" Something sharp pokes my middle finger. Aisling holds my hand in place to keep me from jerking it away.

"What'd you do?" Julian demands, stepping closer to the counter.

"I told her it would pinch." As she moves her hand, the safety pin she stuck me with falls to the counter. She rubs my finger along the chain of the bracelet. Tiny smears of blood dull the silver links.

"What the heck? What are you doing?" Julian reaches over and tries to help me pull my hand away. I shake my head.

"It's okay." He looks at me like I'm crazy, but I shrug. To Aisling, I say, "You could've been a little more specific."

She grins. "Better to ask forgiveness."

She releases my hand and clasps the bracelet in place. I see her lips move, but I can't hear what she's saying. As soon as the silver is resting against my skin, I feel a pulse of warmth travel up my arm. It's a slightly tingly feeling, but not bad. Almost pleasant. Like sitting near a nice fire on a cold night after spending too much time out in the snow.

I twist my wrist, admiring the bracelet, before looking at Aisling. "You're not going to tell me why you just did that, are you?"

"Nope!" She closes her eyes and holds her hands out in front of her, palms up. "A witch must have her secrets."

"You're not a witch," Julian says. "You're crazy, but you're not a witch."

Aisling opens one eye. "Coming from you, I'm really not sure if that's a compliment or an insult."

Before he can say anything, she reaches under the counter. "Here. This one's for you." She tosses a black velvet bag at Julian and he catches it against his chest. "I'd make you promise, but I don't trust you to keep it."

Julian's jaw clenches, but his eyes stay on the velvet bag in his hand. When he unties it and turns it over, a purple stone on a thick silver chain lands in his hand.

"Pretty. What is it?" I ask.

Aisling glances at me and smiles. "This is purpurite." Reaching out, she lifts the stone, rolling her fingers underneath it to make it dance. "It's particularly good at helping you see the truth of things."

The stone is a few shades of purple, all of them on the darker end of the spectrum, with spots of white and gray. An inverted, uneven triangle only about the size of a silver dollar, it's secured to the chain with a solid silver cap and crisscrossing silver wires. It's pretty, but Julian is eyeing it and Aisling like they both might turn into snakes and bite him.

She tugs Julian's hand until it's over the counter. "This will come in handy eventually. You willing to trust me?"

I wish I could read their expressions. They're both excellent at keeping their emotions masked and right now their faces are blank. Eventually, Julian shifts his weight and lowers his eyes, nodding. The movement seems heavy—almost reluctant—but Aisling accepts it.

Pricking his finger, she runs the small drops of blood along the silver chain and then presses his finger to the chunk of purpurite. Like with me, her lips are moving quickly. I still can't hear what she's saying. After a moment, she lets the stone and his hand drop.

"Happy sixteenth, Glowstick."

Julian stands there looking between Aisling and the necklace for a second. Slowly, his lips twitch into a smile. He shakes his head as he lifts his hands to clasp the necklace in place.

"I want a different nickname," he says. "Vasha gives me enough crap about the lightshow up at Abra. I don't need it here, too."

"How's it going with him?" I ask.

"Better, I guess." Julian shrugs. "After I yelled at him in Russian he's taken to avoiding me instead of antagonizing me, so that's an improvement, right?"

"You yelled at him in Russian?" I ask before realizing there's a more important question. "You know *Russian?*"

Julian's mouth twists into a sly smirk. "I learned it just for him. I don't think he liked being insulted in his mother tongue."

"Like I said. Little bigots," Aisling says. "Especially that one. Poor kid. Sometimes I think he doesn't know how else to talk to people."

Julian snorts. "Yeah. I've noticed."

"So." Aisling leans her elbows on the glass counter, her focus on me. "You wanted to ask me something when you walked in."

My forehead wrinkles. "How did you know?"

"Oh, it was burning a hole in your head earlier. I distracted you, but I could see it, like …" She purses her lips and flaps her hand in the air. "Like it was buzzing around you."

"Well?"

Aisling's blue eyebrows rise. "Well *what?* I may know a lot of things, Sparkles, but I'm not Lexi. If you want an answer, you'll have to actually, you know, ask a question."

"Oh." I take a deep breath and stuff my hands in the front pocket of my hoodie to hide the fact that I can't stop fidgeting with my new bracelet. "Okay. Um, do you find the kids with some … *extra* help? Before I got here, did you know about the rebels?"

Aisling's lips quirk up on one side and she nods once. "Yep and yep."

"How long have you known?" I ask, hoping to get a little more detail.

"A *long* time." Aisling nods once, almost for emphasis.

"Why didn't you tell anyone?" If she had mentioned the rebels to Johanna earlier, maybe they wouldn't have been so distrusting that first night. And maybe they would've cut Julian some slack.

"Because I haven't met anyone ready to listen yet."

"Listen to what?" I step closer to the counter. "Is there more?"

"Of course there's more." She looks at me as though that answer should've been obvious. "There's always more. This is *life*. It's impossible for there not to be more than you think there is."

Julian tilts his head slightly as though changing the angle he's watching Aisling at might help him understand. "That's … very vague."

"I'm *excellent* at vague." She says it with a grin, like it's a source of pride.

"Will you tell us everything?" Whatever she has to say could be important. Vital. I just don't know how or why.

"No."

I blink. "Oh."

"Why not?" Julian asks, eyebrows pulled together.

"Because it's not the right time. I'm still waiting."

"For what?" Julian and I say at the same time.

"The right sign. The right person." Aisling circles her hands in the air. "I'm not even sure what I'm waiting for anymore. Something."

"And it's not us?" I ask. "Even though we've met them? Even though we know you're telling the truth about the rebels?"

"Nope." She shakes her head. "It's not you guys. Sorry, Sparkles. Nothing personal."

"Johanna's not going to like that answer." I rub my eyes with the heels of my hands.

Aisling snorts. "Johanna doesn't like much of anything."

"Okay, then. Great." Julian claps his hands together and smiles a big, obviously fake grin. "This has been a productive visit, hasn't it? So glad we cleared everything up."

"Are you sure you can't give us anything else?" I ask.

For the first time, Aisling looks serious. Even a little sad. She sighs and shakes her head slowly. "I'm sorry, Nadette. Information is power and if I don't share mine with the right person at the right time…" She presses her lips together so hard the edges turn white.

"And now's not the time?" Julian's face is just as solemn as Aisling's now.

"Now's not the time. But tell Johanna something for me, okay?" Aisling waits until I nod to continue. "Tell her she has to let go of the way things have been done, because things are going to change soon. For better or worse, I'm not sure, but there's something coming. Something big."

"Again with the vague," Julian mutters.

"What can I say?" she says with a heavy sigh as Julian and I head for the door. "It's a finely honed gift."

I park the car in the clearing and get out, shivering a little when the breeze hits. It's only the beginning of October, but the weather is cooling off fast. It's already in the fifties today. Sure, nowhere near freezing, but for a girl raised in Florida it's pretty damn cold. I don't know what I'm going to do when true winter hits.

I look across the hood of the Bronco at Julian. He seems strangely hesitant, like he's thinking something he's not sure he wants to say. Then he smiles, a real smile, and tilts his head toward the woods.

"Want to take advantage of our freedom and go for a walk? Who knows when Johanna is going to let us out again."

"Probably the next time you have sentry duty. You signed yourself up for, like, every shift possible."

"Yeah, and thank Sinatra for that." He walks around the hood. "Playing sentry is pretty much all that's kept me from feeling completely claustrophobic this weekend."

"But you still want to walk."

"It's a beautiful day, it's my birthday and going for a walk just for the heck of it is different than being stuck in one area making sure hikers don't find us."

"I guess so."

He smiles and I follow him into the trees. It's beautiful and green and wild here. So different from Florida. Especially South Florida. In the past two weeks, my stamina has picked up. I've gained some weight, but it's all muscle I never had before. Being here has been good for me in a lot of different ways.

But that doesn't mean it's home.

"Did I tell you that it's been six years since anyone bothered doing anything for my birthday?" Julian says. "And that was the year my Uncle Frank managed to get away from work to visit."

My stomach clenches. My family threw me a huge party back in July. My birthday is only a week before my twin sisters', Honor and Dorothy. They turned twenty-three. My sweet sixteen took precedence. Our joint party was almost solely focused on me. Presents, friends, and siblings who travelled hundreds of miles to come home for the occasion.

I had all that and Julian's mother can barely remember she has a son.

"It won't always be that bad," I insist. "You've got friends now. Next year I might go with the surprise party idea."

Julian looks at me, his smile growing. "Next year?"

I grin back as we hike along a ridge that travels up the mountain. "Surprise parties are apparently a lot of work. Might take me a year to plan one."

"Not too much of a surprise if I know it's coming, though, is it?"

"Maybe I'll ask Beth to erase this whole conversation from your head."

He laughs. With how well he can keep people out of his head, Beth's power won't work on him any more than mine does.

Neither of us say anything else for a while. We're busy concentrating on keeping our feet from slipping on piles of fallen leaves, tripping over raised roots, or knocking ourselves out on low-hanging branches.

"Hey, um … I just …" Julian blushes fiercely, a brighter red than I've ever seen on him. My forehead wrinkles. Before I can ask him what's wrong, his hand comes up to my cheek. That's the only warning I have before he leans in and presses his lips against mine.

His skin is soft and warm, but that's it. Just like the one other time I tried kissing a boy, there is no fluttering heartbeat, no shiver, and *definitely* no fireworks.

I freeze. It only takes him a second to open his eyes and stumble back. Fast.

His head smacks into the tree branch behind him. He flinches, muttering something to himself as he rubs the back of his head. He won't meet my eyes. I don't know what to say. The last thing I want to do is hurt him, but I'm also not interested. At all.

Julian sighs. "Sorry. I should—I'll just …"

He turns to leave, but I grab his wrist and hold him here.

"No, wait. Don't be sorry, it's just …" I search for a gentle way to let him down. The only words that come to mind are trite but way too true right now. "You're not really my type."

"Your type?" His lips purse and the color hasn't faded from his cheeks at all. I can't tell if he's more hurt or mad. I can't blame him for either. It's not exactly what someone wants to hear on their birthday. Or ever. "What? Am I too short? Too young?"

"Too, um … male?"

My predilection for honesty means that my family has known I'm gay since I figured it out when I was thirteen. It was easy with them because they'd accepted Jake when he said he was gay, so I knew they wouldn't have a problem with me. All they did was tease me about following in my favorite brother's footsteps. Over the last three years, I've had to explain my orientation a few dozen times. Despite all the practice I've had "coming out," sometimes it's still awkward as hell to say out loud and worse to wait for a reaction. Like now. I watch Julian's face carefully, hoping he takes it well.

His eyebrows pull together, creases appearing around his eyes and across his forehead. The confusion clears fast. "Oh!" His eyes widen and he glances in the direction of the caves before looking back at me. He's silent for another few seconds, but then he clears his throat and asks, "Have you told Lexi yet?"

I wish I could pretend I don't know what he's talking about.

"No." I'm sure my face is as red as my hair right now. "And I'd rather you didn't either."

"Why not? Now that I know what the deal is, it's obvious. It's kind of stupid that I didn't figure it out sooner." Julian almost smiles as he shakes his head. "I mean, how likely is it that she doesn't know already?"

My throat closes. I stare up at the sky through the leaves rustling above our heads. "Exactly."

When the telepath you've had a crush on since the moment you met her doesn't give you a single sign she's interested in being anything more than friends, you kind of have to assume it's not gonna happen. She likes me, but something keeps her from ever saying so. Maybe the age difference is too much. I just turned sixteen. Lexi is already six months past her eighteenth birthday.

Two years isn't a lot in the scheme of life, but *these* two years make a difference.

"If you ask me, she likes you." Julian's voice is quiet but confident. His cheeks are still red and he's holding himself away from me a little bit, a tinge of awkwardness in the air between us, but he hasn't run off. Despite the embarrassment obviously still forcing color into his cheeks, Julian stays and comforts *me* over *my* unrequited crush. "Think about it. How often does she hear things in people's head they'd never admit out loud? How does she know for sure you wouldn't freak out if she came up and asked you out?" He looks around and the corner of his lips tug up into a smile. "I mean, asked you out to *where* I don't know, but you get the picture."

"Hey!" I grin and nudge him toward Abra. We took the long way around to get here, but we're not actually that far away from the caves. "Nature walks are very romantic, you know."

"Yeah." He glances at me. "I know."

I bite my lip and look away. Dammit. I know he still feels a little alienated in Abra. The last thing I want is to hurt him. Dammit, dammit, *dammit.* Now Julian is upset and just … Shit. This was supposed to be a nice day.

I'm lost in my own crappy thoughts. I stop paying attention to where I'm going until Julian's hand on my elbow jerks me to a stop. I blink and look up. Right into Lexi's bright hazel eyes.

How far does her ability reach? How much of the last few minutes has she heard? Is there a rock I can crawl under to die?

"Happy birthday, Julian." Lexi holds out a small wrapped package and smiles. Her eyes keep flicking to me. "It's from me and Beth."

Julian's entire face relaxes as he takes the present, his smile almost coming back. "Thanks, Lexi." He edges toward the arch. "I'm gonna go find Beth and thank her too. Bye!"

He sprints off. And I'm left facing Lexi, my head spinning and chaotic and my hands trembling.

"Would you—um ..." Lexi's face flushes pink. She smiles just enough for her dimple to appear. "You want to go for a walk?"

I remember what I just said about romantic nature walks. And immediately try to forget what I said about romantic nature walks. *Oh, God. She really did hear everything.*

"Yeah." I swallow and try to keep my head from bouncing like a bobblehead. With effort, I keep my thoughts somewhat blank. "Um. Yeah, okay."

Her hands are tucked into the pockets of her coat—the same sapphire-blue one she let me borrow my first day in Abra—but she's smiling as she heads north. Neither of us says much for the first couple of minutes, hiking through the woods and enjoying the early autumn in the air. Her head tilts every so often like she's looking for something. Or maybe listening for something. I don't know what it is. I'm willing to follow her until she finds it.

"It's hard sometimes, separating what people think and what they say." Lexi glances at me, still walking and not seeming to expect an answer. Then she takes a breath and keeps talking.

"People think things they'd never say. Never act on. Deny if anyone ever called them on it." Looking straight ahead, Lexi shrugs. "When I react to something I hear in someone's head, especially someone I just met and *especially* when they're thinking something they never even hint at in words, it blows up in my face about seventy percent of the time."

My mouth goes dry. The shaking in my hands gets so bad I stuff them into the pockets of my jeans. Is this a way to let me down easy or … I don't even want to think the "or." Getting my hopes up that much will only hurt when it doesn't happen.

Lexi's head tilts again and she stops. Reaching for me, she puts her hand on my shoulder. I can't feel her touch through my jacket, but it doesn't matter. I'm so aware it's there.

She brings her other hand up to my cheek. I freeze, but I can't resist as she gently tilts my head up. I don't want to resist. The soft brush of her fingers down the side of my neck sends shivers across my entire body.

There's no way she can *not* know how I feel about her, what I think about every time I see her. But this is the first moment I can let myself believe that Lexi *liking* me could turn into something more.

"Believe it," she whispers, her full lips sliding into a smile as she leans closer. Closer.

I close my eyes just before her lips touch mine. Warm and delicious. For a moment, it's sweet and soft and reassuring. When I let myself relax and slide my hands around her waist, something shifts.

Lexi sighs and inches closer, pulling me against her and brushing her tongue along my bottom lip. Her fingers dig into my red curls. I slide my hands under her coat, feeling the heat of her skin through her shirt. Pulling her closer, I wish it was warmer. I wish she wasn't covered in so many damn layers of fabric. I follow her lead, letting everything else disappear. All we are is heat and touch and this kiss.

I don't know how long I stay wrapped in her arms. Eventually she slows, pulling away bit by bit. When we finally separate, I sway on my feet, dizzy and out of breath. I don't want to let her go. I want more. My head is buzzing. I feel warm and fuzzy. And happier than I've been in a long, *long* time.

It's not like I have a ton of experience with kissing, but I'm pretty sure this one is going to be hard to beat.

Lexi chuckles and kisses me again. This one brief and light.

"What took you so long?" I huff, tightening my hold on her.

She blushes and brushes my hair out of my face, her fingers trailing down my cheek. "You're really careful, Nadie. You always stop yourself when you feel like you're crossing a line because you know I'm listening, but it's hard to tell why. Because you're ashamed of having the thoughts, or because you're just embarrassed for me to hear them?"

"Not because I'm too young?"

"Well, yeah. The age gap kept me back too, a little—but only a little." She's still smiling, but this time the expression is a little sad.

Yeah, because no one who survives what we have can claim to be young. Not in the ways that matter. I remember Linus's helpless cry just before he fell. The etched stress lines on Mom's face as I slowly lost my mind. My siblings tiptoeing around me like I'd become some kind of psychopath.

But I remember the times before that, too. My family may be too big and a little dysfunctional, but they love me. I've never gone this long without talking to them. I haven't seen them in almost three weeks.

She sighs and pulls me closer. I let my head rest on her shoulder as she strokes my hair. "It's okay to miss them. Brian hasn't seen his family in years and he still misses them."

"I hoped you were going to tell me it gets better," I mutter into her jacket.

"I would, but you're kind of hard to lie to, Nadie." I pull back and look up at her. Lexi raises an eyebrow and adds, "Plus, the headache I get from those bells of yours isn't worth it."

I know she's joking, but my heart sinks into my stomach like a rock anyway.

"Are you sure?" I whisper. "I mean, can you really put up with someone who can catch you even when you're lying to yourself?"

Lexi shrugs. "Can you put up with someone who can pull thoughts out of your head before you even process them? I can't help it sometimes. And I can't always keep from reacting to something you never said or did."

I relax a little, pulling her closer. "Kind of seems like a fair trade to me."

"Yeah?" Lexi smiles and rests her forehead against mine, her nose brushing my nose. "I was hoping you'd think that."

"Great. So, um, does this mean you'll come with me when I tell Johanna what Aisling said today?" I widen my eyes pleadingly.

She laughs, the slightly hoarse chuckle of hers that always sends shivers over my skin. "Of course I will." Lexi kisses the tip of my nose and straightens, her hand slipping into mine. "I can't say I'm all that surprised Aisling knew about the rebels. It makes a lot more sense than any other theory we've had about how she found all of us."

"Except Kelsey," I correct as we walk back to Abra.

Lexi nods. "Except Kelsey. Our little prophet found herself."

"Johanna isn't going to be happy about any of this." In fact, "not happy" will probably be an understatement.

"Yeah. She doesn't like being kept out of the loop." Lexi glances at me. "And Aisling hid a pretty important loop."

I don't respond. Really, what else is there to say?

Twenty-One

Julian

Sunday, October 5 – 1:46 PM EDT

Any semblance of a smile falls away and my steps slow as soon as I'm inside the tunnel.

Kissing Nadette was a stupid idea. It's not often I misread something as badly as I did with her. Why did I do that?

And why am I not more upset that it didn't go well?

The kiss was … nice. Warm. Comforting. Pleasant. A lot of other nice-like adjectives. But that's it. I didn't want to press for more and when she said I wasn't her type, the initial pang of hurt didn't last long. After that it was kind of a relief.

Groaning, I try to run my fingers through my hair, forgetting the small birthday present in my hand until the corner of the box clips my forehead. Closing my eyes, I drop my hand and take a breath.

"You okay, Julian?"

My body jerks at the unexpected question. I hadn't heard any footsteps. My answer is automatic. "Um, yeah. I'm fine."

"Actually fine, or I-don't-want-to-talk-about-it-so-go-away-now fine?" Beth asks, her sympathetic smile lit only by the flickering flame in her oil lantern.

I almost lie. My mouth is open and the lie is on the tip of my tongue, but the truth comes out instead. "Somewhere between the two? I don't even know right now."

Her eyebrows rise a little, like she was expecting me to brush her off. "If you want to talk about it, I don't mind listening."

"It's … awkward. And it's not just about me."

Confusion creates a ridge between her eyebrows, but then her gaze jumps from me toward the mouth of the tunnel. I can almost see the second she realizes Nadette and Lexi were supposed to follow me inside.

Beth brings her full attention back to me. "The offer still stands. If you want to talk, I'll listen. It's hard to keep secrets around here. Sometimes it's best to just spit out the news."

"Ugh. It's not news. Or a secret, really. It's just..." My mouth keeps moving, but the words aren't there. I've always been able to rely on my quick thinking and a quicker tongue to get me out of trouble, but now I can't even form a single coherent sentence. My greatest strength is deserting me. It feels like I've been left to balance precariously on a tightrope strung over a ravine. My pulse jumps, my breaths quicken, and my eyes silently plead with Beth to just make this stop.

The face Beth makes is half-smile, half-grimace. "C'mon."

She puts her hand on my shoulder and steers me through the tunnels until we reach the Dorm. My body has calmed down a bit (probably because I'm no longer searching for words my brain seems to have erased), but I still feel jittery. We don't stop at the room I share with Vasha.

"I think this is probably our safest bet," she says as we walk into the room she shares with Lexi. Gently she nudges me to sit on Lexi's neatly made bed with the bright yellow comforter.

I take a deep breath, my eyes scanning the walls. Above us, the roof of the cave has been painted to look like the sky, clear blue with puffy white clouds. Along the edges of the painting are enough shadows and dimensions to trick my brain into thinking that it actually *is* the sky, that this whole room is open to the world. And hanging in the middle of the space is a single light bulb encased in a bright yellow, sun-shaped shade, casting a soft glow on the room.

"Anya did that for us a while back," Beth says, her gaze following mine. "It helps us feel a little less..."

"Trapped?" I ask.

Beth smirks. "I was gonna say 'like mole people,' but 'trapped' works." The smile doesn't disappear when her eyes meet mine, but it softens with concern. "What happened?"

"How do you know when you have a crush on someone?"

I blink. Did I just say that? Why did I say that? When did I completely lose control of my tongue?!

Beth looks almost as surprised as I am. "Huh. That's not quite where I thought this conversation was going to go." She settles onto her mattress and thinks it over. "That's hard to answer because it's different for everyone. Even with one person it's different every time it happens. Because, you know, the person you're crushing on is going to be different and you're going to be older and in a different place in your life and, wow, I need to stop using the word 'different.'"

Huffing something distantly related to a laugh, I shake my head. "That doesn't help me."

"Yeah. Indefinability is one of the downsides to emotions."

"There's an upside to them?" I lean forward, resting my elbows on my knees. One of the only emotional upsides I've ever noticed is that they make people easier to manipulate. Pluck the right heartstring and you can get them to do pretty much anything. I have a feeling Beth wouldn't quite agree with that assessment, though.

"Lots of upsides. But that wasn't what you asked. Let's see ..." She goes quiet for a few seconds, then shrugs. "Well, there's usually some kind of fluttery feeling when you get close. A lot of people are more nervous or awkward around someone they're crushing on. Oh, and dreams? Everyone I've ever crushed on has definitely starred in a dirty dream or two."

She grins, but I can't grin back.

"And it's like that every time?" If that's what a crush is supposed to feel like, then ... yeah. I guess that wasn't what was happening with Nadette. Maybe. The fluttery thing I understand. A little. Everything else? "I've never felt that about *anyone*!"

"Anyone?" Grin gone. Confusion back. And that isn't helping me calm down *at all*. "Not once?"

"No." I run my hand through my hair. The motion doesn't help. I push to my feet and pace the open space between the two beds, trying to burn off the restless energy burning through me. "Is that weird? It seems like you think it's weird."

"Not weird exactly, but usually puberty hits and people—guys especially—end up crushing on *someone*. But usually doesn't mean always. There's nothing wrong with not having a crush." She pauses like she's waiting for me to say something, but I don't know what to say. Nadette is apparently the closest I've ever gotten to a crush, and that wasn't even in the ballpark according to Beth's parameters.

Beth's next question stops me cold. "What do you think about sex? In a general sense."

"What? Seriously?" I stare at her. She doesn't take the question back or even try to clarify it. She just sits there. Waiting. "It's ... I don't know. A biological and evolutionary imperative."

As Beth's smile grows, the expression hovers between amused and sympathetic. "Have you ever heard the term asexual?"

"Like a worm? Or an amoeba?"

Her laugh echoes through the room. "No, not like an amoeba. Keep in mind this is another one of those 'everyone-is-different' things, but on the scale of human sexuality, asexuality can mean that you're not sexually attracted to *anyone*. Girls, boys, trans, genderfluid— no matter what form humans take, you have no desire to have sex with them."

"That's ..." My mouth is dry. It feels like my heart has stopped. I have to swallow a couple of times before I can create words. "That's a thing? People do that?"

"Yeah. It's a small portion of the population—like one percent or something, maybe less—but if that's how you feel, you're definitely not the only one."

"But ..." The word spins through my head as I look back at my life. I figured I never wanted to sleep with anyone because I poured all my focus into staying financially steady. I thought I pushed it aside by choice. But looking back on the last few years, when all the guys I knew were suddenly obsessed with finding someone (anyone, really) willing to sleep with them ... I never had to push that hard. It never felt like I was sacrificing anything. But still ...

"I liked Nadette. I ... well, I thought I did. But then I kissed her and when she told me she liked Lexi I felt ..."

Beth's smile softens. "A little relieved?"

"*Yes.*"

She nods, almost like she expected that answer, but she doesn't say anything for a minute. She's thinking, though, and I'm willing to wait. For the first time I'm letting myself talk about something that always made me feel like even more of an outsider than I already was, and I may have found someone with *answers.*

"I don't want you to get offended by this question, but it's relevant to the conversation, okay?" She leans forward, her hazel eyes serious. "Let me ask it, and then think about it for a minute before you answer."

She watches me, waiting until I slowly nod to ask.

"Have you ever had a friend, Julian? A real one. Someone you actually connected with and cared about and trusted. Before you came here, before you met Nadette, did you have anyone even close to that in your life?"

Have I? If I work off of her definition, Orane was the closest I came, and he was more of a mentor than a friend. And he turned out to be neither one in the end. Uncle Frank and the guys I conned into playing poker with me came close. Kind of. The kids at school were more acquaintances than anything else and that's … it.

I shake my head. I don't really want to admit it out loud.

"Society expects a guy your age to fall in lust with girls. Pop culture tells you guys and girls can't be friends without romantic feelings involved." She pauses, her eyes on mine like she's making sure I'm focused. "But, Julian, what if what you were feeling for Nadette had nothing to do with wanting to kiss her and everything to do with finally having someone in your life you trusted? Someone you could talk to. Relate to. What if it was friendship? Or even platonic love. You *can* love someone without wanting to see them naked."

The long breath I finally take feels like the first oxygen I've had in ten minutes. Could this be that simple? Sitting back down on Lexi's bed, I let the concept and the label percolate. When it finally starts to settle in, I have to admit that it doesn't feel wrong. I don't know that it's totally right, but it doesn't feel wrong.

"So I'm …" I force myself to say the word, to see how it feels on my tongue. "I'm asexual?"

"Maybe." Beth's smile is soft. "There's a whole spectrum of labels and orientations. You might be graysexual or demisexual or something else entirely. Besides, sexuality isn't always fixed. I don't think picking a label you're going to cling to the rest of your life is the important part right now. Today all you have to know is that you're not strange or weird or wrong or broken or anything even close to that just because you kissed a girl you kind of liked and didn't want to take it any further."

I take another breath, this one shakier than I want it to be. "How do you know all this?"

Beth relaxes, the slight shift of her shoulders and additional ease to her posture suddenly cluing me in to the nervousness I somehow missed. "I had a friend growing up who identified as demisexual and talking to her about that got me interested in human sexuality in general. I started doing a lot of reading on my own." She shrugs and leans back against the wall of the cave. "I think if I'd gone to college, I would've gone for a Ph.D. in psychology so I could examine the less studied orientations and the psychological impact of growing up in a society with impossibly dichotomous sexual expectations and standards."

I stare at her, blinking. She sounds like she's reading from a textbook already.

Noticing my blank look, Beth grins. "Sorry. I don't get to talk to people about this much. It still fascinates me, but it's not a subject that comes up in conversation too often."

"Well ... thank you. I ..." I take a breath, my brain still trying to catch up with the conversation. "Really. Thanks."

"And now you know you can come find me if you have questions. There are some books that I can show you if you want, but I think for now you should just sit with the concept and let it soak in. There's no rush, right?" She glances at the curtained doorway and around the small room. "I mean, it's not like you have a lot of dating options here."

I laugh and nod, but I can't think of anything to say. New vocabulary is taking up too much space in my head. Asexual. Not only for amoebas, apparently.

"So ... you gonna open that?" Beth asks, nodding toward the bed.

"Huh?" I look down. My present is sitting on Lexi's bed, still wrapped. "Oh! Yes, definitely. I kind of forgot about it."

"Understandable. You had other things on your mind."

I snort and mutter, "You can say that again."

One pack is from the Sands, and the other the Golden Nugget; both are hotels where a young Frank Sinatra performed, once upon a time. I peel off the wrapping paper and inside is a thin brown box. I lift the top off and find two decks of cards. Both of the boxes are timeworn and faintly weathered. Genuine antiques or very good reproductions. "Holy crap." The words escape on a breath. "How old are these?"

"Not ancient, definitely not dating back to the grand openings. But they're cards that were actually in play at the casinos." Beth smirks. "And considering how often you swear to Sinatra, Lexi and I thought you might appreciate it."

"This is … this is seriously the coolest thing anyone has given me." I've gotten presents before—mostly from Uncle Frank—but they were always things I needed. Clothes. Books. Money that I ended up using to pay bills. This? This is an entirely different kind of gift.

I pick one of the packs up and gently take it out of the box. The weight feels right in my hand and it looks like all of the cards are in good condition. There's writing from the dealer on the inside of the pack and I run my finger over the letters, grinning.

When I look up, Beth is watching me with a matching smile on her face. "So, you like?"

"I love. This is amazing. Thank you guys so much." I shuffle the cards, the sound as familiar and soothing as a lullaby. I raise an eyebrow at Beth. "Want to learn to play poker?"

Her smile widens. From the edge of her bed she pulls up a small box. Inside is a wheel of plastic poker chips and two brand new, still-in-the-plastic packs of cards.

"I was hoping you'd ask that."

Twenty-Two

Nadette

Sunday, October 5 – 1:46 PM EDT

We keep walking, hiking back to Abra the way we came. This time, though, Lexi's fingers are laced through mine and I don't have to fight the urge to rest my head on her shoulder. Or worry that she'll catch me watching the shape of her legs under her skirt. She has a thing for skirts and today's is gray with blue, purple, and green stripes running across the fabric in varying widths, an almost-random pattern. The fabric is thick, but it still manages to flow around her as she walks, the toes of her boots poking out from under the hem with every step. She seems to have a hundred of them, all in crazy bright colors and patterns. I love each and every one of them.

Lexi squeezes my hand, her smile growing wider. I know she hears my rambling, but this time I don't try to hide it. It doesn't embarrass me anymore.

We track down Johanna in the Training Room with Anya and a slew of colorful, intricately detailed canvases. Johanna glances up when she hears us approach. Her sharp gaze takes in everything, lingering on our linked hands longest. She nods a greeting before turning back to Anya.

"We're trying to see if she can paint an illusion," Johanna explains. "Something that will look one way to people who have never touched the dream world and another way to those who have."

"Like a secret message in invisible ink?" I ask. "That's kind of awesome."

"Yeah." Anya snorts. "And it's kind of *not working*."

"Well, how can you tell?"

All three of them blink at me. "What do you mean?" Johanna asks.

"All of us have seen the dream world. How would *we* know what 'normal' people see when they look at these?" I look at the painting. It's incredibly realistic. A picture of a group of kids who all glow with a faint blue light. Behind them there's a doorway of orange flames leading into blackness. The girl in the front of the group has a sign that says, "You are not alone." There's an email address too. I guess, possible threat or not, Johanna has decided to keep reaching out to other survivors. Or at least preparing for the attempt.

"Right. Good point. Excuse me while I go bang my head against a wall." Anya chucks her brushes in a big white painter's bucket and sighs. "I'm done for tonight. I'll come back for everything else after I clean these, Johanna." Then she stalks out, muttering to herself.

Johanna watches Anya go, her lip twitching when Anya's annoyed grumbling floats back to us. Then her laser-intense gaze focuses on me.

"I expected you back a while ago. You saw Aisling?"

"I told you I would."

Johanna nods in acknowledgment. "Let me get the others so you'll only have to tell the story once."

We pick up Tanner from the kitchen, which is pretty much his domain. Julian and Beth are perched at a nearby table with a plate of cookies, two decks of cards, and a wheel of plastic poker chips. Julian winks at me as he shuffles the deck. He handles them like a professional dealer, making the cards fly from hand to hand. Beth frowns as she looks down at the deck in her hands, obviously trying to work out how to copy the trick.

From there, we find Clarke and Kelsey in the Whatever Room. Johanna doesn't say anything, just catches their attention and crooks a finger. They drop what they're doing to follow her out of the room. She leads us all to her room, where everyone takes the same positions they were in last time. As soon as we're all settled, I start talking. No need to draw this out.

"Beth was right," I tell them. "Aisling knows. And she's known for a long time."

Johanna's lips tighten into a thin line. Clarke shakes his head, looking pissed, but no one else really reacts.

"What else did she say?" Johanna asks.

I repeat the conversation. In the silence after, as the information sinks in, I shift restlessly on the end of Johanna's mattress. Lexi puts a hand on my knee and presses down, forcing stillness, forcing patience, and passing on some of the calm that always seems to surround her. It seeps into me through the pressure of her palm. Just that touch and I can breathe a little easier.

"Does it change anything?" Tanner runs his long fingers through his shaggy brown hair. Then, he clarifies, "Anything that we have control over."

Though it looks like Johanna would rather swallow acid than admit it, she shakes her head. "Not a damn thing. We're still safer in Abra than anywhere else and there's still nothing we can do to make it more secure. Or stop whatever they're planning. *If* they're planning anything."

"Great. One more vague, faceless worry to haunt me." Tanner pushes himself to his feet. "Unless you guys have something else to give me daymares, I'm going back to the kitchen."

He leaves, shoving the thick curtain aside and stalking down the tunnel. Johanna frowns as her eyes follow him. She looks concerned for a second. The expression vanishes with a quick jerk of her head and a couple of blinks.

"Is there anything else?" Johanna asks me.

I look down at my wrist. Shifting my hand makes the bracelet jingle. "Aisling gave me this. Made me promise to never take it off, no matter what."

Holding out my arm, I let Johanna look at the silver charm bracelet. Kelsey and Clarke move closer too. I glance at Lexi. She's frowning slightly, but doesn't move.

"Did she say why?" Lexi asks.

"Only that it was important. She gave Julian a purpurite pendant for his birthday, too."

Johanna's eyes widen. "Purpurite? That shit is expensive."

"Is it?" I shrug and pull my hand back. "She didn't say."

"I don't like this." Clarke's entire face is taut, an angry flush adding a deeper layer of red to his russet skin. "She gets all weird with gifts and then says she knows about the rebels but won't tell us and Kelsey can't see shit—"

"Hey! I'm *trying!*" Kelsey protests.

Clarke rolls right over her. "—and there's *something* that *may* be coming from *some* direction at *some* point and just—shit." He grinds his teeth and shakes his head, running his hand over his short hair. "Fuck, this sucks. I need to go hit something."

He gets up and blows out of the cave. Within seconds we hear the steady thump of Clarke going to town on the punching bag in his room. Johanna flicks her eyes up to the ceiling and purses her lips, but doesn't comment.

"It's all still static," Kelsey says, her voice quiet and her eyes downcast. "And it's getting worse, not better."

Johanna opens her mouth. A tiny piece of gravel hits her in the cheek. If I hadn't been sitting pressed against Lexi, I never would've noticed her move to flick that tiny rock at Johanna. She flinches, glaring at Lexi, who glares right back, shaking her head. Probably nixing whatever Johanna had been about to say.

It takes a second for Johanna to sigh and back down. "It's not your fault, Kelsey. Just let me know when anything changes, okay?"

She stands and nods slowly, but doesn't seem quite as defeated as she did a second ago. "I will." On her way out, she glances at Lexi and me. Her smile comes back. "About time."

Then she's gone and it's just Lexi, me, and Johanna.

"So," Johanna says, glancing between us. "You two, huh?"

I grip Lexi's hand tighter. Is she going to tell me we can't be together? Lexi's thumb strokes mine as she meets Johanna's eyes and nods.

"We don't really encourage relationships, you know. Things get complicated when you're around each other 24/7. It's happened before and when it ends the whole family gets awkward."

I open my mouth—to protest, to promise, to plead, I don't even know. Johanna holds up a hand to stop me.

"I said we don't *encourage* it. I never said I was going to try to stop you."

The tension that had been tightening my shoulders rolls away.

"Just, you know. Don't be stupid," Johanna says, raising her eyebrows and pinning us with her almond eyes. "Either of you."

I glance at Lexi. She's still looking at Johanna, a smirk on her face. "Don't worry. I think we'll be okay."

Johanna stares at us for a second and then her expression softens. She doesn't smile, but she doesn't look quite as blank as usual either. "Know what? I actually think you will."

Lexi pulls me to my feet fast enough to keep my jaw from dropping open. We say goodbye, leaving Johanna alone in her room.

"Why do I feel like I just got a blessing from the Pope or something?"

Lexi laughs and pulls me closer. Wrapping her arm around my shoulders, she kisses my cheek. "It's not far off. For a minute there, I wasn't sure which way she'd go on us either."

Us. I like that, like hearing that. That there is an "us."

Lexi stops. Turning me to face her, her eyes are surprisingly serious. "It's not too much, is it? I know this has been sudden, like we're kind of jumping from one end of the spectrum to the other, but …"

"But how do we hold back?" I finish for her. I can't lie. She can't lie to me. And she can see exactly what I'm thinking. There's no hiding, no holding back, no half-measures. When a telepath meets a walking polygraph, it's all or nothing. And that's totally fine with me.

Relaxing as I slip my arms around her waist, Lexi pulls me closer. She rests her cheek against my temple, rocking slightly as we stand there. That's all we do for a while, just stand there wrapped up in each other's arms, but damn. Right now it's enough. More than enough. It's everything.

Twenty-Three

Julian

Saturday, October 18 – 1:07 PM EDT

Every once in a while, I have a moment where it hits me how much has changed. Like right now, when I'm walking up the side of a steep, rocky hill in the chilly October air. A little less than five weeks ago, I was waking up in a hospital wondering if Lynnie would show up and why Orane had disappeared. Now I'm studying the confusing recesses of human psychology and sexuality thanks to Beth (and a stack of textbooks from eBay) and I have friends. Real, honest-to-Sinatra *friends*. Sure, my roommate still pulls his disappearing act whenever I walk into a room, but that only means I don't have to deal with muttered Russian insults.

It's *awesome*.

My sentry shift ended an hour ago, but after Beth checked in to take over, I walked up the side of the mountain toward a lookout I discovered last week. Luckily, by now everyone has pretty much accepted that I need time in the open air to keep myself sane. Usually I drag my watch partner with me, but Johanna finally gave me permission to wander alone as long as I swore to always carry the backpack of stones.

I reach a ledge that looks out over the valley. From here I can see the road leading from Alaster to Abra and, in the distance, the cluster of buildings that makes up the town. Especially now that the trees have begun to change color, the view is incredible. A riot of reds, browns, golds, and greens spread out in front of me. Sometimes I stand here and imagine building a glass-walled house right on this spot so I never have to leave.

It's been too long since I spoke to Pheodora (it took the last eighteen days for Johanna to relax her stringent adherence to the twenty-four-hour-a-day buddy system), so today I stuffed my backpack with an extra sweatshirt instead of the gemstones. A calculated risk that Pheodora will find me before a Balasura like Syver or Orane. The doorway opens and Pheodora appears before I even call for her, as if she was waiting for me to show up.

"I do not have much time, Julian. The crystals I gave you are not enough for what is coming." As she speaks, the ground in front of me ripples and a pile of the same matte-black crystals appears at my feet. "You must take these and do as you did before. Hide them as best you can."

"What's wrong?" I pull the sweatshirt out of the backpack and begin to place the crystals inside. "What's coming? And you still haven't told me what these *do*."

Pheodora shakes her head. "I cannot tell what is coming. There is a haze hanging over this place. Too many possibilities converging in one spot make the future unclear. It is a time of action and consequences. We must prepare as best we can to face anything."

My heart pounds harder and I grip the strap of the backpack tight.

"Events may unfold quickly now, Julian." She's frowning, but her eyes are lit up, glowing brightly in the shady woods. "You must be on guard."

"Against *what*?" I ask the question, but I don't get an answer. The mirrors behind her flash blue and white and red and black and the doorway closes faster than I've ever seen. I'm left standing in the woods staring at empty air with my mouth still hanging open.

What the heck just happened? And who is she running from? I hope it isn't Syver who has her on edge like this. The way Nadette talked about him made him seem utterly ruthless, capable of *anything*. As far as I can tell, whatever fight is brewing on their side of the doorway is getting closer. And bigger. And more dangerous. I hold my breath as I fill the rest of the backpack with Pheodora's crystals, sending up a silent prayer to anyone that might be listening. *Just let us get through this alive. Let us survive whatever is coming for us.*

Grinding my teeth as I exhale, I shake my head. Pheodora's tendency to leave before giving me answers is getting on my nerves.

I touch the zipper of the backpack to close it.

"Oww!"

Sparks jump from the bag to my fingertips. Actual *visible* sparks. The electric shock shoots up my arm, makes my entire body tingle, and completely derails my train of thought.

Wow, that was harsh. I shake out my hand, trying to get the feeling back. Static electricity, I guess. The air *is* getting drier. It's weird that the shock traveled so far that even my pendant seems warm against my skin, though.

Tentatively, I reach out to touch the bag again. This time it doesn't try to zap me into oblivion.

Whatever. I guess as annoying as Pheodora's vanishing act is, it's better than not getting the chance to check in with her at all. And it isn't like any other rebels are lining up to help us out. I have to take what Pheodora is able to do and hope it'll be enough.

I swing the bag over my shoulder and start walking, taking a meandering path that will eventually lead me back to Abra. The leaves crunch and slide under my feet as I climb, but I keep my eyes up, looking for sky through the canopy of the forest and the birds fluttering overhead, free and joyous as they twirl in the currents of air.

When I was a kid, I watched *Forrest Gump*. Jenny's prayer stuck in my head and played on loop for months. The repetitive plea to transform into a bird and escape the life fate had handed me.

I don't believe there is a God, but I whisper that prayer to myself every time I see a bird. Or I did until recently. Now, if I suddenly turned into a bird, I wouldn't go anywhere. I couldn't leave Abra or anyone in it behind. Especially Nadette.

It took me a while to accept that Beth may have been right (or mostly right, anyway) about the asexuality thing. It was watching Nadette and Lexi that made me realize what I felt for Nadette wasn't even close to what they felt for each other. It doesn't mean I don't love her in a different way, though. I could never leave her behind. She's the best friend I've ever had, and the reason I found this place.

I smile. For the first time in my life, I'm somewhere I don't want to escape from.

Stepping through a narrow space between two trees, I stumble backward when I find Vasha waiting for me.

"I'm not going to hurt you, *urod*," he mutters, his eyes on the forest floor.

"Sure, *mudak*." I take another step back. "That'd be a little more believable if I wasn't alone in the middle of the woods with a guy who enjoys threatening me in a foreign language."

His head doesn't move, but his eyes flick up to meet mine and his pale cheeks seem a tiny bit pink. "Good job learning it, by the way. No one else has ever bothered."

I blink. "Umm ... thanks?"

Vasha nods, his chin coming up a little more. "It's kind of stupid, right? That they didn't learn it, I mean. How hard is it for us? Elephant memories, Kelsey calls them, and no one else has bothered looking up Russian."

"Well, no one else thought you were threatening their lives in Russian either," I remind him. "I had more incentive than most."

This time he flinches, his eyes dropping closed and more color rising in his face. He's taller than me and older by a few years, but right now it doesn't feel like that. I have the most absurd urge to pat him on the head, tell him it's all right, and let bygones be gone. Except touching the guy who sparks (especially without getting his permission)? Yeah ... that isn't a good idea.

"I wasn't actually going to hurt you, you know." He says it in a quick, staccato burst of words as his head finally lifts and his eyes fully meet mine. Then he bites his lip and glances away like he's already regretting the outburst.

"That's good to know." I swallow, trying to wet my suddenly dry throat. "Though I'd recommend not threatening death by electrocution if you don't actually mean it. Just, you know ..." I wave a hand, trying to figure out what I want to say. "For future reference or whatever."

"Sorry." Vasha ducks his head again, his dark hair covering his eyes. "I'm still not used to being around people. Even after a year and a half. No one could be near me when I showed up because I kept fucking sparking and I just ..." He shrugs. "This is the only place I've come close to fitting in, and even the people here were scared of me. It's better now that I've got the random lightning bolts under control, but I still don't know how ... and then you show up glowing half-orange and telling us the Balasura know where we are. This place may not be much, but it's the only home I've got. I don't want you or anyone else fucking that up for us."

"It's fine." I take a deep breath and force myself to step closer. "I get it. I couldn't bring friends home because if they told their parents about my mom, social services would pay us a visit and then *boom*. Everything gone. I don't want to do that to anyone."

"Yeah." He clears his throat and shifts his weight, his feet shuffling slightly. "So, we good?"

"That'd be a nice change." His lip almost curves into a smile and I nod, a little knot of the tension I've been carrying around with me since Nadette and I showed up at Abra finally unraveling. "You gonna stop calling me *urod*?"

"You gonna stop calling me *mudak*?" he counters, his expression inching closer to a true smile.

"Only if you stop acting like one."

"We'll see. Just 'cause I'm not gonna kill you doesn't mean we're gonna be having slumber parties and painting each other's toenails."

I snort and smile back as we head toward Abra. "I'd be terrified if you even suggested it."

Just as I switch places with Clarke after my sentry shift on Monday, Nadette's voice makes me jump.

"Mind if we come with you today, Julian?"

I turn to find her and Lexi walking toward me, their hands tightly linked.

"Sometimes you're gone so long I start getting scared you're lost," Lexi says, smiling down at me from higher on the mountain.

"I do get lost sometimes," I admit. "But I like getting lost." I beckon them down, heading toward the ridge where I last met Pheodora. "You find the best spots when you aren't looking for them."

It's only a couple hundred yards from the sentry position, so it doesn't take long to reach. Even when I'm not alone and can't meet with Pheodora, I come here as often as I can. The view always calms me.

"This is cool." Lexi smiles and breathes in deep. I mimic her, savoring the pine and woodsmoke in the air. "I can see why you keep sneaking off."

"Just got to be willing to get lost to find them," I tell her. "It's really pretty at sunset when—"

"Ohmygod!" Nadette grabs my arm. I jump and look at her, but her eyes remain locked on the road below us. "Do you know cars, Julian? Is that a black 1969 Camaro SS with silver racing stripes?"

I squint my eyes. They usually have classic Camaros at the Vegas Auto Show. I can't be sure it's a '69 or an SS, but it's definitely an older-model Camaro. "Um, I don't know cars *that* well, but, yeah. I think so."

The car turns up the road that leads to Abra. Nadette gasps. "Holy shit!"

She jumps off the rocks, slipping but catching herself on a tree branch and sprinting up the steep hill.

"Nadie, wait!" Lexi shouts, running after her.

I catch up with Lexi, but Nadette's head start makes it impossible for either of us to reach her. She's *quick* when she wants to be.

"What's so special about a '69 Camaro?" I huff as we run. Something about that car either scared or excited Nadette. Maybe it was a little of both.

Lexi opens her mouth to answer, but we're running too hard. All that comes out is a breathless, wordless noise. She shakes her head and pushes faster.

Nadette reaches the clearing first and skids to a stop just as two people get out of the car.

The driver is a guy who somehow keeps getting taller and taller. Although he's not as broad as Clarke, I'm pretty sure he's a few inches taller than our resident giant. He's got buzzed-short white-blond hair and tons of scars on arms showcased by a short-sleeved shirt despite the forty-degree weather. But then I notice the girl on the other side of the car and my heart stops.

She has golden-blonde hair long enough to brush the back of her thighs, and golden-brown eyes. It's been years since I've seen her, but it doesn't matter. She looks exactly like her mother. Exactly the way I remember her.

My heart jumps. I blink again and again just to make sure my eyes aren't playing tricks on me. Mariella woke up. She's awake and she's *here*. Somehow she found me.

"How the hell did you get my grandfather's car?" Nadette shouts across the lot at them. Nadette's face is bright red and I can't tell if it's from the cold, the run, or her anger.

What? Her grandfather owns a '69 Camaro? That's kind of awesome.

The big guy doesn't look in the least surprised as he glances at Mari. She nods and he grins, turning back to us.

"Nadette?" His voice is deep, and the smile only highlights the scar on his chin and the other one along his hairline. Mari is here. And if Mari is here, this has to be Hudson, the boyfriend Frank told me about.

Nadette's head jerks back an inch and she looks at Lexi. Lexi shakes her head. I recognize the look on Lexi's face because she looked at me with the same furrowed-brow confusion the day we met. Wow. She can't read them either?

"How do you know my name?" Nadette asks slowly.

"I was with your grandfather, Horace, when he found out you'd run away," Hudson says. "Your family is pretty frantic. They're still looking for you."

"You came here looking for *me*?"

He shakes his head. "No. Didn't even know you were here."

Nadette's forehead wrinkles. "How did you find us then?"

"Aisling gave us directions," Mari says.

My entire body tenses. Holy Sinatra. She's awake, she's here, and she's *talking*? Her voice is exactly like I remember it from when we were little—musical even when she's talking. Her eyes are still locked on Nadette, but I can't wait any longer. I couldn't stop myself if I tried.

I step forward and Hudson's attention locks instantly on me. Even with his eyes blocked by dark sunglasses, I can *feel* it. Mari's gaze follows in the next second. And then her eyes widen.

"Mari?" I ask even though I've never been more sure of anything in my life.

"*Julian?*" she says at the same time.

I run across the clearing. Locking my arms around her waist, I pick her up, relief and adrenaline giving me extra strength. She's crazy thin and only a couple inches taller than me. She laughs and kicks until I put her down, but I can't believe it! She's here! She's here and she's okay!

"I thought you were in a coma!"

"And I thought you were hiding out in *Vegas!*"

"So is this place some magnet for runaways?" Hudson asks.

Mari laughs and looks up at the big blond. "Must be. Julian, this is my boyfriend Hudson."

The introduction confirms my guess, but what catches my attention more is how she says his name like it's something precious. That level of affectionate reverence is a strange emotion to attach to this giant. Up close, his scars are even worse, covering his arms and crossing over each other in layers. Some of them are clean and thin, but others are so warped and bumpy it seems like the skin must have nearly torn off his bones to look that pink and shiny and gross. But Mari's eyes sparkle when she looks up at him.

"Hudson," she says, resting her hand on his elbow and pulling him forward. "This is my cousin, Julian."

"Jacquelyn's runaway in the flesh," he says, smiling again. I look up into his face as he slides his sunglasses to the top of his head ... and I wish I hadn't.

His eyes are black. Horror movie black. Like someone replaced his eyeballs with two globes of oynx. Not even Aisling's eyes are as all-encompassingly dark as Hudson's. Hers are just the iris. Hudson's are black from corner to corner, top to bottom. I freeze, my jaw dropped and my heart skipping random beats, until Nadette's voice shatters the tension coiling in me.

"Wait ... Your name is Hudson? Hudson *Vincent?*" Her face flushes and her eyes get wide. Is she happy or scared?

Hudson glances at her and nods.

Emitting a squeaking squeal, Nadette rushes across the distance between them. Throwing her arms around his neck, she hangs on his neck and hugs him tight. "Thank you, thank you, thank you!"

Hudson looks happily stunned as he returns the hug, and next to me Mari is smiling. Nadette drops back to the ground and steps back to give him some space. Her voice has gone all shaky, but she's smiling. "I always wanted to meet you. Thank you in person. The whole family did. Grandpa never knew where you went after the trial."

"The last few months have been ..." Hudson looks away and shrugs, his left thumb tracing something on the inside of his right wrist.

"Nadette, you *know* him?" I finally have to ask.

"I never got to meet him, but ..." Nadette shakes her head, her eyes shining, "Hudson saved my grandfather's life."

Hudson opens his mouth, only to snap it shut and glance at Mari. He narrows his eyes, and she shakes her head. He raises an eyebrow and exhales. An entire conversation with words we couldn't hear. Is she like Lexi? Or is he? I'm even more grateful for the walls Pheodora helped me build now. The idea of anyone (even Mari) rooting around in my head makes my skin crawl.

"Speaking of Horace, you should really let him know you're okay," Hudson says a couple seconds later.

Nadette bites her lip and glances at Lexi. Whatever Lexi hears in her thoughts is enough for her to put her arm around Nadette's shoulders.

"She's still finding her footing," Lexi says. "Nadette was being tormented at home."

"Not by her family." Mari steps away from me and stands by Hudson's side as they face Lexi and Nadette together.

Suddenly I'm on the edge of a battlefield watching the lines being drawn in the sand.

Mariella stands with her feet apart and her hands in the pockets of her black leather jacket. The longer I watch her, the harder it is to look away. Is the air around her ... shimmering?

"They hired a private detective who traced her as far as New Jersey," Mari explains. "When he lost her trail, the police in Trenton started combing shelters and then bringing in dogs to search the parks for bodies. Your family *needs* to know you're okay, Nadette."

There's something different about Mari. Something magnetic. Listening to her voice is soothing and even before the meaning of her words has time to filter through my brain, I find myself believing what she says. Agreeing with her. I feel it, but I notice it and can take a step back. I'm aware of it. Because of Pheodora's walls? Or because, according to the Balasura, I have the same skill—to *make* people believe me.

I look closer and try to pick out other differences. The more I notice, the more I realize I don't know the girl standing in front of me. Her eyes seem to take in everything even when they're staring straight ahead and she's standing so still it seems unnatural.

The Mari I knew was always in motion. She always had a plan or a game or a story, and she always dragged you into it whether you wanted to join or not. Maybe it's just the years that have passed, but something has changed in her. My heart clenches when I think of Orane. If it screwed with *my* head, what must it have done to hers? I'm used to people abandoning me. Betraying me. Mari isn't.

"I hurt Linus," Nadette whispers. My chest tightens in sympathy when she shakes her head and wraps her arms tight around herself. "They should stay away."

"Linus wants to see you more than any of them," Mari says. "He feels responsible for your disappearance. He'll never forgive himself if something happens to you."

"You've seen him?" Nadette steps forward, drawn toward the mention of her family.

"No, I haven't."

"Then how do you know what … ?"

Mari and Hudson glance at each other again, another silent conversation passing between them.

"It's complicated," Mari says. "I've picked up a slew of useless junk, and I'm still trying to sort it all out."

Before Nadette can ask another question, Hudson cuts her off.

"Can we at least call Horace?" Hudson asks, pulling out a cell phone. "I don't feel right keeping this from him."

She hesitates, but I already know the pull of family will be too strong for her to resist. And why shouldn't it be? Nadette actually has a family who cares about her. They sent out private detectives and police looking for her. Lynnie would never care enough to do that for me.

"It's too dangerous." Nadette takes a deep breath, her body shaking as she releases it. "If I leave, the Balasura will find me. Syver will go after my family again. He threatened my nieces!"

"Then you won't leave. Horace will come here in a heartbeat to see you," Hudson says. His phone beeps as he brings up a phone number and shows it to Nadette. "Can I call him?"

At the first hint of acquiescence, Hudson presses "call."

Nadette's family loves her. If they try to take her home, will she go? If she does, Syver will come for her. She won't be safe.

And she'll be gone …

"Nadette is okay," Hudson says seconds later. Even from a few feet away, I can hear the shouting on the other side of the phone. Hudson cringes and holds the phone away from his ear, but he's smiling a little. I shudder and look away. His smile reminds me of a shark.

"Do you want to talk to her or are you just gonna keep yelling at me, old man?"

Nadette takes the phone when he holds it out, her voice octaves higher than usual when she squeaks, "Grampa?"

She walks away from the group, the phone pressed tight to her ear.

"Aunt Jacquelyn isn't doing too great either, Juli."

I jump and my pulse takes off. Mariella is standing less than a foot away, watching me. Guess I was so locked on Nadette, I didn't notice her moving closer. Her expression is carefully neutral (expert poker face neutral) except for the tightness around her eyes. That little bit of tension reminds me of the look Lexi gave her earlier. It feels like she's staring at me and trying to figure something out. She's studying my face and the air around my body (the lightshow I still can't see, probably). I don't like it. And I don't like that nickname either. Never could get her to stop using it, though.

I snort derisively and shake my head. "She got evicted again, didn't she? Lynnie never remembers to pay rent on time." Or at all.

"Yeah, but she's had everyone she knows out looking for you. She never thought you'd leave the city," Mari says. "For the first week she was convinced that you were at a friend's house, hiding out to punish her for something. After she tracked down the guys you played poker with and the kids you knew from school, she called my dad. He talked her into calling the police to report you missing."

"*Lynnie* called the *cops?*" Even if Frank told her to, it's hard to believe. She hates the cops.

"At least consider calling her, Juli." Mari smiles, her gaze straying toward Nadette and back to me. "Even if you don't tell her where you are, let her know you're safe."

I'm about to agree when Mariella tenses, her head whipping toward the treeline. It's a good ten seconds before I see what caught her attention. Johanna, Clarke, Tanner, Sarah, Beth, and about six others are spread out along the higher ground between us and Abra.

Hudson comes up behind Mari, one of his huge hands circling her waist and his dark eyes trained on the newcomers. Out the corner of my eye, I watch Lexi's eyes lock on Johanna as she moves closer to Nadette, who still hasn't noticed the tension growing in the air.

Johanna signals to everyone else to stay put and she steps forward, walking slowly down the hill.

"It's not often we get visitors," she says, her stare switching between Mari and Hudson.

"Not surprising." Mariella steps forward a few feet, Hudson close behind her.

"It's also not often our seer overlooks unexpected guests." Johanna stops a few feet back, her arms crossed over her chest.

Mari shrugs. "I'd apologize for that if it was in any way my fault."

Johanna hesitates for a second, then nods. Her expression is still too serious. Too tight. I don't think she trusts Mari. She definitely doesn't like another set of people finding Alaster without Aisling's guidance. If I don't do something, Beth may end up rearranging their memories and sending them on their way.

"Johanna, this is my cousin, Mariella. I told you about her when I came here, remember?"

Johanna's eyes widen. "You came out of the coma?"

Mari nods. "After a month. It wasn't a coma. Not really." She smiles and looks around at everyone. "Are we getting an invite in or not? We drove across the state to find you guys."

"I can vouch for Hudson," Nadette says, putting her phone call on hold. "He saved my grandfather's life a few years ago."

Johanna takes it all in, her brown eyes studying me, Nadette, Mariella, and Hudson in turn before she slowly nods.

"All right. No promises, but we can go inside to hear you out."

My chest is buzzing with an uncomfortable, nervous energy. Mari's here. She's safe. I should be excited, but I'm not.

Why do I feel as though the storm we've been waiting for has just appeared on the horizon?

Twenty-Four

Nadette

Monday, October 20 – 3:15 PM EDT

Not since the night Julian and I arrived have so many of us been in the same room. Everyone is always too busy. They have jobs in town and chores and sentry shifts and hobbies. We even eat meals in shifts. Today, Mariella and Hudson's arrival brings in *everyone*.

Mariella is strikingly pretty, with thick golden hair and large doe eyes. The thing I can't take my eyes off of is the slight difference in the blue light that surrounds her. The glow is the same cerulean shade as everyone else's, but Mariella's has more depth. It sparkles like the glint of a well-cut gemstone under jewelry-store lights.

"So are we really doing storytime?" Mariella asks. "Mine might take longer than you think."

"What? Why? How old were you when they first showed up?" Vasha demands.

Mariella looks at Vasha, only the smallest twitch in her expression giving away her stress. "Eight."

More than one person sucks in a horrified breath. Even Vasha's normal scowl fades. "*Eight?*"

Eyes flashing and jaw tight, Mari nods. "Yes, eight. But everything relevant to this conversation happened in the last two months."

Hudson takes her hand and runs his thumb over her knuckles. As soon as he touches her, a little of the tension eases out of her shoulders. She glances at him. I recognize that look, the conversation without words happening between them. I've seen it on Lexi's face a lot in the past month. Lexi might not be able to read Hudson's thoughts, but

Mariella definitely can. Mari takes a breath and shakes herself out a little. Her grip on Hudson's hand gets so tight her knuckles turn white.

"Right." Her lips twitch into a smirk as she looks up at him. "I think we can skip over the intervening years. Start where things get interesting. That's your cue, isn't it?"

Hudson's smile gets tight. He runs his free hand over his close-cropped white-blond hair. Whatever he's thinking makes Mariella press a kiss to his arm. A twitch of his lip, a breath, and he plunges forward. As though saying it fast will make it easier.

"Calease showed up when I was fourteen. I'd been on my own for two years." He holds out one arm, twisting it to show us the scars that cover his skin. "Couldn't keep my ass out of trouble, so my parents kicked me out."

"At *twelve?*" Beth asks as though she's not sure she believes him. Everyone here has a sob story of one variety or another, but few of them were jettisoned from their homes that young.

My skin feels cold. This is a piece of his story I never knew before. *Damn.* Grampa Horace told us the kid who saved him was in a rough place, but I never knew it was *this* bad.

I poke Beth, glaring when she turns around. "Let him talk. I'll tell you if he's lying."

Lexi puts a hand on my shoulder and pulls me closer to her. "Relax," Lexi whispers, kissing my cheek. "They'll listen."

Well, they will now, I silently tell her.

Up front, Hudson smiles at me before he picks up where he left off.

"A few months before I met Calease, I saved this old man, Horace—Nadette's grandfather—from becoming the wrong end of a gang initiation ritual."

I stiffen and lean forward. I feel everyone's attention shift toward me. This wasn't part of the story I told them that first night. I didn't think it mattered at the time.

I can still remember visiting my grandfather in the hospital. He was so bloody and bruised. Those three assholes almost killed him. They *would have* killed him if Hudson hadn't been there. He saved Horace, and then his testimony helped send them to prison. Gramps wanted to return the favor, help Hudson out of trouble and off the streets, but Hudson disappeared.

"Calease made me promise not to fight and I listened to her for four years. Until my past caught up with me one day." Hudson shifts incrementally closer to Mariella.

"Were you out on your own that whole time?" Tanner asks, his eyes wide.

Hudson blinks, almost like he forgot we were here, and shakes his head. "About six months after I met Calease, she gave me a glass pendant—this olive-branch wreath. That's when I made the promise. Everything started getting better. My parents let me come back. I got to meet my little brother, J.R. He was just a baby then."

Mariella rubs his arm. Her hand looks incredibly small on his bicep. The more Mariella strokes Hudson's scarred skin, the easier he seems to breathe. But the pain etched into his face and those demonically black eyes doesn't ease much. When he starts talking again, I know why.

"The guys who beat Horace?" His head tilts toward me, but for less than a second "They got out of juvie in April this year." Hudson's voice is dead. Already low, now he sounds almost as inflectionless as Julian. "They came looking for me. Only took 'em a few weeks to find me. It wasn't hard because I didn't know I should've been hiding. I couldn't remember who they were, but I knew they weren't there to thank me for something. They attacked, and J.R. caught a switchblade meant for me." He swallows and closes his eyes. "He was only four."

The room is silent and still except for the crackling of the fires. My grip on Lexi's hand tightens. He's telling the truth, but holy shit. I wish he wasn't. His brother died because Hudson helped my grandfather? If Horace knows that, it must be killing him.

Hudson shrugs like he doesn't notice the tension hanging in the air. "I was willing to break my promise to Calease that day, but when I tried—"

He may pretend to be unaffected, but I can see his throat convulsing as he tries to keep speaking. And I see the concern in Mariella's eyes. She's not watching us anymore. Her attention is entirely focused on Hudson. Her head tilts back to watch his face. Still holding his hand, she wraps her other hand around his forearm and holds tight.

"But when you tried you suddenly couldn't move or think or breathe and you had to watch your worst nightmare unfold in front of your eyes," Sarah says, her face pale and her eyes wide.

Hudson stares at her for a second and nods. "Yeah."

It takes him a second to start up again. Mariella slides closer, wrapping her arms around his waist and tucking herself under his arm. She's about a foot shorter than Hudson. She looks tiny in comparison, but somehow it seems like Mari is what's holding him up and keeping him going.

After a shuddering breath, Hudson says, "I went in to Abivapna that night and—"

"What's Abivapna?" Johanna asks.

Hudson and Mariella both turn toward Johanna, their heads cocked at almost identical angles. Mari is the one who says, "You didn't know that's what the Balasura call their world."

"That's what *they* call it? How did you—Wait a second." Tanner's jaw drops. "Did you say you *went in?*"

Three other people shush him before I can. Hudson looks at Tanner, talking directly to him as he says, "I went in and got everything back. My memories *and* the ability she tried to steal. Just ..." He looks down at Mariella. Another silent conversation happens before our eyes. "Kind of lost my temper and tried to strangle her. That olive-wreath pendant Calease gave me was in my hand and it linked us. I pulled out a lot more than what she took from me." He waves a hand over his face. "Hence the eyes."

"You touched her?" Johanna is standing in the back of the room, her arms crossed and her eyes narrow. "You went *in* to the dream wo—to Abivapna? After realizing the Balasura were full of shit. Then you *touched* one of them and somehow made it out *alive?*"

Hudson raises an eyebrow. "Yeah."

"Why didn't you just break the pendant?" Kelsey asks.

Hudson and Mari glance at each other. This time it's Mari who answers. "We didn't know that was an option."

Vasha snorts. "That's the first thing I tried. No way in *hell* was I going back in there."

"Is that what you did too? Go back in there?" Tanner asks Mariella.

"Like I said, we didn't know there was any other option."

There are murmured conversations circling through the group, but no one seems able to raise their voices loud enough to ask another question or disturb the strange tension hovering over us all. Mari's gaze takes it all in, scanning over everyone, until she takes a breath deep enough to shift her shoulders under her leather jacket. The she starts talking.

"Orane found me when I was eight, so he knew he had plenty of time to wait. He dug into my head and completely screwed with my mind. He hid memories and edited my entire childhood." She presses closer to Hudson—the motion so small it's almost imperceptible. "He took happy years and made me think I'd spent them miserable, mistreated, and alone. He made me forget the people I grew up with and everyone who loved me. Anyone who might help me."

"What about your parents?" Julian asks, confusion and sadness obvious in his voice. "I saw you when you were, what? Eleven? Everything seemed fine. You remembered them and me."

She smiles at her cousin. "I did remember you. I never forgot my parents, either—I couldn't, honestly. I saw them every day and they aren't the kind of parents to let themselves fade into the background." Mariella purses her lips slightly. "It was more gradual than that. And it didn't get horrible until I was fourteen. That's when I promised Orane I'd stop talking entirely."

"Whoa." Beth opens her mouth and then closes it, shaking her head. "I think I would have failed that on day one."

"I know I would've," Kelsey says.

"It was hard," Mari agrees, "but Orane was basically in complete control of my head by then." Her grip on Hudson noticeably tightens and their gazes meet. Mariella takes a long breath and she seems to draw the strength to keep going from Hudson.

"Hudson found me two weeks before my eighteenth birthday. He had a dream telling him to come to Swallow's Grove, the town I live in. He moved there with your grandfather, Nadette," she says, her eyes locking on me. "After Hudson moved to town, he had another dream. One where he saw me burning alive."

"Prophetic dreams?" Kelsey asks. Hudson nods and she sighs, dropping her chin on her hand. "Those suck sometimes."

Mari nods. "He showed up and basically barged into my life with enough amethyst and malachite and black jade to open up a chain of New Age stores until he could force me to listen to what he had to say." Her lips quirk up when she looks at him. Hudson squeezes her tighter against him. "He tried everything he could think of to convince me Orane was a bastard, but I couldn't believe him. Orane literally wiped the uncertainty from my mind every time the doubts surfaced. For that whole first week Hudson was in Swallow's Grove, I thought I was losing my mind. It felt like I'd lost *weeks* of my life."

I shudder. I don't like thinking about what any of the people here have survived, but what Mariella is describing literally sounds like Hell. To have someone so deep inside your head that they can control what you think and what you believe? So deep that you can't ever question your reliance on them? Never ever see their lies? I can't even imagine it. I don't want to.

"Finally Hudson followed me into Abivapna one night to prove Orane was lying to me."

"You went in *again?*" Sarah asks.

Hudson nods toward Mari. "Twice with her."

Jesus. I think I'm the only person in the room who doesn't know what it's like to step through that fiery archway into another world or dimension or universe or what-the-hell-ever. I shudder now, thinking about the possibility. Pressing closer to Lexi, I try to soak up her warmth and her calm.

"I saw what was happening to her—it was like a war zone in the lights surrounding Mari, but getting her to actively fight …" He trails off, his expression going bleak for a second. "That was the hard part."

"So, wait … your eyes are because of the Balasura, right?" someone asks Hudson. "What can you see exactly?"

For a couple minutes, Hudson talks about what he calls vision filters, different ways of looking at the world that show him the energy left over from Abivapna, let him magnify the world like he's looking through binoculars, and even one that lets him see a person's soul.

We're all stunned, but Hudson runs his hand along Mariella's arm and shrugs. "Those were easy. It was trying to figure out how to deal with all the other shit that sucked."

There are a couple beats of silence as those words sink in. I can't not ask, though. "What other shit?"

Mariella's eyes narrow and she glances around the room. Her eyes rest on each person for a fraction of a second. Then she sighs and drops her head against Hudson's chest, muttering something I can't hear.

"Wait—none of you have more than *one?*" Hudson asks.

"One what?" Johanna demands.

"Ability. Power. Whatever the hell you want to call it." Hudson's eyes are wide open. I still can't see any whites. They really are *entirely* black.

"Of course we don't." Johanna raises an eyebrow. "You're saying you do?"

Mariella starts laughing, but it's a little hysterical. Hudson looks pale.

"Uh, yeah." He glances at Mari and back at Johanna. "Finally figured it out last week. I ended up with eight."

"How is that even *possible?*" Johanna's hands drop to her hips, her face tight. "There's no way you'd be able to survive with that much locked inside your head!"

"Oh, that's nothing." Mariella finally stops laughing. Pushing her ridiculously long hair out of her face, she straightens, a grim smile on her lips. "I have twenty-three."

"You're joking."

Mari shakes her head. "I can also speak and read twenty languages. Just to make it weirder."

Johanna glances at me. I swallow, trying to beat back the dryness in my mouth. "They're telling the truth."

Johanna's bronze skin is almost white. She's trying to hide it, but her hands are shaking. She doesn't like being wrong. Or dealing with the unknown. Now she's facing two living examples of something she thought was impossible.

"What happened to you?" Johanna asks Mari. Only the slightest tremor in her voice confirms her fear. "How did you end up with all that?"

"We loaded up on crystals and stones and went in on her birthday." Hudson looks down at Mari, his lips thin and his eyes focused on her necklace. "Which I never would've made her do if I knew all I had to do was take a hammer to the fucking thing."

I can't see Mariella's pendant from here, but I *can* tell that it doesn't have the orange glow Peter's did. If that's the necklace Orane gave her, it's not connected to the Balasura anymore.

Mari pats his cheek. I can't tell if it's a gesture of reassurance or telling him to hush. "Our plan worked. We just weren't prepared for what would happen when it did." She holds her breath and lets it out in a quick *whoosh*. "We thought I had to do what Hudson had done— touch the Balasura with the pendant between us. When I did and I pulled out what he'd taken from me, it was like …"

"It was like the entire world imploded," Hudson finishes for her.

"It did." Johanna's voice has more than a little ice in it now. "Did you know your cousin in *Vegas* ended up in the hospital because of his connection to Orane?"

"Hey!" From the back of the room near Johanna, Julian protests, wide-eyed. "Leave me out of this, I'm glad she—"

"*And* Nadette! The blowback from whatever you did hurt her, too," Johanna says, ignoring Julian. "And those are just the ones we know about. If this demon was as powerful as it seems, do you even know how many people you hurt with that stunt?"

Mari's eyes widen and her head snaps toward Julian. "You were in the hospital, Juli?"

"Frank didn't tell you?" Julian stuffs his hands deep into the pockets of his jeans. "Uh, yeah. I saw the end of whatever happened between you and Orane and then I blacked out. I was in the hospital for a weekend. They couldn't figure out what was wrong."

"Yeah. They didn't know what happened to me, either." She swallows and smiles, but it's a tight, sad smile. "I was unconscious for a month because my head overloaded. Everything I took out of Abivapna was too much. It took that long to figure out how to get it to work together enough for my mind to work without exploding."

Johanna steps closer. "That doesn't make what you did okay."

Hudson stiffens. Mari's eyes narrow and her voice is as harsh as her expression when she speaks. "I'm sorry, but is there some rule book you have that I never got? 'Cause I thought this was a figure-it-out-as-you-go kind of thing." Johanna opens her mouth. Mari cuts her off. "If you don't like the way I saved my own life, tough shit. You should have been the one to teach me how to do it. We worked with what we had."

Her face flushes, but Johanna doesn't say a word. At least, not about that. "How did you find Alaster?"

Mariella relaxes. Hudson doesn't.

"Did you know that this is the only town in the state to go without a single welfare recipient, social services case, or crime report for the past ten years?" Mariella asks, one eyebrow raised. "Add that to the fact that the local New Age store is the base of operations for the most highly regarded blog on the internet for information on the paranormal, and a few alarms start going off if you know what you're looking for."

Johanna crosses her arms. "How did you convince Aisling to give you directions to Abra?"

Mari glances at Hudson and back at Johanna, confused. "We asked nicely?"

"Can we go back to the beginning for a second?" Everyone looks at Tanner, but his eyes are on Hudson. "You barely survived your own run-in with these things and you went looking for more of them? Are you suicidal or something?"

"Not anymore." His expression is dead serious, before it splits into a smirk. "Though I don't think I'd have an easy time killing myself now even if I wanted to."

Tanner's eyes narrow. "What do you mean?"

With a quick glance at Mari, Hudson reaches into his jeans, pulls out a pocket knife, and draws the blade across his forearm. Mariella sighs as blood runs down his hand and drips onto the stone floor. With a flick of her hand, a roll of paper towels flies across the room toward her. By the time she's torn a few sheets off and passed them to Hudson, the blood has stopped flowing. When he holds up his arm, there isn't even a scar. Not a new one, anyway.

"He's even better than Kyle," Clarke says.

"Shut up," Kyle mutters from the back of the room.

"Can only heal myself." Hudson wipes off the rest of the blood and bends down to clean it off the floor. "Mari's the one who can heal everyone else."

Beth laughs. "Jesus. Telekinetic *and* healer. That's two. What else can you do?"

Mariella brings up her hand. Energy crackles in her palm, a blue-white orb of electricity building there. Her wrist twitches. The energy turns into fire. She flips her hand over, like she's bouncing a basketball. The flames crash to the floor, dissipating into a poof of smoke that changes colors and swirls up with a motion of Mari's hand. When the smoke clears, it looks like a tiny tree is growing out of the stone floor. Only the slight red haze hovering over it tells me it's an illusion.

Holy shit. My eyes bug out and the air leaves my lungs in one gust. Electricity, pyrokinesis, illusions, telepathy, telekinesis, and healing. And that's only a *part* of what she can do? Hell. And I thought my bells were hard to deal with.

"*What?*" Sarah's exclamation shatters the tension in the room.

Julian laughs, a huge grin spreading across his face. "Mari, you'd make a killing in Vegas."

She smirks. Even Hudson relaxes a little. "I'll keep that in mind," she says. The break in the stress doesn't last long. After only a second or two of silence, Mari sighs. "Orane spent a few thousand years trying to turn himself into the perfect weapon. He used the talents he gathered against the kids he stalked and the other Balasura."

Her smile is gone. It's like she's staring at all of us at the same time, her attention somehow focused on every single person in the room.

"The thing is, their war isn't with us. We're pawns in the battles they've been fighting among themselves for millennia. Orane was one of the leaders." She lifts her hand, this time pressing her palm out like she's touching a pane of glass. The air in front of her and Hudson sparkles. I hear the faint buzzing of electricity. It looks like the shield Clarke can create. "That's how I ended up with all of this when we took him out."

Julian gets up and walks across the room to Johanna, then whispers something in her ear. She nods, her eyes flicking toward Tanner, who is already watching them closely. When she jerks her head toward Julian, Tanner gets up. I follow his path, blinking when he and Julian leave the room. Where are they going?

"Julian offered to go talk to Aisling," Lexi whispers. "He knows Johanna won't trust them until she confirms Mariella's story."

Makes sense. Johanna knows I can't lie to her, but she's not one to cut corners. If there's a way for her to triple-check, she will.

Mariella's eyes follow Julian, but her expression is blank.

"What do you want from us?" Johanna walks forward, her arms crossed. "Protection? You went and stirred up the hornets' nest and expect us to hide you?"

"No." Mari meets her stare for stare. "We have plenty of stones. My house is as fortified as I can make it."

Johanna blinks, but that's the only surprise she shows. "So why are you here?"

"We need information. And volunteers, if anyone is willing."

"Volunteers?" Johanna's jaw tightens.

Mari nods. "My best friend K.T. has an older sister named Emily who's been in a coma for four years. There's also a neurologist named Lucas Carroll whose twin brother, Jamie, has been in a coma for almost a decade."

She looks away from Johanna, her eyes carefully scanning the rest of her audience.

"Dr. Carroll has started working on a way to track down the Balasura through their connection to the comatose victims. If we can get enough information about how this all works, we might be able to find a way to break the link to Abivapna and wake them up. All of them."

Twenty-Five

Julian

Monday, October 20 – 3:32 PM EDT

Tanner and I take the tunnel on the north wall of the kitchen, the longer route that Anya claimed as her canvas. Ever since she started painting here, its status as an off-limits route slowly vanished. I think only Johanna and Clarke refuse to use it. There's more art than only the first painting Beth showed me now, a lot more, but I pause when I reach that first one, staring at it and letting the colors wash over me. Calm me. New shapes rise up out of the swirl (like Mari standing next to her giant of a boyfriend) and I can't keep the smile off my face.

I have to run to catch up with Tanner.

"Bold move," he says once we're out of Abra.

Tanner looks at me, *really* looks at me, and I try not to fidget. He's like the ultimate spy. He's got vision better than an eagle's and hearing more sensitive than a bat's. All of his senses are amped up like crazy and he's good at using them to his advantage. Tanner can hear your pulse and smell your fear. He's almost twenty-eight, two years older than Johanna, and he's been in control of those super-senses for eleven years. By now he's so good at reading people's expressions and pulses and scents that his power is almost as scarily intrusive as Lexi's. And I have no way to block Tanner. It didn't matter when I first arrived in Abra, but now I have secrets. Every time I'm in the same room as Tanner I feel like those secrets are written on my forehead with Lynnie's over-bright red lipstick.

"What do you mean?" I force myself to ask.

"Offering to spy on your own cousin, kid. That's pretty ballsy."

I shake my head as we walk along the path to the clearing. "I'm not spying. I want to make sure Johanna doesn't freak and kick her out. Mari's family."

"We're all family here," Tanner says after a second. "What the Balasura did to us means a lot more than shared genetics."

I snort. "Trust me. You guys are already more important to me than Lynnie ever was, but Mari's different. She needs this place. I want to make sure she gets to stay."

Tanner claps my shoulder. "Fair enough. Let's go prove your cousin isn't a liar."

His backpack of crystals and stones clacks as he shifts it higher on his shoulder. I shift mine. It's *way* too light. *Oh no.* I screwed up and grabbed the decoy, the one with only a sweatshirt stuffed inside it.

Crap. Biting my lip, I cross my fingers and hope that Tanner doesn't notice. The stones he's carrying plus the ones in the car should be enough to protect us both, but it'll be almost impossible for me to explain how I managed to leave Abra with an empty backpack.

I hold my breath and follow him through the forest.

The store seems empty when we enter. The tinkling of the wind chime tied to the door blends with the music playing in the background, but otherwise the whole room is quiet and still.

"Tanner I expected, but I would've bet money on Jojo sending Clarke with him." It's Aisling's voice, but I don't see her. Then her blue head pops up over the shelves in the back of the store where it looks like she might be reorganizing a display.

"Hey, Ace." Tanner crosses over to her and presses a kiss to her cheek. I can't believe she lets him. Not only lets him, but smiles. "You're looking pretty as ever."

Aisling pats his cheek. "You're a good kid. When are you going to take my advice and move on with your life? Stop letting her string you along like this."

Tanner shakes his head. "I'm hopeless. Give up on me."

"Such a waste." Aisling *tsks* and shakes her head, but her attention turns to me soon enough. "Did you volunteer or something?"

"Yes."

Her eyes widen a little and I smile. I surprised her. That's a new one. I have a feeling Aisling isn't often surprised.

"Came down to hear my version of events?" Aisling rolls her eyes and goes back to rearranging the display. "I kinda hoped Jojo would stop this whole triple-checking thing now that Sparkles is there."

"You know Johanna," Tanner says. "She's nothing if not thorough."

I wander toward the back of the store, running my fingers along the shelves and holding my breath, waiting for Aisling's answer.

"Well, whatever Mariella said is true."

The air rushes out of me and I grin. I knew Mari was telling the truth, but for Aisling to say *that*? That's huge.

Tanner raises an eyebrow. "That's a lot of trust to place in someone who just showed up out of nowhere."

"You want specifics?" Aisling sets the last little glass figure on the shelf and strides toward the register. "They found me through the blog, showed up all glowing blue, and said pretty things."

I follow her to the front of the store. "You run a blog?"

"Not *a* blog, *the* blog." Aisling clicks a couple things on the computer and swings the screen around to show me a mostly white blog with "The Mystical Demystified" written across the top in bold letters. "It's *supposed* to be anonymously run, but Mari and Hudson are, what? The third and fourth people to find me through that damn website in the past year? At least Valari and Willem didn't ever intend on sticking around."

"It's technology, Ace. Not magic," Tanner says. "We did what we could, but hackers will always find a way around firewalls and decoys."

Aisling smacks the monitor back into place. "Whatever." She keeps clicking. "They found me through the blog, showed up trying to find survivors, and I sent them up to Jojo. That's about it."

"You couldn't have sent up a warning first?" Tanner asks. "You know how Jo—"

Aisling clicks something and the volume of the speakers cranks to full blast. I flinch, but Tanner slaps his hands over his ears and screams, "Shut it off!"

"I hate computers!" Aisling smacks the monitor again.

Tanner is pale as he drops his hands. His voice is too loud when he says, "Let's not do that again, okay?"

"Sorry. I was just trying to switch songs," she mutters. "Pressed the wrong button."

I try to force the conversation back on track. "So you gave Mari directions to Abra. Right?"

"Yup." Aisling glances at me. "Are you disappointed or relieved?"

"What? Relieved. Definitely relieved." Mariella needs to stay where I can keep an eye on her. And where she can help me protect Nadette and the others if anything happens. "Now Johanna doesn't have an excuse to kick her out. You know how much she values your opinion."

"We'll see if that's true this time." I expected sarcasm, but Aisling's serious expression reminds me of her face when she mentioned waiting. Waiting for the right person to show up. Does she think Mari might be that somebody? Before I can ask, Aisling keeps talking. "Tell Johanna to listen to these two, all right?"

"We'll tell her, right, Tanner?"

We both glance at Tanner, but he's shaking his head like he's trying to get water out of his ears. He blinks when he sees us both watching him and shouts, "What?"

"Never mind!" I shout back. That music blast must've been worse for him than I thought. He better not try to contradict me when I give Johanna a recap. I take a breath and open my mouth to say goodbye—

And then the world jumps.

It's just a second (less than that, maybe) but it's as though everything around me is slowing down, slowing, slowing … slowing … moving with the implacable patience of a tree's growth. Colors get brighter. Details stand out, like the small scratches in the glass display counter and the slightly glittery specks of dust in the air. The purpurite pendant warms up against my skin.

It's just a second, a hiccup, and then it's gone. Whatever "it" was. I think I might be the only one who noticed, but then Aisling's eyes narrow and her head tilts like she heard something she can't quite place. Shivering a little, confusion in her eyes, Aisling grabs a jacket from below the register and slips it on.

"You felt that?" I ask before I can stop myself.

Aisling pulls back a little, her expression guarded. "Felt what?"

"That…I don't know. Whatever just happened." She keeps staring at me and I fidget under the sudden weight of the silence. Taking a breath, I ease toward the door. "Never mind. Must've been my mind playing tricks on me or something. I should get Tanner back to Abra." I touch Tanner's arm and point toward the door. He nods, still poking at his ear.

I expect Aisling to stop me, to call me back, but she doesn't.

"Don't forget to tell Jojo what I said." Aisling sounds distracted. When I look back at her, her fingertips are rubbing circles on her temples like she's fighting off a headache.

"I will," I promise as we leave.

"Jesus. I don't think I'm gonna hear right for a week," Tanner mutters as we walk toward the car. "My head is still ringing."

I follow slower, taking a few seconds to enjoy the feeling of having sky over my head instead of stone. A bird screeches, something that sounds like a hawk or some other kind of hunter, and a smaller bird shoots out from one of the trees, streaking across the pale blue sky. Right over my head, it stops.

The pause is longer this time, more than a blink but less than a second. Pressure builds against my ears as though I've suddenly climbed a few thousand feet. Sound doesn't stop, but it warps and distorts like I'm hearing it through a wall or six feet of water. The sunlight is tinted orange, casting a fiery glow on the world.

And then it's done. Gone. And no one else seems to have seen a thing. The breeze kisses my cheek with icy lips, the birds serenade me from the trees lining Main Street, and Tanner continues poking at his ear and muttering to himself, apparently oblivious.

Tanner glances over his shoulder and stops when he notices I'm not following him. "Julian? Everything okay?" His voice is still too loud. Overcompensating. "You look freaked."

I take a breath. It rattles in my chest, my lungs squeezing as though my heart is suddenly taking up too much space. I should tell him. I should.

When I open my mouth, the words don't come. My throat locks and I realize I don't know what to say. What do I say happened when I don't *know* what happened?

"I'm fine," I yell so he can hear me.

I just wish I could convince myself.

Twenty-Six

Nadette

Monday, October 20 – 5:06 PM EDT

"You're impossible," Johanna says after the umpteenth demonstration of Mariella's skills. Sound manipulation this time, making us all believe a full-blown orchestra was playing somewhere nearby. Only the extra bells that were slightly out of sync with the rest of the music told me it was a lie. Johanna doesn't seem thrilled that someone else's illusions are better than hers. "Someone like you shouldn't be able to exist. Not in human form."

"Uh, no? Because ..." Mariella puts her hands on either side of her head, patting herself like she's checking to make sure she's real. "Yeah. I'm here. Obviously not impossible."

I glance at Lexi. She's biting her lip and fidgeting with the folds of her red skirt. Her eyes dart around the room, jumping from face to face as she follows their thoughts. I scoot closer. The room is getting tenser, the stress gathering in the air like static electricity that could spark at the wrong word.

The voice that dares break the silence isn't one I expected to hear.

"Were you serious about what you said? About waking the others up?" Beth asks.

Mari turns slightly to face her, but Hudson keeps his attention on the other side of the room. Like he's worried we'll attack if he lets down his guard.

"Of course I was serious." Johanna's mouth opens like she's about to spout more protests. Mariella's expression hardens. "Don't you *dare* tell me I can't help them. Just in my small town, there are *two* people who need us. It's been four years for K.T.'s sister Emily. It's been a *decade* for Dr. Carroll's brother. What makes them so worthless to you? Why are their families, who have done *nothing* wrong, not worth helping? And what the sun-dappled hell makes *you* the one who gets to make that decision?"

Johanna's body tenses, and the jingling of the metal charms on her bracelet gives away the tremor in her hands. Her voice is calm, almost dead, when she speaks. "And then what? So *what* if you wake them up? The Balasura are *immortal*. They'll keep coming after—"

"After we're dead and rotting and gone. That's why we're not just figuring out how to wake everyone up." Johanna's mouth snaps shut at Mariella's words. From the stillness around me, I don't think I'm the only one holding my breath. "We want to find a way to shut down the borders between our worlds forever. We want to make sure this can't ever happen again."

No one speaks. No one moves. I still can't hear anyone breathing.

Mariella looks as us like we're a math problem she can't figure out how to solve. "Isn't that worth it? Aren't there some things that mean more than hiding? Than just *surviving* for however long your lives last?"

"Goddammit." Johanna's chin drops to her chest. She runs her hands over her short hair, her shoulders shaking. "Do you know how much work it's taken to set this place up? There were only four other people here when Aisling brought me to Alaster ten years ago. Four. And two of them? What happened with the Balasura and their families was just—" She cuts herself off and shudders, a visceral full-body tremble. "Something broke in Kathy and we couldn't fix it. She almost destroyed this entire sanctuary when she took herself out. And she took Paul with her. Keeping this place safe has been a struggle ever since, and what you're planning could demolish *everything* we've built."

There's a beat of silence. Mariella's lip and eyebrow twitch, but an actual expression never settles on her face.

"So that's it? Screw the rest of the world because you have to keep your walls up?" Mariella grows so still I don't think she's even blinking. "You feel safer letting everyone else go straight to hell? They're not strong enough to avoid the demons or escape, so they don't matter.

And if they can't drag themselves out here, then they aren't worth protecting. How noble."

"You are *not* pulling my family into your suicide mission!" Johanna shouts, but Mari doesn't flinch. "I don't care what you can do. I want you out. Gone. Go find some other group of people to brainwash into dying for you, because you are *not* recruiting here."

My heart skips a beat when Kelsey stands.

"They need to stay, Johanna." Kelsey's voice is deeper and more resonant than I've ever heard it.

Johanna's shoulders sag. When she speaks, her voice is low. "What do you see, Kelsey?"

Kelsey shakes her head slowly, her eyes unfocused and distant. "There's still too much static. Too many possibilities are about to converge. But there will be bad things if they leave."

"Bad things," Johanna deadpans. "Like ... ?"

The pain in Kelsey's eyes is sharp and jagged, like a knife of broken glass. "Like a graveyard. A graveyard of bad things."

Johanna laughs harshly. "Fantastic. Anyone have more bad news to pile on? Now's the time. Are we in for a freak hurricane tomorrow? Is nuclear war coming next month?" The muscles in her jaw can't seem to stop jumping.

Lexi pokes me and whispers, "Horace."

Oh, shit. I really don't want to bring that up right now. But Lexi is right. It's too important to wait.

"A few months ago, Hudson told my grandfather about the Balasura." I swallow uneasily when Johanna turns her angry eyes on me. "I, um, called to let him know I'm, you know, alive. And now he's ... well, he'll be here tomorrow."

Johanna's hands clench like she's thinking about wrapping them around my neck. "God*dammit*!" She stalks through the room, heading for the south tunnel and the Dorm. "Great. Fine. Family weekend coming up. Sentries, make note so we don't give the old guy a heart attack. Jesus, this day *sucks*. If anyone needs me, I'll be working on the budget in my room."

The silence that descends is unexpectedly broken by the echo of footsteps coming up the east tunnel. All eyes shift toward the archway.

"Aisling said that—" Julian stumbles as he takes in the tension in the room. "What happened? What'd we miss?"

He looks at Tanner for confirmation that something is off.

"What?" Tanner shouts.

Mari sighs. She crosses the room, her steps light and her movements somehow both graceful and efficient. Stopping in front of Tanner, Mari holds her hands up to frame either side of his head. When he nods his assent, Mari places her hands over his ears. Faint white light glows around her hands. Tanner sucks in a breath, almost a gasp, then exhales in relief.

"Oh my God, that is *so* much better." He glances around in confusion. "Where's Johanna? What happened?"

"This is going to be a long fucking day," Hudson mutters as Mariella offers Julian and Tanner a quick summary. He eyes the rest of the group. Some of them are getting up and wandering off, but others linger. I can't tell if it's curiosity or fear keeping them in place.

Hudson walks closer, takes an empty chair across from Lexi and me, and then leans his elbows on the table. God, his arms look even worse up close. I didn't pay attention before, but his scars are hard to miss now. And those solid black eyes. I press my head against Lexi's shoulder. Just looking at his eyes makes me think he can see into my soul.

"How did Horace find you?" I ask after a couple of seconds of uncomfortably heavy silence.

"He saw the article in the paper after my little brother died. It took him five weeks to hunt me down. I was flying pretty low under the radar then."

"Why'd you tell him about everything? All the dream world stuff?" It's hard to imagine my practical grandfather listening to a story about parallel universes and demons and what-the-hell-ever.

"Kinda had to." He waves a hand in front of his eyes then lets it drop. "They used to be blue. Pale blue. Horace thought I'd gone blind."

I squeeze Lexi's hand tighter just to make sure I can still feel it. It's like my entire body is numb. The shock of everything that's happened—meeting Hudson and Mari, talking to Grampa, watching Johanna lose her shit—has made it hard to process anything. Lexi presses a kiss to my cheek.

"And he's okay with it all?" I ask. "When I talked to him today he sounded … freaked."

"He's been *completely* freaked. He thought you might be dead, Nadette. He's not exactly a fan of the whole mental abduction by demons thing, but he's been doing whatever he can to help us stay safe." A small smile curves Hudson's lips, softening his face. "You should see what he's been doing to the junker of a house he bought. This huge Victorian. He spent a fortune on gemstones just to put them inside the damn walls of every single room."

"That sounds like Horace." I want to smile. "No one in my family half-asses anything once they make a commitment."

He nods. "I've noticed."

Biting my lip, I look away from his intense stare and let my gaze wander around the room. "Do you really think it's okay for him to come here? I ran away to keep my family *safe*. I don't want to drag him into my mess."

"If you think anyone can *drag* Horace Gregory Lawson III anywhere, then we're not talking about the same person," Hudson says, amusement in his voice. "He's already involved, and coming here won't change that. As for the rest …" He trails off, his amusement fading. "I guess we'll see what happens tomorrow."

I pace the clearing and try not to wring my hands. Jesus effing Christ on a life raft, this is gonna end *so* badly. Why did I let Hudson and Mari talk me into this? Horace shouldn't be coming here. I don't want that crotchety old man anywhere near this shit.

Behind me, Lexi sighs. "It'll be fine, Nadie."

Over the past few weeks, I've gotten used to Lexi digging into my head. Usually she can calm me down. Right now, it's annoying.

"No, it's not," she says. Even without looking at her, I know she's smiling. Her voice always drops a little when she smiles.

I skid to a stop less than six inches from slamming into Lexi. Sure enough, she's smiling.

"You're really cute when you're annoyed, you know that?"

Without permission, my face flushes. "I am not," I mutter, looking away.

"Liar." She smirks when she hears the bells ring in my head at the word.

Lexi puts one hand on my shoulder, the other on my cheek. The air is biting—it dropped into the twenties last night and it's not much warmer now—but my entire body warms up under her touch. Her hazel eyes gleam as she leans in and kisses me.

This one doesn't start slow or soft. This kiss devours me the instant her lips touch mine. Like I'm propane and she's a lit match. Her fingers dig into my hair and her other hand slides under my jacket, up my back. I melt in her arms and come back together stronger. Sliding my hands around her waist, I burrow under her shirt until my hands find bare skin. My fingers are cold. She shivers when I touch her, but she only pulls me closer.

The kiss seems to go on forever and it still ends too fast.

Lexi kisses my nose and my forehead. She's breathing just as hard as I am.

Resting her forehead against mine, she smiles. "Now, will you please relax? You're not alone. We can protect Horace."

I nod, trying not to be pessimistic. It's hard because … well, shit happens. Bad people exist, and some of those people are more powerful than you can imagine. I wish I could believe that Syver isn't one of those people. Beings. Creatures? I know Lexi and Johanna and Mari and Hudson and Julian will *try*, though. Try to protect themselves. Try to protect me.

I glance at Lexi and smile, but she blinks and looks away. Her head cocks to the side a little. She does that when she's listening to something I can't hear.

"Apparently there's an old man driving way too fast for safety who just passed the sentries," Lexi says, her lips twitching. I sigh and shake my head. It's shocking that Gramps hasn't ever crashed. He drives like a bad rally racer. And he knows it. And he doesn't care.

Within a minute, Horace's rental car comes tearing up the road. We step well out of the danger zone until he's safely locked in park.

"Girl, get your be-hind out here!" he yells before he's even all the way out of the car. His bald head and white ring of short curls appears over the roof of the car. He glares at me across the clearing. "You make me come any farther than I've already driven and I ain't gonna be responsible for the consequences!"

Lexi smothers a laugh as he opens his arms wide. I crash into him, breathing in his familiar scent—wood polish and Old Spice—and holding him way tighter than most people would dare. He looks more fragile than I remember, but there's no frailty in the arms that wrap around my waist and no weakness in the man who lifts me straight off the ground.

"You ever run away like that again, I'll kill you. And then I'll disinherit you." Horace's voice is gruff and I feel tears on his cheek. I pull back. He's frowning at me, but his blue eyes are laughing. "Or I'll just go off and have a stroke and make you feel guilty for the rest of your life."

"Please, don't." My throat feels thick and the first tears have already escaped my eyes. He's here. He's really here. I wasn't sure I'd ever see him again.

"Nah. I plan on bein' immortal just to piss off that brother of yours," Horace says, smiling down at me and wiping my cheeks dry with his soft gloves.

"Which one?" I have a lot of brothers, but only a few of them seem to be counting down the days until the old man kicks the bucket. "Scott?"

"Nah, other one."

"H.G.?" He shakes his head. There's really only one other option because it's definitely not Jake or Linus. "Phillip?"

Horace snaps his fingers and pokes me in the shoulder. "That's the one. Always expecting something for nothin', that boy." His eyes narrow at me. "Unlike his little sister, who can't seem to remember how to ask for help even when her damn *life* depends on it!"

The lump in my throat that had almost vanished returns. Bigger. "Grampa, I didn't—"

"Want to trouble anybody or put them in danger and blah, blah, whatever other B.S. is about to tumble out your mouth." He reaches out and grabs my shoulders, shaking me just a little. "If you'd just called me, Nadie, I'd have whipped you up to New York faster than you could slap a bird in the beak."

I blink. "Why would I want to slap a bird—"

"Don't interrupt me!" Horace puffs up, but I know the old man is all bluster, no bite. I'm about to call him on it when his eyes lock on something behind me.

"And now you're gonna let me stand here yammering without even introducin' me to your friend?" Horace drops his hands and starts walking toward Lexi. "I'd think wild wombats raised this girl if I didn't know better." He takes her hand, smiling. "Although, honestly, my boy Greg always did sort of seem wombat-ish to me."

Lexi chuckles, that throaty, full laugh I like so much, and my swirling emotions begin to calm. I can tell Horace is charmed. He's also the least likely person in my family to force Lexi to submit to an official inquisition and full background check once he finds out we're dating.

"Lexi, this is my grandfather, Horace Lawson. Grampa, this is Alexandriana George."

Horace looks between the two of us for all of five seconds before a grin spreads across his face. "Finally found someone you could stand for more than five minutes, eh?"

His bushy white eyebrows waggle. Lexi blushes. Right now I'm *really glad* I don't know what's going through the old dog's head.

Sorry, Lexi, I think. She doesn't look at me, but her lip twitches and she gives the smallest of shrugs to tell me that she doesn't mind.

"We should go inside."

I spin around. Hudson and Mari are standing a little higher on the hillside watching us. Hudson is smiling, but Mari's eyes are locked on the little piece of sky visible through the surrounding trees.

"There's a storm coming soon," she says, her voice soft. Almost disconnected. "We need to be under cover before it hits."

"Don't go all soothsayer on us, girl," Horace calls up to Mari. "There're coalsmoke-black clouds up there. Telling us a storm's comin' ain't as impressive as you think."

The distance drops from Mariella's expression and she grins. "Good to see you too, Horace."

Everyone has been treating Mari with a mixture of awe and suspicion since yesterday. It's jarring to hear Horace talk to her like she's normal. Then again, that's how he's always treated me, too. Not worth more or less than anyone else, just different.

I link my arm through Horace's. Partly to be close to him and partly to help steady him up the hill. Lexi holds my other hand.

We don't even get halfway up the hill before Mariella turns, her eyes narrow. "Wait here."

Lexi stares at her, then cocks her head, listening. "For what?"

"Someone's coming."

"The sentries didn't see anyone." But Lexi's gaze follows Mari's anyway.

"She knows a way around them," Mariella says, her voice distant again.

Lexi's hand tightens on mine so fast I flinch. "There isn't a way around them."

I cringe as Lexi's words send up bells in my head. Lexi winces.

"There's a way around them?" Lexi's eyes widen. Mariella remains too focused on the woods to respond. It's only a minute before Lexi's look of faintly disturbed confusion turns to surprise. "Aisling?"

Mari nods confirmation.

We're standing there for another couple minutes. The sky above us gets darker, thick clouds rolling in fast as the wind picks up speed and the temperature drops. I press against Horace for warmth. Growing up in Florida didn't prepare me for temperatures like this. With the additional wind-chill, it can't be above ten degrees right now.

Within a couple minutes, Aisling's bright blue hair appears in the distance.

"I've decided to take Jojo up on her offer," Aisling calls as soon as she's within earshot. "Still have room for me?"

"Seriously? She's been trying to talk you into coming up here for years!" Lexi says. "What changed?"

Aisling stops a few feet in front of us, her dark eyes narrow and her hands stuffed in the pockets of her lime-green coat. "The store isn't safe anymore."

"Why not?" Lexi asks.

Erica Cameron

"If I knew that, I would've fixed it instead of dragging my ass up here!" She rolls her eyes and keeps walking. "Betcha didn't expect to see me again so soon, huh, Mari?"

Mariella smiles and falls into step next to Aisling. Hudson is only a pace behind. "No, but I'm glad you're here. Johanna isn't exactly a fan."

"That girl does what she does well, but ask her to leave the way she sees the world behind and you might as well be asking her to murder her firstborn." Aisling shakes her head. "Like I told Sparkles a couple weeks ago, the kids up in Abra are little bigots."

"They have their reasons," I point out, trying to be fair.

Aisling's lips thin. "Doesn't make it right."

Kelsey must have warned Johanna we were coming because she's waiting for us at the entrance to the caves.

"I'm moving in for a while," Aisling says as she brushes past Johanna, whose attention is focused on Horace.

I gave him my crystal key so that he could see the entrance to Abra. Unfortunately, right now, that includes the distinct lack of welcome on Johanna's face.

"Gramps, this is Johanna Espy. She's the one in charge of Abra." I try to smile, but I'm nervous. I don't want this visit to end with Beth wiping Horace's memories. "Johanna, this is my grandfather, Horace Lawson."

"It's nice to meet you, Mr. Lawson," Johanna says.

"Girly, you call me Horace. Or Grandpa." He ambles forward and pulls Johanna into a hug before she can react. Her eyes are wide over his shoulder, but she doesn't fight it when he hugs her tight and kisses her cheek. "I can't ever thank you enough for takin' care of Nadie for us. Have a feelin' more than a few of these kids owe you their lives."

I hold my breath as he pulls away.

"I did what I could," Johanna says, looking distinctly uncomfortable with the praise.

"Well my family owes you a debt for steppin' in like you did. If there's ever anything you need, you just let me know."

Coming from my grandfather, that's an offer with serious weight. Although my dad Horace Gregory Lawson IV is technically head of the family's businesses now, most of the Lawson fortune is still firmly in the hands of Grampa Horace and he's got connections that would make a politician squirm with envy.

Johanna leads us into the caves to give Horace the tour Julian and I got our first day. He asks all the right questions and showers praise on how organized everything is. With every single comment, my grandfather expertly weasels his way into Johanna's good graces. I think. I hope. With Johanna it's hard to tell.

"She definitely likes him," Lexi whispers as we near the end of the tour.

"It's hard not to." I smile, more than a little relieved. "He doesn't really give you a choice."

Though I may not be able to see the rest of my family, having Horace here helps. He'll figure out how to ease their worry without giving too much away. And if Mariella and Hudson really are trying to shut down the portals between our world and Abivapna, maybe I can go home one day. Eventually.

I hope.

Twenty-Seven

Julian

I wish I could be there when Horace arrives, but I need to clear up some details with Pheodora, so I volunteer to take Nadette's sentry shift instead.

Pheodora appears closer to Abra than usual. I look around, trying to pinpoint my location. I could have sworn the caves' energy reached a hundred yards farther than I am right now.

"Was I correct?" Pheodora asks, pulling my attention away from the geography.

"About what?" I stare at the energy of the arch. Something is different about it. Is it ... blurry? Maybe it's the fading sunlight through the gathering storm clouds changing the hue of the light, but something is definitely off.

"Have things started changing?"

I nod and wrap my jacket tighter around me. The storm clouds above us don't look pretty. The wind was pretty bad before the portal opened, too. I'm going to have to run back as soon as we're finished here if I don't want to get soaked.

And thinking of Abra reminds me ... "I need to warn everyone about what you said, that the Balasura are getting closer."

"No." Her voice snaps and her eyes glow. I tense and step back. Golden light flashes in my peripheral vision, and chills roll across my skin. Was that lightning? I glance up at the sky, but the clouds haven't moved. Time in my world has stopped. It couldn't have been lightning. I roll my shoulders and try to remember what Pheodora just said; I'm oddly relaxed despite the goosebumps lingering on my skin. The purpurite pendant is warmer than usual against my chest, though. I lift my hand and shift it under my clothes. In front of me, Pheodora is smiling regretfully, shaking her head. "Telling them what you know will only put you and everything we have worked for in danger, Julian. It will only put *Nadette* in danger."

The words roll through my body with a force unlike anything I've ever felt before. Emptier than the moment I finally let go of Lynnie. More painful than Orane's betrayal. More disorienting than accidentally drinking water dosed with Ecstasy. I try to clear my head, regain control, but I can't seem to process what she said. "What? How is that even possible?"

"Hudson and Mariella's actions sent shockwaves through Abivapna." She wrings her hands and glances over her shoulder where those strange mirrors are hanging. Right now, they're all blank. "There are dangerous creatures tracking them, and they will follow Hudson and Mariella directly to Nadette unless we are extraordinarily cautious."

My heart stalls. Nadette doesn't talk about Syver much, but it's impossible to forget how haunted she looked in Trenton. Being stalked would traumatize anyone. Being stalked inside your own head? It's not something anyone gets over. I guess the same thing happened to all of us, but Nadette was the only one who *knew* it was happening. How do you get over something like that?

"Does Syver know where she is yet?"

"Do not worry about him." Pheodora looks up the mountain, toward Abra. "We are getting closer, but it is still not enough. Julian, you must spread more stones both inside and outside the compound." Her gaze locks on mine and my breath catches in my throat as her sage-green eyes glow. "We must act before things get worse."

I have so many questions I need to ask, but before I can say another word, there's a pile of crystals at my feet and Pheodora is gone.

I make it back to Abra just before the storm breaks.

For a few minutes I stand under the protection of the archway, watching the lightning flash and the wind rip through the trees. This storm is vicious and I'm glad my sentry shift is over.

Pheodora's words are still ringing in my ears as the thunder rolls overhead.

"We must act before things get worse," she said.

Maybe it's just the storm, but it's like I can feel the tension in the air. Feel the tick of the clock as we race to keep the Balasura away from Nadette. Sinatra bless it, I wish Pheodora would stop disappearing before I had a chance to ask her *anything*. Does she assume I understand what's happening, or is she so stressed that she honestly doesn't notice that she keeps bailing? If she could just give me something concrete to tell everyone, I would warn them all. But I have nothing except Pheodora's stones and the secret of her name.

Heavy footsteps thud behind me and I turn to see Clarke running up the passage.

"Oh, good," he huffs when he sees me, pulling his hood up over his head. "Thought you got lost again."

"Are you going out to get the others?"

He nods, eyeing the storm. "Kels says this one'll last a while."

"Be careful."

Clarke glances down at me and winks. "Don't worry, kid. I'm invincible."

Raising his hands, he pushes against the empty air and a globe of energy forms around him, keeping him dry as he dashes toward the first of the sentries.

Thunderstorms aren't unheard of in Vegas, but they're not common either. I've never seen one like this. Lightning flashes and thunder rolls right on its heels, so close the entire mountain trembles. I take a step back and shiver as the wind shifts, blowing rain straight at me.

Time to go.

I take the long way through the caves, stowing the crystals Pheodora left with me in whatever dark corners and crevices I haven't already filled with all the *other* crystals I've hidden.

After placing the last one in a deep crack near the Dorm, I drop the now-empty backpack in my room and almost run straight into Aisling in the tunnel.

Backpedaling fast, I stare at her. "What are you doing here?"

"I've temporarily gone insane and joined Jojo's little cult." She makes a face as she pulls her long hair into a ponytail. "The things necessity drives us to do."

"Necessity?"

Aisling shakes her head. "Don't worry about it, Glowstick. Just show me how to get to the food."

I grin as I guide her toward the kitchen. "What, you don't have the layout memorized already?"

"This place is a miserable rat warren." Aisling stuffs her hands in her pockets and wrinkles her nose. "I refuse to learn my way around because I won't be here long enough for it to matter."

"For your sake, I hope you're right," I tell her as we approach the kitchen. "Though, if it makes you feel any better, it's really hard to get lost here."

"Don't be so sure. Losing your way is easier than you think."

I blink at that. Her words sound heavier that they should have, weighed down by layers of implications. Swallowing, I have to wonder … could Aisling have any way of knowing that I'm still in contact with the other side?

Aisling barely glances at me as we keep walking. The kitchen is already half-full when we step through the entrance, but it only takes me a few seconds to notice something strange.

Mariella is fidgeting, messing with her hair and twining her fingers together and pacing. Something broke her stillness. Hudson watches her carefully, but doesn't try to hold her in place. It isn't until Vasha comes in a few seconds later that she sighs and quiets for a moment.

"You can feel it too?" she asks.

I don't know what she's talking about, but Vasha doesn't seem to need an explanation.

"If this lasts much longer I'm going to tear my own skin off," he mutters, grabbing a roll from the pantry and ripping it into tiny pieces that he pops into his mouth one by one.

His shaggy black hair is standing on end and it takes me a second to see why. He's *sparking*. Little tiny bolts of electricity are running across his skin, but most of them are concentrated in his hair. He shudders, and his entire body tenses as the sparks get worse.

"This isn't a normal storm." His voice is strained and tense. Our truce has held the last couple of days, but seeing him this stressed out isn't good. I'm not going to test his resolve when it looks like he's on the verge of losing control. I back away. Luckily, Vasha doesn't even glance at me. "Even the worst thunderstorm I've seen up here hasn't been anything like this."

Mariella stares at him, her head cocked to the side. Spinning around, she strides toward one of the exits. "Come on, let's go."

Vasha follows, then skids to a stop halfway across the room. "Wait. What?"

"We both need to literally burn off some energy or someone's going to get hurt." She says it through clenched teeth, her hands tightening into fists when thunder crashes again. "Training Room. Now."

She starts walking again and Vasha jogs to catch up with her. As soon as they're gone, everyone left in the room breathes a sigh of relief. Except Hudson, who follows Mariella like a lost puppy. I stare after them, trying to decide if his absolute devotion is more cute or strange coming from someone who could be a body double for Thor.

"Do you still have the necklace I gave you?" Aisling asks.

Glancing at her, I hook my thumb through the chain and pull the purpurite pendant out from under my layers of clothes.

Aisling nods. "Kind of surprised you've kept it on this long, but good. Make sure it stays there."

"Any particular reason?" It hasn't done much yet, but it hasn't hurt either. I've gotten used to wearing it.

Before she can answer (or decide she's not going to answer), Nadette waves at me, a huge grin on her face. She looks happier than I've ever seen her.

"Julian, come here! I want you to meet Horace."

The old man is thin and wrinkled, but when he drags me into a tight hug I realize he's a lot stronger than he looks.

"Just wanted to thank you for bein' such a good friend to my girl," he says, pulling back and patting my shoulder as I sit down at the table across from Nadette. "She's been tellin' me some about you. I know it ain't easy to put your own troubles away to help out someone else. Takes a certain kind of person to do somethin' like that."

I force a smile onto my face, trying not to think about Pheodora's warning.

"We must act before things get worse."

"She's helped me out, too," I tell Horace.

Horace grins and leans down to kiss Nadette's forehead, ruffling her hair. She blushes and bats his hand away, but I can tell she loves it.

"All right, girls." Horace kisses Nadette's forehead again and then Lexi's. "I'm claimin' an old man's right and takin' a nap. I'd say you should get some rest, but if you're anything like Hudson and Mari, you'll sleep an hour and think that's too much."

Lexi grins. "Probably."

"Don't do anything I wouldn't do while I'm gone," he says with a wink.

"So do whatever we want?" Nadette asks.

"Don't be cheeky, girl," he grumbles without heat before passing a stretch of wall where Anya has been hanging her paintings. Horace's head turns toward the pictures as he passes, but he doesn't pause to study them. Until he reaches the end of the line and sees Anya's latest work.

Horace stops, turns toward the wall, and leans forward.

"You okay, Gramps?" Nadette calls across the room, starting to get up.

He waves her back into her seat, shaking his head. "It's nothin'. Just the old eyes of an old man playin' tricks." Horace studies it with an odd intensity. Then the image flickers and I'm doing the same thing. "Thought for a second this one was of the Grand Canyon. Seemed out of place, is all."

That *isn't* what the picture is? Even from here I can see the rocks and the canyon and same bright blue sky I remember so well from Vegas. Then the purpurite pendant warms against my skin and the painting flickers (almost like an old holographic card). I see a flash of something else. A group of people surrounded by a blue glow and a doorway ringed in orange flame. It's back to the landscape before I can blink.

A strangled squeak from the other table makes me look. Anya is sitting there with wide eyes and both of her hands clamped over her mouth as she bounces slightly in the chair. Horace doesn't notice. He shrugs off the oddity of the changing painting and shuffles toward the tunnel, but stops at the edge of the kitchen.

"Don't you go nowhere," he says to Nadette. He smiles when he says it, but the lines around his eyes make it pretty clear he's not joking. He really is worried she's going to disappear.

Nadette nods, her smile gone. "Promise, Gramps."

At the next table, Anya jumps up and runs over to Johanna, whispering excitedly. I'm guessing whatever Horace thinks he saw in her artwork is a big freaking deal. I don't get a chance to ask about it because Beth slides into the chair across from me, a deck of cards in her hands and a grin on her face. "What do you say, sensei? Care to test what I've learned?"

The cards snap as she shuffles them and expertly deals out five cards for each of us. Smiling, I settle into the game to pass the time, but it's not enough to keep my mind from wandering. And worrying.

The thunder crashes overhead again and I cringe. I can feel it in the air. Time is running out.

I just hope I've done enough.

Twenty-Eight

Nadette

Wednesday, October 22 – 5:01 PM EDT

Lexi and Julian are on watch, Horace is reading, Hudson went for a run, and I feel twitchy. There's something in the air that reminds me of the way my skin felt when Syver was watching me. Which is ridiculous. I haven't seen or heard him ever since his threats forced me to leave Linus in a bloody heap at the bottom of the stairs.

I rub my hands along my arms, trying to get rid of the feeling. And the memories.

I'm so lost in my own thoughts, I barely notice at first when Mariella falls into step beside me.

"Johanna would never let anything happen to this place," she says. No bells. She's not lying, but still ...

"There's a reason they classify paranoia as irrational," I mutter.

"Good point. But you *know* I'm telling the truth." She veers slightly to the left, guiding us down another tunnel. The pause in the conversation only lasts a couple seconds before Mariella asks, "Do you want to learn how to turn it off?"

"Turn what off?"

"The bells. Your ability." She veers right and we're in the Training Room. "It has to get annoying. No TV. No *movies* ..."

My eyes widen. It didn't happen when I was really little, but even before Syver and the rest of the Balasura started stalking me, the bells wouldn't leave me alone long enough to watch anything. Actors are, after all, professional liars. Even songs with lyrics can be impossible unless the singer wrote the song from personal experience. But that doesn't explain ... "How did you know I can't watch TV?"

Mari raises one gloved hand and wiggles her fingers. "It's another one of my new talents. It tends to freak people out, so I don't talk about it much."

"I don't understand. Freaks people out how?"

She glances at me like she's trying to measure how I'll react. "When I touch someone, I can see flashes of their past."

Whoa. That's … I want to ask her if she's joking, but I already know she's not. I've gotten used to telepaths, but they can only read your immediate thoughts, not see your entire past laid out like a documentary.

"Sorry." Mari rubs her hands together and then hides them in her pockets. "It's a touch-activated ability, so it's part of the reason I wear gloves most of the time. I can't keep *all* of these abilities switched off."

Right. I can't even handle *one* ability. Can't really blame Mari for her almost-two-dozen powers getting a little out of control. I push past the strangeness and concentrate on the important part.

How awesome would it be to turn this off like Lexi can? To go through a day without cringing at bells. To be able to listen to music with lyrics and actually *enjoy* it. I've dealt with the ringing for so long the idea of being without it is a little like imagining life without my arms. Just a hell of a lot more appealing.

Mariella smiles and I know she heard my train of thought.

"Once you get the hang of turning it off, you might even be able to expand the ability more," she says. "You're powerful now, but I think you can hone it. Get more specific. Read more into what *kind* of lie it is. Maybe even turn off only half of it so that you can lie to everyone else, but they can't lie to *you.* You might be able to play with it."

"Screw playing with it! I want to know how to shut it off!" I lean closer. "Can you really teach me?"

Her head tilts a little, almost a sideways nod. "It's more like I can show you how to do it yourself."

"I don't get the difference."

Mariella wrinkles her nose and runs a hand over her long blonde hair. "How do I explain this?" She bites her lip and shrugs. "You've always been able to turn it off, you just never made the connection. Like your brain is full of buttons and you haven't pushed the right one yet."

"And you can show me how to find the right one?"

"Yep." She meets my eyes, both eyebrows raised. "You have to be willing to let me into your head, though."

I open my mouth and close it. Into my head? What does that even mean?

"I have to go into your head the same way the Balasura do in order to guide you where you need to go."

My heart stalls. I hold my breath. I've spent the last two years trying to keep people *out* of my head and she wants my permission to go in?

"I swear that's the only thing I will do. If you want out, want *me* out, all you have to do is say so and I will leave. I promise."

Is it worth it? She's telling the truth, but it feels like a huge leap of faith.

"It's not a decision to take lightly," Mariella says. "I definitely wouldn't recommend letting just anyone stroll through your head. And I won't be offended if you say no. Although, if we do this, I can also show you how to keep people like Lexi and me *out* of your head."

"I don't … I mean, I shouldn't just let you …" I bite my tongue to keep from starting another sentence I don't know how to finish. God. Let her *into* my head? How would I even do that? Should I let her try it? I guess it comes down to one question—do I want to learn what Mariella can teach me more than I fear saying yes?

Before I can second-guess the decision, I nod. "Show me."

Smiling, Mariella guides me to the center of the cavern. Once we're settled on the floor, she whispers, "Close your eyes."

The whole process is so gradual I'm in the middle of it before I realize it's started.

Syver's energy trying to latch onto my mind felt like fishhooks. Or knives. Or huge-ass spears. Mariella's touch is softer. Like someone reaching out and taking my hand. Once I accept that touch, I feel like we're sinking into a pile of warm, really fluffy blankets.

I follow Mariella's gentle pull. We fall deeper into my own head, down paths I never knew existed and across roads I didn't know I could travel. Except for periodic flashes of light, sound, and memory, everything is black. The deeper we travel, the darker it is between flashes of light. I'm not scared, though. It's warm and safe here and Mari is guiding me.

Imagine a room, somewhere comfortable with plenty of storage space, Mariella says.

Almost before she finishes speaking, a pinprick of white in the distance appears, quickly growing larger and brighter. It's hard to tell if we're getting closer to it or it's getting closer to us. It keeps expanding, spreading out and changing colors until I'm standing in front of an opaque glass door bordered in white-painted wood.

Before, I seemed to be formless, just floating through the space as … what? A ghost? Energy? Now I look down and see hands and a body. Mariella is standing next to me, smiling.

"Are we going in?"

Nodding, I reach out and push down on the silver handle. The door swings open and we step into … my mother's home office?

Mariella turns in slow circles, taking in the walls of cherry wood shelving and the large desk, the armchairs and the accents of butter yellow and royal blue. "This is cozy. A lot more manageable than what I've got locked in my head."

I'm not sure I want to know what the inside of her mind looks like. "What is all this?"

"A mental representation of the information in your head." Mariella picks up a black book and opens it. Without looking at the pages, she hands it to me.

I drop it.

Syver is staring at me from the page. My heart starts pounding, my hands shaking. It takes me a few seconds to realize it's just a picture. A memory.

Mariella picks up the book and closes it, but I can still see his face and that Cheshire smile, his beetle's-wing hair and those deep emerald eyes. I shudder.

"Sorry." Mariella tries to hand me another book. I can't make myself take it. She steps closer, offering it again. "It's not all bad."

I still can't take it. Opening the book, she shows me another picture. It's from when I was little. Linus is standing behind Mom as she scolds Sophia for playing in her makeup, and she hasn't noticed yet that he used her lipstick to turn her favorite blouse into part of his superhero uniform.

"This room is your life," Mariella says. "Everything you know, everything you've seen, everyone you've met. It's all here somewhere. Everything you can do, too."

Putting the book down, she beckons me toward the desk. Mari glances at the computer and points to an icon that looks like a magnifying glass. It's labeled "Insight."

"Open that," she says.

I sit down in the leather chair and touch the icon. Not sure what I expected, but it's definitely not a white screen with two buttons—a green one on top that says "ON" and a red one below that says "OFF."

"It can't be that easy."

Mariella laughs. "Nadette, do you know what the method of loci is?" She waits until I shake my head. "It's an ancient memory technique that helps people remember things by organizing their minds into rooms or files or books or whatever is easiest to manage. It's this— what you instinctively did here after I showed you how to find this deep meditation and mentioned, just *mentioned*, creating a room."

She looks around the room. I follow her gaze. Every wall is covered floor to ceiling with jam-packed bookshelves. I guess, for me, books were the easiest to imagine. When I catch Mari's eye again, she smiles.

"You used a technique most people can't master, found a place most people don't know exists, and now you're looking at a computer screen inside your own head to help you control an ability most people will never understand. That's definitely *not* easy."

"Well, yeah, but come on." I look at the screen, my finger hovering over the OFF button. I've lived with this curse since birth. It's only gotten worse over the years. Or better, I guess. I've gotten better at reading lies and my ability has gotten stronger. Could turning it off have always been this simple?

"You're inside your own head. This is going to be exactly as easy as you make it for yourself." Mari shrugs. "Right now you want to know how to turn the ability off, so that's what your mind is showing you. One day, if you want to come back and figure out what else you can do with this ability of yours, this screen will look completely different."

"Oh." In a strange way, that makes sense. As much as anything here makes sense. I run my hand along the grain of the cherry wood desk. It feels so real.

Mariella grins. "Hard to believe this is all in your head, huh?"

Glancing at the buttons on the screen one more time, I push out of the chair. I thought I'd want to jab the off button and get the hell out of here. Now that I see it I'm not so sure. Turning it off feels wrong.

I stall, giving myself time to think by walking along the shelves and picking up a book at random. When I open it to a page in the middle, I'm looking at a transcript of my first meeting with Peter. So much has happened that I forgot about him. And Tessa, since it didn't seem like anyone in Abra could help her. No one has ever heard of anyone coming out of the coma. But Mariella is different. Powerful. And she's looking for answers instead of hiding from what's happening around us. Looking for a way to wake up people like Tessa.

"Mari, you said you knew a neurologist?" I ask.

Mariella's eyes lock on mine and I hold my breath. They're just eyes and she's just a girl, but every time she focuses on me like that I feel young and small. Like my life experience is insignificant next to the power in those honey-brown eyes.

"Your psychiatrist, huh?" She asks the question before I can even explain why I brought it up. "Tell me about him."

I take a breath and show her pictures of Peter and of Tessa's glass pendant while I explain everything.

"Do you think Dr. Carroll might be able to help?"

Mariella nods slowly, her eyes locked on a point over my shoulder. "Having another expert to look over the results can't hurt either, right? It's worth a phone call."

I sigh in relief before walking back to the computer and staring down at the screen. The buttons are still there. Glaringly bright red and green buttons.

Can I do it? *Should* I do it?

"You don't have to decide now." Mariella puts her hand on my shoulder. "You can think about it and come back."

I release a long breath and nod. "Okay."

"Only one more thing, then." Mariella heads for the door and I follow. Once we're outside, she closes the door behind us and gestures to the handle. "Lock it. The stronger you build this door, the less likely it is that anyone will be able to infiltrate your mind uninvited. And not just telepaths like Lexi and me. If you build it strong enough, you should be able to keep even the Balasura out."

I freeze, staring at the glass door. "Really?"

Mari nods. "Think of it like your mind is a doctor's office. All this space out here, this is the waiting room. Any information left in the open is available for visitors to peruse, but the important stuff? The patient files and medical records and everything? That's under lock and key."

"That ... actually makes sense."

"I manage to do that every once in a while." Her smile turns wry for a moment before she shrugs. "Even if you build yourself an impenetrable barricade here, you can still communicate with Lexi or any other telepath by leaving your conscious mind on this side of the gate. Your memories and your subconscious, though, the core of who you are, that'll all be protected."

Turning toward the door, I imagine it changing. The pane of opaque glass ripples and gets darker. The color spreads outward until I'm looking at a solid metal door. Thick metal bars lock it into the walls on either side and in the center is a digital pad that looks like a palm scanner from a spy movie.

Behind me, Mariella laughs. "Wow, that's thick. I'm not sure if I should be impressed or insulted you think I'm that much of a threat."

"It's not you. Or Lexi. It's ..."

"Yeah. I know, Nadette. Trust me, the door in my head is even worse. Or better. You know, depending on how you judge these things." She sighs. I glance over, trying to decide if it's resignation or determination I see in her face. "Ready to go?"

I nod, but then something occurs to me—I'm missing one very key piece of information. "Um, I don't know how to get here without you."

Mariella's hands cup my cheeks. "Close your eyes and concentrate on how it feels to be here."

At first I don't get it. Even outside the room, it smells like my mom's office—leather oil and her perfume and whatever incense she's burning that week. After I acknowledge that and move past it, I feel what Mariella meant. There's a soft vibration in the air, one that's familiar and soothing. It brushes against my skin in a way that reminds me of a purring cat. Once I recognize it and fix it in my memory, I hear Mariella's voice.

Whenever you want to come back, close your eyes and feel for that energy. It will lead you straight here.

I feel a nudge upward. I follow her advice in reverse, holding on to the energy. It pulls me back into consciousness.

When I open my eyes, I check my watch. Wow. Only two minutes have passed? It felt like a couple of hours. "Wish we could learn everything like that."

Mariella rolls her eyes as she pushes to her feet. "I know, right? School feels like such a waste of time now." Running a hand over her long braid, she nods toward the door. "C'mon. Lexi should be back in a few minutes."

We walk toward the kitchen, neither of us saying a word. I'm not sure what keeps Mari silent, but I appreciate the quiet. I don't feel different, exactly, but I do somehow feel anchored. More solid. The twitchiness I'd felt earlier isn't as intense, either. I can breathe easier and I'm not as restless as I was.

Mari was right—unsurprisingly. Both Lexi and Hudson are back by the time we reach the kitchen. Hudson's attention locks on Mari immediately, but he refocuses on Kelsey after a second. He and Kels are a study in contrasts together. Tiny and ginormous. Dark and light. Bright and solemn. It's kind of adorable to watch the way Hudson leans down and listens intently to everything she's saying.

Mariella smiles when she sees them and heads in their direction. "I'll see what I can do for Tessa, okay?" she tells me as she walks away. "Promise."

I smile as Lexi steps closer and kisses my temple. Mariella promised and she meant it. Even if she can't wake Tessa up, I feel so much better knowing that at least someone will try.

Twenty-Nine

Julian

Thursday, October 23 – 6:12 PM EDT

Moving quietly is a habit I picked up young. Avoiding Lynnie's attention, or the focus of whatever guy she was dating, was always a good idea. It's become natural most of the time, unthinking, which is probably why Johanna and Clarke don't hear me coming.

"Today? And there's *how many* of them?" Clarke asks, his deep voice echoing slightly in the tunnel.

"Nadette's one of ten kids, Clarke." Johanna sighs. "Plus her parents."

"Fucking A," Clarke mutters. I move closer, trying to make sure I'm not missing any softly spoken words. "They're all coming here. Today. And we're letting them?"

"We're taking precautions, but yes."

"*Why?*"

"Because they've already been threatened by the Balasura. Because her younger brother has already been hurt by them. Because I'm apparently running a damned bed and breakfast now. Who the hell knows?"

Footsteps thud softly against the stone and their voices are getting louder. I walk backward, staying within earshot and out of sight.

Clarke grumbles something I can't make out and then says, "Maybe they'll come, she'll remember that she used to live somewhere with doors, and they'll take her back home. Maybe we'll get lucky just this once."

My blood runs cold. I wait for Johanna to argue, to insist Nadette stays where it's safe, but nothing comes. They walk closer. I stay just out of range, hoping their conversation will end before I run out of tunnel to hide in.

"Trouble or not, I don't want to see her leave," Johanna finally says. "The past couple of weeks, Lexi has been happier than I've ever seen her. And Nadette is a good kid."

"And that skill of hers doesn't hurt either, huh?" Clarke asks.

"That too."

There's a pause before Clarke asks, "Do you think she'll go?"

"I figure it's fifty-fifty right now. She hasn't been here all that long and she actually came from a family. A TV-show-perfect family, if Horace is any indication." Something rustles, but I can't tell what. "Lexi and Julian are the only real connections she has to this place, but if her parents ask her to come home? I don't know."

I come to a break in the tunnel and I have to make a decision—take the long way around, through the Whatever Room and the kitchen to get to the entrance, or walk past them as though I haven't been eavesdropping this entire time. In the second I hesitate, I lose the chance to hide. They're too close. I adjust my backpack and widen my stride, fixing my expression into something between "lost in thought" and "in a hurry."

I make myself stumble slightly when I see them. "Oh. Hi, sorry." Taking a breath, I tilt my head and blink like I'm noticing something off. And it *is* off. Clarke's body is tense and Johanna's lips are more pursed than normal. "Everything okay?"

"You haven't heard?" Clarke asks.

"Nadette doesn't even know yet," Johanna tells him.

Clarke's straight eyebrows rise so high they almost look arched. "I thought you said she asked permission for her family to come."

Johanna shakes her head. "Not Nadette. Her grandfather. He's the one who asked."

"He's kinda cool for an old guy." Clarke says. That's practically a ringing endorsement coming from him.

"Her family? When will they be here?" I ask casually, as if my best friend isn't in danger of being ripped away from me.

Johanna checks her watch. "Around seven. They flew into Albany, so Aisling and Tanner are already on their way to get them. Horace rented passenger vans for the occasion."

"Damn this has been a weird week," Clarke mutters. "Too many strangers showing up."

Johanna exhales, the sound half-sigh, half-groan, and runs a hand over her hair, pulling at her tightly wound curls. "It's not the strangers that worry me as much as the attention."

"And in a nowhere town like this, a dozen strangers get noticed," I finish for her, my heart beating faster. I already know the Balasura are closing in. If Nadette leaves … I shudder and wrap my arms around myself. If she leaves, they'll be waiting outside the gates to grab her.

"Don't say anything to Nadette if you see her," Johanna tells Clarke and me. "Horace is going to tell her soon."

"Yeah. No problem." I swallow and force my expression to relax and my lips to smile. "I was going to take a walk, so I probably won't see her until later anyway."

Johanna glances at Clarke and he rolls his eyes. "I'm not exactly a gossip."

"Keep an eye on the weather," Johanna says when she turns back to me. "It's been strange lately. That electrical storm, then the snow, and now a perfect autumn day?" She shoves her hands in her pockets and shakes her head. "I don't like it."

She's right. The weather this week has been switching so fast it's practically giving us whiplash.

"I'll let you know if I see anything, but my meteorological skills extend about as far as saying 'It's cold and grey outside today,'" I tell her.

Johanna's lips tilt up at one corner, almost a smirk. "That's more than I know from in here."

Promising to bring her back a weather report, I move past them, jogging for the exit. The impending invasion of Nadette's extended family has each footstep jarring my entire body, shaking thoughts loose. Worries. Possibilities.

What if she leaves?

What if Pheodora can't protect her out there?

Why is it that when I finally find a real friend I might not get to keep her?

By the time I'm outside and moving through the trees, the thoughts have built up to a nearly panic-inducing flood.

What if? What if? What if?

Questions I can't answer and problems I can't solve. My shaking hands clench. I move faster.

As soon as I'm almost certain I'm out of range of everyone's extrasensory abilities, I run. I've spent more than a month crawling all over this mountain, so I know the terrain well. I got here just before the seasons shifted, just in time to watch the green landscape burst into bright fall colors and fade just as quickly into the more desolate scenery of winter. Only five weeks and the entire world has changed.

Once I start whipping past the nearly bare trees and the piles of rocks, it only takes me a couple of minutes to find the place where Pheodora's doorway is open. She's waiting for me.

My pendant heats up against my chest and the edges of the doorway flare orange. I blink and skid to a stop, my feet sliding on the frozen earth. What was that? Did I just—

Pale gold light flashes on the edges of my vision. My head swims. My pendant burns hotter, but I ignore it. I needed to tell Pheodora something. Something important ... Sinatra bless it, what was it?

Oh!

"Nadette's family is coming here. All of them." I expel the words around panting breaths. "I think they might ask her to go home with them. And that she might say yes."

"Would she?" Pheodora asks. There are more mirrors this time, some small, some as tall as Pheodora, and they all hang on some invisible wall, floating in midair and reflecting nothing. "You said she feels safe here. And we told her to stay where she is safe."

"Yeah." I nod and swallow, straightening a little bit. "I can remind her of that, but it's her *family*. I know she misses them. She's gonna want to go if she can."

She glances at the mirrors. "You must convince her to stay, Julian."

About to agree, I pause. Everything with Nadette's family almost pushed the other news I wanted to tell Pheodora out of my head.

"Aisling is here," I tell her. "She said her store wasn't safe anymore but didn't tell anyone *why* the store wasn't safe. Did the Balasura try to get to her?"

If the Balasura are closing in on this place, maybe it *would* be safer for Nadette to leave with her family. If she leaves, I can always go to

Swallow's Grove with Mariella. Even if it means volunteering myself for whatever tests their pet neurologist wants to run.

Pheodora's green eyes are grim. "All I know is that, by the time we reached for her, she was gone."

"I think she's scared. And she didn't seem like the type to scare easily."

"Everyone has something they fear, Julian." Pheodora shakes her head, her pink hair swinging behind her. "Even someone who appears as strong as Aisling."

"It's getting worse, isn't it?" I ask. "The war you're fighting."

"It is not going as we had anticipated," Pheodora admits. For the first time I notice the lines on her face and the small spots of dirt on her dress. She looks worn out and that, more than anything else I've heard today, sets my teeth on edge. "But so long as you all stay here, there is hope. We may be able to recover yet."

"How long?"

"We need more time, but not much." Pheodora grips her hands together so tight her already pale skin grows whiter. "Does Nadette's family plan to stay long?"

"I have no idea." If they're anything like Horace, it might be hard to get rid of them once they get here. "Maybe."

Pheodora steps closer, so close she fills up the doorway and my vision. It's as though only the two of us exist.

"What do you need me to do?" I ask.

She smiles, her entire face relaxing as her eyes softly glow. "Just once more, I need you to reinforce the stones."

"There isn't anything else?"

"It is enough," Pheodora says, the doorway already starting to close and a new pile of crystals appearing at my feet. "It is more than enough."

Thirty

Nadette

Thursday, October 23 – 6:26 PM EDT

There's an honesty to winter that I love. A lack of pretension when the bones of the world are laid bare. Evergreens give the mountain a little bit of color and life, but a lot of the trees are just thin fingers stretching toward the sky. The missing leaves make the rises and valleys of the mountain plain, and the weird-ass snowstorm last night coated the world in white. I take a deep breath and smell pine and woodsmoke. Despite the chill, I think it's beautiful.

It'd be a lot more enjoyable if I could get rid of the twitchiness that popped up stronger than ever this afternoon. I feel like there are wayward threads brushing against every inch of my body. Every time I check, there's nothing there. It gets worse outside the caves. The tiny threads turned to spiders crawling all over my skin about twenty feet outside Abra. I wanted to find Julian—Clarke said he'd gone for a walk—but I can't make myself move beyond this point.

I hear footsteps in the tunnel and turn to see Horace. He's smiling, but it's the grin he gets every time he has a secret. Right now I'm not sure if I like the idea of Horace having secrets.

"Don't get your knickers in a knot," he warns, "but everyone you love will be here in about half an hour. Maybe less by now."

I swear my heart tries to leap up my throat.

"What?! They can't come here!" It's bad enough that I'm putting Horace in danger. "I can't believe you told them without asking me!"

"Nadette Elizabeth Lawson."

I cringe as soon as I hear my middle name. I hate being middle-named. Especially by Gramps. Horace's eyes narrow and he crosses his arms over his chest.

"I don't remember anyone appointing you guardian of the globe, and I ain't asked anyone's permission for anything since your grandmother passed. My son's been worrying himself *sick* over you and if you thought I'd just sit here and keep silent then you don't know me very well at all, do ya?"

Taking a breath, I try again. "It's not like I don't want to see them, I just don't—"

"Want anyone to get hurt." His expression softens. He steps closer, putting his rough, wrinkled hands on my cheeks and staring into my eyes. "You're a compassionate girl, but you ain't thinking this through. They're my family too. Think I'd want to get any of 'em in trouble?"

I flush and shake my head. "Of course not, but—"

"But that don't mean you're not worried. And you should be, but we got it planned. Johanna agreed they could come as long as they all swore to keep this place a secret."

My skin chills even more. "Is she going to have Beth wipe their memories?"

"Not quite." Horace grins and tugs on my earlobe before sliding his hands into the pockets of his coat. "Apparently Mari taught her a couple new tricks. Beth can set up a trap in people's heads that will only wipe Abra out of their memories if they're 'bout to betray it."

Oh, please tell me I understood that wrong. "Beth is going to booby trap their *brains?*"

"Pretty damn cool, huh?" He wiggles one bushy white eyebrow, grinning like a kid with a new toy. "Had her test it out on me this mornin'."

I cover my face and laugh. Because it's either that or scream. "I wish you were kidding."

"Nadie, don't go stressin' about this." He wraps his hands around my wrists, pulling my hands away from my face. "Aisling and Tanner are gonna meet them at the airport and drive them up here in vans. With covered windows. They won't even know how to get up here. And they've got more gemstones then you can shake a stick at. They'll be safe as long as we're all smart."

I swallow, close my eyes, and bow to the inevitable, even though I seriously doubt it'll be that simple.

I was nervous the day Horace arrived. It's ten times worse now. Even Lexi doesn't try to calm me down as I pace the edge of the clearing. It's not just the prospect of seeing my family, it's the way my skin crawls under the open air. Not even a backpack stuffed to bursting with crystals stops the itch. I thought I'd gotten over the fear Syver had left me with. Obviously not. My hands won't stop shaking. I feel like I'm being watched. I want to go back to Abra.

"Girl, quit twitchin' or I'll strap you to one of these rocks," Horace mutters. "It's exhausting just watchin' ya."

Lexi winces. "Horace, don't—"

"Hey!" I march over and stare the old man down. "*You're* the one who brought them up here. If you didn't want me to freak out, you should've given me more time to adjust to the idea. I mean, booby traps, Horace? How the hell can I expect them to let us—"

There's a new sound in the air. An approaching engine. Oh, shit. I've run out of time.

Turning, I see two black passenger vans coming up the road. I chew on my lip and walk closer to the edge of the lot. Both vehicles have something black coating the passenger windows and a black curtain dividing the front of the van from the back. Jesus. Johanna *really* isn't taking chances.

Aisling swings the van around so the passenger door is facing me.

"Are we *there* yet?" I hear Linus's sarcastic drawl from inside, but the first person I see when the door slides open is my mom.

"Nadie!" She bursts out of the van and runs the three feet separating us, slamming into my chest so hard only her tight grip keeps me from tumbling backward. "Oh, thank God!"

Another thump and my father's arms wrap around both of us. He kisses my cheek and I see tears running down his face. I've never seen him cry before.

Another thump and I feel someone pressed against my back.

"If I'd known you planned to scare us like this, I would've stolen sedatives from the hospital and drugged your stupid ass," Jake mutters into my ear. "Hippocratic oath be damned."

I smile when the bells ring in my head.

I'm pulled away and passed around the rest of my family like a stuffed animal. The faces and the hugs pass by quickly, but it's been so long since I've seen everyone that they all stand out in my memory.

Everyone is here. Both of my workaholic parents and all nine of my siblings. They all came across the country just to see me. Just to see for themselves that I'm okay.

The last one I face is Linus.

It's been four weeks and five days since I've seen him. His cast is still on. I want to hug him, but I hold myself back.

"I'm sorry, Linus." My voice cracks on his name. "I didn't mean to hurt you. I didn't know it was you and I didn't—"

"If you don't stop apologizing, I'm going to hit you with this thing." Linus turns slightly to the side and wiggles his injured arm at me, his entire face scrunched up in fake concentration.

He looks so utterly, beautifully ridiculous. I laugh. Then promptly dissolve into tears.

Once I start crying I can't make myself stop. They're here. They're all here and they don't hate me. *Linus* doesn't hate me.

"Aww, shit, Nads." Linus wraps his good arm around me and holds me against him, his injured arm trapped between us. "It was a bad joke, but it wasn't *that* bad."

"When are you going to accept that you're not funny?" Sophia says behind me. "It'd save us all a lot of headaches."

"Shut up, Soph." Linus lifts his hand and I know he's flipping her off. "Just 'cause *you* were born without a sense of humor—"

"If you two don't knock it off right now, I will lock you in the van. Together," Mom threatens.

I grin against Linus's shoulder, tears still running down my face. So much has changed in the past five weeks, but not this. Never this.

Linus pulls away, but Mom takes his place.

"We were so worried about you." She puts her hands on my cheeks, her green eyes boring into mine. "How did you even find this place?

Your grandfather makes it sound like some top-secret government installation."

I wipe my eyes and smile. "You're not that far off. It'll be easier to show you."

Taking a breath, I hold Mom's hand and look for Lexi. I want to get any awkwardness out of the way. Lexi steps up behind me and presses a comforting hand against my back.

"Lexi, these are my parents, Grace and Greg. Guys, I want to introduce you to Alexandriana. Lexi is ..." I glance at Lexi, asking for permission to explain everything. She grins the lopsided smile that brings out her dimple, and nods. "Lexi is my girlfriend."

"Oh!" Mom smiles slowly, studying Lexi closer. "Girlfriend, huh?"

And just to get it all out at once. "She's also a telepath."

My dad's blue eyes bug out of his head. "*Telepath?* Like a mind reader?"

Lexi's hand tightens on my waist as my entire family stares at us with slack jaws. Aisling and Tanner move next to me and for a second it feels like battle lines are being drawn. Us versus them.

Then Horace laughs. "Mind reading is nothin'. Just you wait until you see what some of the other kids can do."

"Other kids?" Jake's eyes narrow as he scans the tree line. "How many people live up here?"

"Twenty-seven after Nadette and Julian joined us," Lexi says. "Twenty-eight if you include Aisling."

"Which you shouldn't," Aisling says, her arms crossed. "I'm temporary."

My parents glance at each other, wide-eyed and weirded out. When they look at me, they're both wearing tight, uncertain smiles.

"Well, sweetie," Mom says. "It looks like we have more to catch up on than I realized."

Thirty-One

Julian

Thursday, October 23 – 7:02 PM EDT

I try to sneak my latest backpack of stones into Abra, but the place is too busy. Too many people and too much wariness. Everyone is on guard with the strangers (the *outsiders*) on their way. I stash Pheodora's crystals in the hollow of a tree a good distance from the caves and fill my backpack with the amethyst and malachite and quartz I left there the first time I had to do this.

Before I reach the entrance to Abra, I hear voices, lots of voices, coming up the mountain. That has to be Nadette's family. No one else would be making this much noise.

Pasting a smile on my face and stuffing my hands in the front pocket of my hoodie to hide my clenched fists, I wait for them to reach me. Might as well meet them in the open. It's easier to breathe out here without the stone walls surrounding me.

Tanner appears first, Lexi and Aisling close behind him. The two brunettes and Aisling's blue hair look incredibly out of place in the sea of blondes and redheads that follows. Nadette is tucked between a woman who looks like an older version of her and a tall guy with slightly graying dirty blond hair.

Aisling notices me first, but all she says is, "Hey, Glowstick."

The nickname must catch Nadette's attention, because she looks up and grins, waving me closer.

"Julian, these are my parents, Grace and Greg Lawson." She looks up at her parents, her green eyes glistening a little. "Guys, this is Julian. I found him in Trenton and he came here with me."

"Are you a telepath too?" Grace asks as I shake her hand. Her eyes are a little wide and her smile a little strained, but overall it seems like she's taking everything in stride.

"Nope. Lexi and my cousin Mariella pretty much have that market cornered."

"Julian's the opposite of a telepath," Nadette says. "He's really good at keeping people *out* of his head. He can even lie to me."

"What?" A guy with strawberry-blond hair and a cast on one arm pushes forward. "Are you serious? Dude! You have *got* to show me how to do that."

I glance at Nadette and bite my lip. "It's not exactly something I can teach."

Tanner whispers something and I glance behind me. Johanna is standing right at the entrance of the cave, waiting. It takes me a second to realize Nadette's family can only see the same dilapidated shack I once did.

Heh. *This* should be interesting.

Johanna takes a deep breath and steps past the arch, walking outside the illusion that protects Abra and into the open.

One of Nadette's sisters screams. More than a few others gasp. The kid with the cast (Linus, I'm assuming) laughs. "Oh, man. This place is *awesome*."

Nadette steps forward, placing herself between her family and Johanna. Her smile is more cautious now. "Everyone, this is Johanna. She set this place up and she's in charge of ... security, I guess? And everything else."

Johanna's lip twitches into the ghost of a smile.

"Johanna, this is everyone. My entire family."

Surveying the group, Johanna's dark eyes seem to take in every single person before she opens the pouch tied to her wrist. Removing one of the crystal keys, she lobs it to Linus. Even with the cast, he catches it easily in his good hand. His eyes nearly bug out of his head when the real entrance becomes visible. Without a word, he holds it out and drops it into his mother's hand. She has the same reaction, except she emits a breathless little, "Oh."

Tanner takes the pouch of quartz from Johanna and passes the keys out. One by one they gasp or laugh or turn a little pale. None of them run. Once they get past the shock, they all take a deep breath and stand firm. It's easy to see where Nadette gets her stubborn streak.

"Wow, Nadette," says one of her older brothers. "What the hell have you gotten yourself into?"

Johanna and Tanner play tour guide while I hover on the edge of the conversation. It's not long before everyone converges around the dining room tables while Horace and Tanner begin dueling for control of the kitchen. The two good-naturedly argue on one side of the long room. On the other, Mariella puts on a show, creating a flock of iridescent, rainbow-colored birds that swoop around the room and lighting a row of candles with a flick of her fingers.

Lexi joins the Lawson family, her way eased by the fact that Nadette refuses to let go of her hand for long. One of her brothers tells a joke and everyone laughs. Nadette's smile is so wide it's almost blinding.

My chest aches, jealousy directed at *everyone* stabbing through me, sharp and sudden. Nadette's barely had time for me lately. Even Mariella, who should be my family and my support, has hardly been around. I try, but it's hard to ignore the vicious voice in my head constantly pointing out how quickly (and easily) I've been replaced.

In the end, it doesn't matter. If Nadette decides to leave, I'll still beg her to reconsider. Literally beg if that's what it takes. I'll even beg Lexi to help me convince her.

I just hope it doesn't come to that.

Mari slides up next to me, a small smile on her face. "I figured that any family that includes Horace would be an interesting group, but my expectations fell short."

"I can't believe how many of them there are." If they'd brought along aunts, uncles, cousins, siblings-in-law, and nieces? The number would be well into the thirties. Maybe the forties. The extended Teagan family would only need a table for seven.

"Yeah. Being an only child doesn't prepare you for family meals like this," Mari's grin only lasts a second. "Speaking of family, though ..."

"How about we don't?"

"I had to tell my dad we found you."

"Oh." I turn away from Nadette's sitcom family to deal with my own dysfunctional one. "That's fine. I never wanted to worry him. Really."

"So will you—"

"No. I won't. There's no reason to call Lynnie." Mari opens her mouth, but I cut her off. "It's time for her to learn how to take care of herself. I can't spend my entire life cleaning up her messes. I won't."

She watches me for a second before she finally nods. "My dad was *pissed* when he found out you were missing."

Though I'm glad she's letting the subject shift, I raise an eyebrow. "Weren't you in a coma when that happened?"

"Yep. But seriously. I've never heard him yell like that. He laid into Aunt Jacquelyn like you wouldn't believe. He said, and I quote, 'You're fucking right, it's your fault.'"

"You heard him say that?" I'm not sure how the image of Frank losing his cool over my disappearance instead of tiptoeing around Lynnie is supposed to make me feel. Like with most things involving her, I'm pretty much numb. I never wanted to stress him out like that, but Sinatra bless it did Lynnie have that coming. But, wait ... "*How* did you hear that? Again, coma. You were in one, right?"

She waves her hand, dismissing her month-long coma like it was as minor as a bug bite. "I could still hear what was going on. Plus, the telepathy kicked in after the first week." She shakes her head as she pulls her long braid over her shoulder. "Let me tell you this, it is frustrating as hell to hear people begging you to wake up when you're so deeply trapped in your own head you can't answer them."

"Wow. Yeah. That would *suck*."

"Bad as it was with Mom and Dad, it was worse with Hudson. He barely ever left the room, and once the telepathy switched on?" Her shoulders come up a little, like she's trying to protect herself from the memories. "Jesus. Listening to him blame himself while he sat there praying and begging and bargaining for me to wake up ..."

She shudders. The air around us grows heavy with memories and guilt.

Needing a change of subject, I look around the room for her perpetual shadow. "Speaking of the Jolly Blond Giant, where is Hudson?"

Her grin slowly comes back. "Hiking with Brian. He wanted to be a Boy Scout when he was a kid because of the camping trips. He's making up for lost time now since he wasn't part of a troop long enough to go."

"Why not?"

"Because he punched a bully. But that kid's parents ran the troop, so ..." Mariella shakes her head. "It was bullshit. Completely unfair. But there's a lot of stories like that in his life."

I think there's a lot of stories like that in *all* of our lives (I mean, isn't that why we all ended up here?), but I keep my mouth shut and go back to watching Nadette's family.

"It's good for her to see them," Mari says a minute later. "She was carrying a lot of guilt about Linus and her disappearance. That's almost all gone now."

She's right (I know she is), but acknowledging it forces me to recognize something else.

The calmer Nadette gets, the more I worry.

Please don't leave.

It's been three days. I still haven't found a chance to bring in the last batch of crystals and I'm starting to worry the Lawsons intend to make this visit a permanent thing.

Since none of us sleep anyway, there are plenty of beds for the Lawsons to borrow. The problem is that with this many people running around the caves, they feel claustrophobic. Overstuffed. Which is why I volunteer for more sentry shifts than usual. Every time I see one of Nadette's family members wandering through the tunnels, I can't help worrying.

What if they don't *leave*?

What if Nadette *does?*

Heading back to Abra from my sentry shift, I crunch through the fresh snow, pulling my hood tighter around my face. There was another brief blizzard last night and everyone keeps talking about how winter's hit early this year. Early and hard. It's gotten cold enough in the caves that Sarah and Brian have added extra fire pits wherever possible. Mari helped Sarah create portable heaters out of some large chunks of quartz, too, but it's still too cold to go without a jacket (and often more than one) inside Abra.

Today isn't any warmer, inside Abra or out. The caves may be colder, technically, but I don't have to deal with the wind inside. Even so, at least there's some sun in the forest. Pros and cons either way.

After my sentry shift, I have to force myself to head back into the caves. Stepping out of the thin sunlight makes me shiver. I look around and listen, waiting. The entry tunnel is deserted. Not a single footstep echoes down the corridor.

Before I can second-guess myself, I turn back to the forest. I head straight for the hollow where the crystals are stashed. It takes a minute to dig them out of the snow. Despite my gloves, my hands slowly go numb until, by the time I try to close my hand around the first crystal, I can barely control my fingers. I wasn't planning on doing this today, but I can't risk waiting any longer. I stuff Pheodora's crystals into the pockets of my pants, jackets, and backpack, slipping them into whatever spaces will hold them.

Hiding them inside the caves is harder. My heart beats a guilty tattoo every time I see someone approaching. I barely manage to find enough hiding places, doubling up the new crystals in some of the spots I've used before. They *just* fit (thank Sinatra) in the dark nooks and crannies of the tunnels and behind furniture in the bedrooms, but if Pheodora changes her mind and hands me another batch, we're going to be in trouble.

Knowing it's done lifts a weight off my chest. I let my mind wander, not bothering to open my eyes until I hear footsteps. Nadette. And for once, she's alone.

"Are you sure you're allowed to walk around without an entourage?" I glance over her shoulder in mock-surprise. "There has to be another Lawson around here somewhere."

"I know." She rolls her eyes, but she's still smiling. "Can't really blame them. I *did* vanish for weeks without anything more than a vague apology letter."

"True."

"Have you called your mom yet?"

I close my eyes and shake my head, my conversation with Mariella fresh in my mind. "I'm sure Frank has sent her an email letting her know I'm fine. That'll have to be enough."

"Hmm."

"Hey. No judging." I poke her in the arm as if I'm not totally uncomfortable right now. As if my pulse isn't racing as I force myself to ask the question that's been haunting me for days. "So do you want to go back with them?"

"Well, yeah. Of course." She blinks as if surprised I even needed to ask. "They invited Lexi to come stay with us. Didn't I tell you that?"

My heart jerks to a stop against my ribcage and it takes every bit of control I learned playing poker to keep the fear from showing on my face. "That's news to me."

Oh, no. Lexi was one of her strongest reasons to stay. If she has the option to take Lexi with her ...

Fear drowns everything out, literally ringing in my ears until I can't hear anything else. My hands tremble, but I stuff them in the pockets of my coat to keep them hidden. Swallowing, I try to shake myself out of it. I need to concentrate. Nadette is still talking and I can't afford to miss a word of it.

" ... But we'll see what happens when it gets to that point," she says with a shrug.

"Well, I hope it works out," I tell her, hoping it's the right response to whatever she said.

Her smile fades a little. "I'm going to miss them. I know they have lives and that I'll eventually get to visit them, but ... I just hope they stay safe. Linus especially. He's not exactly one to take things seriously."

Her words replay in my head. The trembling in my hands stops and it's like suddenly everything becomes clearer. Brighter. Better. She's not leaving! I can barely contain my grin. *She's sad about this. Do not sound too excited*, I remind myself as I say, "After what Linus has seen here? He'd have to be incredibly stupid to laugh it off."

Her lip twitches. "You sound like Horace. He said almost the same thing."

"He's right. You should listen to him." I pretend to think that over. "I'm glad you're staying, though. Blue told you to stick around here, right? So that can't be a bad plan."

"I know. I keep reminding myself of that, too." She looks toward the kitchen. "You coming? It'll be dinner time soon and I think Horace is making something special."

"I just gotta get something from my room. I'll be there soon."

"Don't wait too long or there might not be much left." She grins at me as she leaves and I smile back, but my smile fades the second she's out of sight.

Nadette is staying, but … ?

Come on, Pheodora, I think even though I know she can't hear me. *Work your magic. She's here for now, but I don't know how much longer that'll last.*

Thirty-Two

Nadette

Monday, October 27 – 2:05 AM EDT

I'm walking through a mirrored hallway. Entirely mirrored. Walls, floor, ceiling, it's all seamlessly connected reflective glass, but frost covers most of the floor and climbs up the walls. I shiver, my breaths crystallizing in the air.

"You hid yourself well." *Oh, God, no.*

I jump and turn. There's no one there.

It doesn't matter. I know that voice. I know that voice.

But it's impossible.

"Not well enough."

Running, I slide through the maze. Fear heats my body, but it barely counteracts the growing chill in the air.

"Run all you want, I will always find you."

I barely stop before I crash into a mirror. Oh shit. Shit! A dead end.

The temperature drops. I shudder. I'm only wearing pajamas. The sweatpants and long-sleeve shirt can't protect me against this bone-chilling freeze.

Turning, I dig my bare feet into the snow and ice covering the ground, almost slipping and cracking my head against one of the walls. I lose the ability to move as soon as I see the person blocking my path.

No. It can't be him. He can't be here. It's impossible!

But somehow he is. My nightmare. A thousand copies of him, his reflection picked up in the glass until it looks as though I'm standing in front of a solid wall of demons.

"Hello, my pet." Syver smiles, his hand reaching out for me.

I scream and throw myself through the mirror behind me, praying for an escape. Or death.

I jerk awake, adrenaline coursing through my veins and my body convulsing. My black jade necklace and my bracelets are hot against my skin. The last time they did this ...

I have to get out of here!

Kelsey jumps like a startled cat when I bolt out of the room, tears streaming down my face. I run half-blind toward Lexi's room.

A hand grabs my wrist and I scream.

"It's me, Nadie! It's me!"

Lexi's voice, worried and frantic, but so wonderfully familiar. I throw my arms around her neck and sob. Words escape, but my sentences are broken. Incomprehensible. It doesn't matter. The dream is replaying in my head and Lexi sees it all.

"Honey, you're so cold."

I'm not cold, I'm numb. So frozen I can't feel my fingers and toes. So scared I can't think.

Lexi guides me into her room, drapes her thickest coat around my shoulders, and then wraps a blanket around that. It's not enough. I'm still shivering, shuddering, and scared.

Lexi strokes my hair and cradles me against her, murmuring, "I'm here. I'm here."

And then she says it.

"It was just a nightmare."

The bells clang through my head. The sound is so jarring it sends shudders through my skull. I wince. Lexi jumps. My tears fall faster. My sobs come so hard and fast my chest feels like it's about to burst. My entire body is shaking and my head is spinning, searching for an escape.

Where do you go when an entire cave of amethyst and quartz isn't strong enough to protect you anymore?

Lexi gasps. "It wasn't ... it *wasn't* a nightmare?"

No bells. This time, she's telling the truth.

"Fuck. No. Oh my god." She pushes up, grabbing my arms and hauling me to my feet. "We need to find Johanna."

I'm crying so hard I can barely see, but Lexi doesn't slow down. The harder I sob, the faster she pulls me through the caves. When we reach the kitchen, it's empty except for Sarah, but Tanner appears a second later, his face tense.

"What happened?" he asks. "I heard her scream."

"Where's Johanna?"

"She's with Anya. They're—"

"I need to talk to her now!" Lexi hisses. "And no it can't wait so just—"

A siren shatters the night.

Tanner slaps his hands over his ears, his entire body curling into itself. Sarah ducks under the table. My tears stop as I listen, trying to figure out where the hell that alarm is coming from. It sounds like—

No. Wait. That's not a siren. That's a *scream*.

They're coming! They found a way in!

Mariella's voice bursts into my head, echoing in my ears and my brain. It's so overpowering—a physical thing pressing down on my head. It takes me a second to figure out what she's trying to tell us.

The Balasura are coming!

Tanner grabs Sarah's arm and drags her out from under the table.

"What? No! That's not possible!" she shrieks, shaking and nearly collapsing. Tanner wraps his arm around her waist to keep her upright, ignoring her shouts.

"Get to the Training Room!" Tanner orders. "We need to—"

We both cringe as bright orange light floods the room. Squinting, I see shapes in the light. People. I hear whispers. The voices of the Balasura. They hiss like snakes and no bells chime in my head. Because they're not hiding behind their façade this time. The masks have come off. Their weapons are drawn. Anyone they capture will end up in a coma like Tessa. Or dead.

Tanner peers into the light and pales. Stepping back quickly, he drags Sarah after him, his eyes still locked on the figures in the light. The ones moving closer all the time.

"Run!" Lexi screams.

I sink into the simplicity of reaction. My brain is quiet, my body numb, acting on autopilot. We sprint through the tunnels, gathering people as we go. Vasha, Julian, and others I can't see. They're just bodies in the crowd. Faceless people who are *not* the enemy. It isn't until they come closer that I notice how the world is shifting around us. Bubbles of warped time spread out from the portals as they open. As Julian and Vasha skirt the edge of one, their movements seem to pick up speed. Faster and faster until they're nearly invisible. We follow them through that bubble because it's the only way to get to the Training Room.

Tanner almost causes a collision when he skids to a stop.

Beth is on the floor, her body crumpled on the cold stone. A glowing copy of her floats through the air, a bright orange rope of light wrapped around her ghostly throat like a noose. She's fighting, screaming silently and flailing as she's dragged through the air. It doesn't matter. Beth is completely at its mercy. They're going to get her if we don't stop it.

I move without thinking. Pushing past Tanner, I reach out to grab her.

"*Don't!*" Hands wrap around my wrist and yank me away from Beth. She brightens. There's a pulse of light. And then she's gone. Something dark and angry grows from the pit of my stomach, feeding on the looped memory of Beth's silent struggle and the moment she disappeared. Gone.

"I could have *helped* her!" I scream, ignoring the bells clanging in my head. Why wouldn't they let me help her?

"You can't touch them," Hudson insists, letting me go when I push away. "If you touch them after they've been separated, they'll get you too."

His words filter through my unfocused mind as he presses a chunk of amethyst into my hand. No bells. He's not lying. If I'd touched her I'd be on the other side of that portal, sitting at Syver's mercy. Another stone appears in Hudson's hand. He's carrying an entire backpack of them. He gives one to Lexi and distributes the rest.

"This isn't going to be enough." He glares at the empty bag like he can fill it by willpower alone. "This isn't just one of them—this is a fucking invasion."

Before anyone can speak, his shoulders drop and he turns toward one of the offshoot tunnels. Less than a second later, Mariella appears at a run, trailing a row of floating backpacks. All the backpacks of stones we take with us when we leave the caves.

"Take one and keep *moving!*" she screams.

Lexi grabs two, shoving one into my arms as she pushes me past Beth and down the hall. I glance over my shoulder, trying to see through the crowd behind me. Before we turn down the next tunnel, I look back again. Hudson and Mari are squatting next to Beth, a forcefield of purple, white, and green light surrounding them. Mari's hands glow as they press against Beth's forehead. Hudson has his fingers pressed against Beth's neck. He looks at Mari, shaking his head.

"Don't look," Lexi whispers, her voice trembling. "Just keep running."

Portals open everywhere. The ceiling. The walls. Orange fire spills from those doorways in waves or shoots out like spears. Like the spears Syver attacked me with. The stones activate, their energy pulsing out in crystalline purple, green, and pure white. When the two energies meet, bright blue sparks fly. The stones are trying to protect us from the fire pouring out of Abivapna, but the entire cave is bright orange. We're being overrun. Overwhelmed.

Someone screams. I try to turn. Lexi drags me onward, tears running down her face.

The scream cuts off too early.

We keep running.

The orange light surges and fades as portals open and close. The demons are probing our defenses, finding the weak spots and picking off anyone left straggling. The backpacks Mari brought us work well, though; we're protected.

Then the tunnel goes dark. We all freeze. But no. It's not dark. Not really. Back to normal. Back to the solid dark walls of stone lit only by the soft white light of Vasha's rigged lamps. Those walls echo back the sounds of our harsh breathing. The sobs coming from all around me. I hear people crying. I think I might be one of them. I feel disconnected from it all, watching and analyzing and feeling nothing.

The darkness remains. We inch forward, closer to the Training Room. I barely have the time to hope that the worst is over before the first bolt of orange lightning strikes.

I scream and duck, cowering against the ground and throwing my hands over my head.

The bolt never reaches us. I peek out from under my arms. The forcefields from the backpacks rise up to meet it, creating a dome over our heads that absorbs the energy. The impacts crack and spark like exploding transformers, but the shield holds. And it only gets stronger when Clarke and Mariella and Hudson add their power to the defenses.

Lexi hauls me to my feet. The group starts to move. Everyone presses as close to Clarke, Hudson, and Mari as we can get without tripping over each other. I watch the light show, tracking the tiny cracks in the forcefield as they move closer together. Lexi grabs my head and locks it against her chest.

By the time we reach the Training Room, we've gathered almost everybody. I try to count, but people are moving too fast. Lexi pushes me to the center of the room and makes me sit. I watch as the others unzip the backpacks and take out the stones inside. They create a circle around us, each stone touching the next all the way around. Clarke is still holding up his forcefield around us; his skin is tinged with grey.

Mariella is standing a foot away from me, her head tilted back and her eyes closed. It doesn't look like she's doing anything, but the air around us pulses with power that makes my hair stand on end and my skin tingle.

Someone tugs on my backpack. My pulse jumps. I hold on tighter until I hear Lexi's voice.

"Let go, Nadie. We need this."

When I release the strap, Lexi tugs the bag off my back and tosses it to Hudson, who's completing the ring of stones near the one entrance to the room.

I look up as one of the bolts strikes directly over my head. I close my eyes, missing the moment it hits. Doesn't matter. The lights are so bright they burn against my eyelids, creating bright red fireworks inside my head.

Arms wrap around my shoulders and lips press against my cheek. Lexi. She wipes my cheeks dry. Was I crying? I can't feel it. I didn't realize.

"Breathe, honey," she whispers to me. "Don't hold your breath like that. *Breathe.*"

Oh God. I exhale and my lungs burn. Sensation creeps back in to my body as I suck in more air. My breaths stutter as my lungs try to remember how to work. Lexi strokes my hair, her hand trembling. The lightning still rains down above us. Mariella still stands next to me, power radiating from her like heat from a fire. I can *feel* it. I shudder again, glad that she's on our side.

Shifting my gaze, I try to find something—*anything*—else to concentrate on. Everyone whose power won't help in this fight is pressed as close to the floor as they can get. They're all huddled, in groups or alone, and their eyes are either wide and watchful or tightly closed as their lips move in silent prayer. Now that they're still, I count. There should be thirty of us here, including Mari and Hudson.

I only count twenty-four.

"Don't think about that right now. We'll be all right," Lexi whispers, holding me tighter. No bells this time, but that's barely a comfort. She's shaking, probably from the effort of dealing with her own fear plus the blasting surround sound of two dozen other minds. I wrap my arms around her and kiss her forehead.

Each orange blow comes so fast that it feels like it's one constant stream of lightning. All I can do is hold Lexi tight and close my eyes.

Lexi whispers in my ear that the Balasura's usual visits only last a minute of our time, but this one feels like hours. No one knows for sure, though. The barrage of power seems to have blown out Vasha's generators and short-circuited every quasi-electrical device in the caves, including our watches.

Even after the lightning stops and the portals close, no one moves. If the Balasura can get in once, they can do it again. No one believes this is over. And no one wants to be the first to test the safety of the rest of the caves. It's nearly pitch black in the Training Room now, the only light coming from the small fires Sarah and Mariella hold in their hands. It feels like time has been sucked out of the room, leaving two distinct markers. Before and Now.

Except Now doesn't feel remotely safe, especially when no one knows how long the chasm between the two has lasted.

It doesn't matter, in the end. Whether it's been fifteen minutes or over an hour, it won't bring Beth back. Knowing won't save anyone.

It's nearly silent for a long time after the Balasura disappear. Silent except for the chattering of teeth and a few broken sobs.

"Is it … Do you think it's safe to go to the bathroom?" The voice is soft and low, but it still makes me jump. And it only takes a second for the impact of that simple question to reverberate through the room.

"*Is* it safe?" Sarah asks. "I'm so thirsty."

"I wouldn't go," Vasha mutters. "They're probably just waiting for us to leave."

Someone starts crying again. My hands shake.

"How did they get in?" Anya asks. "I don't get it. *How* did they get in?"

No one has an answer. Silence falls, but this time it only lasts a second before it's shattered.

"This is *your* fault." Johanna's voice is steady, but there's ice dripping from her words. Bells ring in my head, but I don't dare stand up and contradict her. Fear and fury burn in her eyes as she gets up and stalks through the crowded room toward Mariella and Hudson. Lexi stiffens, her eyes flicking between Johanna and Mari.

Mari doesn't move, just looks up from within the cradle of Hudson's arms. "Do you even hear what you're saying? How is this *my* fault?"

"Abra has been safe for *fifteen* years." Under the honey tones of Johanna's skin, she's going red. Bright red. Hudson stiffens, but Mari puts her hand on his arm and he settles back down. Johanna doesn't notice or doesn't care. "You're here barely more than a *week* and everything goes to hell!"

"Just to make sure I'm following, did I invite them here or did they follow me?" Mari asks.

"Be very careful about what you say next," Hudson growls, his low voice rougher than ever.

Johanna blinks, stunned into silence. But not for long. "Are you *threatening* me?"

"No more than you're threatening us."

"Hudson," Mariella says sternly. Her boyfriend loosens his grip on her as she stands to face Johanna.

They stare at each other for a moment. Then something passes between them. Something no one else can see or hear. It's there, though. Something must have happened, because Johanna droops. It's slight, but after that motion, the balance of power between the two of them shifts. Before they were almost on equal footing, but after? After, Johanna somehow looks smaller, a child throwing a tantrum while the patient parent waits for her to tire herself out.

"Defense won't work anymore, Johanna." Mari's voice is soft, but it carries throughout the cave. "If we don't figure out how to stop them, they're going to tear through our planet until there's nothing left."

"Fifteen years, Mariella. This has been a safe haven for *fifteen* years." Johanna stands straighter, her hands clenched in fists by her side. "For the last eight, my defenses were enough. More than enough. Until you showed up."

My attention is so locked on the battle of the wills playing out in front of me, it takes me a moment to catch what else is happening. First it was Tanner and Clarke, but others quickly join them, positioning themselves behind Johanna like a guard. Or an army. Not everyone picks a side, but no one stands behind Mariella. Julian almost does, inching closer to her than anyone else, but even he doesn't seem ready to openly declare allegiance to his cousin. There are too many coincidences stacked up against her. I don't believe Mari let them in on purpose. I *know* she didn't. At the same time, everything was fine until she and Hudson arrived. Everyone was safe.

"Don't be naïve, Johanna." Aisling steps up to Mari, her dark eyes flashing. "I've been telling you for years that hiding won't do anything but waste time and—"

"Stay out of this," Johanna barks.

Aisling blinks. "If you're stupid enough to get rid of them, I'm leaving too. You'll be on your own."

A little bit of the color leaches out of Johanna's face. It feels like everyone in the cave is holding their breath, waiting for her decision.

"I want you out of here, Mariella." Her voice is hoarse but strong and steady. "Before daylight. I want both of you gone." She glances at Aisling, her voice a little less steady as she says, "You too, if you're going with them."

Aisling shakes her head, her lips tight. "You're making a mistake."

Johanna's entire body tenses. "No. My only mistake was letting them stay this long."

Mariella barely acknowledges Johanna's verdict or Aisling's support. Instead, she looks at Julian. "You can come home with me, Juli. I know Dad wants you to come stay with us."

Julian's eyes widen. He looks at me. Even without him saying a word, I know what he's thinking. He wants to go, but he won't leave without me. And I can't leave without Lexi. I can't make myself do it.

Looking up at Lexi, I silently ask, *Would you go, if I went?*

Lexi's hazel eyes look so sad. "This is home, Nadie. I can't leave my family when they need me."

Her answer doesn't surprise me, but a little pang of regret bites my stomach. I turn back to Julian and shake my head. It could have been so nice. I could have lived with Horace, helped fix up the dilapidated Victorian he bought—the "junker" Hudson mentioned. Julian and I might have even been able to carve out a sliver of normalcy for ourselves there. But leaving Abra now would feel like betraying the people who took me in when I had nowhere else to go. I can't do it.

Julian calmly shakes his head. "I know where you live," he tells Mari with a strained smile. "I'll find you if we change our minds."

Mari steps closer and puts her hands on his cheeks. "You be careful, okay, Juli? My parents will kill me if anything bad happens to you."

His smile grows wider. "They might try. I don't think they'd actually succeed."

"It's the thought that counts." She kisses his forehead and hugs him tight. "Promise you'll find me if you need me. And don't do anything stupid."

"Promise."

Mariella releases him and glances around the room, meeting everyone's eyes in turn. "The same goes for everyone. Find me if you need me. And please don't take unnecessary risks just because you're scared. *Please.*"

Then she leaves, walking out of the room with Hudson and Aisling trailing her. My stomach clenches as they disappear down the tunnel, each of them carrying a full backpack of stones with them.

Lexi's grip around my waist tightens. It doesn't stop the worry building in my mind.

Why do I feel like I just made a huge mistake?

Thirty-Three

Julian

Monday, October 27 – 5:52 AM EDT

We're all huddled on the couches in the Whatever Room when Vasha and Nicole manage to turn the lights back on. I wish they hadn't.

Seeing the bodies laid out on the floor shatters the last of my control.

As I force myself to walk toward the dead, the shaking in my hands spreads up my arms and into my chest. Cold worse than anything I've felt in my life encases my body. I can't stop shivering.

Mariella, Hudson, and Aisling are gone, banished from Abra. I could've walked right into my most tightly-clutched fantasy life if I'd tagged along, but I couldn't bring myself to do it. Not without Nadette. As much as I'll miss her, Mari's exile is a whole lot easier to accept than the six bodies in front of me.

They're not in comas. They won't maybe, possible, *someday* wake up. They're dead.

Beth is dead.

My poker buddy. My confidante. My friend. She's just … gone. I barely knew the other five. Trevor, Raychel, Chloe, Madison, Joey. They were names I learned that first week and faces I passed in the tunnels, but they had their routines and I had mine. Our paths rarely crossed. I assumed I'd get to know them eventually.

My eyes are burning, but I'm not crying. I can't. My entire body feels dried out.

"Are you okay?"

I turn toward the voice, but it takes a few seconds for my eyes to focus on the person in front of me. Is that Vasha?

Vasha's eyes narrow and he touches my shoulder, shaking me a little. "Julian, are you all right? Did you get hurt?"

"What? No …" I look down just to make sure I'm right. There's a hole in my jeans where I tripped while we were running. My knee is a little scraped up, but otherwise it looks like I'm in one piece. Physically. "I'm …"

I can't even tell him that I'm fine. I am so far from fine.

"I can't believe she's gone," I whisper. None of the dead have any obvious injuries. Not a single scrape, cut, or burn. It looks like they're sleeping. Kneeling next to Beth, I take her hand and squeeze it. She's so cold. Even colder than I feel. The tightness in my throat makes it nearly impossible to force speech. "Beth never treated me like a freak, Vasha. Never. She was nice."

The tears start rolling, dripping onto Beth's brown coat.

Vasha shifts closer, kneeling beside me as tears run down his own cheeks. "She deserved better. They all did. They thought they were safe here. Why couldn't we protect them?" He looks at me, his dark eyes drowning in tears and guilt. "What use are powers if we can't protect our friends?"

Exactly. What good are their powers or *anything* I've been doing since I got here? People died. And Pheodora wasn't here to stop them. Tremors wrack my body as I stand, my hands clenched into tight fists. "I have to—I have to go."

I grab one of the backpacks of stones and sling it over my shoulder. I consider heading into the forest, but it's too far. Too big a risk. Instead, I turn toward my room. As soon as I push through the curtained entrance, I close my eyes. I sink into the mental room Pheodora showed me how to create and slam my hand against the golden symbol she left behind.

Except it's not gold anymore. It's glowing orange. Like it's on fire. Vines of orange light extend from the sign she burned into the wall, stretching past the glass divider I built and into the part of my mind no one is supposed to have access to.

No way. After the attack tonight, I'm taking *no* chances. It only takes a second of concentration to change the dividing wall from glass to reinforced steel. I shove the original walls (the ones infected with the vines that shouldn't be there) back and replace them with stronger fortifications. The place isn't as cozy (more panic room than dream home now), but I don't care. Not if it keeps the Balasura out. I don't need pretty, I need safe.

And I need Pheodora to answer my freaking call.

Outside my über-fortified cell, I slap Pheodora's symbol one more time. This time the light pulses under my palm, so I open my eyes.

The air in front of me ripples and brightens. I bite my tongue to keep from screaming. The doorway is the wrong color. Twining through the pearl-white light of the gateway are vines of fire-orange. They hover along the edge of the doorway, twisting and writhing like serpents. The purpurite pendant heats up against my chest. It's nearly scalding, but it doesn't burn me. I ignore the heat, keeping my eyes on Pheodora. She stands just inside the gate, her green eyes glistening as jewel-like teardrops roll down her cheeks one by one.

Her tears should make me sympathetic. They don't. Each one pisses me off. What is *she* crying about? She didn't know them. She never met Beth or any of the others. Never tried.

"You were supposed to protect them." My voice is stronger than I expect it to be.

"I am so sorry, Julian." Her voice sounds distant, almost distorted. Because of the orange flames surrounding the doorway, or the energy rising from the crystals in my backpack? I can't see it, but I feel the force field's energy vibrating against my skin.

I stay back, tightening my grip on the strap of my bag. "What happened? How did they get past you? The crystals were supposed to protect us!"

"There are so many of them." Her hands spread out, both an apology and a plea. "We could not hold them back."

"People *died* here." I picture Beth lined up with the others on the stone floor and the tears start falling again. Faster than before. "Six people died."

"I know. I could not stop it." Her hands cover her face as she sobs. I take a shaky breath and step closer, swallowing around the lump in my throat.

I have never caught a glitch in Pheodora's emotions or expressions before, but this feels … overdone. It's too much. Too perfect. A performance. But Nadette would have told me if the information Pheodora passed on was wrong. She would've caught it, wouldn't she? The only thing I kept back was Pheodora's name. Everything Pheodora told me, Nadette believed.

So did Nadette miss something or is (I swallow hard and *make* myself think it) … What if, knowing Nadette could read the truth of what I said, Pheodora only gave me information she knew Nadette would believe?

Oh, God. Is Pheodora like Orane?

That possibility sits like an acid-dipped lead weight in my stomach as I ask, "Can you bring them back?"

"No, Julian." Pheodora shakes her head and wipes her cheeks dry. "That is beyond anyone's power."

I rub my eyes, digging my hands in like I can force the tears to stop. My chest constricts. Is there even air in this room? I force myself to breathe and drop my hands, wiping them on my jeans.

"Time has run out, Julian. You must act now. We can still save Nadette."

A glass vial stoppered with a glass cork appears on the ground in front of me. Inside is a liquid that shimmers with a slightly iridescent glow.

"What is it?" I'm not willing to touch it yet. The purpurite pendant begins to throb, the scalding heat rising and falling in a steady rhythm. I fight the urge to run.

"A sleeping potion."

I blink. The purpurite's pulses get quicker. Sharper.

That doesn't even make sense. Dreams are where these demons operate, how they dig into your head and take what they want. Putting anyone to sleep sounds like the opposite of a good idea. "What am I supposed to do with it?"

"You must use it to save Nadette."

"How will a sleeping potion save Nadette?" At my feet, the glow of the vial gets brighter. Only an ounce or two of liquid. Only enough for one. "What about the others?"

"We cannot save them all. To even mention this world while tensions are so high will start a panic. No one will listen. You will lose your chance of saving Nadette's life."

"But what if we told them—"

"No. Not after what happened here tonight," she says. "If you tell them anything, you will lose your chance, Julian. And it may be your *last* chance."

I stare into Pheodora's eyes, unsure. This feels wrong.

So, so wrong.

Thirty-Four

Nadette

Monday, October 27 – 5:59 AM EDT

It's been three hours since the Balasura's attack ended and I still can't stop shaking. I press closer to Lexi. She tightens her grip on me. Her hands aren't much steadier than mine.

We ended up in the Whatever Room once we could bring ourselves to move. Guess someone figured that if we were going to huddle in fear, we might as well huddle on couches. The stones from the six now-ownerless backpacks are spread in a circle around the edge of the room. Everyone else is wearing theirs or holding it in their lap. No one wants to be out of reach of as many crystals as they can carry. The Balasura haven't been back yet, but why take the risk?

A loud *clang* makes us all jump.

"Sorry." Tanner flushes, picking up the iron kettle he dropped and refilling it with water.

I take a breath and look around. Everyone is here. Except …

"Where's Julian?"

Lexi blinks like she's coming out of a fog. "He was here a minute ago, wasn't he?"

From the next couch over, Vasha says, "He said he had to leave."

"Leave?" I straighten, my heart pounding. "Like, *leave* leave?"

Vasha shrinks back slightly, shaking his head. "I don't know. He was with Beth and he …"

Oh, God. Beth. Everyone is mourning, but Julian *loved* Beth. Apart from Lexi and me, she was the only one here who really treated him like family and now she's gone. There's no way he's handling that well. Especially not if he's alone.

"Is he in the caves?" I ask Lexi.

Her eyes crinkle at the edges as she concentrates, searching through the minds within Abra. She told me once that even though she can't read Julian's mind, she can still sense his presence. Almost like the absence of something that *should* be there.

I should've been paying more attention to him. No. Damn. Not even that. He shouldn't still be here. Why the hell didn't I talk him out of staying? He had a shot at being with family and I didn't bother convincing him to go even though I knew—*knew*—that I was his only reason for staying.

God, I'm a shitty friend.

"He's in his room, I think," Lexi says. "Or close to it, anyway."

"C'mon. We should go make sure he's okay." No one should be on their own tonight. Vasha shifts like he's going to get up and I pause. "Are you coming?"

He takes a breath and for a second it seems like he's going to say yes. Then he sinks down and shakes his head. "No, he's—he'll be happier to see you guys. We're still not ..." Vasha looks away and shrugs.

Lexi squeezes his shoulder as she gets up, but doesn't say anything.

I take her hand and pull her as close as I can without tripping over her. I need her warmth and the reassurance that I'm safe.

Dammit. Now I feel worse. Julian probably needed that silent support too and he didn't have it.

Just as we reach the entrance to the Dorm, a pulse of energy hits me. My skin prickles and my body tenses. I look at Lexi, just to make sure she felt it. Her jaw is clenched and her hand trembles in mine. She feels it. And she knows exactly what it means.

There's a portal open nearby. And Julian is the only other person on this end of the caves.

No.

I start running.

If he's already within the energy bubble those portals create, time is moving exponentially faster for him. Even running, even though it'll take us less than a minute to get to his room, it might be too late.

It can't be too late. I can't lose anyone else.

Not again. Not tonight.

Thirty-Five

Julian

Monday, October 27 – 5:59 AM EDT

I stare at the vial on the floor and I can't make myself touch it. But I can't wait for much longer. I have to make a choice before someone finds me and I lose the chance entirely.

This should be easy. I've spent my whole life reading people and situations and predicting reactions and events. Now my head feels fuzzy, and no matter how I try to arrange the information I know, it refuses to fall into a pattern that makes sense. I can't see the answer.

Panic. I'm about to freaking panic. My breath comes faster until I'm on the verge of hyperventilating. Right or wrong? Has Pheodora been playing me or can I trust her with this?

It's like the truth is on the tip of my tongue. Like I'm seeing it out of the corner of my eye. I'm going to have to make an educated guess here. Am I willing to trust Pheodora now if taking that chance means risking Nadette's life?

"No." I can't lose anyone else. Especially not Nadette.

Pheodora's head tilts. "No?"

"I can't do it. I won't." The more I say it, the stronger the conviction feels. The fog begins to clear. This is right. "I'm not going to drug Nadette."

"It is the only way to keep her safe, Julian."

I shake my head and run my hands over my hair. "I should've talked her into going with Mari. You weren't the one who protected us during the raid. Mariella and Hudson did. *They* kept us safe even though it was somehow too much for you."

She doesn't say a thing.

It's like my refusal is the starting gun.

Orange light tinged with gold flashes in my periphery, shooting across my field of vision like a meteor. There's a buzzing in my head like a swarm of locusts. It gets louder and the building heat in my purpurite pendant pulses in time with my rapidly beating heart. Then the orange-gold light bursts like a thousand simultaneous fireworks. My vision washes out. I flinch away, closing my eyes. It doesn't help. The light is so bright it bleeds through my eyelids. Or it's already inside my head.

It takes a few seconds for my vision to clear. When it does, my body tenses and I fight the urge to *run*.

There's no white left in the doorway. The orange light extends like flames, and ropes of that light extend across the room, reaching for me. Where it brushes against my skin, blue sparks fly. I look down at my hands. For the first time I can see the glow clinging to my skin. The mostly blue light has veins of orange running through it like a constantly shifting spider web. Where the orange vines hit, the veins running over my skin glow brighter. They spread and split and grow, trying to beat back the blue. Trying to suffocate it.

The full truth hits me like a blast of desert heat. The purpurite pendant burns against my chest and the confusion and the shell of stupid denial Pheodora managed to build in my head cracks, shatters, and falls away.

Pheodora isn't going to do anything to save us. She's *never* been here to save us. Ever since I met her, Pheodora's been using me to get something she couldn't. They wanted Nadette. And I almost handed her over. I look down at the vial near my feet and shudder. I almost gift-wrapped her for them.

But it also means that even though everything Pheodora told me about the rebel Balasura is true, that's not who I've been working for. It means that I did my very best to destroy Abra, the only safe haven the survivors have ever found. It's unstable now. Unsafe. And they've lost *six* members of their family. Beth died because of *me*.

Oh, fucking hell.

What have I done?

I stare at Pheodora and she slowly smiles, the glittering tear drops disappearing along with every trace of sorrow in her eyes.

"Do you finally see?" she asks that with a stupid level of calm disinterest, like we're talking about the weather. "It is highly fortunate it took so long for you to wake up. Fortunate for me, at least."

"You won't get Nadette." My hands clench and my body trembles, rage and adrenaline tearing through me. "I'll tell her everything. You'll never touch her."

Pheodora laughs. "Child, she was doomed the moment you entered her life. It is far too late for you to save her now."

Her eyes travel over my shoulder. I hear something behind me. A voice that's distant and warped, but it's still recognizable.

Nadette is calling my name.

Oh, no.

I try to step back, away from the portal and Pheodora, but I can't move. Dammit! I struggle harder, silently begging. *Please go away. Turn around. Go back to the others. Hide.* Run. *Forget you ever met me and run!*

Pheodora laughs. "Always too little and so often far too late."

I start to turn. I open my mouth to scream at Nadette, "Stop! Go back! Run like hell!"

Pheodora was right. It's already too late.

Before I can utter more than her name, before I'm even halfway facing the door, Nadette slams into me. Her arms wrap around my waist. She tries to pull me away from the portal, but the impact throws us both off-balance. Teetering on the edge of Abivapna, I flail. My hand almost closes on the edge of the dresser, but my grip slips. My foot catches Nadette's.

We both go tumbling down.

The air is warm and smells of gardenias. I land on my knees next to Nadette, my fingers digging into the bright green grass.

"Nadie!" Lexi calls. "NO!"

The air around us shudders. The portal closes as Lexi screams Nadette's name.

My heart drops into my stomach. Despite the warm air, I'm freezing. My chest clenches.

"Julian ..." Nadette trails off, her face pale and her lip trembling.

Pheodora stands in front of us with a man I've never seen before. Nadette stiffens, her eyes bulging. In an instant, she's back to the twitchy, stressed-out, paranoid girl I met in Trenton. Her eyes are locked on the guy with the deceptively dark hair that seems almost green in certain slants of light. It's only one word, a name, but it escapes her as something between a resigned sigh and a frightened whimper.

"Syver."

My entire body shudders. Syver? This is *Syver*?

I nearly choke on a hysterical laugh. Of course it is. Pheodora has been using me the entire time. Of course she's working with the very creature Nadette left her family to flee.

"You did well, Julian." Pheodora steps closer and smiles. "Not quite as well as I hoped, but it is enough."

That pulls Nadette's eyes away from Syver. I wish it hadn't.

"No. You—" Her mouth keeps moving, but her head jerks like she's choking and her eyes shut. Nadette folds over her legs, her shoulders shaking.

I'm watching her fall apart, but I feel nothing. Not even the grass under my hands.

This can't be happening to me. Not again. Not if Nadette is going to have to suffer for it.

"You've been working with them." She sits up slowly, like ten-ton weights are fighting her for each inch. Her eyes are hollow. Broken. "They told you to find me. You gave me just enough truth to keep me from figuring it out. Julian, *why*? This whole time…"

I can't say a thing. The most important moment in my life, and words have utterly failed me. My mind is blank, my tongue heavy, and my body shaking. Her words trail off when we catch movement in the corner of our eyes. Syver is smiling as he strolls closer.

"Welcome back, my pet." Syver bends slightly to be eye-level with Nadette. My heart pounds. "Did I not tell you I always get what I want?"

Pheodora laughs, the chime-like sound ringing through the air. She steps up behind him and runs her hand over his dark hair, her smile taking on a hard edge.

"If you get out of this alive, tell Lexi I love her." Nadette's voice is empty. As dead and lifeless as her eyes looked when she realized how I'd betrayed her. She takes a deep breath, her gaze never leaving

Syver's, but I know she's talking to me. "And tell my family, too. Tell them I'm sorry."

"A sweet thought, but pointless, really." Pheodora brushes her hand down her flowing dress, black this time, the color stark against her pink hair, and then her glowing eyes meet mine. "He is not going anywhere, child. Neither of you are."

Fuck. That.

I push to my feet and face them both, keeping my face as blank as I can make it. My body is still and calm, but my mind is working like mad.

Leaving isn't an option. They'll kill us before they let us escape. They wanted Nadette badly enough to send me across the country to spy on her, but when they finally attacked, Mariella and Hudson were able to hold them off. I can't imagine they liked that much. But *I* do. I can use their fear of Mari in our favor. I can convince Pheodora to keep us alive with a very judicious application of the truth.

All I have to do is play my cards, place my bet, and hope I can bluff well enough this round to come out on top.

"Don't worry." I'm talking to Nadette, but my words are meant for the demons. "They're not going to kill us. Not yet. Not for a long while."

Nadette winces. The motion is incredibly slight, but I've gotten used to watching for it. I was right, then. They intend to kill us. Good to know. It means I have absolutely nothing left to lose.

"Your faith in our benevolence is sadly misplaced." An amused smile twists Pheodora's face. "Or do you still cling to the belief that we are on your side?"

I snort. "Fuck no."

Nadette glances at me. Even in the midst of this nightmare, a curse word leaving my lips obviously surprises her. I ignore her as much as possible, keeping my focus on Pheodora and Syver.

"You're on your own side. You want to win whatever little war you've got going on. That's why you're going to keep us alive. And safe."

"I have been waiting a long time for Nadette to step into this world," Syver says, his eyes flashing a brighter green.

"And you'd be waiting now if my cousin had her way. She was about to completely fuck up your plans."

Their expressions don't change, but Pheodora and Syver both go still.

"And what is that to do with you, child?" Pheodora's words are sweet but her tone drips with disdain. "Your little tricks are nothing to us."

"And less than nothing compared to what Mari can do." I step closer and slightly to the side, easing myself between Nadette and the Balasura. "That's why you're going to keep us alive. Mariella is my cousin, and family is important to her. Even more so with Hudson. He'll fight for Nadette with his life. If you keep us alive, you might be able to distract them. They'll try to save us and you might—just *might*—have a chance of winning when you face them."

I let that sink in before I make my final point, lay my last card down on the table.

"But if we're dead when they come looking for us?" I say, my voice low and even. "Honestly, I wouldn't even give you long-shot odds of surviving what'll come your way when they break into your world. Because they *will* get in. We both know that." I raise one eyebrow and cross my arms. "They've already destroyed Orane. You really want to give them the chance to wipe you both out too?"

Then all I can do is hold my breath and wait for the biggest gamble of my life to play out.

Acknowledgements

This book literally would not have existed without a push from my editors, Danielle Ellison and Patricia Riley. I came to them with a vision and they showed me how much more there was to the story than even I knew. Nadette and Julian have life because of them, but their awesomeness doesn't end there. I couldn't have asked for better champions or friends than I've found in these ladies. Thank you both for absolutely everything.

Many thanks are due to my agent, Danielle Chiotti. You're like a fairy godmother, a knight in shining armor, and a therapist all rolled into one wonderful person. Your patience, guidance, and support mean the world to me!

Finding the shape of *Deadly Sweet Lies* wasn't easy and took me a while to pin down, but I had help along the way. Thank you so much to everyone who offered edits and advice including my mom Corey (whose reaction to the end of the first draft will forever be one of my favorite memories of this book), my sister Haley, and my sister-of-the-heart Asja Parrish. I also have to thank my fantastic friends like Tristina Wright, Quinton Brown, Jenn Marie Thorne, Livia Blackburne, and my soul-sister Lani Woodland.

I'm especially grateful on this book to Marni Bates. She saved my sanity several times while I was working on edits, gave me just the right kind of encouragement to keep going, and offered feedback and advice that was indescribably invaluable. Thank you for everything. And yes, Marni. I'm still to blame for everything forever. ;)

To everyone from the OneFour Kid Lit debut group, thank you for your phenomenal support. I am so proud to share my year with such a tremendously talented group of authors! Here's to 2015 being only the second of the many amazing years we have ahead.

Thank you to Britta Gigliotti, Meredith Maresco, Cindy Thomas, Rich Storrs, Jessica Porteous, Kate Kaynak and the entire staff of Spencer Hill Press for all the work they do behind and in front of the scenes. You guys all make it possible for me to share my words with the world. Thank you.

So much love goes to my entire far-flung family who have been excited, supportive, and absolutely amazing through everything! My parents and my sisters, my aunts and uncles, my cousins—they have all turned into book pimps for me and I cannot tell them all in words how much their enthusiasm means to me. I love you guys!

And, last but by no means least, I owe a huge debt of gratitude to every single reader and blogger who picked up *Sing Sweet Nightingale* and helped me spread the word. People like you are what make this a dream career.

About the Author

Photo by Lani Woodland

After a lifelong obsession with books, Erica Cameron spent her college years getting credit for reading and learning how to make stories of her own. Erica graduated with a double major in psychology and creative writing from Florida State University and began pursuing a career as an author.

Erica is many things but most notably the following: writer, reader, editor, dance fan, choreographer, singer, lover of musical theater, movie obsessed, sucker for romance, ex-Florida resident, and quasi-recluse. She loves the beach but hates the heat, has equal passion for the art of Salvador Dali and Venetian Carnival masks, has a penchant for unique jewelry and sun/moon décor pieces, and a desire to travel the entire world on a cruise ship. Or a private yacht. You know, whatever works.

In addition to the *Dream War Saga*, Erica is also the co-author of the *Laguna Tides* novels with Lani Woodland. You can find out more at ByEricaCameron.com.

CPSIA information can be obtained at www.ICGtesting.com
Printed in the USA
LVOW06s0349191115

463276LV00002B/2/P